The EMPIRE CLUB MURDERS

A DI MATTHEW STANNARD NOVEL

C.K. Harewood

Blue Laurel
Press

ISBN (Hardback): 978-1-912968-46-6

ISBN (Paperback): 978-1-912968-40-4

ISBN (eBOOK): 978-1-912968-39-8

THE EMPIRE CLUB MURDERS

C. K. HAREWOOD

Chapter One

'Ladies and gentlemen. If you could resume your seats for the charity auction, please.'

Thomas Yates turned to wave at the waiters standing behind him on the dais and instead struck the microphone stand, sending it flying. He lunged for the stand, flailing desperately with both hands, his pale blue eyes wide and startled beneath his white eyebrows. One of the waiters came to his rescue, took hold of the stand, and set it by the elderly treasurer. Yates nodded his thanks and mopped his brow with a handkerchief.

Silly old buffer, Dickie Waite thought, leaning against the rear wall of the function room where he could be out of the way of the club's revellers. They had stopped paying him any attention some while ago, had ceased to cast disdainful looks at his shabby dinner jacket and trousers, bought second-hand the year before for a cousin's wedding and not at all the proper attire for such a fancy do as this. He was quite obviously out of the wrong drawer, an oddity in their club, and the members had dealt with him by pretending he didn't exist.

1

Dickie didn't mind; it suited him this way. It meant he could watch.

And watch he did as the evening wore on and the members of the Empire Club gave themselves up to fun. Balloons that had been pinned to the picture rails now floated around the room, only to be kicked away when they reached the floor by feet encased in patent leather pumps or elegant silver and gold satin heels. Streamers dangling from the crystal chandeliers tickled the bare shoulders of the women while men tugged others down to pile on their slick-backed hair or hang around their necks like paper boas, giggling at the ridiculous figures they cut.

His editor, Bill Edwards, had sent Dickie to cover the event for the newspaper, telling him while he was there to sound out whether some of the members would be interested in featuring in some profiles about the area's most eminent residents. He'd told him who to talk to and given him a camera to take some snaps. Dickie had asked if it was such a good idea. With the world as it was, with so many people struggling to make ends meet as work dried up and investments dwindled to nothing, did Edwards really want to fill the pages of *The Chronicle* with stories about the upper classes and how wonderful and exciting their lives were?

'You're bloody right I do,' Edwards had retorted. 'People want to be taken out of themselves. They love reading about glamorous parties and nobs living it up.'

And Dickie, looking around the room, had to admit his editor was right. Women readers would want to know about the dresses the female club members were wearing, what colour feathers they had stuck in their sequined headbands, the size of the jewels they wore, while male readers would be interested in knowing how their betters earned a living, what brand of cigarettes they smoked, which cocktails they drank. If only Dickie could be as interested, but covering society affairs, even if it was for charity, wasn't why he'd become a reporter.

As soon as the four-course dinner was over – Dickie swiped a menu to see what they'd had and raised his eyebrows at the smoked salmon, pate de foie gras, sirloin of beef and peaches in Chartreuse jelly listed there – the mingling began. Dickie saw men bend over other men's wives, their hands surreptitiously brushing bare skin even as they carried on a conversation with the husbands. The women's expressions gave nothing away, but their bodies responded, pressing back against the fingers, rosy flushes creeping up their throats to deepen the rouge rubbed delicately into their cheeks. How many of those trespassing fingers would be allowed further liberties later? Dickie wondered.

At Yates's plea, the men returned to their seats, lighting the cigarettes stuffed into Bakelite holders clenched between their wives' teeth before lighting their own. The room quietened as Yates banged a gavel.

'Ladies and gentlemen. As you know, every year, we at the Empire Club hold an event to raise funds for a local charity. This year, we are raising money for the poor and needy children in this borough. A very worthwhile cause. I'm sure you'll all agree.' There was a faint murmuring, lacking in any sincerity, and Yates cleared his throat before continuing. 'I would like to offer a very heartfelt note of gratitude to all of you and to the local businesses who have donated tonight's auction items. So, let us begin.'

First to be auctioned were bottles of wine and champagne, all excellent vintages, Yates assured his audience, but they fetched unremarkable sums. The Cole Porter, Irving Berlin and various jazz gramophone records were bid on more enthusiastically, but it was when theatre tickets came up that the members really grew lively. *The House That Jack Built*,

Ivor Novello's show playing at The Adelphi, won plenty of bids, while *La Traviata* at Drury Lane struggled to find many takers but still made more money than Dickie earned in a month.

Yates was struggling to keep up with the bids and his calls for order were drowned out by the cheers the members made each time someone shouted a sum. He banged his gavel furiously as a man jumped onto the dais and elbowed him out of the way.

Dickie recognised him. This was Christopher Fairbank, dealer in fine art and antiques, and one of the men his editor wanted him to write about. A good-looking man with a square jaw, Fairbank could have passed for a film star, though one occupying an unmistakable middle age, and many of the women focused an admiring gaze upon him.

'Let's make this a little more interesting, shall we?' Fairbank said, snatching the microphone away from Yates and angling it towards himself. 'Ladies, what say you sell your kisses for charity?'

Squeals of delight greeted this suggestion and women clapped their hands like children being given a treat. Some even bounced on their chairs in excitement. The men seemed less taken with the idea. They smiled awkwardly at one another and busied themselves with their drinks.

Yates said something in Fairbank's ear. Fairbank laughed and waved Yates away. The elderly treasurer stepped down from the dais and sank into his chair. His wife touched his arm and asked him something, but Yates shook his head, folded his arms firmly over his chest and turned his face away. Was he put out because Fairbank had deposed him, Dickie wondered, or because he disapproved of the direction the auction had taken?

'So, come on,' Fairbank called. 'Who wants to be the first to sell themselves for a good cause?'

A sudden shyness came over the company and no lady admitted to being game. Fairbank's brow creased and his square jaw hardened in irritation. Another man jumped up beside him. This, Dickie knew, was Archibald Ballantyne, an ageing Lothario if ever he'd seen one. His tails were perfectly tailored, but they couldn't hide the expanding waistline, nor could the winged collar conceal his double chin. But what Ballantyne lacked in looks, he more than made up for in charm, a talent Dickie had witnessed for himself in court when Ballantyne the defence barrister would rise, resplendent in wig and robes, and expertly pick apart a witness's testimony. Ballantyne's preferred method of attack was to convince a witness they were wrong about what they thought they saw or overheard rather than batter away mercilessly to find the flaws in their statements. It was a method more often successful than not. Many a prosecution barrister's case had been lost because they couldn't compete with Ballantyne's persuasive charm.

'Now, come on, ladies. Don't be shy. Marion,' Ballantyne held out his hand to Mrs Stephen Goodall sitting at one of the front tables. 'You're a sport. Why don't you show your friends how it's done?'

Marion needed no further persuading. Ignoring her husband's attempt to grab her wrist, she joined Ballantyne and Fairbank on the dais and presented herself to the crowd.

'Look at this beauty,' Ballantyne declared. 'Now, who wouldn't want a kiss from this goddess?'

Two men seated at a table a few feet away from Dickie sniggered. 'Plenty of us have already had one,' one said.

'Had more than a kiss, old boy,' replied the other. 'Archie's drawing it mild by calling her a sport.'

Men were calling out their bids, and Marion's cheeks were rounding with pleasure as they continued to rise, stopping at five pounds. Fairbank declared the prize won and

Marion stepped down to deliver herself up to the winner. This lucky man pulled Marion onto his lap, wrapped his arms around her waist, slid a hand over her rump, and the two kissed to the cheers and applause of the onlookers.

The shyness was gone. Two more women offered themselves, one fetching two pounds, the other three. Marion Goodall was glowing with delight that she had fetched more. Then Dickie saw Fairbank wink at an attractive strawberry blonde, and she stepped up beside him obediently.

'The delicious Sophie Sutton, gentlemen,' Ballantyne cried.

Men cheered, and bids came in thick and fast. Dickie saw Marion Goodall's expression harden as the younger, prettier woman quickly surpassed her five pounds. Dickie shifted his gaze to the man who had been sitting next to Sophie Sutton and who he guessed was the lady's husband. Mr Sutton's face was stony, his jaw hard and tight, the hand resting on the table clenched into a fist.

The bids were slowing – eight pounds had been offered so far – when Fairbank waved his arms and quieted the room. 'Twenty pounds,' he cried, and grinned at Sophie. Her hands went to her mouth as a cheer, the loudest of the evening, burst from the audience. No one attempted to up the bid – was it too high a price to pay or was it understood Fairbank was not to be bettered? – and Fairbank took out his pocketbook and withdrew the requisite notes, slapping them down on the lectern in triumph. Then he held out his hand to Sophie and she went eagerly to him. His arms around her waist, Fairbank planted his lips on hers. Her hands gripped his shoulders, her body arched beneath his.

The kiss lasted too long. The cheers and laughter became muted. Men looked at each other, eyebrows rising. The women's lips parted as they stared at the couple, fingers stroking their own collar bones distractedly, wishing themselves in Sophie's place.

Andrew Sutton leapt to his feet. 'FAIRBANK!'

A hush fell. Everyone was waiting to see what would happen next.

Fairbank withdrew his lips from Sophie's with a practised laziness. 'Yes, old chap?'

'Enough,' Sutton growled. 'Sophie!' He clicked his fingers at his wife and directed her to her chair.

Fury and indignation blooming on her face, Sophie disengaged herself from Fairbank and resumed her seat. She looked at no one as she grabbed her champagne glass and threw the contents down her throat.

They'll have an almighty row later, Dickie thought grimly, glancing back at Ballantyne and Fairbank, who were grinning at one another. Yates had had enough. He jumped up onto the dais and gestured angrily at a nearby waiter to clear everything away. He spoke to Ballantyne, shaking his head in disapproval, and Ballantyne put a hand on his shoulder and nodded in agreement. Satisfied, Yates strode away, disappearing into the corridor. A few moments later, he returned with a three-man Ragtime band and busied himself with ordering them around as they set up on the stage.

Despite the general gaiety caused by the impromptu auction for kisses, Yates wasn't the only one who didn't seem to have enjoyed himself. Dickie noticed that quite a few of the members talked earnestly to each other, watching warily as Fairbank and Ballantyne moved around the room. There was a couple shaking their heads and stubbing out their cigarettes, disapproval evident in the erectness of their heads, the tightening of their lips and the critically raised eyebrows. Dickie's eyes fell on another couple. These two stood out, being younger than the others, and the woman looking a good deal more stylish in her simple forest green silk-crepe dress than her overdressed, middle-aged companions. She was tall and willowy, with blonde hair curled in finger waves in the latest fashion. They were huddled together near one of the large French windows and it seemed to Dickie the woman was imploring the man to leave. She kept gesturing towards the doors, and when he grabbed hold of her hand, shaking her head as if she didn't want to hear what he had to say. Maybe they wouldn't be renewing their membership in the new year, Dickie mused wryly.

His gaze returned to Ballantyne and Fairbank as they chatted with members, lighting cigarettes and kissing hands, unabashed and unapologetic about the scene they had caused. They worked their way to the back of the room where Dickie stood, there joining three other men who nodded greetings at their approach. Dickie knew these three as well: Adrian Foucault, Donald Spencer and Eric Hailes.

'Enjoying yourself, Kit?' Spencer asked with a sly smile.

'It's my aim in life,' Fairbank said, taking a glass from the tray of a passing waiter, following him with his eyes, an amused yet strangely inquisitive expression in them. Dickie stared after the waiter, wondering what there was about him to pique Fairbank's interest.

'Twenty quid's a bit steep, though, isn't it?'

'It's an investment, Don. You'll see.'

'I don't think her husband was amused,' Foucault said, sipping at his champagne. 'He'll ask you to step outside later.'

'Andrew hasn't got the guts,' Fairbank sneered, looking over his shoulder at the Suttons, sitting silently side by side, their bodies rigid with anger.

'And the succulent Sophie?' Hailes asked with an ugly leer. 'You think she'll play ball?'

'After spending twenty quid on her? She better. I'll tell you all about it, Eric.'

8

'I might have a go myself,' Hailes said. The others laughed at his ambition. 'I could,' he protested.

Ballantyne patted Hailes on the arm. 'Aiming a bit high there, Eric. But don't worry. We'll find some shrivelled old virgin who won't mind your clumsy fumbling. Now, I must get back to Florrie or some devil will be trying his luck with her.'

'You still on for later?' Spencer called as Ballantyne wandered away.

'Oh, rather,' Ballantyne said. 'I wouldn't miss that for the world.'

The other four moved off, and Dickie checked his watch. It had gone ten and he really couldn't stand much more of watching these people enjoy themselves. He would call it a night, but he decided not to leave empty-handed, and wandered into the kitchen where the waiter who Fairbank had eyed with curiosity was emptying the remains of the dinner into the bin. He stared at Dickie out of the corner of his eye.

'Mind if I take some of that?' Dickie asked, gesturing at the leftovers on the kitchen table behind them.

'Help yourself,' the young man said and carried on scraping.

'Thanks,' Dickie said, pocketing vol-au-vents and wrapping wedges of cheese in his handkerchief. 'What do you think of them?'

'Who?' the waiter frowned.

Dickie jerked his head at the door. 'The members.'

The waiter jerked a shrug. 'Not much.'

'Give good tips, though, I expect.'

'Not this lot. You're lucky if you get so much as a thank you.'

'The upper-middle-class,' Dickie nodded understandingly. 'They're all the same.'

'You're not with them, are you? I heard Mr Yates say you're a reporter. So, what are you doing here?'

'I'm supposed to be writing about them for the 'paper.'

The waiter made a face. 'Why would you want to do that? What's so special about them?' He didn't wait for an answer, but picked up the stack of plates and carried them through to the scullery.

Dickie watched him go, thinking it was a bloody good question.

Chapter Two

14th January 1930

Matthew Stannard pushed open the door of The Fiddler's Retreat and elbowed his way through the patrons to reach the bar. The barmaid, busy pulling pints, glanced up, ready to tell him to give her a minute because she only had one pair of hands. But when she realised who it was, her frown turned to a toothy smile.

'Well, hello, stranger!' Ruby put a hand to her frizzy hair, making sure no strands had come loose. 'Where have you been hiding yourself?'

Matthew took off his hat and smiled politely. 'Nowhere, Ruby. Just busy.'

Ruby tutted. 'You're always busy. You'll work yourself into the ground if you're not careful. You know what they say about all work and no play.'

He shook his head at her concern. 'I'm fine. Where's Fred?'

'He went down to put a new barrel on. So, what you having? Or are you going to tell me you're on duty?'

'I'm not on duty tonight, but I'll have a drink upstairs.'

'Oh, go on, have one with me. My birthday treat.' Ruby leaned forward over the pumps, toying with the buttons on her blouse. 'Or we could go on somewhere after closing time, if you like?'

'Well...' Matthew cleared his throat, feeling his cheeks growing warm as a man at the bar, still waiting for his pint, turned to him, looking him up and down to see what had got Ruby so worked up. 'I'll be up with Mum tonight, and I've got an early start, so I... Fred!' he halloed rather desperately as his brother-in-law came up behind Ruby.

'Now, now, Ruby, leave Matt alone,' Fred said with an amused smile. 'How about serving the customers? You know? What we pay you for?'

'All right,' Ruby said sulkily. 'See you later,' she promised Matthew as she wiggled away.

Fred raised his eyebrows at Matthew. 'See you later, eh? Play your cards right, Matt—'

Matthew held up his hand. 'Don't start.'

Fred chuckled. 'You better get upstairs quick or she'll be trying to give you a birthday kiss next. Go on. They're waiting for you.'

He lifted the wooden bar flap and Matthew stepped through, moving into the hall and climbing the carpeted stairs leading up to the private area of the pub, feeling the rumble of the train that sped along the track at the rear of the building beneath his feet and hearing the familiar sound of his mother and sister arguing. He peered through the gap between the sitting-room door and the frame and saw his mother set a bottle of wine (got in especially for him, he knew) down near the edge of the dining table his sister was trying to lay.

'No, Mum,' Pat snapped. 'Not there. It'll get knocked off.'

Amanda slammed the bottle down in the middle of the checked tablecloth. 'Nothing I ever do is right, is it?'

'There's no need for you to do anything. You just want to interfere.'

'I want it to look nice for Mattie.'

'It will look nice,' Pat insisted. 'Not that Mattie will notice, anyway. Now, shift yourself. You're in me way again.'

Matthew took a deep breath and stepped into the room. 'Hello,' he said, forcing a smile onto his face.

'Mattie!' Amanda shrieked and threw herself at him, clamping her arms around his neck and giving him a noisy kiss on the cheek.

'Oh, put him down, Mum,' Pat chided as Matthew disentangled himself. She kissed his other cheek and used her thumb to wipe away the smear of bright red lipstick their mother had left. 'Happy birthday, Mattie.'

'Thanks. No Georgie?'

'He'll be home soon.' Pat straightened the salt and pepper pots. 'You'll get your presents then.'

'I've told you before,' Matthew said as Amanda peeled his overcoat off him. 'I don't need presents.'

'And I've told you before, you're getting presents, so shut yer face.' Pat snatched his hat from his hand and thrust it at their mother to hang up with his coat.

Matthew shrugged, giving in. 'They better be good ones, then. What's for dinner?'

'Your favourite,' Pat said, going through to the kitchen at the far side of the room. 'Steak and kidney pudding.'

'Sit down with me, Mattie.' Amanda took his arm and steered him to the settee. 'Tell me what you've been up to.'

Matthew lit a cigarette and told her about his work, leaving out anything that would make his mother fuss and implore him to be more careful, or worse, to leave the police and get a nice, quiet, safe job. He was dying to tell her his best news, but he bit his tongue, wanting to wait until all his family was together, and so let his mother rattle on, ignoring

13

her plea that he move nearer so she could see him more often. He was glad when he heard the stairs creak and Fred came in with Georgie. Amanda, annoyed she no longer had Matthew all to herself, rose and went into the kitchen.

'Hello, Mattie. Happy birthday.' Georgie smiled, and Matthew was struck as he always was by his young brother's resemblance to their father. There was the same dark hair and blue eyes that all three children shared, but Georgie was the only one who had inherited their father's square jaw and dimpled chin.

'Thanks. How are you getting on at work?'

'Oh, it's all right,' Georgie said dismissively.

'It's bloody marvellous, Matt,' Fred said, oblivious to Georgie's lack of enthusiasm for his job with the local butcher. 'You should see what he brings home. Sausages, chops. He even manages steak sometimes. You should ask him to get some for you.'

Matthew glanced at his brother and saw the unease on Georgie's face. 'I don't need anything.'

Fred clicked his tongue in impatience. 'I know what you're thinking, but he's not stealing it. Mr Bennett tells him to take what won't keep.' He sniffed the air. 'Blimey, that smells good. One good thing about you coming round, Matt, I always get a decent dinner.' He went whistling into the kitchen, leaving the two brothers alone.

'Does Mr Bennett say you can take it?' Matthew asked.

'Mostly,' Georgie nodded, 'but Mum keeps on at me to bring home more, so sometimes—'

'That's stealing, Georgie.'

'It's only now and then.'

'I don't care if you've only done it once. I'm a police officer, for God's sake. How's it going to look if my own brother gets arrested for theft?'

'I won't do it again, Mattie. Promise. But can you tell Mum and Fred to stop asking me?'

'I'll talk to them,' Matthew promised as the others came back into the room.

'I've told Pat we're giving you your presents now,' Amanda said, delving behind a cushion and pulling out a parcel wrapped in brown paper and tied with blue ribbon. The others held back, knowing Amanda wanted to give Matthew her present first. 'Do you like it?' she asked anxiously as Matthew peeled back the wrapping paper.

'I do,' he said, holding the cricket jumper against his chest and smoothing down the blue V-neck collar.

'You said you needed a new one.' Amanda tugged the bottom of the jumper to make it hang straight. 'It's the right size, isn't it?'

'It's perfect, Mum. Thanks.' He leaned forward to give her a kiss, feeling guilty because he knew it must have taken his mother, suffering with arthritis, months of painful endeavour to knit.

'This is from me and Fred.' Pat deposited a boxy parcel wrapped in the same brown paper, only this time tied with string, on Matthew's lap. He opened it to discover a set of six Hardy novels, leather-bound with only minor scuffing to the covers. 'You haven't read them, have you?'

Matthew assured her he hadn't, hoping the second-hand books hadn't set Fred and Pat back too much. He was still working his way through the set of six Dickens novels they had bought him four years before and doubted he would get on to the Hardys any time soon.

'Me now.' Georgie thrust his present at Matthew. This one was wrapped in tissue paper and contained a set of three cotton handkerchiefs with his initials, MJS, embroidered in the corner.

'They're lovely, aren't they, Mattie?' Pat said, her eyes insisting he agree.

Matthew smiled up at his brother. 'They're just what I need, Georgie. Thanks.'

'I wasn't sure about the initials,' Georgie said shyly, 'but the lady in the shop said everyone's having them done like that.'

'They're very smart. Thank you all.' Matthew put his presents to one side and took a deep breath, trying not to grin like an idiot. 'Now we're all together, I've got some news to tell you.'

Amanda's face fell. 'You're getting married.'

'Oh, Mum!' Pat scolded.

'No,' Matthew said with a sigh, 'I'm not getting married. My promotion came through. I've made inspector.'

His family erupted into congratulations. Pat grabbed him and gave him a cuddle. Fred clapped him on the back. Amanda took his face between her crabby hands and kissed him. Georgie held back, unsure what to do, but said, 'That's brilliant, Mattie.'

'How's that for a birthday present?' Fred declared. 'Detective Inspector, eh? Who'd have thought it?'

'I would have thought it,' Amanda cried indignantly. 'I always knew Mattie would get on in the police. Not like his father. He never got further than sergeant.'

'Mum,' Pat shook her head, a warning not to bring their father into the conversation. She turned to Matthew. 'You staying put or they moving you somewhere else?'

'Moving me,' Matthew said.

'Oh,' Amanda gave a little cry. 'Not far away?'

'Craynebrook, Mum. Not far.'

'Why can't you stay at Hackney?' Fred asked, taking up the wine bottle and twisting the corkscrew into the cork.

'There'll be too many inspectors. Craynebrook's a smaller station but one of their inspectors has retired.'

'How much smaller?' Pat asked.

'Well, there's a superintendent in charge, and in the CID, two inspectors, including me, two sergeants and three constables.'

'And when do you start?'

'Tomorrow.'

'Blimey. They don't give you much time to get ready, do they? And Craynebrook is posh.' Pat picked up his presents and stacked them neatly on the sideboard. 'You'll have to watch your p's and q's there, Mattie.'

'No hiding there, either,' Matthew said ruefully.

'What do you mean hiding?'

'If I cock things up,' he explained, trying to hide his anxiety behind a laugh, 'everyone will know.'

Pat smacked his knee, a reproof for his coarse language but also for worrying; his laugh hadn't fooled her, he knew. 'You won't mess anything up. Why would you?' Before he could answer, she carried on. 'I mean, you're good, aren't you? One of the best. You caught that beast killing all those women when no one else had a clue how to get him. Craynebrook should be blooming glad to have you. Oh, that reminds me. Has Mum shown you her scrapbook? Mum, show Mattie.'

Amanda took up a large book lying on the table beside her armchair. She beamed at Matthew as she passed it to him and Pat nodded to open it. 'You just take a look at that.'

The scrapbook was thick, but Matthew could see that all the pages had already been filled. He caught his breath as he opened it and saw the newspaper clippings pasted in by Amanda. He recognised some of the headlines.

'I've cut out the article every time your name's been in the newspaper,' Amanda said proudly. 'I used to keep them all in a box, but Pat came home with this scrapbook the other day so I could put them in there.' She flipped the book back to the first page and tapped. 'The first clipping goes back to when you were in Uniform. See?'

'Oh, now you've done it, Mother,' Fred said. 'Matt's gone all red.'

'It's hot in here,' Pat said, heading for the kitchen. 'I'll need to get Mum another scrapbook now you're a detective inspector, Mattie. You'll be all over the newspapers, I'll bet.'

Matthew gave the scrapbook back to his mother, embarrassed by the pride his family took in his achievements and knowing his sister had tried to cover his blushes.

'Hurry up with dinner, Pat,' he called, a little too loudly. 'I'm starving.'

Chapter Three

Sidney Mills took a deep breath of the crisp morning air and stamped his feet, enjoying the sound of the brittle grass breaking beneath his shoes. This was more like it; he had room to stretch himself. He should have done this weeks ago instead of moping indoors, getting under Kathy's feet. How long had he dreamed of retiring, of not having to get up at 5 a.m. and going into work, of having whole days to do whatever he wanted? And now he had retired and had all the time he could want, he didn't know what to do with himself and wished he was back at the factory. His mother had always said he was hard to please.

He set off across the common, intending to explore. Although the great expanse of ground was practically on his doorstep, just a ten-minute walk away, he couldn't remember ever walking it before. He'd passed it often enough on his way to work, and he remembered how it had been used by the military in the Great War, but he'd never appreciated just how big it was. Winter wasn't the best time to see it, though. It was never a pretty place, not even in summer, but winter made it bleak with hard dirt showing through the grey, brittle grass and the trees barren of leaves. Not that dogs seemed to mind, he thought, smiling as a Labrador and a Yorkshire terrier nearby barked and ran around one another while their owners tried to call them to heel. Maybe he should get a dog, Sidney mused, and walked on.

As he walked, he reluctantly admitted to himself that Kathy had been right to make him wrap up well; it was still damnably cold, despite it warming up over the last week or so. Kathy had made him put on two pairs of socks, and though he had told her to stop fussing over him, he was glad she'd insisted, for he could already feel his toes starting to numb. He wouldn't have a very long walk, he decided, amending his plan of that morning. Half an hour or so would do. Sidney walked quickly, feeling the first twinges of cramp in his calves. Cramp was new. Thirty-five years he'd spent on his feet, walking the factory floor, and he'd never got cramp or needed a sit-down then. This was what retirement had done to him. Made him lazy. Made him old. Made him realise he had nothing in common with his wife.

He needed a hobby, that was it. Something to pass the time and challenge his mind. Kathy had suggested wood-working, but that was no good. He had trouble banging in nails, let alone making things. Stamp collecting? Sounded dull to him; he didn't see the attraction. But then, what else was there? Sidney sighed heavily and, looking about him, frowned, not knowing where he'd come to. His mind had been wandering, and he hadn't been paying attention to where he walked. He'd come to an odd sort of corner of the common. It looked less travelled than where he'd come from, though the area got some traffic, for the hardened mud he was standing on had been churned up while wet and there were tyre marks criss-crossing the ground. Why would a car come this way? he wondered. There was no road or access to houses here.

Sidney pushed back the cuff of his overcoat and examined

his wristwatch. He'd been out for nearly thirty minutes, and he was cold and wanting a cup of tea. Time to go home. He shoved his gloved hands into his pockets and sniffed. His nose wrinkled and his brow creased. What was that smell? Sweet, sickly? He looked around. It seemed to come from somewhere to his left, beyond the clump of bushes. He stepped over to them. The smell was definitely stronger here. He stood on tiptoe, peering over the top of the bushes.

'Oh my God,' he gasped and stumbled backwards. It couldn't have been… no, he'd been mistaken. It wasn't… Gingerly, he stepped up to the bush again, hardly daring to breathe. He craned his neck over the top and looked down. He put his gloved hand to his mouth as he felt his gorge rising.

What was he to do? *Think, think*, Sidney ordered himself. The police, that was it. He had to call the police. But from where? The houses at the edge of the common or a telephone box? He'd passed a box on his way, hadn't he? Yes, he remembered, just before he set foot on the common. Casting an anxious look back at the bush, Sidney hurried away as fast as his frozen legs would carry him, ignoring the curious stares of the dog-walkers he had passed earlier. Relief flooded through him when he caught sight of the red telephone box. Yanking the door open, he snatched up the receiver.

'Number, please?' the operator asked.

'Police,' Sidney shouted into the mouthpiece, and the operator made the connection.

'Craynebrook Police Station,' a voice declared.

'You've got to come,' Sidney panted. 'You must come to the common.'

'Calm down, please, sir,' came the reply, and Sidney obeyed, taking a few deep breaths, audible to the policeman, who waited patiently for him to finish. 'Now, tell me your name and what the matter is.'

'My name's Sidney Mills and I was walking on Crayne-brook common when I...' he gulped. 'When I found a dead body.'

The king was looking down at Matthew censoriously, as if judging him just as much as Superintendent Howard Mullinger.

Matthew had arrived at Craynebrook Police Station at half-past eight, a full half hour before his meeting with the station's superintendent, and was seated on a bench in the entrance lobby beneath the station's notice board with its warnings against pickpockets and a list of helpful local tele-phone numbers. To help pass the time, and if he was honest, to help calm his nerves, Matthew had reread the letter he had received from Eliot Campbell, his first guvnor when he had started in the police force as a wide-eyed police constable and who was now the Assistant Deputy Commissioner. Campbell had made it his business to keep an eye on his former protégé's career and had sent this letter congratulating Matthew on his recent promotion and, as ever, offering a few words of sage advice. As he always was, Matthew was grateful for the advice but doubtful he would remember to take it. Campbell asked for Matthew to keep him updated on how the new posting was going, and Matthew hoped he wouldn't let him down. He almost wished Campbell wouldn't take such a keen interest in his career. It made him even more nervous than he already was. He cursed Fred for insisting they open a bottle of champagne to celebrate his promotion. The one bottle had turned into two, and he'd been more than a little drunk as he made his way home. Still feeling the effects, and nervous about the day ahead, he hadn't been able to eat breakfast that morning, and had instead relied on three cigarettes to wake him up. If Pat were here, he mused as his

22

right leg jiggled up and down, she'd tell him he had nothing to be nervous about, but then she didn't understand his situation. Matthew just knew that his new colleagues, aware of his reputation, would be waiting for him to make a mistake.

At ten minutes past nine, the telephone behind the desk rang and Matthew was told by the constable on the front desk that the superintendent would see him now. He was led up two flights of stairs to the superintendent's office, where a secretary in her late twenties greeted him with a smile. There was a red indent on the bridge of her nose where her spectacles had rested before she snatched them off and hid them from view.

She rose and knocked on the superintendent's door. A voice barked out, 'Come in.' She opened the door, said to Matthew, 'There you go,' and hurried back to her desk.

Matthew stepped inside and closed the door. A man in his early fifties with a long bulbous nose and close-set black eyes looked up over gold-rimmed spectacles. 'Detective Inspector Stannard?' he asked in a deep, gravelly voice.

'Yes, sir,' Matthew said.

Superintendent Mullinger pointed to the chair in front of the desk. 'Sit down.'

Matthew obeyed, and Mullinger pulled out a buff-coloured file from a pile on the edge of his desk. 'So, you're joining us today?'

'Yes, sir.'

Mullinger's finger ran down the first piece of paper in what Matthew could see was his personnel file. 'From Hackney Police Station, I see. Well, you'll find it rather different here, I expect. Not so rough. You joined the force in early 1914.'

'Yes, sir.'

'And been in it ever since.'

'Yes, sir.'

'You didn't serve in the war?'

Matthew's jaw tightened. 'No, sir.'

'That's rather odd,' Mullinger said, taking off his spectacles. 'Most men of the age you would have been then were very keen to join up. Couldn't stop them. The police force was severely depleted by our men enlisting as soon as war was declared. Why didn't you?'

'I believed the police force needed me to stay where I was. I did my duty, sir. I just did it in a policeman's uniform rather than in a soldier's.'

Mullinger put his spectacles back on his nose and resumed his reading of Matthew's file. 'Assistant Deputy Commissioner Campbell speaks very highly of you, and you received a personal commendation for your part in the capture of the Marsh Murderer.' A bushy eyebrow rose. 'Got your name in the newspapers for that, didn't you?'

Matthew caught the note of disapproval. 'I wasn't the only one, sir.'

'But you got most of the attention. Did you enjoy that, Stannard? The publicity?'

Matthew took a deep breath; out of sight, his hands curled into fists on his knees. 'I did my job, sir. Any attention paid to the investigation by the Press was not of my doing.'

'Didn't mind it, though,' Mullinger said. Not a question this time, a statement of fact. 'I don't approve of the men who serve under me having too close a relationship with the Press, Stannard. We, of course, cooperate with the local newsmen, but I will not have my officers speaking to reporters about gossip and rumour and speculation. If the Press is to be told anything, then they will hear it from me. Is that understood?'

'Yes, sir. Understood.'

'Good.' Mullinger took off his spectacles again and tossed them onto his blotter. The paper in the blotter was immaculate, not a trace of ink upon it. Mullinger drummed his fingers

24

on the edge of the desk, leaning back in his chair, contemplating Matthew.

'The Marsh Murders. Those were very unpleasant, I believe. Fortunately, we haven't had any murders like that here. Craynebrook's not that sort of place, not like where you've come from. Decent people live here, Stannard. What crime there is, and of course, there will always be crime, amounts to mostly petty thefts, burglaries, the occasional fistfight when the public houses close. I doubt if there will be any opportunities for you to get your name in the 'papers again.'

'That has never been my intention, sir.'

'I'm glad to hear it. Well, let me explain how things work here. To begin with, Craynebrook is not Hackney. What I'm saying, Stannard, is that a different type of policing will be required of you here. What may have been appropriate behaviour where you've come from is unlikely to be appropriate in Craynebrook. This area requires tact and diplomacy, not the size ten boot in the door. I won't have you blundering in where angels fear to tread.'

'I try not to blunder, sir, and I've never been one for kicking in doors. I'll be as tactful as the work allows.'

Matthew knew he sounded petulant, insubordinate even, but Mullinger had got his back up. He decided he didn't care for the superintendent and found his mind travelling wistfully back to Hackney CID where about now Powell would be scraping out the barrel of his pipe, Davies would be telling one of his blue jokes, Bennett would be tutting to himself as he tried to master the typewriter while Hunter asked for his help in filling out an arrest form. Matthew had never imagined he would miss them, but sitting here with disapproval coming off the superintendent in waves, he was beginning to wish he hadn't got his promotion. He'd never asked to be in the newspapers. That was something that had just happened as the investigation unfolded. And his superiors at Hackney hadn't objected. In fact, they had done all they could to encourage reporting of Matthew's great success. After months of bad press because the Marsh Murderer seemed to be running rings around the police, his capture had been something to shout about. The top brass were keen to get the Press and the public back on the side of the police, and articles about a brave detective sergeant arresting a homicidal maniac single-handedly got the police a great deal of good publicity. And Matthew a great deal of ribbing from his colleagues, not all of it good-humoured. He had hoped that his celebrity, such as it was, would fade with this move to Craynebrook; now he was wondering if he would have to carry it around with him forever.

There was a knock and the door opened. Mullinger growled, 'What is it, Miss Halliwell?'

'Sorry to disturb you, Mr Mullinger,' the secretary said, 'but a body has been found on the common and Inspector Lund is in court all day.' She glanced at Matthew. 'The front desk was wondering if Inspector Stannard could attend.'

Matthew got to his feet, buttoning up his jacket. 'Of course,' he said before Mullinger could speak. *Anything to get out of here*, he thought. 'If that's all right with you, sir?' he conceded, taking a step towards the door.

'Well, I do need to show you the station,' Mullinger said sulkily.

'I'm sure I'll find my way around,' Matthew assured him, adding that he would like to get straight to work, knowing it was a claim the superintendent wouldn't be able to find fault with. Yet Mullinger's expression suggested he wasn't at all happy at being abridged in this way and he paused for a long moment before agreeing Matthew could go. Matthew hurried out and Miss Halliwell closed the door behind him.

'I'm sorry to have pulled you out of there,' she said, returning to her desk.

'There's no need,' he said with sincerity. 'Could you tell me where the CID office is?'

'Down the stairs, the door directly opposite. You'll be sharing an office with DI Lund. Lucky you,' she muttered.

Chapter Four

A call had come into *The Chronicle*'s switchboard at twenty past nine, just as Dickie had deposited his mug of tea on his desk and sat down in front of his typewriter, with the news that the police were all over Craynebrook common. Dickie had volunteered to go, bored with trying to write his profiles. He knew he should let *The Chronicle*'s new reporter cover the story, but tough! Young Teddy would have to cut his teeth on something else.

And now, Dickie was hunkering down in his overcoat, sinking his chin into his red tartan scarf and keeping his hands firmly in his pockets as he kept his eyes on the corner of the common where all the action was. Over the years, he'd perfected the art of standing around, learning how not to waste his energy during cold weather with feet stamping or blowing on frozen hands. 'Stand still, wear layers,' he'd told Teddy a week earlier when the young man had been sent to cover a story about swans at the local pond, 'and think of somewhere warm while keeping your eyes peeled.'

Dickie had found *The Chronicle*'s informant and stroked the man's dog as he asked what he knew. That source of information quickly drying up, he had ambled over to the constable on guard, who was doing his best to keep back the crowd of onlookers that had gathered.

'Morning, Sam,' Dickie said to PC Samuel Rudd. The young man looked chilled to the bone. 'I heard a body's been found. Who is it? A tramp?'

'I can't tell you anything, Mr Waite, you know that.'

'I know,' Dickie nodded. 'Mr Mullinger wouldn't like it. At least tell me who found the body.'

PC Rudd considered a moment, then nodded back at the crowd. 'See that bloke with the check cap? That's Mr Sidney Mills. He found the body. Now, do me a favour, Mr Waite, and bugger off. If the Super finds out I've told you that much—'

Dickie held up a hand to show he understood. 'Thanks, Sam. Next time I see you in The King George…' he nodded meaningfully, and the young man nodded back with a smile. He wandered back to the crowd and stood next to the man PC Rudd had pointed out. 'Mr Mills?'

'Yes?' Sidney looked at Dickie warily.

'Dickie Waite, *The Chronicle*. I understand you found the body?'

Sidney nodded, the saggy skin beneath his chin wobbling. 'That's right. And I don't want to see anything like that ever again.'

'Let's hope you never do. I don't suppose you know who it is, do you?'

'Couldn't tell. He was a right state. Face all bashed in. I expect his own mother won't be able to recognise him.'

'Bashed in, you say? Dear, dear,' Dickie tutted. 'Why would someone do that to a poor tramp?'

'Tramp?' Sidney frowned. 'He isn't a tramp. Not dressed like that.'

'Dressed like what, Mr Mills?'

'He has evening dress on. You know, white tie and tails.'

29

Dickie licked his lips. A dead gent on Craynebrook common! Now that made the story more interesting.

'Reporter, you say?' Sidney asked, his eyes narrowing at Dickie. 'This is going to be in the newspaper, is it?'

'Yes. Front page, I should think.' Dickie waited, knowing what Sidney Mills would say next.

'Will you mention me?' Sidney asked after a moment.

'Of course. You're the man who found the body. Tell me, how did you come to find him?'

Sidney cleared his throat and stood a little straighter. 'Well, I was out for a walk, you see, and I got over there, and I smelt something funny.'

'Funny?'

'Sickly and sweet. I wondered what it was, and I looked over the bush where the smell was coming from, and I saw him.' He shuddered at the memory.

Dickie made a note in his notebook. A sickly sweet smell meant the body must have been there for some time. 'Anything else you noticed?'

'Not really. I got away from there as fast as I could and called the police. God knows where my wife thinks I am. I should have been back half an hour ago, but the copper there told me I've got to wait in case the detectives want to talk to me. Why they can't come to me at home, I don't know.'

'Well, that's very interesting, Mr Mills, thank you,' Dickie said, putting his notebook away.

'Here, you will get my name right, won't you?' Sidney asked as Dickie turned away. 'Sidney Mills. M-I-L-L-S.'

'Don't you worry, Mr Mills,' Dickie said, trying not to smile. 'I'll get it right.'

Detective Sergeant Justin Denham tucked his scarf inside the collar of his overcoat and opened his mouth in a wide yawn.

The baby had been crying most of the night and he'd hardly got a wink of sleep. He could have done without spending an hour or so freezing his backside off on Craynebrook common.

'All right, Sam?' he asked as he approached PC Rudd, banging his gloved hands together.

'Bloody freezing, sarge,' PC Rudd replied.

Denham nodded. 'What we got?'

'Bloke over there found the body behind that bush. Called us straight away. I got a statement from him.'

'Body been there long?'

'Smelt like it had.' Rudd shook his head. 'It isn't pretty.'

'I don't expect it is.' Denham peered at the bush where a couple of uniformed officers were staring at the ground. 'Got the duckboards coming?'

Rudd nodded. 'On their way, sarge. Should be here any minute. What about your lot? When's Inspector Lund going to get here?'

'He isn't. Inspector Lund's in court all day today. Could be all week if the case goes the way he expects. No, we've got the new bloke coming down as soon as Old Mouldy's finished with him.'

'That's the Stannard fella, ain't it? The one from the 'papers?'

'That's him.' Denham waved at two men getting out of a police van. 'Get the duckboards down and be careful not to mess up any of the ground,' he called, watching as they followed his orders. 'All right, Sam. I'll leave you to it. If the crowd gets any bigger, give me a shout and I'll get you some help.'

'Thanks, sarge.'

Denham made his way over to the scene, stepping carefully to make sure he wasn't doing what he'd warned his colleagues about and messing up any evidence on the ground.

31

He was confident there was nothing of interest this far out from the body; the ground was hard as stone. As he drew nearer, however, he saw tyre marks etched into the dried mud. A vehicle had driven this way.

Denham was about to head over to the bushes to inspect the body when he heard an unfamiliar voice. He turned to see a smartly dressed man in a dark blue overcoat and matching trilby showing a warrant card to PC Rudd. He headed back towards the crowd, realising the new inspector had arrived.

Matthew put his warrant card away and stepped forward to meet the man coming towards him. 'Sergeant Denham?' he asked.

'Yes, sir,' Denham said. 'Good morning.'

'Morning. I'm Matthew Stannard.'

'I know who you are, sir. Read all about you in the newspaper.'

'Right,' Matthew said, and nodded over Denham's shoulder. 'Good to see the duckboards are down.'

'Yes, sir,' Denham said. 'There are tyre tracks showing a vehicle drove this way and over to where the body is. They must be quite old because I don't think it's rained for a week or more.'

'Footprints?'

'Not that I've seen so far. But I haven't actually been near the body yet.'

'Let's take a look, then.' Matthew started for the scene and Denham filled him in on some details.

'Mr Sidney Mills found the body. He telephoned the station at 9.03 this morning. PC Rudd has taken an initial statement but advised Mr Mills to stay in the vicinity in case you wanted to question him.'

'Police surgeon and photographer?'

'On their way.'

They drew near the bush, and Matthew stepped onto the duckboards, studying the ground. 'You're right. The tyre tracks lead to the bushes. The car parked and they got out.'

'They, sir?'

'Two different sets of footprints,' Matthew said, pointing. 'Either side of the car. Then, look here. They come together and head towards the bush.'

Denham cursed under his breath. 'We need a ruler, sir. To measure the footprints. I don't have one.'

Matthew put his hand in his overcoat pocket and drew out a tailor's tape measure. He handed it to the sergeant. 'Always keep one of those in your pocket, Denham. They come in handy.'

'Yes, sir.' Denham took the tape measure and bent down to the footprints.

Matthew sniffed the air. 'I can certainly smell him.'

'Yes, sir. Very ripe, I'd say.' Denham finished his measuring and rose, following Matthew behind the bush.

Matthew looked down at the body and his hand went to his mouth. It wasn't just the smell that was turning his stomach over; it was also the bloody mess that had been the man's face.

'Mr Mills said he'd been messed up,' Denham said in a hushed voice.

Matthew tore his eyes away from the man's bashed-in head. 'There's no sign of a struggle, here or out there. So, possibly he was killed somewhere else and brought here in a car by two men. They lifted him out of the car – he'd been on the back seat or in the boot – and dumped him here.'

'Sounds plausible.'

'It's just a theory,' Matthew said. 'Check his pockets for any form of identification.'

Denham bent down and examined the body's pockets,

33

those he could get to without disturbing it too much. 'Nothing, sir,' he said. 'It could be a robbery gone wrong.'

Matthew nodded. 'Could be.'

He glanced up and saw two men approaching. Both carried bags, and Matthew knew the photographer and police surgeon had arrived. They introduced themselves and Matthew and Denham stepped aside while they carried out their work. The police surgeon confirmed the man was dead, estimating the body had been there for two weeks at least, and left, allowing the photographer to take his pictures. When he was done, when Matthew was satisfied that every angle had been caught, he told Denham the body could be taken to the mortuary and scanned the common, settling his gaze on the row of houses at the edge.

'Get Uniform started on the house to house,' he said. 'Tell them to ask if anyone's seen a car crossing this ground in the last month. That should be an unusual enough sight. Then meet me back at the station.'

Denham nodded. 'Yes, sir.'

Chapter Five

Matthew's first visit to the CID office earlier that morning had been fleeting, just enough time to nod a hello to the two detective constables sitting at their desks before hurrying back out of the door. When he entered CID this time, only one of the junior detectives was still there, and he stood to attention as Matthew walked in.

'Apologies for not introducing myself properly earlier,' Matthew said, 'but I was in a hurry.'

'That's perfectly all right, sir,' the constable said. 'I knew you were on a call.'

'Thanks. And you are?'

'DC Simon Barnes, sir. The other chap you saw is DC Gary Pinder. He's been called out to a burglary. Everyone else is out. I'll expect you'll see them later.'

'Well, I'm very pleased to meet you, Barnes. I hope we'll work well together.' The words, practised the night before, rolled off Matthew's tongue with ease. They were the same words used by his guvnor when Matthew had joined Hackney CID. He'd always thought they sounded good.

'I'm sure we will, sir,' Barnes replied. 'Can I get you a cuppa?'

'Yes, thank you.' Matthew pointed to a small, partitioned section of the room. 'Is that my office?'

'Yes, sir. You're in there,' Barnes followed Matthew into the small office, 'with DI Lund.' He gestured at the desk to the right.

Matthew caught Barnes's eye as he studied Lund's desk, and they shared a look of disdain. Lund was obviously a messy worker, for there didn't seem to be an inch of space on the desktop free of clutter. The top sheet of the blotter was a mass of blue and black ink, backwards words and blots, and should have been thrown away by now. Pencils were scattered around the telephone, desk lamp and paper trays, but all of it seemed to have been moved to one side to make way for Lund's refreshments. A cup and saucer of a half-drunk tea was on the right hand side, scum on the top of the liquid. In the saucer were the remains of a biscuit, and a crinkled greaseproof wrapper containing the curling crusts of a sandwich was next to it. A photograph of a rather plump, severe woman was perched precariously near the edge of the desk and the ashtray to its side was overflowing.

'DI Lund is in court all day,' Barnes said as Matthew moved to the hatstand and hung up his overcoat and hat.

'So I understand.' Matthew emptied his pockets, putting his notebook and packet of cigarettes on the desk. He sat down and opened the drawers. They were mostly empty save for three pencils, a pencil sharpener, a knotted collection of treasury tags and a half-empty bottle of aspirin. Matthew pointed at the typewriter sitting on the blotter. 'Does that have to be here?'

'Oh,' Barnes said, and heaved the Imperial into his arms, turning to set it down on a narrow table against the wall. 'DI Lund's not keen on typewriters. It takes him half an hour to type two words, so he usually gets one of us to do the typing. Do you type, sir?'

'When I have to, constable,' Matthew said, not ready to admit he wasn't much better at typing than Lund. Now he was an inspector, he could enjoy delegating such administrative tasks to the junior ranks. He looked up at Barnes and raised his eyebrows. 'That tea?'

'Just getting it, sir,' Barnes said and hurried out.

Matthew pulled the In tray towards him, the only item on the desk that gave any indication of having a previous owner. The tray was filled with buff-coloured folders, and paper-clipped to the topmost was a handwritten note. It said 'Good Luck' signed off with the initials BC.

Barnes came back with the tea. 'That's from DI Carding, sir,' he said, putting the cup and saucer near Matthew's right hand. 'He was here before you.'

'Good luck? For these cases or in general?'

Barnes shrugged. 'I couldn't say, sir.'

'Are these all ongoing cases?' Matthew asked, opening the first folder.

'I believe so, sir. I think some of them may have been started by DI Lund, but he...'

Barnes didn't need to say anymore; Matthew understood Lund had used the opportunity of his predecessor's departure to dump all his unwanted case files on the new boy's desk. He asked Barnes for the Missing Persons register and settled down to see if he could find his dead man in its pages.

A moist warmth engulfed Dickie as he entered *The Chronicle*'s main office. The radiators were on full blast and smoke filled the air, courtesy of the chain-smoking secretary who barely looked up from her typewriter when Dickie came in. Light filtered thinly through the windows marred by dirt, forcing desk lamps to be turned on even this early in the day.

It was an unpleasant, rather dingy office, but to Dickie, it felt like home.

He had lingered on the common for another hour while the police carried out their investigation, watching as the mortuary van arrived and took away the body, laid out on a stretcher and covered by a thick woollen blanket. He'd seen the uniformed officers knocking on the doors of the row of houses that bordered the common, talking to the occupants and scribbling down information on clipboards. But he hadn't been able to gather any more information than that Sidney Mills had supplied, and he wondered how many column inches he would manage to fill when Bill Edwards shouted from his office, 'Dickie! Get in here.'

Dickie unwound his tartan scarf and took off his coat, hanging them over the back of his chair, before going in to see what his editor wanted. 'Yes, Bill?' he asked, moving around the editor's desk to hold his frozen hands over the radiator.

Edwards tapped his cigarette against the ashtray and stuffed it back in the side of his mouth. 'Where's my profiles?'

'I'm working on them.'

'Let's have a look at them, then.'

Dickie turned and leant against the radiator, a pleasurable warmth radiating through his backside. 'I haven't actually written anything yet—'

'I know you haven't,' Edwards growled. 'I've been through your desk and found nothing.'

'What are you doing going through my desk, Bill?'

Edwards was unmoved by Dickie's outrage. 'I've given you a job to do, Dickie, and you're not doing it.'

'I will write them, but I got that call this morning.'

'The body on the common? You should have let Teddy take that one. He needs the experience.'

Dickie toed a cigarette stub he'd discovered by his shoe and Edwards heaved a sigh.

'Do the profiles, Dickie. I know it's not the best assignment in the world, but it's got to be done. You've had weeks and you haven't even set up any interviews.'

'I've got a list of names I'm going to work through.' An idea suddenly occurred to Dickie that might mollify Edwards. 'And I'm going to try to get a meeting with Superintendent Mullinger this afternoon.'

'Well, that's a start.' Edwards tapped a pencil on the desk as his eyes narrowed at Dickie. 'What's the story on this body? Dead tramp?'

'No. A gent in evening dress, apparently. Beaten bloody according to the fella who found him.'

'Murder, then?' Edwards' interest was piqued. 'Get anything from the coppers?'

Dickie shook his head. 'Mullinger's got their mouths sewn up tight.'

'See what you can find out from Mullinger when you see him, if you can get him to talk about anything other than himself.' Edwards shook his head indulgently at Dickie. 'Write up the piece about the body, then. Can you make something of it for the front page?'

'I don't have much, but I could give it an angle. It's being investigated by the new inspector. Name of Stannard.'

Edwards frowned. 'Why do I know that name?'

Dickie gave him a hint. 'Hackney? Last year?'

'Stannard, Stannard...' Edwards banged his desk. 'Got it. The Marsh Murderer. Stannard's the copper that caught him.'

'The very same. Been made up to inspector and started at Craynebrook this week.'

'Is Stannard on your list to interview? Because if he isn't, he should be.'

'If Mullinger will let me talk to him. You know what he's like.'

'Try to get him. Stannard's would be a profile even I'd like to read.'

'I'll do my best,' Dickie promised.

Denham rapped on Matthew's open office door. 'I'm back, sir,' he declared.

'Get anything?' Matthew asked, gesturing Denham to come in.

Denham dragged a chair over. 'The only thing that came out of the house to house enquiries was a husband and wife at No. 15. The Carpenters were in bed when they heard a screech of car tyres and got up to look out of the window. They saw a car driving off the road and onto the common. This was a week or so before Christmas in the early hours of the morning. They didn't see where it went or whether it stopped. They just thought it was someone mucking about and went back to bed.'

'Did they recognise the car or see the person driving?'

'Didn't see the driver, but the husband said the car was black with a light canopy. Couldn't say what make or model, though.'

Matthew lit a cigarette, his fourth of the day, then remembering Denham, offered him the pack. Denham held up a palm in polite refusal. 'How long for the pictures to come back from the photographer?'

'He'll be developing the prints now, so by the end of the day, I should think.'

Matthew nodded, satisfied with the answer. 'The mortuary called. Postmortem's at three, so I'll need a car to take me down there.'

'I'll sort that out, sir,' Denham said, rising and putting the chair back where he had found it. He noticed the Missing Person register on Matthew's desk. 'Any luck finding the dead man in there?'

'No. There's a couple that are roughly the same height and build, but the hair's the wrong colour. They're brown-haired and our chap's a redhead. We'll have to wait on the fingerprints, and as soon as we have them, get them off to the Yard to check against their records.'

'Do you want me to come with you to the post-mortem?'

Matthew shook his head. 'You've got enough to be getting on with here. Type up Mr Mills' witness statement and all the others. And telephone the local stations. Check on their Missing Persons, just in case. Someone, somewhere, must be missing this man.'

Chapter Six

Matthew pushed open the doors to the mortuary and recoiled at the stench that hit him, a mixture of chemicals and decaying flesh. His head was already throbbing with a headache and the smell made his head swim. He cursed himself for not having eaten anything before he left the station as his stomach flipped.

'Hello,' a voice said, making Matthew jump, for he hadn't seen the white-coated young man standing by the sink. 'Dr Wallace will be here in a moment.'

'Thanks,' Matthew said, fishing in his pocket for his cigarettes. He lit one, closing his eyes as he took the smoke down. It didn't get rid of the stench, but it certainly helped.

'Put that out, please,' a low, clipped voice said.

Matthew opened his eyes to see another man in a white coat standing on the far side of the ceramic slab where the dead man was laid out beneath a sheet. He was in his fifties with dark hair turning grey around the tips of his ears and a square, craggy face that exuded authority.

'It helps with the smell,' Matthew explained.

'I don't allow smoking in my examination room.'

The young man who had greeted Matthew strode over and

presented him with a stainless steel kidney-shaped bowl. He glanced from Matthew's hand to the bowl and Matthew reluctantly threw his cigarette into it.

'Detective Inspector Matthew Stannard,' Matthew said, moving towards the older man and holding out his hand over the corpse.

The older man took it. 'Leo Wallace. Pathologist. You're new, aren't you?'

'Yes. It's my first day, actually.'

'In at the deep end, then,' Wallace said, indicating the body beneath the sheet. He nodded at his assistant and the young man whipped the sheet away. 'So, what do we have here? A body found this morning on Craynebrook common, I believe?'

The assistant nodded. 'Presumed killed elsewhere and deposited at the scene.'

Wallace looked over at Matthew. 'Why the presumption it was a deposition site and not a murder site?'

'There were tyre tracks suggesting a car had driven to the spot. There were also footprints but no drag marks, which makes me think he was carried and dumped.' Matthew took out his notebook and held it up. 'Mind if I make my own notes?'

'Not at all,' Wallace said, and nodded to his assistant. 'I'm ready to begin the visual examination of the body.' His assistant stood ready, pencil poised. 'We have a man of between twenty-five and thirty-five years of age, five foot eleven, red-haired, well nourished.' Wallace opened the mouth. 'Teeth are in reasonable condition. Two fillings to rear molars. No sign of gum disease.' He took up a magnifying glass and examined the hands. 'The hands, as well as the face, appear to have suffered from animal predation. Nails are clean and filed. No obvious sign of anything beneath the nails, such as skin or hair. Clothes are sodden. Decomposition is advanced. The subject has obviously been dead for some time.'

'How long, Mr Wallace?' Matthew asked, looking up from his notebook.

Wallace gave him a withering glance and Matthew guessed the pathologist wasn't used to being interrupted. 'That is what the post-mortem will tell me, inspector.'

'But at a guess,' Matthew pressed. 'The police surgeon estimated a minimum of two weeks.'

'Between three and four weeks, I'd say, but you will have to wait for my report before you hold me to that.'

'Of course,' Matthew said with a grateful smile, and nodded for Wallace to continue.

'Massive damage to the back of the skull. A severe depression over the crown. Bone has splintered, probably entering the brain. Almost certainly the killing blow. Contusions to the face. Looks like the left cheekbone has been fractured along with the nose. Lips have been split open.' He peered through the magnifying glass. 'Possible shoe print spanning the left jawline. Right. Let's get him stripped.'

The assistant put down his clipboard and picked up a pair of scissors. Wallace stood back as he cut away the clothing, revealing the body beneath. Matthew winced. The man's torso was a mass of bruises and broken skin and he felt his gorge rising. He caught Wallace looking at him and turned his head away.

'Mind if I take a look through those?' Matthew asked, pointing at the clothing the assistant was carefully putting into a metal tray.

'Help yourself,' Wallace said, moving back to the slab. 'Shoe prints visible on the torso amongst the extensive bruising. Three ribs on the left have been broken, one rib on the right.'

Matthew took the metal tray to a workbench on the opposite side of the room, glad to have an excuse to turn his back on the body while Wallace prodded and poked. He picked up the man's pair of black patent leather pumps, noting the lack of mud on them, supporting his theory that the dead man hadn't walked across the common, as well as the manufacturer's name stamped on the inside. They were the kind of shoes a man could buy in any high street shoe shop. The socks, vest and underpants were of similarly ordinary provenance, but Matthew was impressed when he took up the black tails and felt the quality of the fabric. He peeled back each side of the front, looking for a label, and his eyes rose in surprise when he found it. He examined the pockets, just in case Denham had missed anything, but found nothing.

The last object in the tray was a wristwatch. It had a silver face with Arabic numerals and a dark brown strap. Matthew turned it over and saw there was an engraving on the metal back plate. It read: *27th August 1928. The day you saved me. All my love forever, N.* Matthew wondered who N was and what the dead man had saved her from. Frowning, he turned the watch over once more. Something was peculiar here. The man's evening dress, his tails, trousers and shirt, were all top quality, but his underwear, shoes and watch were work-a-day garb. A man who could afford the best in evening wear surely could afford the best in everything else.

'I am now going to make the first incision,' Wallace said, and Matthew turned to see the pathologist putting the blade of a scalpel to the dead man's chest.

A moment later, there was the sound of gas escaping, as if from a punctured tyre or football, and a noxious smell filled the room. Matthew's vision blurred, then darkened. The last thing he saw was the cold, tiled floor of the mortuary smacking him in the face.

· · ·

Miss Halliwell set the tea tray on Superintendent Mullinger's desk. 'Will there be anything else, Mr Mullinger?'

'No, thank you, Miss Halliwell,' Mullinger said, and took the nearest cup and saucer as she closed his office door behind her. 'Well, Mr Waite, how does this work?'

Dickie reached for the remaining cup, helping himself to two of the five digestive biscuits on the plate, placing one in his saucer and dunking the other in his tea. 'I ask you questions and you answer them.'

'What kind of questions?' Mullinger dropped two cubes of sugar into his tea and stirred noisily with his spoon.

'Well...' Dickie munched on his biscuit, giving himself time to think. Although he had planned to interview Mullinger at some point, he hadn't intended to do it so soon and hadn't prepared any questions. 'Tell me about when you began in the police.'

Mullinger needed no further prompting; he talked and talked. Dickie learned about his earliest days as a police constable, his rapid but entirely deserved rise through the ranks until he reached the lofty position he now occupied. Mullinger told him all this with a fair amount of name-dropping, not meaning to but telling Dickie his career owed as much, if not more, to the friends he had made as to his ability as a policeman. Dickie took down as many of Mullinger's words as he could, but his hand began to cramp and he took a sneaky glance at his watch. He'd been listening to Mullinger for almost three-quarters of an hour and the man had hardly paused for breath. Time to shut him up talking about himself and move him on to the men who served under him, Dickie reckoned.

'That's excellent, Superintendent,' he said, cutting Mullinger off in mid-sentence. 'That's lots of excellent material for your profile.'

'You're sure you have enough?' Mullinger asked.

'Plenty about you and your background,' Dickie assured him. 'But what about running a police station? How do you go about doing that as well as you do?'

Mullinger frowned and toyed with the handle of his teacup. 'Well, I've always felt it's important to set standards for the men to aspire to. You have to understand, most of the men who join the police force come from the lower classes and as such, do not possess the manners I believe are requisite when dealing with the better members of society, such as are to be found in Craynebrook.'

Dickie nodded understandingly while thinking what an insufferable snob Mullinger was. 'And how do you set the standard?'

'By making it quite clear when they start that I won't have rudeness or informality from them, not to myself nor to the public. Why, only this morning, I told my newest officer – he's been transferred from Hackney, you understand – that he must employ tact and diplomacy when dealing with the public in Craynebrook. Those were my very words.'

'Your newest officer would be Detective Inspector Matthew Stannard, I believe?'

'That's correct.'

'The man who caught the Marsh Murderer.'

Mullinger's mouth tightened. 'Yes.'

'You must be delighted to have such a detective at your station,' Dickie said, unable to resist goading the superintendent.

'Delighted?'

'Well, he is something of a celebrity,' Dickie said with a smile. 'My editor would be over the moon if I could get a meeting with DI Stannard. He'd make an excellent subject for one of the profiles, you see.'

Mullinger put his cup and saucer back on the tray. 'That won't be possible.'

'It would only take about half an hour—'

'Inspector Stannard is on an enquiry, Mr Waite. I'm certainly not taking him off a murder investigation to talk to you.'

'Perhaps he would be prepared to speak to me when he's off duty?'

Mullinger cleared his throat. 'I'm afraid that's all I've got time for.' He pressed a button on his intercom. 'Miss Halliwell? Mr Waite is leaving.'

Dickie could take a hint. He screwed the cap back on his pen, tucked it and his notebook into his inside jacket pocket, and rose as Miss Halliwell opened the door. 'Thank you for your time, Superintendent Mullinger.'

'Not at all. You will let me see the piece you write before you go to print?'

'Of course,' Dickie nodded, knowing Mullinger just wanted to make sure Stannard's name didn't creep into the article and risk eclipsing him. 'Good afternoon.'

Matthew was sitting with his head in his hands on the bench outside the mortuary. He'd come to there, stretched full out on the wooden slats, with the overhead lights hurting his eyes and an overwhelming sense of shame.

'Here. Take this.'

Matthew accepted the mug with hands that shook a little. 'Thank you,' he said and tasted the tea, his face screwing up at the sweetness.

'Three sugars,' Wallace said, sitting down next to him on the bench. 'Drink it all up. You need it.'

Matthew took a few more mouthfuls. 'What must you think of me?'

'Oh, none of that.'

'I should be used to post-mortems by now. I've made a fool of myself.'

'Not a bit of it. You're not the first policeman to faint in my mortuary and I daresay you won't be the last. Feeling better?'

Matthew nodded. 'The tea's helping.'

'Nothing better than a good cup of tea. Except maybe a whisky.'

'You don't have one of those, do you?' Matthew asked, only half jokingly.

Wallace patted Matthew on the shoulder. 'You'll be right as rain once you've rested a little.'

'Did you finish the post-mortem?'

'Lord, no. You haven't been out that long. I'd barely got started when you dropped.' Wallace gave Matthew a sideways glance. 'Will you be coming back in?'

Matthew ran his hand over his hair, patting it back down where it was sticking up. 'I'd rather not, if you don't mind.'

'I don't mind at all. I'll be working on the most unpleasant part and I don't want to have to pick you off the floor again.'

Matthew leaned back against the tiled wall and stared at the ceiling, taking a few deep breaths. His headache was even worse than before. 'Did I hear you right? The killing blow was the crack on the head?'

'You did. I'll be able to confirm that once I open up the skull.'

'Any idea what the weapon was?'

'Something flat and wide. A small plank of wood, perhaps. Whatever it was, I suspect he would have gone down like a sack of potatoes.'

'Killed him instantly?'

'Very possibly.'

'What about the damage to his face and torso? You mentioned shoe prints. He was kicked?'

'Repeatedly, the poor fellow.'

'That's very helpful, Mr Wallace. Thank you.' Matthew drained his mug and set it down on the bench. He made to stand up, but Wallace put out a hand.

'Wait a moment, inspector. Try your legs before you stand.'

'I'm fine,' Matthew assured him with a grateful smile. He put his hands flat on his knees, took a deep breath, and stood, spreading out his arms to prove he was balanced.

Wallace nodded, satisfied. 'Sweet tea always works.'

'I'll get back to the station.' Matthew reached down to the bench to pick up his hat and coat, which had been thoughtfully put beside him. He folded the coat over his arm and was turning to go when Wallace's amused voice made him turn back.

Wallace had got to his feet and was holding up an envelope. 'Don't you want these, inspector? Your dead man's fingerprints?'

Matthew took the envelope with a shake of his head. 'I'm not making a very good first impression, am I?'

'Not at all, inspector. I actually like people to be upset by a cutting up. Having to determine a cause of death for a person on my slab can sometimes diminish my faith in human nature, knowing another human being put them there. To know there are still people who can be horrified and upset by sudden and violent death is rather reassuring.'

'I'm glad to be of some use,' Matthew said with a wry grin. 'Before I go, Mr Wallace, I wonder if I can ask a favour?'

'You may.'

'Can I ask you to keep my passing out to yourself? It's my first day at Craynebrook, as I said, and if it got around the station that I'd fainted... Well, I could do without their mockery.'

Wallace patted Matthew's arm and nodded. 'Your secret is safe with me.'

Matthew, knowing part of the reason he had a headache was because he hadn't eaten, stopped at a bakery on the way back to the station and bought himself two Bath buns. They were a little on the stale side, but they went some way to stopping the shaking of his hands.

Walking into CID, he told Denham of Wallace's preliminary findings and handed over the envelope containing the fingerprints, telling him to despatch them to Scotland Yard with all haste. Denham said he would see to it and informed Matthew he had turned nothing up regarding Missing Persons registered at other local stations.

'Why do you think he was done in, sir?' Denham wondered as Matthew took out the bottle of aspirin from his desk drawer and tipped two pills into the palm of his hand.

'Well, he didn't have any money on him, no pocketbook, no money clip, so it might be robbery,' Matthew said, wincing as he swallowed the pills dry. 'But it seems a lot of trouble to go to, to simply rob a man. Have the photographs come in yet?'

Denham disappeared to his desk and came back a moment later with a file. He placed it before Matthew. 'What are you looking for, sir?' he asked as Matthew studied each picture carefully.

'The pathologist believed the weapon was something like a narrow plank of wood. I'm just seeing if there's anything at the scene that could be a match. No, there's nothing here. Get Uniform to extend the search to all of the common, just in case the weapon was flung away further afield.'

'Yes, sir.'

'And I'm going to need a car first thing in the morning.'

'Of course, sir. Where will you be going?'

'Savile Row,' Matthew said, and saw the sergeant's eyebrows rise in surprise. 'The tails our dead man was wearing were made by a Savile Row tailor.'

'It's not much to go on, sir,' Denham said doubtfully.

'At the moment, it's all we have.'

Matthew looked out into the main office as the door opened and a man he hadn't seen before shuffled in. He was short and plump with brown hair thinning on top. His tie was askew and one tail of his shirt was untucked.

Denham followed his gaze. 'DI Lund,' he murmured and returned to his desk, nodding a greeting at the incoming inspector.

Matthew got to his feet, wincing as his brain rocked inside his skull.

'Hello!' Lund said in a surprised tone, halting at the door and looking Matthew up and down.

Matthew extended a hand. 'Matthew Stannard. Pleased to meet you.'

'Raymond Lund,' Lund said, shaking it. His hand felt soft and clammy and Matthew resisted the urge to wipe his own on his jacket.

Lund turned to his desk, taking a toffee from his jacket pocket and unwrapping it. 'I've been in court all day.'

'Yes, I know,' Matthew said, resuming his seat.

'Going to be an all-weeker, I reckon,' Lund said gloomily, his mouth making smacking noises as he chewed on the toffee. 'You ever had one of those?'

'Once or twice.'

'Bloody hate them when they're like that. Sitting around all day, waiting to be called. I hear you've got a dead body. That's bad luck on your first day.'

'Bad luck on any day.'

'More so for him, though, eh?' Lund grinned. 'Know who he is yet?'

'Not yet.'

'I hate those too. Unidentified bodies. It can take ages to find out who they are, if you ever do.'

'I'm sure I'll find out who he is.'

'Yes, well,' Lund gave Matthew another appraising look. 'I expect it'll be a piece of cake for the man who caught the Marsh Murderer.'

Chapter Seven

A police car was waiting for him at the front of the station when Matthew arrived the next morning. He poked his head through the window of the passenger door, introduced himself to the driver and climbed in.

It took over an hour to reach Savile Row, the police driver having to fight his way through the heavy London traffic. Matthew, who hadn't slept well the night before, his mind refusing to switch off, tried to focus on the notes he'd made in his notebook, but his eyes closed and his chin sank upon his chest. He jerked awake when the driver said loudly, 'We're here, sir.'

Matthew cleared his throat, annoyed with himself for drifting off, and knowing it would soon be all around the station that he had been asleep on the job. He put his note-book away and smoothed a hand over his hair before opening the door.

Telling the driver to wait, Matthew strolled down the street, not wanting to rush and so deny himself the pleasure of window-shopping, and using the cold morning air to wake him up properly. It irked him a little that window-shopping was all he could do. His salary would never be enough to enable him to afford a Savile Row suit; he would have to continue to make do with old Mr Hoberman of Mare Street, Hackney.

Matthew chided himself for the thought the very next moment. To think he was making do was unkind; there was nothing at all substandard about Mr Hoberman's tailoring. He had done Mr Hoberman a service some years back, catching the gang who had beaten up his son in an anti-Semitic attack, and after seeing Matthew eye his suits with a fierce longing, had offered to make him a suit free of charge. Matthew had refused, politely and reluctantly, informing Mr Hoberman it was against police regulations to accept gratuities. But the tailor wouldn't take no for an answer and Matthew finally agreed to have a suit off him at a greatly reduced price. The suit Matthew wore beneath his overcoat, and the grey one hanging in his wardrobe, were both Mr Hoberman's work, and he knew they were as good as anything a Savile Row tailor could produce.

Matthew stopped at a shop with a sign bearing the name Rose & Harper. He opened the door, and a bell tinkled overhead. He walked into a shop that seemed nothing but gleaming mahogany and rich colours, all illuminated by soft, pale yellow lights. Waistcoats adorned half-mannequins, cravats were tied around their stunted necks, and gloves were fanned out invitingly on trays.

A tall, thin man, immaculately dressed, stood behind a long counter. He gave Matthew an appraising glance and said, 'Good morning, sir. Can I help you?'

Matthew put his hat down on the counter and held up his warrant card. 'Detective Inspector Stannard.'

The man's expression turned to alarm. 'Police? Is something wrong?'

'I'm hoping you'll be able to help me, sir, in identifying a person of interest. Could I have your name?'

'Adam Gibson, I'm the manager here. I'm not sure I can be of any help.'

'Well, we'll see.' Matthew smiled. 'The man is mid-twenties to mid-thirties, red-haired, five foot eleven, medium build. He was wearing black tails made by this establishment.'

'That's not much to go on, inspector,' Mr Gibson said, relaxing a little now, Matthew guessed, it was clear neither he nor the shop was in any trouble.

'I appreciate that, sir, but the tails were of a recent design, I'd say, so perhaps you can think of any person who matches the description who might have purchased them in the last year, say?'

Mr Gibson tutted. 'I can't think, inspector. You have to appreciate how many men patronise this establishment. Do you have a photograph of this man?'

'I don't,' Matthew said, 'but perhaps you have a list of your customers you could consult to see if the names ring any bells?'

Matthew saw Gibson's reluctance to divulge his client list and was preparing to insist when the manager ducked beneath the counter and drew out a large ledger, banging it down on the worktop and flipping it open.

'One year, you say, inspector?'

'To begin with.' Matthew watched as Gibson ran his forefinger down the column of names, first on one page, then another, and another. He was becoming disheartened when the forefinger tapped a particular line. 'Mr Gibson?' he prompted.

'This might be your man. Mr Rupert Caine. He had a full evening suit from us in August of last year.' Gibson's brow furrowed. 'Let me see. Yes, he was an inch or two shorter than me, so that would fit your five foot eleven. I would put him at about thirty-two years of age. Mr Caine had red hair and, judging by the measurements here, I would class him as medium build.'

'Do you have an address for him?' Matthew asked. 'I expect all your clients have credit accounts here?'

'Naturally,' Mr Gibson said indignantly, affronted by the idea that any of his clients would ever demean themselves by paying for their clothes with cash at the point of sale. 'I have an address for Mr Caine.' He read it out and Matthew jotted it down.

'Was the evening suit the only items Mr Caine bought from you?'

Mr Gibson flipped another page in the ledger. 'He also bought several ties and a Prince of Wales check suit.'

'All on credit?'

'Yes, of course.'

'Do you usually give credit facilities to anyone who walks in here, off the street, as it were?'

'Certainly not. We either know the gentleman in question or he comes with a reference from another of our gentlemen. We would not extend credit facilities to you, for example.'

It was a dig, Matthew knew, a deliberate show of disdain from the manager. 'Because I'm a policeman?'

'Because you do not have a reference, inspector. I'm afraid a warrant card from His Majesty's Constabulary is not quite good enough for this establishment.'

'And Mr Caine had a reference?'

'He must have done, inspector, else he would not have been extended credit.'

'Do you have the reference?'

'I'm afraid not.' Mr Gibson's expression suggested he wasn't sorry at all. 'I handed it back to Mr Caine.'

'You didn't make a note of the referee?'

'That is not our accustomed practice.'

'Do you remember who wrote it?' Matthew persevered patiently. 'Presumably, it was from someone you had already sold suits to.'

There was a falter in Mr Gibson's expression and Matthew knew then his check of the reference had been less than thorough. Perhaps there had been an 'Honourable' in the title, and Mr Gibson had thought that, unlike Matthew's warrant card, that was good enough.

'I cannot recall, inspector,' Mr Gibson said, and there was a genuine note of apology in his words this time. Or was it regret? 'But I am sure the reference was perfectly good. After all, Mr Caine had a Rolls Royce motor car and a driver. He drove up in it just out there.' He pointed through the window to the street.

'You didn't get the registration number, I suppose?'

'No, inspector,' Mr Gibson sighed.

'Can you describe his driver?'

'The driver? Really, inspector. All these questions.'

'If you could bear with me, sir.'

The brow furrowed again. 'I didn't get a very good look at him, but I suppose he was young and slender. He had blond hair, I think. I remember it poking out from beneath his cap. That's all I can tell you, inspector. The driver got out of the car to open the back door for Mr Caine and then got back into the driver's seat.'

Matthew noted these details down. 'Is Mr Caine's account up to date? Did he pay for his clothes?'

Mr Gibson consulted the ledger. When he looked back up at Matthew, his cheeks were red. 'All of Mr Caine's bills are currently outstanding.'

Matthew nodded. He had suspected this would be Gibson's answer. 'And I think they're unlikely to ever be settled.'

Mr Gibson stiffened. 'And why is that?'

'I believe Mr Caine is dead. If only you'd taken a note of his referee, you could apply to him for payment.' He smiled at the manager. 'Thank you for your time, Mr Gibson. Good afternoon.'

Chapter Eight

The address Mr Gibson had given Matthew for Rupert Caine was a large, terraced house on Coleman Street in Marylebone. A sign in the front downstairs windows declared 'Rooms to Rent'.

In Matthew's experience, there were two types of landlord. The type who didn't care who they rented rooms to as long as their tenants paid their rent, and the type who insisted on references and laid down rules, determined to keep as respectable a house as was possible when accepting complete strangers into their home.

Mrs Paige-Ross, Matthew decided, was the latter type. An army widow, he guessed, whose husband's pension wasn't enough to make ends meet. She reminded him a little of his mother with her soft grey curls and the neat skirt and blouse, a jewelled brooch, probably paste, pinned to her tweed lapel. He resolved his mother would never have to take in lodgers to keep her head above water.

'Good afternoon, madam,' he said, wincing a little as rain dripped around the brim of his hat to slither down his neck. 'Sorry to bother you, but I wonder if I could ask you a few questions about a tenant of yours?' He held up his warrant card.

A wrinkled hand went to her throat. 'Of course,' Mrs Paige-Ross said nervously and stepped back, holding the door open for him to enter. He noticed her checking the street as she closed it, hoping no one had seen her give entrance to a policeman. He felt like telling her the police car parked outside would give him away but decided it wouldn't help to draw her attention to it.

'Let me take your hat and coat,' she said, holding her hands out. He handed them over. She hung them on a large oak wall unit and gestured him into the front sitting room where a coal fire blazed in the fireplace. 'Would you like tea, inspector? It won't take me a moment. The kettle's already boiled,' she asked as he sat down.

He said yes, partly because he was dying for a cup and partly because he knew it would give her time to relax a little. Decent people found a policeman in their home unsettling, and he wanted her to be at ease to answer his questions. Mrs Paige-Ross returned in a few minutes with a tray bearing a teapot, two cups and saucers, a milk jug, sugar bowl and plate of biscuits. Matthew rose to take the tray off her and set it down on the coffee table between them. His stomach rumbled at the sight of the biscuits.

She poured out the tea and told him to help himself to the biscuits. Matthew did, taking two digestives and propping them in his saucer. He took a sip of the hot tea and a bite of a biscuit, resisting the urge to dunk it. He had the feeling Mrs Paige-Ross would consider that a common thing to do.

'Which tenant?' she asked, holding her cup and saucer in her lap as she perched on the edge of her armchair.

'Mr Rupert Caine,' Matthew said, brushing crumbs from his trouser leg.

'Oh,' she said, and her expression drooped. 'Mr Caine.'

'He has a room here?'

'Had. He hasn't lived here for several months. He left at the end of August.'

'Did he leave a forwarding address?'

'Inspector,' she sighed, 'he left with no notice at all. He packed his bags and left in the middle of the night.'

'He did a moonlight flit?'

Mrs Paige-Ross shrugged at the vernacular. 'If that's what it's called. He owed me two months' rent. I never would have thought he'd do that. He seemed such a gentleman.' She sounded disappointed rather than angry.

'How long was he your tenant?'

'Three months. He paid the first month's rent upfront, even offered me the second month's rent, but I refused to take that.' She heaved a breath. 'Of course, if I'd known...'

Matthew nodded. He had a clearer picture of who Rupert Caine was. He presented himself as a gentleman, had good references, probably forged, seemed to have means and money, and so people took him to be a gentleman. Once he had their trust, he abused it. A con man. That's who Mr Rupert Caine was.

'Did he have a car?' he asked.

Mrs Paige-Ross took a sip of tea. 'I never saw one.'

'Did he have any visitors?'

'No.'

'No women came calling?'

Mrs Paige-Ross drew herself up. 'I don't allow my tenants to have women in their rooms, inspector.'

'Quite right,' Matthew said with an apologetic smile. 'But you didn't see him with a chauffeur, for example?'

'No. Mr Caine was out most days, and he went out a great deal at night. But he was always very pleasant when our paths crossed, very polite. As I say, I would never have suspected he would treat me so badly. And not just me, it seems. He gave this address out to others. I'm still receiving letters from his creditors.'

'Do you still have them?'

Mrs Paige-Ross rose and went to the bureau in the corner of the room. She opened the top drawer and took out a thin wadge of envelopes. She handed these to Matthew and resumed her seat with a sigh.

Matthew shuffled through the envelopes, noting the stamp of Rose & Harper, Savile Row, on the front of one. There was also a letter from a tobacconist, one from a barber's and another from a dentist, all asking for his bills to be settled. There was another paper, not a demand for payment, but a handwritten request for Mr Caine's shirts to be laundered.

'Is this Mr Caine's handwriting?' Matthew asked, showing Mrs Paige-Ross the note.

'Yes.'

The note was written on cheap notepaper in blue ink. The writing was almost clumsy, inelegant. Not the hand of a gentleman, Matthew thought. 'I'd like to keep all these, if I may?' he asked, already putting the bundle of envelopes into his inside jacket pocket.

'Of course. If you could get them to stop writing to me, I'd be grateful.' She sniffed. 'Why are you asking me about Mr Caine, inspector? Is he in some sort of trouble?'

'I'm afraid I believe Mr Caine to be dead, Mrs Paige-Ross.' Matthew saw her eyes widen, her lips purse, but she seemed to take the news with equanimity. 'A man's body was found in Craynebrook yesterday morning without identification upon him, and I have reason to believe he is Mr Caine.' *Or the man you knew as Mr Rupert Caine*, he mentally added, for he doubted it was his real name.

'I see. Do you have a photograph of him? I could tell you if it is him.'

This surprised Matthew. He wouldn't have expected a

lady like Mrs Paige-Ross willing to look at the photograph of a dead man. 'I'm afraid a photograph wouldn't help. You see, he was rather badly beaten and his face…' he paused, wondering how to describe the mess Mr Caine's face had become.

But Mrs Paige-Ross nodded understanding. 'I suppose I should say "poor Mr Caine", but after the way he treated me…' Her voice trailed off as she turned her gaze to the burning coals.

Mrs Paige-Ross had a harder heart than Matthew had taken her for. 'Well,' he said, 'if there's nothing more you can tell me about Mr Caine?' he asked over the rim of his teacup.

'Nothing I can think of, inspector. I really saw very little of him, as I've said, and it turns out I knew even less of him than I thought I did. He was a stranger, in every sense, it seems.'

'Then I shan't take up any more of your time. Thank you, Mrs Paige-Ross. You've been a great help.'

She saw him to the door and handed him his hat and coat. He hurried to the waiting police car, trying to dodge the raindrops.

Chapter Nine

Matthew's next stop was the police station on Marylebone Lane, hoping Mr Rupert Caine's activities had become known to his fellow officers. He introduced himself to the constable on the front desk and asked to speak with a detective.

A young man with a wispy moustache stepped forward to greet Matthew as he was shown into the CID office. 'DC Davis, sir. I understand you're from J Division. You're quite a bit off your patch.'

Matthew wasn't sure if there was an accusation in the young man's words – protecting a division's jurisdiction was practically Rule No. 1 in every police station he'd been in – but he chose to take it as just a polite remark.

'I don't want to tread on anyone's toes,' he said, 'but I could do with some information on an enquiry I'm working on.'

'Whatever I can do, sir,' Davis said, and dragged a chair over to his cluttered desk and gestured Matthew to it.

Matthew sat down, grateful the young man was prepared to be obliging. 'It's a murder enquiry,' he said, taking out his notebook and propping it on his knee. 'I have an unknown dead man in Craynebrook, but who might have been a Mr Rupert Caine. Do you recognise that name?'

DC Davis shook his head. 'It's not ringing any bells.'

'Well, he seems to have been a conman, so it's possible Rupert Caine may have been an alias. Any reports of cons in the area in the last year, specifically between June and August?'

Davis considered a moment, then moved to the bank of filing cabinets behind his desk and pulled open one of the drawers. 'There was a spate of reports of a man obtaining money by deception.' He rifled through the files, found the one he was looking for and pulled it out. 'Yes, here we are. There were four complaints made against a Mr Cyril Pargeter, one of which was dropped when the complainant decided he didn't want his wife to find out what he'd done.' Davis grinned. 'Mr Patterson, Mr Walton and Mr Black. This Mr Pargeter persuaded them to buy his car. He was letting it go for a song and they jumped at the chance. They hand over the money – six hundred pounds apiece – and Mr Pargeter disappears.'

'And the car?'

'Never got their hands on it. We traced the car to a rental company. They'd rented it out to a Mr Stephen Carter who matched the description of Cyril Pargeter.' Davis pulled out a piece of paper and showed it to Matthew. 'That's the signed agreement. Mr Carter returned the car to them at the end of the rental period.'

'And they didn't have an address for him?'

'No. Didn't need to take one, they said, as Mr Carter paid upfront.'

'Description?'

'Red hair, a little shy of six feet tall, medium build. Sound like your man?'

Matthew nodded. 'Anything else?'

'Pargeter or Carter, whoever, was well spoken, seemed like a gentleman, had all the right clothes, the manners. Charming. That seems to be the overriding impression everyone got.'

'He'd have to be to get all that money out of them. Can I have a look at that?' Matthew asked, and Davis handed the file over. 'And nothing since August?'

'Nothing. The last complaint against him was made on the fifteenth of August. We haven't had anything since so…'

'You assumed he moved out of the area,' Matthew finished.

'And into yours, apparently,' Davis nodded. 'Have you had complaints about a confidence trickster?'

Matthew shook his head. 'Not that I'm aware, but I've only got this information today and I haven't been back to the station yet. But my dead man sounds like he may have been this Rupert Caine or Stephen Carter or Cyril Pargeter. Could I take this file with me?'

Davis nodded. 'As long as you sign that you've taken it out and send it back to us when you're done.'

Matthew assured him he would, and thanking the young detective, bid him good day.

Henry Patterson was in his late fifties, an upright, soldierly type with gunmetal grey hair and a pencil moustache. He welcomed Matthew into his office with a nod and a hand-shake, but there was an air of embarrassment about Patterson as he waved him to a seat and told his secretary he wasn't to be disturbed.

'Thank you for seeing me, Mr Patterson,' Matthew said, taking out his notebook and pen. 'I'm investigating a suspi-cious death of an as yet unidentified man. Certain clues suggest he may be the man you knew as Cyril Pargeter, and I wonder what you can tell me about him?'

'I have told the other detectives.'

Matthew inclined his head apologetically. 'I'd like you to tell me, if you don't mind.'

Patterson sighed, smoothing his fingers along his moustache. 'I met Cyril Pargeter in the American Bar at the Savoy. I was having a drink after work and we fell into conversation.'

'What did you talk about?'

'Various things, inconsequential,' Patterson shrugged. 'How awful the weather was. The décor at the Savoy. The drinks available. Eventually, we got onto the subject of cars, and he told me he owned a Rolls Royce Phantom that he'd only bought the year before but was having to sell it because he was going abroad and couldn't take it with him.'

'Did he say where abroad?'

'Kenya, I think.'

'On business?'

'I believe so. He said he was a civil engineer.'

Matthew made a note. 'Please continue.'

'I told him I was thinking of getting a car and he joked I could buy his.'

'It was a joke?'

'Pargeter said it as a joke, inspector, I suppose so as not to seem pushy. Anyway, I asked him how much he wanted for it. He prevaricated for a while, saying he didn't like to talk money, but I rather pressed him.' Mr Patterson shook his head at his own gullibility. 'He named a price. Six hundred pounds.'

Matthew frowned. 'And that didn't strike you as cheap for a year-old Rolls Royce?'

'I know what you're thinking, inspector. That I was a fool not to have seen Pargeter for what he was, but I didn't.'

'I don't think you're a fool, Mr Patterson,' Matthew assured him. 'It's just my opinion that if something sounds too good to be true, then it usually is. But confidence tricksters know how to make an implausibility sound plausible, and they rely on the people they trick to be decent-minded, not even considering that another person may be up to no good.'

'Kind of you to say so, inspector,' Patterson gave a weak smile. 'So, there were other men he cheated? I didn't know that.'

'At least two others. Both defrauded the same way.'

'I see. Anyway, I told Pargeter I was very interested and asked to see the car. We left the bar, and he took me to where the car was parked. It was just as he'd described it. Beautiful. I said I wanted to buy it without a second thought. He asked if I was sure or just pulling his leg. I told him I was sure, and he said that if I really was keen to buy, then he would sell it to me. He wanted it to go to someone who would appreciate such a car. Buttering me up quite shamelessly, but I fell for it. We agreed to meet the next day at the Savoy. I would hand over the money and he would give me the necessary documents and keys. We met at the appointed hour. Pargeter bought me a drink, showed me the documents, and I gave him the six hundred pounds. He bought me another drink, drank half of his, then said he needed to visit the gentlemen's convenience and that when he came back, he would take me to the car and give me the keys.'

'But he didn't come back?'

'No. After fifteen minutes, I went into the lavatory to see if he was still in there. He wasn't. I went back to the bar. He wasn't there either. He wasn't anywhere. I asked the porter on the front doors if he'd seen Mr Pargeter and he told me he'd seen him leaving fifteen minutes previously.'

Matthew nodded. 'Immediately after he left you. Did you look for the car?'

'I walked up and down the road and there was no sign of it. I reported the whole miserable affair to the police and have been waiting for something to happen.' He looked meaningfully at Matthew. 'Is something happening? Has he been caught?'

Matthew thought of the body lying in the freezer at the mortuary and considered telling Mr Patterson that, in a way, Cyril Pargeter had been caught, but not by the police. 'I'm afraid I have nothing to report regarding your case, Mr Patterson.'

'I see,' Mr Patterson said unhappily.

'Was anyone with Mr Pargeter?'

'Not that I saw.'

'When you looked at the car, you didn't see a driver?'

Mr Patterson frowned. 'No. I suppose that should have alerted me, shouldn't it? A car like that, a man like that, would have had a chauffeur.'

The conversation was making him miserable, Matthew could see, and he'd got all he needed. He put his notebook away and got to his feet. 'Well, thank you, Mr Patterson. I won't take up any more of your time.'

Patterson rose, buttoning his jacket. 'Tell me, am I likely to see my money again?'

'I think it's unlikely,' Matthew admitted. 'I'm sorry.'

Patterson nodded. 'I'm resigned to the fact that the money has gone, inspector, and that, despite your words, I've been a damn fool. I know because my wife tells me so every day.'

Chapter Ten

After Henry Patterson, Matthew visited Alan Walton and Roger Black. Both told him the same story, of how Cyril Pargeter had engaged them in conversation and agreed to sell them his car, and both were just as embarrassed as Patterson by their gullibility. It was gone six by the time Matthew got back to the station and he was yawning as he walked into his office.

'Long day?' Lund asked.

Matthew jumped. He hadn't realised the office was occupied. 'Yes,' he said, hanging up his overcoat and hat. 'Lots of driving around and lots of talking to people.'

Lund took a mouthful of coffee. 'Get anywhere?'

'Maybe.' Matthew sank into his chair. 'Tell me. Have there been any reports of confidence tricksters in the area in the last year?'

Lund wiped his lips with the back of his hand. 'I don't think so. Why?'

'I think my dead man was a con artist.' Matthew ran the names Caine, Pargeter and Carter by Lund, but the detective shook his head and said they meant nothing to him. Matthew was disappointed. He'd hoped there would have been complaints made at Craynebrook similar to those made in Marylebone and that he would have his dead man's real name before the week was out. He sighed and made a mental note to have Denham check the names in the morning. Maybe something would turn up.

'Well, that's me done for the day,' Lund said, smacking his hands down on his desk and pushing himself up. He took his coat off the stand and pulled it on, dropping a homburg on his balding head. He turned to Matthew. 'Fancy a pint?'

Matthew knew he should accept the offer, that to turn his fellow inspector down would seem unfriendly, but he wasn't in the mood to spend an hour in the pub with Lund. And besides, he wanted to follow up on an idea he had. 'Not tonight, thanks. I've still got things to do. Maybe tomorrow if you're around.'

'Yeah, maybe. See you then.'

'Before you go,' Matthew halted Lund before he got out of the door. 'Where do Craynebrook's top drawer people go of a night?'

'The Super's sort, do you mean?' Lund considered. 'I'd say there's three places. The Conservative Club; that's on the high street. The golf club on Benston Drive, and the Empire Club on the corner of St Jude's Avenue. Why you asking?'

'My man played his cons on rich men he met in bars. I thought it might be worth seeing if he's been doing the rounds in Craynebrook.'

Lund nodded. 'Not a bad idea. But a word of warning. You might bump into the Super at either of the first two and he won't like you asking his friends questions about conmen.'

'But he won't be at the Empire Club?'

'He's not a member,' Lund grinned, 'no matter how hard he tries. But you're not going to these places tonight, are you? It's time to clock off, Stannard. You've done your day's work.'

'I will,' Matthew said, 'once I've been to the clubs.'

Lund shook his head. 'Rather you than me.'

Dickie knew his eyes were glazing over and diverted himself with a puff of his cigar. His face screwed up at the taste of it. He would have preferred to smoke his pipe, but the Member of Parliament for Craynebrook had insisted on the cigar, and smoke it Dickie must if he wanted to get Alexander King to talk about himself.

Not that it had been difficult. Like Mullinger, King had no shame talking about himself. Dickie was tempted to use 'garrulous' to describe King's manner when he wrote his profile piece, but that was a mild term for the narcissistic oratory that had been flowing from the lips of the politician for the past hour and a half. Dickie glanced down at his notebook lying on his right thigh. He had more than enough for the article. It was time to call it a night.

Dickie leaned over and balanced his cigar on the ashtray stand by the side of the leather armchair, catching out of the corner of his eye a figure entering the hall just beyond the open door of the room. He did a double take, doubting it was who he'd thought it was, and was surprised to see he had been right the first time.

'Well,' Dickie said, taking the opportunity of King quietly belching to rise, 'that's all excellent material for my article, Mr King. Thank you very much.'

'Oh,' King said, frowning as Dickie gathered up his things. 'You have enough, do you?'

'More than enough,' Dickie said with sincerity. 'And, of course, I'll send you a copy before it goes to print.' He could see Matthew moving away from the open doorway, further down the hall. He said a hasty goodbye and hurried after him.

Matthew was at the far end, speaking to a waiter. 'Inspector Stannard?' Dickie hailed.

Matthew turned at the call. 'Yes?'

'I thought it was you. I was on the common yesterday morning when you found that dead fella. One of the constables told me who were you and, of course, I recognised your name. Sorry. I should introduce myself. I'm Dickie Waite from *The Chronicle*.'

Matthew took Dickie's hand. 'Pleased to meet you, Mr Waite, but I'm afraid you'll have to excuse me. I'm on enquiries.'

'The dead man?'

'Yes, the dead man.' Matthew tried to step around Dickie, but the reporter moved to intercept him.

'I don't want to disturb you, inspector, but I wonder if we could sit down together sometime?'

'I can't talk about the case.'

'I know. That's not why I'm asking. I'm actually writing a series of profiles on eminent figures in Craynebrook and I thought you'd make a good subject.'

Matthew snorted. 'I'm not eminent, Mr Waite, and I doubt anyone will want to read about me.'

'That's false modesty, surely, inspector? You are, after all, the man who caught—'

Matthew didn't want to hear the words Marsh Murderer again. He cut Dickie off. 'I can't give you an interview, Mr Waite. Even if I wanted to, which I don't, Superintendent Mullinger would never allow it. Now, please. I really do need to get on.' He gestured for Dickie to move out of his way.

'Stannard!'

Matthew groaned as he looked over Dickie's shoulder and saw Mullinger striding towards him, a brandy glass in one hand, a cigar in the other. The dinner jacket he wore was straining at the buttons.

'What the devil are you doing here?' Mullinger demanded.

'I'm following up on enquiries, sir,' Matthew replied, stepping pointedly away from Dickie.

Mullinger glared at the reporter. 'After all I said to you, Stannard, you're talking to the Press?'

'No, sir,' Matthew protested. 'I—'

'I just happened to be here in the club, Mr Mullinger,' Dickie cut in. 'In fact, Inspector Stannard was doing his very best to get rid of me when you came along.'

'I see,' the superintendent said, his eyes narrowing. Mullinger didn't entirely believe Dickie, Matthew could tell.

'In fact,' Dickie went on, 'it's time I was off. Very nice to meet you, inspector,' he said, grabbing Matthew's hand and shaking it warmly, 'and good night to you both.'

Mullinger watched him go out the front door before speaking again. 'You better explain yourself, Stannard.'

'I'm following up a lead, sir,' Matthew said, cursing Dickie. 'I have reason to believe the dead man may have come here.'

'Here?' Mullinger looked around the hall as if trying to work out what a dead man whose body had been unceremoniously dumped on Craynebrook common could be doing at such a place as the Conservative club. 'You think he was a member?'

Matthew shrugged. 'I don't know until I make enquiries.'

Mullinger looked uneasy. 'Do you really have to? I'm sure you're wrong about this. No one here will know this dead man.'

'What's this about a dead man?' A short man with round spectacles, a bushy moustache and oiled hair poked his head around Mullinger. 'It all sounds very interesting.'

'No, not at all, Ian,' Mullinger said. 'This is to do with work.'

'Not the chappie found on the common, is it? I heard about that. This one of your men, Howard?' he asked, scrutinising Matthew.

'Yes, he is.' Mullinger made no attempt to introduce Matthew.

'How do you do? Ian Sterling.'

'How do you do, sir,' Matthew said.

'Have you come to question us?' Sterling said with a silly grin. 'I didn't do it, officer. Don't put the cuffs on me.'

Matthew smiled politely. 'I won't, sir. Not unless you're guilty.' It was said as a joke, but his words made Sterling's smile falter. 'I would like to ask you some questions, if I may.'

'Oh, ask away,' Sterling said, suddenly serious. 'Anything I can do to help.'

'Thank you.' Matthew ignored Mullinger's glare. 'The dead man is as yet unidentified, but he was between twenty-five and thirty-five, around five foot eleven, medium build, had red hair. He may have only recently come to the club. Do you know anyone like that?'

Sterling frowned. 'Well, I might be wrong, of course, but it does rather sound like that Calthrop chap.' He looked at Mullinger. 'You remember Charles Calthrop, don't you, Howard?'

Matthew stared at Mullinger. Mullinger was looking uncomfortable. His nose had reddened, and his Adam's apple bobbed as he swallowed.

'Calthrop?' Mullinger said, 'I don't remember—'

'Yes, you do,' Sterling said. 'You were chatting to him just before Christmas. Didn't you say he was going to put you onto a good thing?'

'I don't think I actually said that.'

'Sir,' Matthew cut in. 'Could I have a word with you?'

'Oh,' Sterling said, looking from Matthew to Mullinger, 'I haven't spoken out of turn, have I?'

'No, of course not.' Mullinger coughed and rubbed his mouth with the back of his hand. 'But I need to talk to Stannard about this. Do excuse me, Ian.'

Sterling nodded and left the two men alone. Matthew opened his mouth to speak, but Mullinger shook his head and turning, led him into a small room, slamming the door.

'Sir, if you recognised—'

'Now, you just hold your horses, Stannard.' Mullinger pointed a finger at Matthew's nose. 'I had no idea that man might be this Calthrop fellow.'

'But you had the report,' Matthew protested. 'You read the description. It must have rung a bell.'

'Why must it?' Mullinger cried. 'That description could have fitted half a dozen men.'

'Hardly, sir. Red hair isn't all that common.'

'I won't be contradicted in this way, Stannard. You don't even have proof that the dead man and Calthrop were one and the same.'

Matthew swallowed down his anger. 'I do need to know what you know about Calthrop, sir.'

Mullinger's mouth twisted in irritation. 'Very well.'

'Was he a member of this club?'

'No. I believe he was thinking about joining but er... well, he never got around to it, I suppose.'

'How often did you see him here?'

'No more than twice, I'm sure. The first time was only in passing. The second, when I popped in and he was already here, and we had a drink together.'

'What did you talk about?'

'Sterling's got it all wrong,' Mullinger said, his voice

rising. 'I talked to Calthrop for no more than half an hour and that was about nothing in particular.'

'It wasn't about a good thing he could put you on to?'

'Certainly not.'

'Or a motor car you were interested in buying?'

'Motor car?' Mullinger made a face. 'No.'

'Do you know who else he spoke to here? Who else I can ask—'

'No!' Mullinger cried. 'I absolutely forbid you to speak to anyone else. No one could tell you any more than I and to think that anyone here might be involved in his death.' Mullinger grabbed the handle and yanked the door open. 'It's unthinkable. Now, I order you to be on your way.'

'But sir—'

'No buts, Stannard. That's an order.' Mullinger made a shooing gesture and Matthew had no choice but to do as he was told. But Mullinger wasn't taking any chances. He escorted Matthew to the door and slammed it in his face.

Matthew glared at the door, resisting the urge to kick it. That Mullinger resented his presence in the club Matthew understood. But for the superintendent to refuse to talk to him, to hinder his investigation, was unforgiveable.

Pulling on his gloves, Matthew started down the path. As he reached the pavement, someone called his name.

'Sorry if I got you into trouble, inspector,' Dickie said. 'I didn't know your superintendent was there.'

'So, you'll understand if I don't particularly want to talk to you, Mr Waite,' Matthew said, pushing past Dickie.

'I get it,' Dickie said, hurrying to catch up, 'but why let him have it all his own way? Come on, inspector, give me something.'

'I can't talk about an ongoing case, Mr Waite, you know that.'

'You could, at least, tell me the dead man's name,' Dickie suggested.

'Actually, I can't. I don't know his name. Not his real one, anyway.'

'So, he's still an unknown dead man found on Craynebrook common,' Dickie said.

'You're talking in headlines,' Matthew said, smiling despite himself.

'Yes, I do that. Do you think we could slow down a bit, inspector? My legs aren't as young as yours.'

Matthew relented and slowed his pace.

'Do you know I could be able to help?' Dickie said, catching his breath. 'A few lines in the 'paper and you could have people clamouring to tell you all about the dead man. You might even find out his real name.'

Matthew glanced sideways at Dickie, acknowledging he might be right. An article in *The Chronicle* calling for information might prove useful. 'All right,' he nodded. 'I'll give you something.' He halted and Dickie did the same. 'The dead man may have gone under several names. None of which I'm telling you until I've made further enquiries. But I can give you a description.'

Dickie took out his notebook and pencil. 'Go on.'

'Five foot eleven, medium build, red hair, twenty-five to thirty-five. I know it's not much,' he added ruefully seeing Dickie's disappointment.

'No distinguishing marks?' Dickie asked. 'Scars, tattoos?'

'Unfortunately not.'

'All right. That will have to do. Who do you want me to attribute this to?'

'You can say it came from me.'

Dickie frowned. 'Are you sure? After the way Mr

Mullinger acted, you might do better to pass it off as someone else at the station.'

'Certainly not.' Matthew set off at a quick pace again.

'Where you off to now?' Dickie again caught up with him, tucking his notebook in his coat pocket.

'The golf club.'

'The golf club's closed tonight. All the staff have gone down with something so they've had to shut up. I was going to go there myself to interview one of the members for the 'paper.'

'The Empire Club, then,' Matthew amended irritably.

'Well, isn't that a coincidence? That's where I was heading.'

'Was it really?'

'I can tell you don't believe me,' Dickie said, grinning, 'but it happens to be true.' They walked on for a few yards in silence before he asked, 'How's it been going for you so far at the station?'

'Busy.'

'But no busier than where you were at Hackney, I suppose. You made quite a name for yourself there.'

Matthew sighed. 'Mr Waite, please don't use this time to get something on me for your newspaper. Not unless you want to end my career in the police.'

'I thought we were just chatting.'

'There's never a just with a journalist. Your lot are always after a story.'

'Now, that's unfair,' Dickie said in mock hurt.

'I'm sorry I've hurt your feelings.'

'No, you're not. Ah, here we are.' Dickie gestured up at the double-fronted, white-painted Georgian house. 'This is the Empire Club.'

They walked through the open gateway and up the paved path to the front double doors. The doors were not locked and there wasn't any porter guarding them on the inside. Matthew was surprised.

'Anyone could walk in here,' he said to Dickie.

Dickie wasn't listening. He was looking towards the end of the hall. 'This chap coming towards us is Thomas Yates,' he said to Matthew. 'He's the club treasurer.'

'I say,' Yates said as he drew nearer, 'can I help you?' He caught sight of Dickie. 'Oh, Mr Waite, isn't it? What are you doing here?'

'I have a meeting with one of your members, Mr Yates,' Dickie said.

Yates looked at Matthew. 'And you?'

'I'm not with Mr Waite.' Matthew flashed his warrant card. 'I'm Detective Inspector Stannard, Mr Yates. I'd like to ask you a few questions.'

'Me?' Yates said incredulously.

'You, sir, and anyone else who might be able to help me.' Matthew turned to Dickie and raised his eyebrows meaningfully.

Dickie took the hint. 'I'll let you get on,' he said, and smiling at Yates, walked away down the hall, turning into the lounge in search of his interviewee.

'I can't think how I or any of the members can be of help to the police,' Yates said.

'If we could go somewhere to talk, Mr Yates,' Matthew suggested, not willing to be put off.

Yates nodded and led Matthew into the smoking room. A few of the leather armchairs were occupied, and the men looked at Matthew with mild interest before returning to their newspapers or conversations.

'Please sit, inspector,' Yates said. 'If you could keep your voice down, though, I would appreciate it.'

'A man's body was found on the common yesterday, Mr Yates,' Matthew began. 'He has yet to be identified, but my enquiries have led me to believe he may have possibly visited clubs in Craynebrook. He was twenty-five to thirty-five, five foot eleven, medium build, red-haired. Do you recognise that description at all?'

'No, I don't believe I do.'

'Do these names mean anything to you? Rupert Caine? Cyril Pargeter? Stephen Carter? Charles Calthrop?'

'No, I don't think so, but I'll be the first to admit, my memory's not what it was.'

Matthew sighed. 'That being so, Mr Yates, I'm afraid I will have to talk to your members to see if any of them recognise the description or the names.'

'Oh, no, really?' Yates looked pained. 'Must they be bothered in this way?'

'I'm afraid they must,' Matthew said. 'This is a murder enquiry, Mr Yates. So, if you could provide me with a full list of your members' names and addresses, please?'

'You want them tonight?' Yates asked wearily.

'Sometime in the morning will be fine,' Matthew said, catching sight of the time from the clock on the mantelpiece and deciding he'd done enough for one day.

Yates nodded, one hand to his head in dejection, and let Matthew see himself out.

Chapter Eleven

Rosie Yates put pink-painted fingertips to her mouth as her lips widened in a yawn. Oh, how she would have liked to stay in bed this morning rather than getting up and shivering in the dining room, but she hadn't been up to bearing the disapproval of Mrs Hughes.

The Yates's cook/housekeeper had a very definite idea of what was right and what was not, and breakfasting in bed was most definitely not right. Not that she ever said so, of course. That would have been an unacceptable familiarity from a paid domestic, but she made her feelings plain in a dozen other ways. Rosie only had to complain of an ache in her back and Mrs Hughes would offer the opinion that her mistress had lain in bed too long. If Rosie expressed fatigue in the middle of the afternoon, Mrs Hughes claimed it was because she had accustomed her body to indolence by remaining in bed when hard-working people had long been up and about. If Rosie had had the courage, she would have told Mrs Hughes to mind her own business, that her opinions were not required, but her insides curdled at the idea of creating a scene, and besides, what if Mrs Hughes took offence and left her employ? What would Rosie do then? Domestic servants were so difficult to get these days. Young girls didn't want to be tied down to the kitchen, at the beck and call of their mistress, when they could have regular hours and better pay working in a factory or in a shop. Rosie supposed the best she would get was a daily, a charwoman who would come in, cook their meals and do the rough housework. Rosie would have to get out of bed to let her in and then she'd have to be around to make sure the daily didn't take liberties. No, she sighed, it was far better she freeze having breakfast with Tommy at the dining table.

Not that he was being much company for her this morning. Rosie scraped butter noisily over her toast and glanced across at him to see if he'd noticed. Nothing changed in her husband's expression. She picked up her coffee cup, took a sip and banged it down on the saucer. Nothing again. There he was, scribbling on his notepad and only looking up to check another piece of paper in the file he had brought home the previous night.

'Tommy, what are you doing?' Rosie demanded to know.

Yates looked up. 'What, my dear?'

'Why are you doing that at the breakfast table?' she cried, pointing at his paperwork. 'You haven't spoken a single word to me.'

Yates's expression became pained. 'I'm sorry, Rosie. This is something I have to do this morning.'

'But what is it? And why are you frowning so much? Is it something to do with the club?'

He threw his pencil down on the table and huffed as he sank back against the chair. 'A policeman came to the club last night. Apparently, a body has been found and no one knows who he is. This detective – what was his name? Stannard, yes, that was it – thinks this dead man might have come to the club. Why he thinks that, I don't know. Anyway, he insists I deliver up to him all the names and addresses of the members before this morning is out.'

'Can he order you about in this way?' Rosie cried indignantly. 'Doesn't he know who you are?'

'It seems he can. If I don't give him the information, he'll come to the club and question the members one by one, I expect, and can you imagine what that would do for the club's reputation? So, you see, my dear, I have to do this.' Yates gestured at the paperwork. 'But I don't like it. Giving out confidential information to the police.'

'You're helping with their enquiries. Isn't that what they call it?'

'Don't say that, Rosie, please. You make me sound like a criminal.'

'Oh, Tommy, don't talk rot. Anyone who knows you knows you're nothing of the sort.'

'And what about those who don't know me?' Yates cried. He picked up the newspaper sitting by his elbow and tossed it across the table. 'It's in *The Chronicle* about this dead man. And this Stannard walked into the club with that bloody reporter, Waite—'

'Language, Tommy!'

'Sorry, my dear. But the inspector came in with that reporter who I had to let in to our charity auction. So, he's going to know the police have been sniffing around and he'll write about it for the newspaper, so that this time next week, everyone in Craynebrook will know I've been questioned.'

Rosie unfolded *The Chronicle*, her eyes scanning the front page for the article her husband alluded to. She found it in the far right column near the bottom, a STOP PRESS article. It read: *POLICE SEEK HELP IN IDENTIFICATION OF DEAD MAN. The police are calling for anyone who recognises the following description of the dead man whose body was found on Craynebrook common on the morning of the 15th January to come forward. The man was between twenty-five and thirty-five years of age, 5'11", of medium build, with red hair and was discovered wearing evening dress. It is understood the man had been dead for three to four weeks when he was found. Anyone with information regarding this person should contact Detective Inspector Matthew Stannard at Craynebrook Police Station. DI Stannard was the officer responsible for apprehending the infamous Marsh Murderer.*

Yates went on talking while Rosie read. 'People will think the club is disreputable. People will say the police questioned Thomas Yates over such-and-such, so he must be up to something, and then they'll start thinking all sorts of things about the club and about me.' He poured himself more coffee, spilling it over the tablecloth. He swore again, to himself this time so as not to offend Rosie, and dabbed the stain with his napkin. 'And who's to say they're not right?'

Rosie, who had not really been listening, looked up at this last. 'What do you mean by that?'

'Well,' Yates said with a grimace, 'you know how some of the members behave. The club sometimes resembles a monkey house, not a respectable, decent place at all, which is what I thought it was when I took over as treasurer. I wouldn't have taken the job if I'd known what it was going to be like. I mean, this is a fine way to spend my retirement, isn't it? Being pushed around—'

'Tommy,' Rosie said sternly, alarmed by the way her husband was talking. 'I won't have you speaking like this. You know perfectly well what a good job you do running the club. Everyone respects you.'

'*They* don't!'

'I don't care what *they* think.'

'Everyone else does.'

Rosie drew in a deep breath, unable to contradict her husband on this matter. 'It will be fine,' she assured him in her most soothing voice. 'Drink your coffee. Don't worry about the stain on the cloth. Mrs Hughes will see to it.'

Grudgingly, Yates obeyed, and Rosie resumed her reading of *The Chronicle.* She remembered the news reports of the Marsh Murderer and his dreadful crimes, and unlike her husband, would have been rather excited to meet the man who had caught him.

'Tommy,' she said slowly as a thought occurred to her. 'This man the detective was asking about?'

'What about him?'

'It says here he had red hair and was wearing evening dress. And that he died three to four weeks ago. Well, that might have been around the night of the charity auction, mightn't it? And there was a red-haired man at the function.'

Yates frowned at her. 'Was there?'

'Yes, don't you remember? He came up to us and introduced himself. Oh, Lord, what was his name?'

'I don't remember any man introducing himself.'

'Oh, you never remember anything,' she tutted testily. 'He was a nice-looking chap, very charming.' She banged her fist lightly on the table. 'Oh, what was his name?'

'Don't worry yourself about it, my dear.'

'But if the police need information, I should tell them—'

Yates banged his coffee cup down on his saucer. 'Absolutely not, Rosie. I forbid you from talking to that detective. I won't have you involved with the police.'

'But I might be able to help.'

'Help, how? You can't even remember this fellow's name. And you don't know the man they found is him.'

'But it might be, Tommy.'

'Rosie,' Yates said, giving her his sternest look, 'no. Now, please, let's drop the subject. I have such a lot to do today. I must complete this list and hand it in to the police. Then I've got to go to the club and interview for serving staff as well as get everything ready for tonight. I really don't need to be worrying about you. All right?'

Rosie sighed. 'Yes, Tommy. All right.'

Matthew threw his hat onto his desk, leaving his overcoat on, and sat down. 'Good morning, Denham. What do we have?'

Denham put a file before Matthew. 'Post-mortem report from Dr Wallace. Came in first thing.'

'Thanks.' Matthew glanced up at Denham out of the corner of his eye, looking for any sign Wallace might not have kept his word and his fainting was common knowledge. But there was nothing in Denham's expression that suggested he knew anything.

'Tea?' Denham offered.

'Not for me,' Matthew said, opening the file. 'I've got to go out as soon as I've read this.'

'Seen the 'paper this morning?'

'Haven't had time,' Matthew murmured. 'Why?'

'Your name's in it. There's an article saying the police are asking for information.'

'I know. I thought it might help to identify our dead man.'

'Oh,' Denham said. 'I'm surprised the Super let you do it. He normally tries to keep stuff like that out of the 'papers.'

Matthew didn't reply, but continued reading the post-mortem report. Wallace confirmed the blow to the head had killed the man but couldn't confirm whether the beating had preceded or followed it. He'd found footprints amongst the bruises and wrote they belonged to a size nine foot. The wound to the head had been delivered from the right, suggesting a right-handed attacker, but that this couldn't be taken for granted. The weapon had been something like a small plank of wood, but the way the skull was broken suggested that whatever it was had had curved or bevelled edges. The man had been a smoker, deposits in the lungs and nicotine-stained fingers attesting to this, and had been in good health.

I've read more conclusive post-mortem reports, Matthew thought despondently. 'Did the search of the common turn anything up?'

Denham shook his head. 'Plenty of twigs and thin branches, but nothing like a plank of wood. Nothing flat. Will you be needing the car again?'

'No. I'm only going to the golf club. I'll walk.' Matthew closed the file and picked up his hat. 'I'll be an hour or so. While I'm out, try calling stations in South Kensington, Mayfair, all around there, and get them to check on their Missing Persons. You never know. He might turn up.'

A steward greeted Matthew on his arrival at the golf club. He showed his warrant card and said he needed to speak to the manager. The steward informed him that the manager was on the telephone, but he'd be with Matthew as soon as he was free and did Matthew want to wait? Matthew said he would and went into the lounge. He'd hardly been waiting two minutes when a short, middle-aged man wearing green plus fours strode in and headed for the window.

'Bloody hell,' Matthew heard him say. 'Why do I do it?' He turned and caught sight of Matthew. He laughed and gestured with his thumb at the window. 'Why do we do it, eh? Play golf on a day like this?'

'I don't,' Matthew said. 'I'm not here for the golf.'

'Too cold,' the man nodded understanding. 'I haven't seen you here before. New member?'

'No. I'm here to see the manager. I'm Detective Inspector Stannard.'

The man looked taken aback. 'The police? Why? What's happened?'

'Nothing to alarm you, sir. I'm just on enquiries. Actually, while you're here, I wonder if I could ask you a few questions?'

The man giggled uneasily. 'Ask me questions? What the devil for?'

'Because you happen to be here,' Matthew said, 'and I trust you won't mind helping the police.'

The man cleared his throat. 'Well, no, of course I don't mind. Why would I?'

'Thank you. If I could have your name, sir?'

'Eric Hailes.'

Matthew made a note. 'Are you aware a man's body was found on Craynebrook common two days ago? And that he is as yet unidentified?'

'I heard about it,' Hailes said, and shook his head. 'Terrible thing.'

'It's possible he may have frequented this golf club.' Matthew described his dead man. 'Does he sound at all familiar?'

'No, I, er, can't say he does.'

'What about these names? Rupert Caine. Cyril Pargeter. Stephen Carter. Charles Calthrop.'

'No. Why do you think he might have come here?'

'He may have come here or gone to one of the other clubs in Craynebrook. The Empire Club, perhaps.'

'Oh, you're going to be going there, are you?'

'Are you a member?'

'Of the Empire Club? Yes, I am.' Hailes tugged at his ear. 'So, you don't know who he is? This man on the common.'

'No. He didn't have any identification on him, and no one has reported him missing.'

'I see.' Hailes made a face. 'Going to be bloody difficult to find out who he was, I expect.'

'We'll identify him,' Matthew assured him with a nod, turning as the steward returned and said the manager would see him now. 'Thank you for your time, Mr Hailes.'

'Not at all, inspector,' Hailes called after him.

Chapter Twelve

The hairdresser was not being gentle. She was dragging the comb through Rosie's wet hair rather than teasing it, making Rosie wince with every tug.

Why don't I tell her to take care? Rosie chided herself, and hissed as her head was jerked backwards again. She endured it for another minute, then the woman set the comb aside. Rosie breathed a silent sigh of relief. She could relax and perhaps even close her eyes as the scissors snipped, cutting off her split ends. Her eyelids drooped. Her head tilted back.

'Have you heard the rumours about Sophie Sutton, Rosie?' Florence Ballantyne, sitting in the chair alongside, jolted her awake.

'What rumours?' Rosie asked.

'About her and Kit.'

Rosie turned her head, only to have the hairdresser tut and twist it back to its forward position. 'Sorry,' she whispered and tried to catch Florence's eye in the mirror. 'Sophie Sutton and Kit?'

'My dear, you saw them at the charity auction.'

'But that was just fun. Kit messing about.'

Florence giggled. 'You're so innocent, Rosie. Fun, indeed. Her husband certainly didn't think it was fun, did he? I wouldn't have liked to be Mrs Sutton that night, I can tell you. You can just imagine the quarrel they had.'

'I rather like Andrew,' Rosie said. 'He seems very nice. A bit stiff, I know, but that may be shyness, them being so new.'

'That's probably why Sophie's tired of him. After all, who wants nice?'

'I do,' Rosie cried indignantly. 'My Tommy's nice and I wouldn't have him any other way.'

'Yes, of course, my dear,' Florence leant over and patted Rosie's hand. 'Tommy's lovely, an absolute darling, but he's not likely to make any hearts flutter, is he? Other than yours, I mean. Whereas Kit…'

'You speak as if you're tempted yourself, Florrie.'

Florence shook her head. 'Not a bit of it. Kit Fairbank doesn't hold a candle to Archie. But he is attractive, that you must own, Rosie.'

'I suppose so.'

'Sophie Sutton certainly seems to think so, and I wouldn't be surprised if she has plans for something to happen between them tonight.'

'Florrie, you don't mean…?' In the mirror, Rosie saw Florence's perfectly plucked eyebrows rise.

'I do mean,' Florence said, sitting up straight as her hairdresser took out the pins in her hair.

'But does Daphne know what's going on?'

'I haven't the faintest idea, but it wouldn't surprise me if she did and doesn't care. You can't blame Kit for having a wandering eye. Daphne's such a cold fish. You can't expect men to go without, can you?'

Rosie didn't see why not. That was the whole point of monogamy, wasn't it? If Tommy ever started noticing other women… but no, Tommy wasn't unkind like that. He wasn't like Kit Fairbank. She glanced at Florence. Nor like Archie, from all she'd heard. She wondered if Florence knew about the women Archie had chased and, so the gossip went, caught.

'I hope your Tommy's done something about the staff at the club,' Florence said, keeping a stern eye on what her hairdresser was doing. 'The ones we had at the charity do were simply dreadful. They had no idea what they were doing. Marjorie Cooper had one of the little fools spill champagne all over her dress.'

'He's interviewing staff today,' Rosie said distractedly. Florence's mention of the charity auction had made her think of the article in the newspaper again. 'Florrie, did you read in the newspaper this morning about the body found on the common?'

'Yes, I did. Dreadful to think something so sordid could happen in Craynebrook, isn't it?'

'The police are calling for information. Apparently, they don't know who the man is.'

'Just some tramp, I expect.'

'Tramps don't wear evening dress, Florrie.'

Florence murmured a reply, but her attention had transferred to her magazine, and she was only half listening to her friend.

'I thought the description of the dead man sounded rather like the chap at the charity auction.' Rosie chanced a sideways glance at Florence while the hairdresser reached for more hair clips, but Florence's expression hadn't changed. 'The dead man had red hair.'

Florence shrugged. 'Lots of men have red hair.'

'Do you think so? I've only known one or two. And well, that chap hasn't been back to the club since that night, has he?'

'I really couldn't say. He might have been there, just not at the same time as us.'

'No, I don't think so. Tommy would have seen him and he didn't remember him at all.'

Florence flicked over a page of her magazine.

'Florrie, what do you think?' Rosie asked impatiently.

'About what, dear?' Florence asked, turning to her with a sigh.

'I wonder if the dead man might be the chap Kit brought along.'

'Did Kit bring someone?'

'Didn't he? I thought he did,' Rosie said, tugging at her bottom lip. 'Oh, well, maybe he didn't, but should I go to the police, Florrie?'

Rosie had caught Florence's interest at last. She turned excited eyes on Rosie, pushing her hairdresser's hands away. 'Go to the police? Oh, Rosie, whatever for?'

'They need information about this man, Florrie. He's dead, and no one knows. What if his wife is wondering where he is? Wouldn't you want someone to talk to the police if your husband was lying dead somewhere?'

'Oh, Rosie, don't.' Florence shuddered. 'I can't bear to think of Archie dying. But would you really go to the police?'

'If I thought it would help. Tommy says I mustn't, but…'

'Oh, you don't want to pay any attention to what Tommy says,' Florence said, grabbing Rosie's hand and squeezing. 'If you know anything, you must go to the police and tell them.'

Dickie put his coins on the pub counter and heaved a sigh of relief that he was out of the cold, for half an hour or so, at least. From his overcoat pocket, he took out his greaseproof-wrapped sandwich – tongue and piccalilli, made for him that morning by his wife – and wrapped his fingers around the handle of the pint mug the barman deposited before him, carrying both over to the table by the fire, which was occupied by only one other man. He sank back in the chair, stretching out his legs and wiggling his stiff toes. He contemplated the dancing flames for a long moment, feeling warmth returning to him.

'Nice to come in here and get warm again, isn't it?'

'Yes, it is.' Dickie smiled at the other man and unfolded the greaseproof paper. The sandwich had been squashed out of shape in his pocket and didn't look particularly appetising, but it would be enough to stop his stomach rumbling. He took a large bite from one corner, enjoying the sharp tang of the piccalilli on his tongue, and washed it down with a mouthful of beer.

Taking out his notebook, he flicked through the pages, growing more despondent with each turn. He had taken copious notes during his interviews with Superintendent Mullinger and Alexander King, but when he read through them, there was actually very little of any worth. Waffle, that's what he had. Pages and pages of waffle. He would have his work cut out finding the nuggets amongst the dross. The interview with the councillor had been little better. He turned another page where he'd scribbled two dates and times. These were the two interviews he had lined up for the following week with a local historian and the vicar of St Benedict's, but he expected them to be dull dogs. What he needed was someone with a bit of glamour about them. Someone who had an interesting story to tell.

'Work or pleasure?'

'I'm sorry?' Dickie frowned at his companion of the fireside. He'd almost forgotten he was there.

The man gestured with his eyes at Dickie's notebook. 'Are you having a working lunch?'

'This?' He waved the notebook. 'Yes, work. I'm a reporter and I'm just going through my notes.'

'Reporter, eh?' The man looked impressed and Dickie warmed to him. 'Up from Fleet Street, are you?'

'No,' Dickie admitted, instantly deflated. 'I'm from *The Chronicle*.'

'Oh, yes? We take your newspaper. What are you working on? If you don't mind me asking?'

'I'm doing a series of profiles on some of Craynebrook's worthies.'

'Are you really? And who are our local worthies?'

'Well, the superintendent of the police station, the MP, Mr King and Councillor Markham. But that's as far as I've got.'

'You didn't look like you were enjoying going through your notes.'

Dickie lowered his voice. 'Between you and me, I was just thinking they were all a bit lifeless and wishing I could find a subject with a bit of sparkle about them.'

The man's expression became thoughtful. 'Worthies, you say?'

Dickie nodded. 'You know someone you think I should interview?'

'I wouldn't call them worthies, far from it, but they've got sparkle. Oh yes, they've got sparkle, all right.'

'Who?'

The man reached for his drink before answering. 'The members call them The Five. Silly name, really, but then they don't have much imagination there.'

'The Five?' Dickie asked, intrigued. 'What members? Where's 'there'?'

'Sorry.' His companion held up his hand. 'I'm going about this all arse-uppards, aren't I? The where is the Empire Club. The members of the Empire Club are the ones who don't have much imagination, and The Five are an exclusive group of those members.'

'Are you a member of the Empire Club?'

'We were. That is, my wife and I, a year or two back. We stopped going.'

'Why was that?'

The man made a face. 'We didn't like the way things were heading. When Tommy Yates first took it over, it was a lovely club. But then The Five joined, and it started to go downhill.'

'Who are these Five?'

'Archie Ballantyne, Christopher Fairbank, Adrian Foucault, Donald Spencer, Eric Hailes.' The man counted them off on his fingers. 'They are The Five.'

'I've been to the Empire Club,' Dickie said. 'They were having a charity auction do and my editor sent me there to cover the event. I saw those men.'

The man raised an eyebrow. 'Then you know what I mean.'

Dickie nodded. 'They were certainly conspicuous. Fairbank and Ballantyne, anyway.'

'Attention seekers, the pair of them.'

'And you left the club because of them? I can't say I took to them myself but what did they do that you disliked so much?'

The man shrugged. 'You know how sometimes there are people who are just not your cup of tea? Well, it was like that, really. Although there was gossip too about what they get up to. Not that I'm going to repeat any of that. No, really, I've said enough. But if you want sparkle, I daresay you'll find it in The Five.'

'Thanks for the tip,' Dickie said thoughtfully as the man unfolded his *Daily Mail*.

Chapter Thirteen

The dead man hadn't been to the golf club. The manager was emphatic that no red-haired man had crossed the club's threshold and had checked that none of the names Matthew put to him had been entered into his membership ledgers. Disheartened, Matthew made his way back to the station.

He sat down at his desk and saw a brown envelope addressed 'For the attention of DI Stannard' sitting on his blotter. He tore the envelope open and pulled out a five-page handwritten list of names and addresses. Thomas Yates had written a short note on blue notepaper. It said: *Inspector Stannard. These are the names and addresses you asked for.*

Matthew began working through the list. Some names he recognised from the golf club membership ledger; others were new to him.

His telephone rang. Matthew snatched up the receiver. 'Stannard.'

'Front desk, sir. Sergeant Turkel. I have a lady here asking to speak to you. A Mrs Yates.'

'Very well. I'm coming down,' Matthew said, wondering why Thomas Yates's wife wanted to see him.

When he reached the entrance lobby, Sergeant Turkel

nodded him towards a petite, pretty woman sitting on the bench beneath the noticeboard, legs crossed at the ankles, her dark blue handbag clutched tightly on her lap.

'Mrs Yates?' Matthew asked.

Big blue eyes looked up at him. 'Yes,' Rosie said nervously.

'I'm Inspector Stannard. You wanted to speak with me?'

'Well, I'm not sure.' She looked around Matthew towards the door, eyeing it as if thinking about fleeing.

'Why don't we go in here?' he said, opening the door that led into a small private interview room.

She hesitated for a moment while he smiled encouragingly down at her, then rose and passed through the doorway, filling Matthew's nostrils with the smell of lilies as her perfume wafted over him.

'Please, take a seat,' he said, closing the door and pulling out one of the chairs at the table for her. He pulled out the other and sat down opposite. 'Now, how can I help you?'

'I think…,' she began, then looked doubtful, 'but I'm not sure. I think I might be able to help you.'

Matthew watched as she opened the clasp on her handbag and took out a newspaper clipping. She passed it to him, and he quickly read it, realising it was the morning's article from *The Chronicle* Denham had told him about. 'You know something about this man?'

Her expression became pained. 'My husband wouldn't like me coming here.'

'Your husband is Thomas Yates?'

'Yes. You met him yesterday.' She nibbled her bottom lip.

'The dead man?' Matthew pressed.

Rosie sighed. 'The description in the newspaper sounds like a man who was at our charity auction in December. At least, he had red hair and was about thirty. I just thought it sounded like him and that if I told you...' Her shoulders slumped. 'But I suppose I'm just being silly.'

'No, you're not,' Matthew hurried to assure her. 'Any information is of help, Mrs Yates. Can you tell me this man's name?'

'Yes, I finally remembered it. Calthrop. Charles, I think.'

Calthrop again. 'And this charity auction was at the Empire Club?'

Rosie nodded.

'What can you tell me about Charles Calthrop?'

'He introduced himself to Tommy and me, we exchanged a few words about nothing in particular, and that was it.'

'Introduced himself? So, he hadn't been there before?'

'No. I think Christopher Fairbank brought him as a guest.' Rosie held up her hand. 'But I'm not sure it was Kit, so please don't take my word for it.'

Matthew remembered seeing the name Christopher Fairbank on Yates's list. 'Your husband said he didn't recognise the description of the man when I asked him.'

'Tommy has a poor memory, inspector, and he was very busy that night. He had to deal with such a lot. I expect he just forgot.'

Matthew nodded understandingly. 'I expect so.'

'Well,' Rosie smiled awkwardly, 'that's all I can tell you, inspector. I really ought to be going.' She rose and looked at Matthew as if she expected him to prevent her leaving.

He opened the door. 'Thank you for coming in, Mrs Yates. You've been a great help.'

The office of Palmer & Knight, Solicitors, was one of the pokiest Dickie had ever been in. Dickie had had to climb the narrowest of staircases, made even gloomier by the dark green paint that adorned the walls, to reach the three rooms that made up the company and it seemed to him that nothing had changed in the two years since he had last visited Joseph Palmer. Even the aged secretary sitting behind her too-small desk looking over an ancient type-writer was the same and looked as if she hadn't moved since that last visit.

The door marked 'Joseph Palmer' opened and a man with a square face and flat nose looked out. 'Dickie?' he said, frowning as Dickie crossed the floor towards him. 'I didn't know we had an appointment.'

'Miss Holden very kindly managed to squeeze me in,' Dickie said, smiling at the secretary who looked at him sternly over the top of her half-rimmed spectacles.

'Well, come in,' Palmer said, leaving the door open as he walked back to his desk.

Dickie entered, wondering how his friend never seemed to suffer from claustrophobia in the small office with its towering bookcases crammed with legal tomes and case files spilling their paperwork. He plumped down in the chair by Palmer's desk, his toes nudging a pile of box files and nearly sending them toppling.

Palmer shifted the papers he had been working on to one side of his desk. 'How's things? Keeping well? Emma all right?'

'Same as ever. You?'

'Myrtle's been having trouble with her stomach again,' Palmer said, making a face.

'Oh, I'm sorry to hear that,' Dickie said without a great deal of sincerity. Myrtle had been having trouble with her stomach for as long as he'd known her, and she never tired of telling everyone so.

'Well, what can I do for you?' Palmer asked. 'Have you finally come to make your will?'

'Not today.'

'You should get it done. Worst thing you can do is keep putting it off.'

'I have nothing to leave, Joe,' Dickie said, tired of hearing about his will and what would happen if he were to die suddenly. 'I'm here for something else.'

Palmer frowned. 'Legal advice?'

Dickie shook his head. 'I'd like to get some information about people I hope you know.'

'For the 'paper?'

'That's right. My editor wants a series of profiles written about some of Craynebrook's most eminent residents, and…' he paused, wondering how to phrase his next sentence. 'I've heard a thing or two about some of them which I think you may be able to confirm or deny.'

'Why me?'

'Because you know everybody. And don't worry. I'm not asking you to betray any legal confidences.'

'Who do you want to know about?'

'Have you heard of The Five?'

Palmer's genial face paled.

'Joe?' Dickie asked, noting the change. 'What is it?'

'What have you heard?' Palmer asked.

'Just that they joined the Empire Club in Craynebrook and some members thought it went downhill.'

'That all?'

Dickie shrugged helplessly. 'I know it's not much.'

'It's nothing.'

'But there's something more to it, I just know it.'

'Journalist's hunch?'

'If you like. I saw them at the club just before Christmas and I didn't like what I saw. Then I was chatting with a man today who used to belong to the club and who said he and his wife left once The Five joined because they didn't like the way it was going. They weren't his cup of tea, he said, and though he refused to repeat gossip, I just got the impression there's something a little dodgy about them. Am I wrong? Are The Five perfectly respectable, upstanding members of the community?'

Palmer drummed his fingers on the desk as he studied Dickie. 'Is this off the record?'

'I'm just after confirmation, Joe, and information, if you've got it. No one will know where it came from, I promise.' He held up his hand and began counting on his fingers. 'Archibald Ballantyne, Christopher Fairbank, Adrian Foucault, Donald Spencer, Eric Hailes. They are The Five. Yes?'

Palmer's jaw tightened. He nodded.

'Ballantyne and Foucault are criminal barristers and you and your partner are criminal solicitors. Have either of you had any dealings with them?'

Palmer let out a breath and nodded. 'It was about five years ago. I was representing the victim of an assault and Ballantyne was the defence counsel. The evidence the police had gathered was good. No, better than good. It was watertight. They'd got the right man. But Ballantyne got him off and my client got nothing.'

Dickie frowned. 'But that just makes Ballantyne a good barrister, doesn't it? It was his job to get his client acquitted.'

Palmer sniffed. 'Ballantyne knew his client was guilty.'

'So what? You're going to have to tell me what you're getting at, Joe. I'm not a lawyer.'

'If a barrister knows his client is guilty, he has an ethical duty not to mislead the court.'

'Give me an example.'

'All right, then. If he knows his client was in the vicinity of the crime at the time, he can't put forward an alibi that says the client was somewhere else. That's misleading the court. You understand?'

Dickie nodded. 'So, you're saying Ballantyne misled the court. How?'

'I didn't know and that was the problem. I just overheard a conversation that made me think so. I was in the Gents after the trial was over, in one of the cubicles. I heard the door open, and Ballantyne and his client came in. The client was thanking him for getting him off and Ballantyne said it was his pleasure and all that, the usual guff. Then the client said, and I quote, "I'll get the money to you by Saturday," and Ballantyne shushed him. Said, "Quiet, you fool." I heard the client laugh and leave. I stayed in the cubicle until Ballantyne had gone, then went straight to the clerk of the court to tell him I needed to see the judge. I told the judge what I'd heard and he said he'd look into it. Next thing I know, bricks are coming through my sitting-room window. One of them hit Myrtle.'

'How do you know it was Ballantyne?'

'It wasn't Ballantyne throwing the bricks, Dickie,' Palmer said scornfully. 'He wouldn't dirty his hands in that way. But it was his doing, all right. I saw him at the courthouse a few days later and he gave me a look that told me he knew I'd overheard his conversation with his client and that I'd told the judge. I'm not a brave man, Dickie. A brick through the window is enough to scare me off.'

'What about the judge? Did he look into your allegation?'

'I never heard another word about it, and I didn't ask. And now I do my best to avoid any cases Ballantyne or his friend might be involved in.'

'Foucault, you mean. What do you know about him?'

Palmer shook his head. 'Nothing but rumours.'

'What kind of rumours?'

'About money, mostly. And about some of his inclinations.' Palmer raised his eyebrows.

'Do you mean sex?' Dickie asked.

Palmer nodded.

'Anything illegal?'

'Not what you're thinking. Just that he has certain tastes in that area and they're not your usual.'

Dickie wondered what those tastes could be. 'And what about the other three?'

'Fairbank's a skirt-chaser, but that's no secret. Word has it his wife has given up on him and they lead separate lives. Has a good business in antiques, knows what he's talking about. Does a lot of international buying and selling, lot of clients abroad. Is he dodgy? Probably, but I don't know in what way.'

'Spencer?'

Palmer's eyebrows rose. 'Not a very pleasant character, by all accounts. Something of a bully boy. Works on the council and there's a lot of rumours he takes backhanders for building contracts, that sort of thing, and isn't averse to throwing his muscle around. Apparently, he used to box when he was younger and put a lad in hospital for three weeks.'

'Hailes?'

'Ah, now, Hailes is the unlikely member of The Five. You wouldn't put him and the others together in usual circumstances — he's a weasel little thing — but I expect it's because he's useful to them. Stockbroker, you see. Gets to hear everything in the City and can probably put them on to a good thing. I heard that Ballantyne had been boasting about how he had a crystal ball and how the Crash hadn't done him any harm. I expect that crystal ball is Eric Hailes.' Palmer shrugged. 'But like I say, Dickie, this is all rumour, gossip. I don't know anything for certain, except that one time about Ballantyne.'

'There's no smoke without fire, Joe,' Dickie said. 'But how do they get away with it? I mean, if these rumours are rife, if everyone in their circle, and people like you, out of their circle, know what they're up to, how do they get away with it?'

'Who's going to stop them? They have friends in high places. They must have, otherwise the judge I spoke to would have done something about Ballantyne, wouldn't he?'

'You think he tipped Ballantyne off about what you'd heard?'

'I didn't talk to anyone else about it. It had to be him. And you're doing profiles about them?'

Dickie nodded. 'My editor wants to call the series 'Craynebrook's Great and Good'.'

Palmer made a face. 'You want to know how they get away with it, Dickie? That's how. They present the right face to the public. You know, your 'paper's always covering some charity work they're raising money for something or other. Hiding in plain sight, it's called.' He gave Dickie a meaningful look. 'Unless someone puts a stop to them. Exposes them. Perhaps in a newspaper.'

Dickie shook his head. 'I don't think my editor would do it.'

'Then they'll go on getting away with it, won't they?' Palmer studied Dickie for a long moment. 'If you're serious about looking into their antics, there is someone you could talk to. Someone who can probably tell you what you want to know about The Five. Willie Dodds. Old-time crook. Retired, now, but he's got the dirt on everyone around this area, and he'll do anything for money.'

'Where can I find him?'

'The snooker hall in Stratford. Now, I've told you more than I should, and if you don't mind, Dickie, I'd rather like to have my cup of tea in peace before my three o'clock appointment.'

· · ·

'Be here tonight by six o'clock, please,' Yates told the waiter he had just hired and took a mouthful of tepid coffee as the young man left his office. Grimacing, he set the cup back in its saucer, shaking his head at the youth of today. None of them wanted to do a decent day's work anymore. All because of the war, he mused. It had changed everything. Women given the vote, wanting to go out to work rather than look after their children and their homes. The working classes demanding this and that, going on strike, holding their employers to ransom. Where was it going to end?

Yates looked at the next name on his list of interviewees and hoped this young woman would be better than the last he had interviewed. That girl had been hopeless. Hadn't even known that she should serve from the left and take away from the right, asking him why it mattered. She hadn't been hired, which meant that this Sally Cooke had better know her onions otherwise he would be a hand short for dinner.

'Miss Cooke?' he called, loud enough for the woman waiting out on the landing to hear.

Sally Cooke appeared a moment later in the doorway. She was tall, and a little on the plump side, with dark frizzy hair pinned back behind her ears, sallow skin and round spectacles sitting on her nose. Yates was disappointed. He liked to have pretty waitresses for the club; it looked better. But then, he supposed, at least she wouldn't be pestered by male members with wandering hands.

'Come in, Miss Cooke,' he said, waving her to the chair by his desk. She sat down without a word. 'I see from your letter that you have waitressed before in various West End restaurants and that you know what to do. That's a great relief to me, you understand. So few so-called waiters and wait-resses have any idea how to wait at table. I also have your character reference here from the manager of the last establishment you worked in and he is very complimentary. Tell me, why did you leave your last place of employment?'

'I wanted a job nearer home,' Sally said.

'I see. And before that you were at a Lyons Corner House in Piccadilly. I expect you were rushed off your feet there.'

She nodded. 'It was very busy.'

'Well, it doesn't get as busy as a Lyons Corner House here at the club, but you'll be busy enough. There are, of course, certain differences to what you'll be used to. There'll be no familiarity with the club members. You're here to wait tables, not chatter. Is that understood?'

'I'm not much of a talker, Mr Yates.'

'Good. And you'll need to be smartly dressed at all times. You'll be given a uniform. Any breakages will come out of your wages. But please, do try not to break anything.' He gave her another look. The eyes that looked out from behind the spectacles were confident and intelligent. Yes, she would do. 'I'm happy to take you on, Miss Cooke. I trust you are available to wait tables tonight?'

'Yes, Mr Yates.'

'Excellent. Pick up your uniform from Mrs Wilkins in the kitchen, and be back here by six o'clock to start setting up. All right?'

Sally Cooke stood. 'Yes, Mr Yates. All right.'

Chapter Fourteen

Daphne Fairbank inhaled the smoke from her cigarette, closing her eyes as it worked its way down her throat and the nicotine soothed her nerves. She looked around her sitting room, at the furniture, at the ornaments, at the paintings on the wall, all of them her husband's finds and all of them perfect. Her home looked expensive and immaculate, but Daphne found it devoid of feeling. Objects, not people, lived in her home. She tapped her cigarette against the ashtray on the sofa beside her, watching as the ash piled up and the front door latch lifted.

'I'm home,' Christopher Fairbank announced, poking his head around the sitting-room door.

'So I see,' Daphne replied, not looking at him.

'"Nice to see you." "Have you had a good day, dear?" Would it kill you, Daphne?'

His wife turned the page of a magazine in answer.

Fairbank sighed. 'I'm out tonight.'

'At the club?'

'Yes, at the club. You don't have to come.'

'I won't. I don't want to spoil your seduction of Sophie Sutton.' She looked at him at last, a narrow, sideways glance.

'Are you wondering how I know about that? All my friends are talking about you and her. They delight in telling me of your amours.'

'Tell them to mind their own damned business,' he said, and moved away from the door.

'There was a telephone call for you,' she called, bringing him back.

'Who from?'

'A Detective Inspector Stannard. He wanted to know when you would be home.'

'The police?'

She enjoyed the concern in his voice. 'Have you finally been found out, Kit? Do the police know what you've been doing all these years? All the people you've swindled?'

'What did you tell him?'

Daphne took another drag of her cigarette. 'That you'd be home by five-thirty.'

'He's coming here?'

'Yes, he's coming here.'

'Did he say what he wanted to see me about?'

'No. And if you're thinking of leaving early for the club to avoid him, don't. I'm not going to lie for you.' The door-bell rang. 'Too late,' she smiled icily at her husband.

'Mr Fairbank?' Matthew asked when the front door opened.

'Yes,' Fairbank said. 'I take it you're Inspector Stannard? My wife said you'd be calling. Come in.'

Matthew stepped inside, taking off his hat, and looked around the hall. He knew nothing about art and antiques, but even he could tell there was money in the house, just from the few pieces on display. Oil landscapes in heavy gilt frames hung on the walls and Regency console tables were set against the walls, although the Chinese vases on the tables looked like the tat given away as prizes at funfairs to him. Even so, he mused, they were probably worth more than he could earn in six months.

'How can I help you, inspector?' Fairbank asked, hurriedly closing the sitting-room door.

Matthew got a glimpse of a hard-faced, dark-haired woman on the sofa before the door closed. He realised he wasn't going to be invited to sit down or offered refreshment and the discourtesy annoyed him.

'I need to ask you about your acquaintance with a Mr Charles Calthrop,' he said to Fairbank, who was standing with his arms crossed over his chest. 'I understand he was a friend of yours.'

Fairbank stared at Matthew, the skin beneath his left eye twitching. 'Calthrop? I'm not sure—'

'I've been told he was a guest of yours at the charity auction at the Empire Club in December.'

'Oh, yes,' Fairbank clicked his fingers. 'So he was.'

'When did you see him last?'

'It was at the charity auction. I said goodbye to him when the evening ended. I haven't seen him since.'

'What's your relationship with Mr Calthrop?'

'Passing acquaintance, that's all. I met him up town and invited him to the club. To be honest, I made the invitation when I was a bit tight, not really expecting to be taken up on it. When he turned up at the club, I was surprised.'

'Did he come alone?'

Fairbank's eyes rolled upward as he considered. 'Can't remember. Memory's a bit hazy round the edges for that night. I drank rather too much, I'm afraid.'

'Where in town did you meet him?'

'A club in Soho. Can't remember the name.'

'You seem to have a poor memory, Mr Fairbank.'

Matthew met Fairbank's eye and held it. He saw anger there, a desire to put Matthew in his place.

'I suppose I have,' Fairbank said, backing down.

Matthew smiled. 'What was his business?'

'Couldn't say, inspector. Never asked.'

'I see. Are you aware that a man's body was found on Craynebrook common on Wednesday?'

'I heard something about it.'

'I have reason to believe that was the man you knew as Charles Calthrop,' Matthew said, watching Fairbank closely.

Fairbank's eyebrows rose and his lips pressed together. 'You don't say? That's awful.'

Matthew couldn't tell whether Fairbank's surprise was fake or genuine. 'Do you know of anyone who might have wanted to do him harm?'

'None at all, inspector. As I say, I hardly knew him. I really don't think I can tell you anything else. You're wasting your time with me.' Fairbank smiled, but the smile stayed on his face for too long, and Matthew knew he was hiding something.

'Well, thank you, Mr Fairbank,' he said. 'But if you do think of anything that might be relevant, you will let me know?'

'I will,' Fairbank assured him and opened the front door.

Matthew had barely set foot on the step before it was slammed shut behind him.

Matthew strode into the CID office. 'Denham, I want you checking the records for a Charles Calthrop.'

'Yes, sir,' Denham said, quickly scribbling down the name. 'And who's he?'

'Possible name for our dead man. Although, I wouldn't be surprised if it turns out to be another alias. And while you're at it, check the records for Christopher Fairbank. See if we have anything on him.'

'Is that another alias?'

'No. It's one of the names on Yates's list.'

'A member of the Empire Club? I doubt if a man like that will have a record, sir—'

'Just do it, Denham,' Matthew snapped.

All heads in the main office turned in surprise at his tone, and Matthew took a deep breath. 'Sorry,' he said, catching sight of the clock. 'It's gone six. Do that in the morning, Denham. Get off home. Unless you want to get a drink?' he offered.

'I would, sir, but my wife's expecting me.'

It hadn't occurred to Matthew that Denham was married. 'Of course she is. Another time, then.'

'Yes, sir.' Denham nodded and said goodnight.

The constables still at their desks kept their heads down when he had gone, and Matthew, knowing he should make an effort to be friendly, extended the same invitation to them. To his dismay, they accepted, and all three made their way to The King George.

Chapter Fifteen

'We were starting to think you weren't coming,' Ballantyne said to Fairbank as he strode into the smoking room at the Empire Club.

Fairbank tugged at his collar. 'I had a visit from the police this evening.'

'There!' Hailes cried at Ballantyne. 'What did I tell you?'

'What?' Fairbank asked, looking from Hailes to Ballantyne.

Ballantyne scratched his temple. 'Eric's also had a little chat with a policeman today.'

'DI Stannard?' Fairbank asked.

Hailes nodded. 'He was asking about the dead man on the common.'

'What did you tell him?'

'That I didn't know anything.'

'Well, that's true,' Spencer said, grinning at Ballantyne.

'This is serious, Don,' Hailes said.

'No, it's not. You told us he was there to see the manager. That he found you there was just a coincidence.'

'Oh, really? A coincidence?' Hailes waved his hand at Fairbank. 'So, why's he talking to Kit?'

Spencer turned to Fairbank. 'What did the copper want?'

'He says they think the dead man on the common is Calthrop and someone's told him I brought Calthrop here to the club.'

'Who told him?' Hailes asked.

'How the hell do I know?' Fairbank retorted.

'All right, chaps, easy,' Ballantyne said. 'Now, Kit. Was this chappie only asking about Calthrop?'

'He asked if Calthrop came with anyone. I said I couldn't remember.'

'And he went away?'

Fairbank nodded.

'That's all right, then. So, we can all calm down. Can't we?' Ballantyne raised his eyes questioningly at Fairbank.

'I suppose so,' Fairbank said grudgingly.

'Eric?'

Hailes nodded unhappily.

'No need to ask you, Don. Adrian?' Ballantyne looked over to the man standing by the window.

Foucault turned his head and blew out a plume of smoke. 'I'm always calm, Archie.'

Ballantyne grinned. 'Good. Now, let's forget all this business with police and dead men.'

Fairbank stuffed a cigarette in his mouth and lit it. 'I'm damn well going to enjoy myself tonight, Archie.'

Ballantyne handed him a glass of champagne. 'Let's all enjoy ourselves.' He clinked his glass against Fairbank's. 'Here's to a pleasant evening.'

It was an awkward hour in the pub. Matthew struggled to find something to talk about with the young men, who seemed rather in awe of him. *Or maybe*, he considered ruefully, *they just don't like what they've heard about me, the copper who always gets noticed.* He made a half-hearted attempt to find out a little about them, but when they were less than forthcoming, Matthew made a show of checking his wristwatch and announced he had to be going. The junior detectives seemed relieved rather than sorry and jumped up to thank him for their drinks.

Buying fish and chips after getting off the bus, Matthew had just fitted his key into the front door lock when he heard the telephone in the hallway ringing. Groaning, he turned the key and opened the door, just in time to see the other tenant of the house, Mr Levitt, lift the receiver to his ear.

'Who d'ya want?' he said into the mouthpiece. 'It's for you.' Levitt thrust the telephone at Matthew.

Matthew took it. 'Stannard,' he said.

'Mattie?'

'Oh, hello, Pat,' Matthew said, watching Mr Levitt as he shuffled down the passage to his front door.

'Don't sound too pleased to hear from me, will you?'

'I thought it was the station calling me back,' Matthew explained. 'Something wrong?'

'No. I just thought I'd give you a call. Find out how your new job's going.'

Matthew frowned, wondering why Pat sounded as if she was grinning to herself at the end of the line. 'It's going all right,' he said cautiously.

'Just all right?' she echoed with a laugh. 'You've got a murder to investigate, 'aven't you?'

'How the hell do you know that?'

'That friend of Mum's, the char? She's got ladies she cleans for in Craynebrook and she picked up the local rag and, blow me, your name was in it, right there on the front page. She brought the 'paper to the pub to show Mum. You didn't waste any time, did you?'

Matthew cringed, knowing Pat had no idea how her

words embarrassed him. Even she seemed to think he wanted his name in the newspaper. 'It was a call for information, Pat, that's all,' he said testily. 'I haven't done anything remarkable.'

'Well, you made Mum's day.'

'I'm glad she's pleased.'

'You sound it,' Pat said, not missing his sarcasm. 'Anyway, you're all right?'

'Yes, I'm fine. You really don't need to check up on me. I'm a big boy now, Pat.'

'Sod you, then. I won't bother next time.'

'Pat!' he sighed.

'All right, all right,' she said, the sulkiness leaving her voice. Pat could never stay cross at anyone for long. 'When are you coming round again?'

'I don't know. Depends how busy I get.'

'It's not me who's asking. It's Mum and Georgie. You know me, I couldn't care less when I see you.'

'A couple of weeks,' he said to mollify her. 'But I better go now. My dinner's getting cold.'

'Right. See you then.'

'See you.'

'And Mattie?'

'Yeah?'

'Don't let them work you too hard.'

'I won't,' he promised and hung up.

Mr Levitt came back into the hall. 'I ain't your bleeding secretary, Stannard,' he said, nodding at the telephone. 'Ringing morning, noon and night, and it ain't ever for me. I've a good mind to complain.'

Matthew mounted the stairs to his flat. 'I've never known you to do anything else, Mr Levitt.'

· · ·

118

Dickie had lost count of the times he'd been in a dive like the Regal snooker hall. Why, he wondered, were the best people to talk to the kind of people who frequented such places?

The Regal was one of the worst. Located in a basement, there was an unhealthy smell of damp about the place. It clung to the nostrils and made Dickie feel ill just by breathing in. The bare brick walls had been painted dark green and the colour was only relieved by sporting posters encased in cheap frames, the paper foxed and crinkled behind the thin glass. The lights that hung low over the snooker tables had dusty, torn paper shades stained yellow by cigarette smoke.

Dickie lit his pipe and asked the man leaning over the nearest snooker table if Willie Dodds was there. He almost hoped he wasn't.

'Over there,' the man said, pointing his cue to the furthest corner of the basement.

Dickie murmured a thank you and made his way over, trying to ignore the less than friendly looks cast his way.

Willie Dodds was sitting at one of the few tables in the room, running a gnarly finger through a puddle of beer. Dickie had reached the table before he looked up.

'Whatcha want?' he asked, giving Dickie a quick once-over.

Dickie thought Dodds qualified for being the ugliest person he had ever seen. He had a squat, pudgy face surmounted by a nose that must have been broken at least three times, a scar on his chin and yellow eyes peering out from a liver-spotted complexion. 'I'm told you're Willie Dodds.'

'What if I am?'

'Then you're who I'm looking for. Mind if I sit down?'

'What if I do?'

Oh Christ, Dickie thought, pulling out a cracked leather covered wooden stool, *it's not going to be that type of conver-*

sation, is it? 'A friend of mine gave me your name. He thought you might be able to give me information on some people I'm interested in.'

'What friend? What people?'

'My friend doesn't matter. As for the people... Archibald Ballantyne, Christopher Fairbank, Adrian Foucault. You know them?'

'What you want to know about them for?' Dodds asked, his eyes narrowing suspiciously. 'Who the bleeding hell are you?'

'Dickie Waite. I'm a reporter.'

Dodd's top lip curled. 'Journalist, eh?'

'I'm working on a piece for my 'paper, and I've heard some interesting rumours about those three. I'd like to find out more, and this friend of mine said that if anyone could tell me about them, it was you.'

'What do I get for talking to you?'

Dickie had been ready for this question. 'A quid,' he said in a tone that implied he wouldn't negotiate the fee.

'All right,' Dodds said, 'and you get the drinks.'

Dickie got the drinks, a double rum for Dodds and a single malt whisky for himself. The whisky looked as if it had been watered down.

'So, what do you want to know?' Dodds asked, drinking half of his rum in one go.

'Anything you can tell me.'

'Well, what have you heard?'

'That Ballantyne and Foucault take backhanders from the villains they defend in court. Is that true or just gossip?'

'It's true, all right. I know men what done it, and word gets around. You get nicked and you got the means, get Ballantyne or Foucault to represent you in court and you'll be all right.'

'You give them money and they get you acquitted? What are you paying for, exactly?'

Dodds shrugged. 'This and that. Jurors scared off. Witnesses persuaded to change their statements. That kind of thing.'

'Can you give me any names of the people they've got off in this way?' Dickie didn't really expect Dodds to give him anything, but it didn't hurt to ask. To his surprise, Dodds did, rattling off a few names. Dickie recognised one or two from trials he'd covered for *The Chronicle*. 'You're not worried about telling me their names?' he wondered.

Dodds coughed into his hand, then wiped the mucus he'd brought up on his trousers. 'What can they do to me?'

'You're ill?'

'Something to do with me lungs.' Dodds took another gulp of his rum. 'Empressemma, the quack called it.'

'Emphysema,' Dickie corrected.

'That's what I said. Anyway, I'll be dead before the year's out.'

Dickie didn't bother expressing sympathy. 'What about Christopher Fairbank? Any dirt on him?'

'He's the antique dealer, ain't he? I heard he's got valuers in his pocket. Someone comes to him with a piece they've got and he recommends a valuer. The valuer says it's worth nothing. They go back to Fairbank and he gives them what seems a decent price for a load of rubbish. He then sells it for its real value, and then some.'

'So, the valuers get a backhander for their trouble?'

'That's it.' Dodds waggled his empty glass at Dickie. Dickie refreshed the rum and asked for valuers' names, but Dodds shook his head and said he didn't know any.

'What about Eric Hailes and Donald Spencer?'

Dodds's brow creased. 'Never heard of Hailes, but I've

seen that Spencer fella.' He made a face. 'Not one to get on the wrong side of, if you know what I mean.'

'I don't know what you mean.'

'Likes to use his fists. I've seen him in bare-knuckle fist-fights. Really ugly fights, and he always won. He also likes the dogs.'

'Racing?'

'Fighting. Can't stand it meself, seeing two dogs taking bites out of each other. But Spencer loves it.'

'Dog fights are illegal.'

Dodds chuckled. 'So's bare-knuckle boxing. Don't bother Spencer.'

'They sound a lovely lot.'

'All their chums up at the pony club would be shocked,' Dodds said in a mock posh voice and drained his glass.

'You're not wrong there,' Dickie murmured, doing the same with his own.

Thomas Yates snatched a glass of champagne, his third in the last hour, from the tray as Norman Kelly passed by. Yates watched the waiter with distaste. It was a good thing the man was competent, otherwise he would have given him the sack weeks ago. A sullen, shifty fellow, he gave the treasurer the creeps. Yates looked around for Sally Cooke and saw her dipping around a table, putting glasses on her tray. At least she seemed to be doing a proper job.

A burst of laughter drew his attention to the dais at the opposite end of the hall and his lips curled in disapproval. There they were, Ballantyne, Fairbank and the others. The Five! The men who had ruined his retirement. He didn't mind Eric Hailes so much. He was all right, when he was on his own, but Foucault and Spencer were just as bad as Ballantyne and Fairbank in their own ways. Foucault with his sneering, looking down on everyone else, and Spencer... well, anyone would think Donald Spencer had been brought up in an East End slum, the way he carried on. And to think these men had got all the credit for the money the club had raised at the charity auction. It had been their names in the newspaper, their faces in the photograph of them handing over a cheque to the children's charity. There hadn't been a word of praise for Thomas Yates who had organised the evening. No, not a single word.

He turned his attention to the dancefloor. Ballantyne danced with his wife, Fairbank with whoever he could get hold of, it seemed. There he was now, twirling Winifred Sloper off back to her husband and eyeing up the ladies who stood around watching the dancing, hoping he would pick one of them next.

Yates stiffened as Fairbank's eyes landed on Rosie. Fairbank put his hands to his hips and crooked each of his forefingers at her, a tease, bidding her to come to him. Yates watched in horror as Rosie smiled and ducked her head down, half embarrassed, half pleased to have been singled out in this way. He took a step forward, his breath catching as he continued to watch, the shout of protestation stuck in his throat. Fairbank was inching forward, keeping his eyes on Rosie, the smile crooked and the more enticing for it. Her friends were giggling, encouraging her to go to him, and Yates saw Rosie put one foot on the dance floor, unsure, hesitatingly, her cheeks reddening in her shyness.

Then Rosie's sparkling eyes caught sight of her husband and the smile dropped from her face. She shook her head at Fairbank and held up her palms to her friends, who tutted in annoyance at her change of heart. She went back to the table and sat down, grabbing her glass of wine and lifting it to her lips.

The Ragtime band reached the end of the number, and

into the quiet that followed, Yates heard Ballantyne's fruity voice call out, 'Now, what do we have here?'

Ballantyne was grinning at Norman Kelly as he moved around the nearest table. He winked at Fairbank, and Yates's throat tightened as he realised Ballantyne was up to something.

'Keep your backs to the wall, gentlemen,' Ballantyne said, his voice rising to get everyone's attention, 'if you value your arseholes.'

Thomas winced. To use such language in mixed company, and no one minding, no one reprimanding him, no one rebuking him with a *Steady, Archie, old man, keep it clean. Ladies present, and all that.* But there everyone was, smiling and laughing, the women hiding their mouths behind their hands, pretending to be shocked, but enjoying Ballantyne's banter all the same.

Ballantyne grabbed a glass from Norman's tray. The tray became unbalanced and Norman nearly dropped it. 'Butterfingers,' Ballantyne said, taking a mouthful of champagne. Yates saw Norman glare at him, then move to back away. 'Oh, not so fast, dearie.' Ballantyne grabbed the waiter by the shoulder and held tight. 'We want to have a proper look at you, don't we, Kit?'

'What is it, Archie?' Fairbank said, stepping forward to look Norman up and down. 'Fish or fowl, do you think?'

'Fish, I'd say.' Ballantyne sniffed. 'Yes, there's a definite odour of eau de haddock.'

Laughter all round. Not Rosie, though, Yates saw with an air of pride. She didn't think Ballantyne funny. Lovely little Rosie. Kind little Rosie.

'Male or female?' Fairbank asked.

'Difficult to say,' Ballantyne said, scrutinising the waiter's face. 'Could be male, but then again…'

'There's one way to find out,' Fairbank grinned at Ballantyne.

'You don't mean take a look, do you, Kit?' Ballantyne cried, pretending astonishment.

'Why not? We could do with a giggle.'

'I'd say. Come on, then, you androgynous thing. Take them off.' Ballantyne gestured at Norman's trousers.

Oh no, this was really going too far. Yates looked around desperately. Couldn't someone stop them? Kelly was trying to get away, but Spencer and Hailes moved to block his path. There was no way out.

'Looks like we're going to have to do it for him,' Spencer said to Ballantyne.

'Afraid so, Don, old thing,' Ballantyne agreed, nodding. 'Who's going to volunteer?' He glanced around at the onlookers. 'Marjorie? Louisa? Oh, come on, Louisa. I know you love taking trousers off.'

A screech of laughter from the women as Louisa buried her face in her hands.

'Oh dear, it's down to us, Kit, old chum,' Ballantyne said. 'Come and give me a hand.'

Ballantyne grabbed hold of Kelly's left arm as Fairbank took hold of his right. The waiter struggled, but they were too strong for him. They forced him face down on the table where Rosie sat and pinned him there. Yates stared at Rosie's horrified face. Then he looked at Ballantyne's and Fairbank's and saw no humour there, only an ugly pleasure.

The sense of fun had left their audience too. There was no laughing now, only unease. No one seemed to quite understand what was happening. Was this part of the joke? they wondered. Were they supposed to find this funny? Men looked at each other with frowns; women kept their eyes on the three men at the table, wanting to look away but unable to.

'Eric, get your arse over here,' Ballantyne yelled, and Hailes hurried over. 'Pull his trousers down. Let's see what he's got.'

Hailes put his hands around the waiter's waist to unbutton his flies. Kelly had stopped struggling now and was whimpering into the tablecloth. Hailes tugged his trousers down to his ankles, revealing his underwear, and stepped back.

'And the rest,' Fairbank ordered angrily.

Hailes looked from Fairbank to Ballantyne, unsure. 'Do it,' Ballantyne roared angrily, and Hailes obeyed, yanking down Kelly's underpants. Two pasty white buttocks were presented to view. The onlookers stared, transfixed by the sight.

Ballantyne and Fairbank laughed, and understanding each other perfectly, turned Kelly over onto his back.

'Well, I'll be damned,' Ballantyne laughed, staring at the waiter's genitals. 'Cock and balls.'

'Pity I don't have my camera,' Foucault called, holding out his champagne glass for Spencer to refill.

Husbands were turning their wives around, pulling them away from the obscene sight. Yates saw Rosie's mouth open, her eyes widen, and the sight of her at last forced him into action. He hurried over, grabbing her hand and pulling her out of the chair.

'We're leaving,' he said into her ear, and propelled her out of the hall.

'That poor man,' Rosie whimpered as he held out her coat for her to slide her arms into.

'That's it,' Yates declared. 'I've had it. No more.'

'Tommy? What do you mean?'

'I mean I'm resigning,' he yelled as he dragged her towards the door.

Chapter Sixteen

Mrs Lillian Briggs unlocked the back door of the Empire Club, shaking her head as she spied the chilblains on her fingers. The skin was cracked and bleeding, the result of too many days dipping them in and out of cold water to scrub floors. And the cold weather didn't help. Cor, but she was chilled to the bone. How she longed for the spring and warmer days when she might not have to spread lard on her bleeding, crooked fingers to soothe them, and not risk falling on her backside on icy pavements.

How much longer before she could pack this cleaning lark in? Lillian wondered. She'd spent a lifetime in service, save for a few, almost blissful years when the children had come along. She'd had dreams of never having to go back, but that had proved wishful thinking. What with three children and Bill's chest condition, there couldn't have been any sitting around for her, not when the extra money came in so handy. How she'd love to be a lady of leisure like the women she cleaned up after. Nothing to do all day but sit around reading magazines and having your hair done, nannies to look after the children, and say to your husband when he came home

what a trial the day had been because the cook had been difficult over the sauce.

'Don't know they're born, they don't,' Lillian muttered as
she took her cleaning caddy from the cupboard with its
dusters and beeswax furniture polish, reaching back in to get
her dustpan and brush. There was no point moaning about it,
she told herself as she climbed the stairs to the first floor,
panting heavily, her bulk making the action not as effortless
as it would have been forty years earlier when she'd been a
tweeny. Nothing would ever change.

Lillian went into Yates's office first, flicking the duster
over the desk and filing cabinets, taking care not to move
anything. The silly old sod made such a fuss if anything was
out of place. She emptied the wicker wastebin into a refuse
bag, then went to the billiard room. The shelves got a quick
dust, as did the frame of the billiard table. The ashtrays were
emptied into the bag, and Lillian crossed the wide landing to
the private dining room.

She was pleased to see the dining room neat and tidy; it
didn't look like it had been used. Not like the other time, she
mused, dipping a second duster in the beeswax and wiping
the table with great sweeps of her arm. God knew what had
gone on then, but she'd had to clear away dirty plates and
broken glasses, and food and drink spilled all over the floor,
and the other things she hadn't liked to mention when she
told her husband about the mess. Took her nearly an hour to
set the room right again. And did she get any extra for that
from Mr bloody Thomas Yates? Not a shilling more. She
hadn't even got a thank you.

She closed the door to the dining room and moved to the
first of the bedrooms. Poking her head around the door, she
saw it hadn't been used, so there was nothing for her to do.
She moved on to the second bedroom and opened the door.

'Oh, 'scuse me,' Lillian said, and backed out. But then she stopped. She hadn't heard anything from inside. No gasp of surprise at her entrance, no creak of the bed frame or springs, no rustling of bedclothes. She pushed the door open again and peered around the side at the man lying in the bed. Her skin prickled. Moving inside, her breath caught in her throat as she saw the man's eyes were open, staring up at the ceiling.

'My gawd,' she whispered as she looked down upon his face. Her fingers trembled as they reached for his cheek. She snatched them away as soon as they encountered his cold skin. Her eyes wandered downwards towards the large, dark stain on the blanket. She pulled the blanket away and staggered backwards, banging into the door she'd left half open and almost falling out into the hall.

Lillian ran into Yates's office and snatched up the telephone.

'Number, please,' the operator said.

'Police,' Lillian gasped into the mouthpiece. 'I need someone to come.'

Denham was busy at his desk when Matthew walked into CID the next morning. The sergeant looked up, nodded a hello, then explained he was working through records for the names Matthew had given him. He looked anxious, as if expecting another scolding. It irritated Matthew a little. He'd apologised for his brusqueness the night before and he hoped Denham wasn't a man prone to sulking.

'Anything on Fairbank?' Matthew asked as he hung up his overcoat.

'Nothing in our records,' Denham said. 'And I telephoned Scotland Yard first thing to check there. They didn't have anything either.'

'Didn't really think there would be,' Matthew muttered unhappily. The telephone on his desk rang and he snatched up the receiver. 'Stannard.'

'Turkel, sir,' the sergeant said. 'Just had an urgent call come in from a woman at the Empire Club. Says she's found a body in one of the bedrooms. Will you attend?'

It took a moment for the sergeant's words to register. Another body? For a split second, Matthew wondered if it was a prank being played on the new boy, and he searched the faces of Denham and the constables as they stared at him for a sign. But there was no hint of merriment in their expressions, and he decided the call must be genuine.

'Sir?' Sergeant Turkel prompted.

'Yes. I'll attend,' Matthew said and banged the telephone back into the cradle.

'What is it, sir?' Denham asked.

Matthew pulled his overcoat back on. 'Get your hat, Denham. We've got another dead body.'

Dickie was yawning as he shuffled into *The Chronicle*'s office. Despite his distaste for the place, he'd played a couple of games of snooker at the Regal with one of the regulars when he'd finished with Willie Dodds, deeming it best if he let him win, and got home after one o'clock in the morning. His wife hadn't moved or said a word to him as he clambered into bed, though he knew she was awake, and she hadn't troubled herself to wake him in the morning. And so, he had stayed asleep until the banging at the windows that signalled the arrival of the window cleaner woke him. He hadn't had time for breakfast, and his only desire was to get a cup of tea inside him. He groaned when Bill Edwards shouted at him.

'Sorry I'm late, Bill,' Dickie called. 'I overslept and the wife didn't wake me.'

'Get in here.'

Dickie slammed down the milk bottle he had been holding, wondering if today was the day when he told Bill Edwards to stick his job up his arse. 'What?' he demanded, leaning against the editor's doorframe, ready for a row.

'Trust you to be late today,' Edwards growled.

'What's special about today?'

'We've had a tip-off. The police are all over the Empire Club. Rumours are a body's been found there. That's what special about today. I didn't know if you were going to show your face, did I? I've had to send Teddy.'

'You're bloody joking?' Dickie cried.

'Who else did I have to send?'

'I don't mean Teddy. A body at the Empire Club?'

'That's right. Why the face, Dickie?'

'It's the coincidence of it,' Dickie said, rubbing his chin. 'I've been talking to people about the members there.'

'Even more bloody reason why you should have been here, then, ain't it?' Edwards lit a fag and tossed the match into the ashtray. 'Go on. Get down there. And don't come back until you've got someone to talk.'

Matthew decided to interview Mrs Briggs before viewing the body and found the cleaner in the kitchen, seated at the big pine table with a mug of tea held tightly in her two hands and a look of horror and disbelief on her face. A uniformed constable stood on guard at the door. Matthew pulled out a chair and sat down.

'I understand you've had a very great shock, Mrs Briggs, but I need you to tell me about this morning,' he said.

Lillian nodded, letting out a shuddering breath. 'I don't ever want to see anything like that again.'

'I hope you never have to.' Matthew flicked a glance at

Denham to make sure he was taking notes, then continued. 'What happened this morning?'

'I got here just after eight. 'ere, don't tell Mr Yates that, will you? I'm supposed to be here at half seven, only I was running late this morning. Me 'usband couldn't get the stove to light and—'

'I won't tell Mr Yates,' Matthew promised, keen to prevent her from recounting her morning troubles that were of no interest to him.

Lillian relaxed a little. 'Well, I let meself in the back door, like I always do.'

'You have a key?'

She nodded. 'I could have done with a cup of tea, but as I was late, I thought I'd better get on with me work. So, I got my cleaning things from the cupboard and went upstairs. I always start at the top and work down. I did Mr Yates's office first, then the billiard room, then the dining room. Not that there was much to do in them. Mr Yates keeps his office tidy, and the other rooms hadn't been used. Nor had the first bedroom. Then I looked into the other bedroom and...' she gulped, 'that's when I saw him.'

'Describe what you saw, Mrs Briggs.'

'I saw him in the bed, blankets pulled up to his chin. I knew something weren't right. I moved closer and his eyes were open. Staring up at the ceiling, they were, and I knew then he was dead. Just to be sure, I put me fingers to his cheek and he was cold as a stone, inspector. Made me go cold too. I should have got out of there then, but I saw the stain on the blanket and I couldn't think what was making it. You see, I thought he must have had a heart attack or something. I never imagined...' Lillian lifted her mug with both hands and took another mouthful, closing her eyes as the hot sweet tea flowed down her throat.

'Go on, Mrs Briggs,' Matthew said, trying to keep the impatience out of his voice.

'I pulled the blanket down, didn't I? And then I saw it. A great big 'ole in his chest and blood all over him.'

'Do you know who the man is?'

'Oh, yes, I know 'im,' she said, nodding. 'His name's Christopher Fairbank. Everyone here calls him Kit.'

Chapter Seventeen

Matthew and Denham exchanged a glance.

'Are you sure?' Matthew asked.

'I'm sure,' Lillian said. 'I've seen him often enough. In the 'paper and throwing his weight around here. It's him, all right.'

Matthew remembered his meeting with Fairbank the evening before and he could well imagine him throwing his weight around. 'Well, thank you, Mrs Briggs. That's been very helpful.' Matthew stood, picking up his hat.

'Is that it? Can I go now?'

'Yes. We have your address should we need to talk to you again. Go home and rest.'

'I will,' Lillian assured Matthew, getting up and pushing her chair under the table. 'My 'usband won't believe me when I tell him.'

'Did you suspect something like this was going to happen, sir?' Denham asked as Lillian left the kitchen. 'Is that why you had me look into Fairbank?'

'I don't have a crystal ball, Denham,' Matthew said wryly. 'If I could predict a murder, we'd be out of a job. Has anyone contacted Mr Yates?'

'Mr Yates, sir?'

'The treasurer of the club. He needs to be told what's happened and I want to speak with him, see if he knew Fairbank was using the bedroom last night. Is the photographer here yet?'

'Yes, sir. He's already upstairs. And the police surgeon's with him.'

'Let's get up there, then.'

Denham instructed a constable to fetch Mr Yates, then joined Matthew climbing the stairs to the first floor. Another uniformed constable was on guard at the top of the stairs and let them through. Matthew saw the flash of a camera bulb and heard the murmur of voices from a room to the left. He stepped inside the doorway and his eyes were drawn to the dead man in the bed. Mrs Briggs was right. It was Christopher Fairbank.

It was far from being the worst murder scene Matthew had been exposed to during his time as a policeman, but he could understand how the sight had horrified Mrs Briggs. There was something very unsettling about a dead body that had the eyes open. The eyes became glassy in death and robbed the body of any personality.

'Good morning, inspector!'

'Mr Wallace,' Matthew said in surprise. 'I wasn't expecting to see you.'

'I take my turn as police surgeon,' Wallace said with a shrug. 'And I can tell you, this fellow is most certainly dead.'

Matthew gave him an appreciative grin. 'From a stab wound to the heart, I take it?'

'Indeed.'

'Time of death?'

'Between midnight and six o'clock.' Wallace clicked his medical bag shut. 'That's me done. I know you'll be impatient for the results of the post-mortem, so get him over to me as soon as you can and I'll do it straight away. Will you be attending, inspector?'

Matthew met Wallace's eye. There was a twinkle in it but nothing malicious. 'Sergeant Denham will attend,' he said.

'Until then, sergeant,' Wallace said and left the room.

'You want me to attend the post-mortem, sir?' Denham asked.

Matthew nodded. 'It's good experience for you.'

'It's a part of the job I don't like,' Denham said with a grim smile. 'I don't understand how Dr Wallace can poke around in dead bodies all day and enjoy it.'

'It takes all sorts, Denham,' Matthew said, looking around the room.

There were two empty champagne glasses on the bedside table, an empty bottle of champagne on its side on the floor by the bed, and a glass ashtray with four cigarette stubs and a mound of ash. Two of the stubs had red lipstick on them and one glass bore the red imprint of lips around its rim.

'He had company. Have you taken a picture of this?' Matthew asked the photographer, pointing to a pair of trousers crumpled on the floor. The photographer confirmed he had recorded the scene and was ready to pack up. 'I want those photographs developed right away,' Matthew said, bending to pick up the trousers and delving into the pockets. He withdrew a pocketbook from one. 'Doesn't look like he was robbed. There's twenty pounds in here.'

'I wonder why he spent the night here,' Denham said, moving to let the photographer pass. 'He lived local.'

'Well, if the woman he had here wasn't his wife...' Matthew said.

Denham nodded. 'I suppose so. What about Fairbank's wife?'

'What about her?'

'Could she be a suspect?'

'Everyone's a suspect until we have more information, Denham. Even Mrs Briggs.'

'Really?'

'Really. But before you ask, no, I don't think Mrs Briggs killed him.' Matthew stared down at the body. 'There's no sign of a struggle.'

'Well, he would have felt safe with a woman, wouldn't he? You don't expect a woman to do this sort of thing.'

'Women are just as capable of committing murder as men.'

'Yes, sir,' Denham murmured, getting out of Matthew's way as he came around the bed to study the bedside cabinet. 'What is it?'

'French letter in the bin.' He pointed to a white powder residue on the top of the bedside cabinet. 'And drugs here. Possibly cocaine. Get this in an envelope and sent off for testing. There'll be envelopes in Yates's office across the landing.'

Denham hurried out and returned a few moments later with a small envelope and a ruler. He used the ruler to scrape the powder into the envelope and sealed it. 'Have you finished in here, sir? I saw out of the window that the mortuary van's arrived.'

Matthew nodded. 'They can remove the body. Let's have a look at the other rooms on this floor.'

'Mrs Briggs said they hadn't been used.' Denham followed Matthew into Yates's office.

'Mrs Briggs is not a trained detective.'

'I didn't mean we shouldn't look,' Denham protested under his breath.

Matthew saw nothing amiss in the treasurer's office and went into the billiard room. All looked as it should. The cues were in the rack, the balls on the baize. He crossed the landing to the private dining room, Denham following at his heels.

'My wife wants a dining table like this,' the sergeant said, looking at the oval mahogany table with admiration. 'How many do you think it seats?'

'Six as it is. Eight with the leaves in,' Matthew said, moving around the table to look out of the window. He saw Thomas Yates coming in through the gates.

'I reckon you could easily get ten around this.'

'Keep your mind on the job,' Matthew said, turning back to the room. Something in the fireplace caught his eye. It looked like a piece of fabric had caught on the back spike of the grate. He reached in and took hold of it.

'Found something, sir?'

Matthew straightened and held up the fabric.

Denham coughed, embarrassed. 'Those are…'

'Knickers, sergeant.'

'Yes, sir.'

'Get them in an evidence bag,' Matthew said, passing the underwear to Denham.

As Denham bagged the knickers, Matthew moved to a room next to the dining room. It must have been a bedroom at some point for there was a disassembled Victorian bedstead in one corner but it was now being used as a junk-room. Scratched and sun-bleached bookcases lined one side of the room, home to boxes of Christmas decorations, old telephone directories, and paper-stuffed files containing receipts and purchase orders made by the club. The other side of the room had boxes piled against three-quarters of the wall inside the door, but there was a space at the far end. Matthew studied the empty space. There were three indentations in the carpet forming a triangle. On the wall where Matthew stood was a cheap framed print of Constable's *The Hay Wain*.

'Anything, sir?' Denham asked from the doorway.

'Something stood here.' Matthew pointed at the carpet. 'A three-legged something.'

Denham stepped over to him and looked down. 'A stool?'

Matthew shook his head. 'The points are too small for stool legs.'

'What then?'

'Camera tripod?' Matthew suggested. 'But why have a camera here?'

'Perhaps it was being stored here.'

'Perhaps.' Matthew frowned at *The Hay Wain*. It was an odd place to hang a painting. 'Or…' He took his handkerchief out of his pocket and lifted the painting off the wall with it. There was a hole in the wall. Matthew put his eye to the hole and saw the mortuary men lifting Fairbank onto a stretcher. He straightened. 'Someone's been spying into the bedroom.' He stepped back to allow Denham to have a look.

'Pervert,' the sergeant muttered.

Matthew went into the bedroom and studied the wall where the hole should be. He found it in the centre of a flower in the wallpaper. He returned to the junk-room where Denham was peering through the hole. 'If you didn't know the hole was there, you'd probably never notice it.'

'So,' Denham said, 'someone was in here, watching and taking photographs while Fairbank and a woman were in there? Did this watcher kill him?'

'There's nothing to say the tripod was there last night,' Matthew pointed out.

'Nothing to say it wasn't either, sir.'

'True,' Matthew conceded, knowing the 'sir' had been added to cover any impertinence. 'Well, there's no point speculating. Mr Yates is here. Let's have a word.'

· · ·

Thomas Yates was pacing in the hall. He strode towards Matthew as he and Denham come down the stairs. 'Inspector. What is going on here? I have a policeman turn up on my doorstep, insisting I come here—'

'I'm sorry you've been bothered, Mr Yates,' Matthew interrupted, 'but I'm afraid there's been an incident in one of the bedrooms. Mr Christopher Fairbank has been killed.'

Yates's mouth fell open. He stared at Matthew, uncomprehending, then suddenly staggered backwards.

Matthew lunged and grabbed at him. 'Hold on to me, Mr Yates,' he said, shocked by the effect his words, so unthinkingly delivered, had had on the elderly treasurer.

'I need to sit down,' Yates gasped.

Matthew jerked his head at Denham to help him, and between them, they walked Yates into the kitchen and sat him down at the kitchen table. Matthew grabbed a glass from the draining board and filled it with water. He put the glass into Yates's hand. 'Drink this,' he ordered. 'Should I call you a doctor?'

Yates shook his head as he gulped at the water. 'I'll be fine,' he said, taking a deep breath. 'It was just... I wasn't expecting that.'

'I'm sorry,' Matthew said. 'I shouldn't have told you like that.' He dragged over another of the kitchen table chairs and sat down by Yates, watching the old man as some colour returned to his cheeks.

Yates turned watery blue eyes on him. 'Fairbank's dead? Murdered here in the club?'

'I'm afraid so,' Matthew nodded. 'Are you up to answering some questions?'

'Yes, of course.'

'You're sure you're all right?'

Yates attempted a smile but managed only a brief turning up of his lips. 'I'm fine.'

Matthew heaved a breath of relief. The kitchen door was open, and he turned to stare out of it through to the hallway as there came the sound of footsteps. The mortuary men were bringing Fairbank's body down. Matthew mouthed at Denham to close the door.

He turned back to Yates. 'Did you know Mr Fairbank was spending the night here?'

Yates shook his head. 'I had no idea. I should have done. It's my responsibility to know. But we left early last night. I didn't even give any instructions for locking up.'

'Why did you leave early?'

Yates straightened. 'We'd had enough, that's all.'

There was something in his expression that interested Matthew. 'Enough of what?' he pressed.

'The members were getting a little rowdy last night,' the treasurer shrugged. 'It wasn't pleasant, and I took my wife home.'

'Which members were getting rowdy?'

'The Five,' Yates sighed heavily.

Matthew shared a quizzical look with Denham. 'Who are The Five, Mr Yates?'

Yates frowned at Matthew, then nodded. 'Of course. You're new here, so you wouldn't know. The Five, inspector, are Ballantyne, Foucault, Spencer, Hailes, and….' his gaze turned heavenward, 'Fairbank.'

Matthew was intrigued. 'What happened?' he asked, adding when Yates seemed reluctant, 'It's important I know.'

'They picked on one of the waiters,' Yates burst out. 'They pulled down his trousers and made obscene remarks. It was really quite reprehensible behaviour and I wanted no part of it.'

'Who was the waiter?'

'His name is Norman Kelly.'

'Did The Five have a reason for picking on him? Did they know him?'

'No, I don't think so. The Five don't need reasons, inspector. They do what they want, when they want here.'

'How long has Norman Kelly worked here at the club?'

'Since mid-December.' Yates frowned. 'You don't think he had anything to do with this, do you?'

'We think a woman did it,' Denham said.

'A woman?' Yates cried in astonishment.

Matthew glared at Denham. Realising he had spoken out of turn, Denham ducked his head down, cheeks reddening.

Matthew turned back to Yates. 'You'll have an address for Mr Kelly in your records?'

'Yes,' Yates said. 'I can get that for you, but do you really think it was a woman?'

'We have reason to believe Mr Fairbank was with a woman in the upstairs bedroom last night,' Matthew said. 'Do you have any idea who that might have been?'

'None. Unless it was Daphne, his wife, but…, no, no. She wasn't here last night.'

'Was it common for Mr Fairbank to spend the night here at the club with a woman?'

'I believe he stayed here a few times. Whether he entertained women here, he never told me, and I never asked. But it is well known Kit Fairbank had an eye for the ladies, inspector. As a member of the club, he was entitled to use the facilities. It was no business of mine who he used them with.'

'Always the same bedroom?' Matthew asked.

'I believe so.'

'Do other members use the bedrooms frequently?'

Yates shifted in the chair, seeming to find it uncomfortable. 'The Five are the most frequent users, inspector. Most of the members are local and have no need to sleep here.'

'So, if any modifications have been made to the bedroom, they are likely to have been made by one of The Five?'

Yates frowned. 'What modifications?'

'We found a peephole in the wall from the room being used for storage looking into the bedroom Mr Fairbank was using.'

'A peephole?' Yates whispered.

'It appears someone liked to watch what has happening in the bedroom. Perhaps even take photographs. There are marks in the adjoining room that suggest a tripod may have been set up at the peephole.' Yates was shaking his head in disgust. It was clear the old man had had no idea of what had been going on in the bedrooms. 'Who has keys to the club, Mr Yates?' Matthew asked.

Yates took another mouthful of water. 'I do. The cleaner, Mrs Briggs, has a key to the back door so she can let herself in. No one else.'

'Are there any spare sets?'

'One. I keep it in my desk.'

'I'm going to need you to check to see if it's still there.'

Yates nodded and rose. Matthew watched him anxiously, making sure the old man was steady on his feet. The first shock seemed to have worn off, and now Yates was suffering only from a dreadful realisation that he had been ignorant of so much.

Matthew followed the treasurer up the stairs to his office, Yates avoiding looking in the direction of the bedrooms. He opened the top drawer of his desk and took out a set of keys.

'They're here.'

Matthew nodded, realising that the keys still being in Yates's possession meant very little. He'd seen for himself that the doors were left open, and if Yates had left early, it was possible that no one would have locked the club up at all. His suspect list could end up being impossibly long, but at the top for the moment were the woman Fairbank had been with and the waiter.

'I'm going to need the names and addresses for all your staff members, Mr Yates. Same as you did for your members.'

The elderly treasurer nodded. 'I'll do that for you now, inspector.'

Chapter Eighteen

A crowd had gathered on the pavement outside the gates of the Empire Club. Dickie found Teddy amongst their number and told him to get back to the office. Teddy had not been pleased and had slunk away with a rebellious look on his face, but Dickie paid him no mind. He kept his eyes firmly on the house, his ears tuned to his neighbours' excited conversations. The cleaner had found the body, Dickie learned, up in the bedroom, this information got from her before the police arrived when she had rushed out into the street, crying for help. Dickie recognised the voice of Frank Greader, the landlord of The King George pub, and pushed his way through to him.

'Morning, Frank,' Dickie said. 'I thought I heard your dulcet tones.'

'You took your time getting here, didn't you?' Greader said, offering Dickie a paper bag containing humbugs. 'I phoned your 'paper more than an hour ago.'

Dickie shook his head at the paper bag and took out his notebook. 'It was you, was it? So, come on. What do you know?'

'The cleaner found the body when she went in this morning. Said he was in one of the bedrooms with a great big hole in his chest. The dead fella's Christopher Fairbank.'

'Do you know the cleaner's name?'

'Lillian Briggs. She and her old man are regulars at the pub.'

'How did she know who the dead man was? I can't imagine they would mix socially.'

'Lil cleans at the golf club. He was a member there too, and she saw him often enough to know him. Said he was a right one.'

'A right one?'

Greader nodded. 'I've heard it said before by others. Him and his mates.'

Irritation swelled within Dickie. Here was more gossip about The Five. Practically everyone he had talked to in the last few days had a story to tell about them, so how come he, a seasoned journalist, was only finding out about them now? *You're obviously not as good as you thought you were, Dickie, old son.* 'What have you heard?' he asked Greader.

'That they're a bit wild, like lots of those nobs are. You read it in the newspapers, don't you? All the parties they have, dressing up in silly costumes and falling into the Trafalgar Square fountains dead drunk.'

Dickie shook his head. 'You're talking about the Bright Young Things, Frank. I wouldn't have thought any of the members of the Empire Club were all that young.'

'They're not, but don't you believe they don't know how to enjoy themselves.'

'In what way?'

'Well, drinking, course. Not that I got anything against that.'

'Seeing as how you're landlord of a pub,' Dickie said with a twinkle in his eye.

Greader grinned. 'But there's other stuff.' He bent his

head towards Dickie and whispered, 'Drugs.' He leant back and shrugged. 'It's what I've heard.'

'Who from?'

'The staff. They come into the pub and they tell us.'

'I'd like to talk to them. Can you give me a name or two?'

Greader pupped his lips while he considered. 'Make it worth my while.'

Everyone has their hand out, Dickie thought ruefully as he slapped a couple of crowns into Frank's outstretched palm.

'Harry Cole, one of the waiters,' Frank said, tucking the coins away in his trouser pocket. 'He's your lad. Got a mouth on him and he knows plenty of what goes on there.'

'And where can I get hold of Mr Harry Cole?'

'I expect he'll be in at lunchtime for a pint. He usually is.'

'I'll pop in at lunchtime, then,' Dickie promised as he saw the front doors of the club open and Thomas Yates step out.

Matthew had told Yates the club was to remain closed for the time being and the treasurer simply shrugged and said he understood. Matthew got the impression he wasn't at all upset at the club being out of bounds to the members, quite the reverse. He seemed glad.

He saw Yates to the front doors and watched him walk down the path towards the gates. He had thought the treasurer pompous before, but now he couldn't help but feel sorry for him as he noted the slumped shoulders and the drooping head.

'Back to the station, sir?' Denham asked, following Matthew as he stepped out onto the path.

'Not yet,' Matthew said, lighting a cigarette, cupping his hands around the flame. 'DC Barnes stays here to carry out a search of the entire club. Tell him anything that looks suspicious, I want bagged as evidence. I also want all the kitchen knives dusted for fingerprints, then sent off to the mortuary for Dr Wallace to examine. Just in case the killer didn't bother to bring a knife and used what was available. I want you to talk to Norman Kelly. You'll have time before the post-mortem. But before that...' Matthew turned to face the sergeant. Denham must have realised what was coming, for he stared down at his feet. 'I'm not going to make this a formal reprimand this time, sergeant, but if you ever again tell a member of the public what we're thinking, especially when I'm in the middle of questioning them, I won't hesitate. Is that understood?'

Denham nodded, a guilty schoolboy caught in a misdemeanour by his headmaster. 'Yes, sir. I'm sorry, sir. It just slipped out, and anyway, I didn't think Mr Yates was a suspect.'

'What did I say earlier? Everyone's a suspect until we've ruled them out. We don't know what Mr Yates is yet. He might be exactly what he appears to be or he might not. You need to learn to reserve judgement and hold your tongue.'

'It won't happen again, sir.'

Matthew nodded, satisfied. 'Off you go to Kelly's digs. I'll be at Fairbank's house telling his wife her husband's dead.'

Chapter Nineteen

Matthew rang the doorbell of No. 7 St Jude's Avenue and listened for movement on the other side of the door. Heels clipped on wooden flooring, and then the door opened to reveal a maid, thin and neat, old and plain.

Her eyes narrowed as she quickly took in Matthew and the uniformed constable behind him. 'Yes?'

Matthew held up his warrant card. 'I need to speak with Mrs Fairbank. Is she home?'

The maid didn't bother to check. 'She is,' she said, and stepped back to let them enter the hall. 'Wait here, please.' She left them to go into the sitting room. Matthew heard her say, 'The police to see you, madam,' but didn't hear the reply.

The maid reappeared. 'You're to come in,' she said and jerked her head towards the sitting-room door.

Daphne Fairbank was sitting on the sofa when Matthew and the constable entered, stroking a Pekingese lying beside her and drinking a cup of coffee.

'You again,' she said, one eyebrow rising. 'I'm afraid my husband isn't here.'

'I know that, Mrs Fairbank,' Matthew said, seeing the constable take up his position by the door. 'May I sit down?'

She pointed her cigarette at the sofa opposite and Matthew sat. 'I have some bad news. I'm sorry to have to tell you that your husband is dead, Mrs Fairbank.'

Daphne leaned forward to put her cup in its saucer. 'What did you say?'

'Your husband is dead,' Matthew repeated, hoping she wasn't about to have a screaming fit. He'd never been very good with hysterical women.

Her eyes narrowed. 'How?'

'He was killed at the Empire Club sometime after midnight.'

'I see.' She gripped the scruff of the Pekingese's neck as she stared at her coffee cup. 'Who killed him?'

'We don't know yet,' Matthew said. 'Are you all right, Mrs Fairbank?'

'I'm not going to burst into tears, inspector, if that's what you're thinking. Was he with a woman at the club?' She smiled. 'You don't have to answer that, inspector. I can see from your face he was. Who? Or don't you know that either?'

'Do you know who he was with, Mrs Fairbank?' Matthew asked, irritated by the 'either'.

Daphne didn't answer at once. 'I have no idea. Whichever woman took his fancy, I suppose.'

Why had she hesitated? Matthew wondered. 'You weren't at the club last night?'

Daphne brushed dog hairs from her skirt. 'I stopped going to the club some time ago. I became bored watching my husband attempting to seduce every woman he could lay his hands on.'

'Were you expecting your husband home last night?'

'I expect nothing of Kit. He comes and goes as he pleases.'

'Did your husband often stay out all night?'

'Very often. Adultery is a hobby of his. Has been ever since we married.'

Matthew noted her incorrect use of the present tense. She wasn't as composed as she wanted him to believe. Perhaps the news hadn't really sunk in. 'Where were you last night, Mrs Fairbank?'

Daphne's eyes bored into him. 'I was here.'

'Alone?'

The Pekingese received a slow stroke up and down its back. 'I gave our maid the night off,' Daphne said. 'I didn't see the need to keep her here just for me.'

'So, you were here alone? From what time?'

'From about six o'clock last night to seven this morning. Hilda stayed overnight at her sister's, I believe. Are you asking these questions because I'm a suspect, inspector?'

'I just need to confirm your whereabouts for the record, Mrs Fairbank.'

'You think I killed him, don't you?'

'I don't think anything at the moment,' Matthew assured her. 'I'm just gathering information. With that in mind, I'd like to have a look around.'

'You want to search my house?'

'It may help me find out who killed your husband.'

'How could it? He wasn't killed here.'

'Are you refusing, Mrs Fairbank?'

'And if I am?'

'Then I'll have to get a warrant.' He narrowed his eyes at her. 'Is there a reason you don't want me looking around the house?'

The Pekingese yelped as Daphne dug her nails into his skin. He jumped off the sofa and scurried out of the room. 'Of course there isn't. I don't like my privacy being invaded, that's all.'

Matthew waited.

'Oh, look around if you must,' she snapped, throwing open the lid of the cigarette box on the coffee table and grabbing a cigarette. She didn't bother with her holder, but just clamped the cigarette between her lips and lit it, tossing the lighter into the corner of the sofa. She folded her arms across her chest and kept her head turned defiantly away as Matthew and the constable left the room.

They started their search upstairs. Matthew discovered Mr and Mrs Fairbank had separate bedrooms, a not uncommon practice for people of their class, he knew, but perhaps more understandable given the husband's extramarital proclivities.

Christopher Fairbank's bedroom was overtly masculine. The walls were papered in a dark blue and gold stripe with heavy blue velvet curtains to match. The furniture was Victorian, heavy and dark, a large wardrobe, chest of drawers, bedside tables. On the walls hung paintings of lithe naked females cavorting in Roman baths. Everything was in its place, to the small stack of books — French novels Matthew couldn't read — perfectly lined up on one of the bedside tables to the hairbrushes on the top of the chest of drawers. Fairbank hadn't kept a photograph of his wife in his bedroom.

Matthew pulled open the bedside drawer on the side of the bed it seemed Fairbank had used. A few pens, a comb and a bottle of aspirin were all that was inside. He shut it again and moved to the chest of drawers. The top drawer held collars, handkerchiefs and underwear, the second socks and shirts, and the bottom, a selection of pullovers. He moved to the wardrobe. Fairbank had four suits: grey, black, blue and pinstripe. Out of interest, Matthew peered inside one for the label and saw a Savile Row tailors' label. Not Rose and Harper, though. Fairbank had patronised H. J. Bennett. He searched through the pockets but found nothing.

A door in the corner led to a small bathroom with a cabinet over the basin. Inside was a toothbrush and toothpaste, razor and spare blades, a powder for treating Athlete's foot and three unopened packets of French letters, the same brand as the wrapping Matthew had found in the wastebasket at the club.

Daphne Fairbank's bedroom yielded nothing of interest. The decoration in her bedroom was feminine but not too flouncy, walnut furniture instead of mahogany, and the books on her bedside table were English Classics. Her bedside drawer contained nail files, an eye mask and two bottles of aspirin, one half-empty. The underwear in the chest of drawers was quality but not designed to be alluring. Two fur coats hung in protective wrappers in the wardrobe along with a quantity of dresses, blouses and skirts. Shoes were laid out neatly on the bottom.

Returning to the ground floor, they searched Fairbank's study. A large oak desk filled up much of the room, and in it, Matthew found legal papers relating to the house and his business, catalogues from auction houses, household bills, a cash box with more than one hundred pounds in notes and coins and a pornographic book filled with luridly painted illustrations.

It took another hour to search the rest of the house but Matthew found nothing that might provide a clue as to who had killed Christopher Fairbank. He went in search of Daphne and found her in the kitchen, discussing lunch with the maid.

'Thank you, Mrs Fairbank,' he said. 'We're all done.'

Daphne turned to him, her jaw set hard. 'And did you find anything?'

Matthew smiled. 'We'll see ourselves out.'

'Will you be seeing my husband's friends, inspector? I'm sure they'll be able to tell you far more than I.'

'I will be seeing them, yes,' Matthew said. 'I believe Mr Ballantyne lives a few doors away at number thirteen?'

She nodded.

'I'll drop in and see him then. Also, your husband's body will need to be formally identified. Will you be able to do that or is there someone else we can ask?'

'I'm quite capable of identifying him, inspector. Just let me know when.'

'I will. Goodbye, Mrs Fairbank.'

Matthew left No. 7, glad he didn't have a wife like Daphne Fairbank.

Chapter Twenty

Denham rapped on the door, still smarting from the telling off Matthew had given him. He knew he'd messed up. Knew it as soon as the words were out of his mouth and Matthew had glared at him. He hadn't needed telling. Perhaps he should have apologised as soon as they were out of the club; that might have looked better. At least prove he knew he'd ballsed up. He shook his head, annoyed at himself and at Matthew. It wouldn't have mattered if he'd been with DI Lund. Lund wouldn't have given a toss what he said. He probably wouldn't have even noticed.

The yellowed net curtains to his right twitched and a woman's face peered out at him. He held his warrant card up to the window and the net curtain dropped back into place. A few moments later, the door opened.

'Yes?' the woman said.

'Norman Kelly. Is he in?'

'What do you want him for?'

'I'd just like a word.'

The woman leant against the door frame and folded her arms. 'Well, you're out of luck. He's not here.'

'Any idea where he is?'

She shrugged.

'When did you see him last?'

'This morning when I brought the milk in. About seven.'

'And how did he seem?'

'Miserable. Same as always. He muttered a 'morning', but I wouldn't have got that if I hadn't said it first. Then he went.'

'Went where?'

'Down that way.' She nodded at the pavement to Denham's left.

'No, I mean, did he go to work?'

'Might have. I don't know what he gets up to.'

'I see,' Denham muttered. He looked up at the front of the house. He asked for the woman's name and was told it was Mrs Coggs. 'You have the downstairs, he has the upstairs?'

She nodded. 'He's got the front room. Another fella's got the back. I got the whole of the downstairs.'

'Are you in charge of the house?'

'No, dearie,' she laughed. 'I'm a tenant, just like the rest.'

'So, you wouldn't have a key to the other rooms?'

Mrs Coggs shook her head. Pity, Denham thought. If she had a key, he could have searched Kelly's room. He could always break the door down, he supposed...

'Do you know what time he came in last night?' he asked.

'It weren't last night, it was this morning. Just gone half-past three. Woke me up, he did, with all the noise he was making.'

'What noise?'

'Snivelling as he went up the stairs. I think he fell up 'em at one point. I heard him crying.'

'Crying?'

Mrs Coggs's top lip curled up. 'He's always snivelling. I can hear him through the ceiling. So, go on. Tell me what he's done.'

156

'We think he might—' Denham began and broke off, an image of being told to learn to hold his tongue entering his mind. 'There was an incident where he worked last night and we're talking to all the staff. That's all.' He checked his watch. If he didn't get a move on, he'd be late for the post-mortem. 'When he does come back, can you tell Mr Kelly we'd like to talk to him?' He handed her a card with his name and the telephone number of the station. 'Give him this and tell him to call me.'

'I'll tell him if I see him,' she said, tucking the card into her apron pocket. 'What if he doesn't call you?'

'Then I'll be back,' Denham promised.

Matthew rang the doorbell of No. 13 St Jude's Avenue. A maid answered it, this one about thirty years younger than the Fairbank's maid and a great deal more coquettish. She looked Matthew up and down, her mouth curving up in pleasure on one side.

'Yes?' she said invitingly.

'Detective Inspector Stannard to see Mr Ballantyne.'

Her smile flattened. 'You better come in.'

A voice called from the sitting room as she shut the door behind Matthew and the constable. 'Who is it, Daisy?'

'It's the police, madam,' Daisy called back and gestured for Matthew to go in. She followed on the heels of the constable. 'This is Detective Inspector Stannard, madam.'

A woman was sitting on the sofa, her feet up. She stared at Matthew blankly as he entered, her *Tatler* magazine held up before her.

'I'm sorry to intrude,' Matthew began. 'Are you Mrs Ballantyne?'

'Yes,' she replied. 'I'm Florence Ballantyne.'

'I'd like to speak with your husband. Is he at home?'

'He's upstairs. Why do you want to speak to Archie?'

'A matter concerning Christopher Fairbank. If he could be called down?'

'Shall I, madam?' Daisy asked.

'Yes,' Florence waved at the girl, 'call him. What about Kit, inspector? Has something happened?'

Matthew made a quick appraisal of Florence Ballantyne and determined she was a very different type of woman to Daphne Fairbank. She had the look of a hysteric, he thought, a woman likely to burst into tears or screams if told of something as horrific as a friend being murdered. 'I think it's best if I explain to your husband, Mrs Ballantyne,' he said.

'Explain what?' a voice said.

Matthew turned to see a tall man with chestnut brown hair, a little portly, standing in the doorway. 'Mr Ballantyne?'

'Yes,' Ballantyne said, casting an enquiring look at his wife.

'It's something to do with Kit, Archie,' Florence said, closing her magazine.

'Kit? Is he all right?' Ballantyne asked. 'Not had an accident, has he?'

'I'm afraid he has,' Matthew said. 'He's dead.'

There was silence for the briefest of moments while this news sank in, then Florence let out a cry and reached for her husband.

Ballantyne ignored her flapping hand. 'Dead? That's nonsense. I only saw him last night. He was perfectly well.'

'I daresay he was. He was killed at the Empire Club last night.'

'Florrie,' Ballantyne said, keeping his eyes on Matthew. 'Go upstairs.'

'But Archie—'

'Upstairs.'

Florence threw her magazine onto the sofa and hurried from the room, taking Daisy with her.

Ballantyne tugged at his cuffs. 'Now, what the devil do you mean he was killed, inspector?'

'Mr Fairbank was stabbed in one of the club's bedrooms.'

'Who by?'

'That's what I'm trying to find out. When did you last see Mr Fairbank?'

Ballantyne shot him an impatient look and marched past him to pour himself a drink from the tray of decanters on the sideboard. He didn't offer Matthew one. 'Last night at the club when we left. That was around twelve, twelve-thirty. We left Kit there.'

'Do you know why Mr Fairbank remained behind at the club last night?'

Ballantyne hesitated. 'No,' he said, taking a gulp of his drink. 'I don't know.'

'You didn't wonder?'

'I didn't care, inspector. I'm his friend, not his wife.' A thought occurred to him. 'Good God, does Daphne know?'

'I've informed Mrs Fairbank. I must say I was surprised by how she took the news. She didn't seem very upset.'

Ballantyne snorted. 'I doubt if she was upset at all. She and Kit didn't get on, inspector.'

'So I gathered. Was Mr Fairbank having an affair?'

'Why are you asking that?'

'Because the evidence suggests he was with a woman last night.'

'Are you saying a woman killed Kit?' Ballantyne cried scornfully.

'I'm not saying that, Mr Ballantyne. I'm asking if you know who he might have been with?'

Ballantyne sank into an armchair and crossed his legs. 'No. I don't know who he was with.'

'I understand there was an incident at the club last night,' Matthew said. 'You and Mr Fairbank assaulted a waiter.'

Ballantyne laughed. 'Assaulted? What nonsense. I'll admit there was a bit of horseplay, but no one was hurt, inspector. It was a joke.'

'Mr Yates didn't seem to find it funny. Nor, apparently, did many of the other club members.'

'Oh,' Ballantyne waved a hand dismissively. 'Yates is an old woman. Doesn't know how to have any fun.'

'Did you know the waiter?'

'No.'

'There was no reason to pick on him in particular?'

Ballantyne's expression lost all its amusement. 'You know, inspector, I don't like your tone. I think you forget who you're talking to.'

'I know exactly who I'm talking to, Mr Ballantyne.'

'Do you?' Ballantyne narrowed his eyes at Matthew. 'Stannard, isn't it? I know that name. Why do I know your name?'

Matthew didn't answer.

'Stannard, Stannard.' Ballantyne clicked his fingers. 'The Marsh Murderer. You caught him, didn't you?'

'That's right.'

'Well, quite the celebrity, aren't you? I expect Mullinger's wetting his knickers having you at his station.'

'I'm not here to talk about me, Mr Ballantyne.'

'What? You don't want to talk about yourself?' Ballantyne smirked. 'What kind of copper are you?'

'The kind who wants to find out what happened to your friend,' Matthew reminded him.

Unabashed, Ballantyne took out a cigarette case from his inside pocket. 'Well,' he said, lighting it and blowing a plume of smoke into the air, keeping his eyes on Matthew, 'I certainly hope you find out who killed poor dear Kit, inspector, but I'm afraid I can't help you. Now, if you don't mind, I think it's time you were leaving.'

Ballantyne remained seated for a few minutes after Matthew and the constable left. He dragged on his cigarette, watching the smoke curl into the air. Then he rose and moved to the hall. Picking up the telephone, he waited for the operator to connect him, his fingers drumming gently on the banister rail.

'Hello?' Adrian Foucault said after a few rings.

'Have you heard about Kit?' Ballantyne asked.

'Heard what?'

'He's dead. Someone killed him. I've just had a policeman here asking questions.' There was silence at the end of the line. 'Adrian? You still there?'

'Yes, I'm here. Killed?'

'I know. I can hardly believe it.'

'But—'

'No, no questions on the telephone, old man. Just come over here as soon as you can. I'll call Donald and Eric to come round too.'

Ballantyne broke the connection and gave the operator another number. He did this twice, giving Spencer and Hailes the same information he had given Foucault. When he put the receiver down for the last time, he sighed and ran his hand through his hair.

'Archie?' Florence, leaning over the upstairs banister, called down. 'Has he gone?'

'Yes, my sweet. He's gone.'

'Is it true about Kit?'

'Seems so, old girl.'

'How did it happen?'

'Don't know all the details yet. That detective chappie didn't seem all that well informed.'

161

Florence put her hand to her forehead. 'He's given me such a headache.'

'Oh, poor love. You have a lie down. I've asked the chaps over, but we'll do our best not to disturb you.'

'You're so sweet, darling. Ask Daisy to bring me up a cup of tea, will you?'

'Will do. Now, off you go.'

Florence moved away as Ballantyne heard a car pull up outside the house. He opened the front door and saw Donald Spencer climbing out of his Alvis.

'I can't believe it,' Spencer declared as he walked up the path. 'I just came past the club. There are police all over it.'

Another car pulled up and Eric Hailes got out. Like Spencer, he hurried up the path.

'There are police at the club. Is that because—'

'Yes,' Ballantyne said, jerking his head for Hailes to step inside. 'Let's wait for Adrian before we talk.'

Spencer and Hailes went into the sitting room. Ballantyne went into the kitchen and told Daisy to take tea up to his wife. As he returned to the hall, he saw Foucault through the glass pane of the front door. He yanked open the door before Foucault could ring the bell.

'You took your time,' Ballantyne said. 'Don and Eric are already here.'

Foucault didn't bother to reply and walked past Ballantyne to join the others in the sitting room.

Ballantyne followed, closing the doors behind him.

'Keep your voices down. Florrie's upstairs.'

'What the bloody hell is going on?' Hailes said in a loud whisper. 'Kit murdered at the club?'

'What did the detective say?' Foucault asked coolly.

'He was asking about that waiter we fooled with,' Ballantyne said, pressing a glass of whisky into Foucault's hands. 'Help yourselves,' he gestured to Spencer and

Hailes. 'And asking why Kit stayed on at the club when we left.'

'What did you tell him?'

'I told him nothing, Adrian, and I think it best if you all do the same.'

'He's not going to talk to us, is he?' Hailes asked, gulping down the whisky he had poured himself.

'Of course he's going to talk to you. The police will probably interview everyone from the club.'

'Why can't we tell him anything?' Spencer wondered. 'If he thinks the waiter did for Kit—'

'I don't know if that is what he's thinking,' Ballantyne said. 'He was asking who the woman was.'

'So?' Spencer shrugged. 'Tell him. Why not?'

'Because we don't know where it will lead, Don,' Ballantyne said.

'Archie's right,' Hailes nodded. 'We could be opening up a whole can of worms by talking to the police. And my nerves won't stand it. It was bad enough when I had that detective asking me questions the other day.'

'But he's going to find out,' Spencer said. 'Someone at the club will tell this detective who Kit was with.'

'Maybe, but it doesn't have to come from us,' Ballantyne said. 'Adrian?'

Foucault considered. 'It might look suspicious if we all claim ignorance.'

'He won't have proof of anything, though, will he?' Ballantyne said. 'I think it may be far worse if we talk and let something slip that we'd all rather keep just between us.'

Hailes had been thinking. 'So did the waiter kill Kit?'

'I don't know, Eric,' Ballantyne snapped.

'Does Daphne know about Kit?' Foucault asked.

'The inspector told her.'

'Is she all right?'

'I haven't the faintest idea, Adrian. But you know Daphne. She won't give a damn about poor Kit, I promise you that, so don't waste your time worrying about her.'

'I'm not worrying about her. I'm thinking it will look odd if one of us doesn't call in on her,' Foucault said.

'I'm not going,' Hailes declared.

'Still scared of her, are you?' Spencer laughed.

'Bloody right, I am,' Hailes said, chucking back his whisky. 'If you're so brave, you go.'

Spencer shook his head. 'Daphne loathes me.'

'I think you ought to go, Archie,' Foucault said, helping himself to a cigarette from the box on the coffee table. 'Take Florence with you.'

'Florrie can't stand Daphne,' Ballantyne protested.

'Florence will want to go, believe me,' Foucault said with a smile. 'She'll be able to tell all those cats at the club how kind she's been and how poor dear Daphne's coping.'

Spencer laughed. Hailes looked as if he wanted to but was too scared of Ballantyne's expression.

'All right,' Ballantyne nodded. 'I'll take Florence to see her. It might not be a bad idea, anyway. I can find out what Daphne's told that detective.'

'And in the meantime,' Foucault said, 'for safety's sake, we should all keep a low profile. Now, if we're done here, I'm going home to finish what I was doing.' He headed for the door.

'Just a thought,' Hailes said, halting him. 'Kit being killed hasn't anything to do with the other one, has it?'

The men all looked at one another, considering this. Finally, Ballantyne spoke.

'I don't see how. And don't, for God's sake, go connecting the two if this detective calls on you, Eric.'

'I won't,' Hailes said, not meeting Ballantyne's eye. 'I'm going too.' He followed Foucault out of the house.

'We should keep an eye on him,' Spencer said to Ballantyne as he watched Hailes drive away. 'He gets scared easily and then he can't stop his mouth flapping.'

'I'll leave Eric to you,' Ballantyne said. 'You're better at intimidation than me.'

Spencer grinned. 'I'll be off. Let me know how it goes with Daphne.'

'I will,' Ballantyne said, pouring himself another drink. He knew it was too early to be drinking, but hell, he needed it after the news he'd had. Poor Kit dead and a copper sniffing around. He didn't like it. He didn't like it one bit.

Chapter Twenty-One

Matthew returned to the club after leaving the Ballantynes to check all his orders were being followed. He found DC Barnes in the hall, checking off items on a clipboard, and he almost saluted when he saw Matthew approach. Matthew asked how the search was going, and Barnes told him it was almost done and that he had had the kitchen knives fingerprinted and sent off to the mortuary. Matthew checked the detective constable's paperwork, had a quick look around, and satisfied, asked for a driver to take him to the other members of The Five.

Spencer was the nearest. A bachelor, he lived in a flat opposite the golf course, and was pulling up in his car when Matthew arrived.

Matthew saw Spencer eyeing him speculatively as he climbed out of the driver's seat. 'Mr Spencer?' Matthew asked, moving towards him. 'Detective Inspector Stannard.'

'What can I do for you, inspector?' Spencer asked, slamming the door.

'Have you heard what's happened at the Empire Club?'

Spencer paused, and Matthew wondered why. 'I've seen

the police are all over it. What's happened? Has someone stolen the silver?'

'I'm afraid it's rather more serious than that,' Matthew said, sure Spencer was lying, that he did know what had happened. Ballantyne, probably, had called him. 'A friend of yours, Christopher Fairbank, has been killed.'

'Ah,' Spencer said, nodding. 'At the club, you say?'

'That's right. You were at the club last night?'

'Yes, I was there. Left about half twelve.'

'Were you aware Mr Fairbank was planning to remain at the club overnight?'

'No, I wasn't.'

There was a carelessness, almost a disinterest, in Spencer's manner. It didn't seem right for a man who had just been told a close friend had been murdered.

'It's almost certain he stayed behind with a woman,' Matthew went on. 'Any idea who that might have been?'

'Could have been anyone. Kit liked women and women liked him. You should ask the women members of the club. If they'll admit to being with him, that is.' Spencer smiled, showing his teeth.

'I understand there was an incident with a waiter at the club last night involving Mr Fairbank.'

'That nincompoop?' Spencer scoffed. 'He got his trousers pulled down, that's all.'

'That was supposed to be funny, was it?'

'It's obvious you didn't go to public school, inspector,' Spencer said scornfully. 'So, that waiter killed Kit, did he?'

'You sound surprised.'

'I am surprised. I didn't think he'd have it in him.' Spencer shrugged. 'Is that all?'

'For the moment,' Matthew nodded. 'If you think of anything that may help the investigation, however, Mr Spencer, I'd appreciate it if you'd let me know.'

'Oh, I'll be sure to,' Spencer said in a tone that made Matthew think he meant the exact opposite.

Adrian Foucault's house was a double-fronted, turn-of-the-century building. It was a big house. Far too big, Matthew thought as he rang the doorbell, for a bachelor. It was opened by a woman in her fifties, neat, scrawny, severe.

'Yes?' she asked.

Matthew flashed his warrant card. 'I'd like to see Mr Foucault, please.'

The woman was unruffled by having a policeman on the doorstep. 'Do come in,' she said. 'I'll inform Mr Foucault you're here.'

She moved off down the hall and knocked on a door, inclining her head as she listened for the reply. It came, and she went in. Matthew heard the soft murmur of her voice, his name, and then she reappeared, inviting him in.

'Mr Foucault?' Matthew asked the man sitting at the large rolltop bureau.

Foucault finished what he was writing before turning to Matthew. 'Yes. Inspector Stannard, isn't it? I've been expecting you.'

'You have?' Matthew asked, taken aback.

'Archie Ballantyne said you'd called. Please, have a seat.' He gestured Matthew towards the ox-blood red Chesterfield sofa in the middle of the room.

'So you know what's happened?' Matthew asked as he sat down.

'Kit Fairbank's been killed, yes,' Foucault said airily, crossing one thin leg over the other and tapping a finger on the arm of his chair. 'Dreadful.'

'You were at the club last night?'

'I was.'

'Until what time?'

'I left the same time as Archie. That must have been after twelve, I suppose. I'm afraid I can't be more exact than that.'

'Were you aware Mr Fairbank was spending the night at the club?'

'No. In fact, I didn't speak to Kit much at all last night, so I have no notion of his movements or intentions.'

He was so cool, so collected. It irritated Matthew. 'I understand Mr Fairbank had a reputation for womanising. Do you know who his current lady friend is?'

'I didn't involve myself in Kit's affairs, inspector. It was really none of my business.'

'So, that's a No, is it?' Matthew said.

Foucault's composure wobbled, just a little. 'That's a No, inspector.'

'What about this incident with the waiter? Were you a part of that?'

'No, I was not.'

'But you witnessed it?'

'It would have been rather difficult to miss.'

'You approved of the bullying your friends indulged in?'

'Did I say that, inspector? I don't believe I did. Is this yet another example of the police putting words in people's mouths?'

'It's me wondering why you didn't do anything to stop it.'

'Why should I?' Foucault shrugged. 'They were having fun. And there were plenty of others nearer who could have stopped Kit and Archie if they were so inclined.'

A thought occurred to Matthew, and he mentally kicked himself for not thinking of it earlier when he had spoken with Ballantyne and Spencer. 'Did you know a Charles Calthrop?'

Foucault uncrossed and recrossed his legs. 'No.'

'Never heard that name before?'

'No.'

'He was an acquaintance of Mr Fairbank. He brought him to the charity auction in December.'

'Did he?' Foucault frowned. 'Can't say I remember.'

'He was a red-haired man, good looking. Charming, apparently.'

'Well, then, I feel sure I would remember if I'd met him, inspector.'

'You don't recall him?'

'I've already said no, inspector. It's going to be rather tedious if you continue asking me questions to which you already have the answers.'

'God forbid I should bore you,' Matthew said, getting to his feet. 'I'll let you get on. I can see you're very busy.'

'Yes, thank you, inspector, I am. Miss Bird will show you out.'

Matthew was still fuming when the police car pulled up outside the home of Eric Hailes. He could now understand why Yates had spoken about The Five in the way he had. They were superior, arrogant and confident. Matthew didn't like them either.

Hailes lived in a much smaller house than his friends. This house was a terrace, well-maintained and perfectly adequate, but not on the same scale as Ballantyne and Foucault. When Matthew knocked on the front door, it wasn't a maid in neat uniform who answered. The door was opened by a woman wearing a scarf around her head with silver hair clips poking out at the front.

'Yes?' she asked, peering at him.

'I'm Inspector Stannard, madam. I'd like to speak to Mr Hailes.'

The brown eyes widened. 'You want to talk to Eric?'

'Yes. Are you Mrs Hailes?'

'Yes, I am. You better come in.' She led him through the house to the kitchen, where she opened a back door and stepped out into the garden. 'He's in the shed,' she explained and called out her husband's name. 'Eric, come out here. There's a policeman to see you.'

Matthew heard a clatter from inside the shed, a muttered swearing, and Eric Hailes poked his head out of the doorway. 'Police?'

'Detective Inspector Stannard, Mr Hailes,' Matthew said. 'But we've met before.'

'Oh, yes,' Hailes nodded. 'At the golf club. Are you here about the man you mentioned?'

'No. A different matter. I think you may have heard what happened at the Empire Club last night?'

'Heard? Yes… that is, no… I've—'

'Oh, do stop babbling, Eric,' Mrs Hailes chided. 'What's happened at the club, inspector?'

'Mr Christopher Fairbank was killed last night, Mrs Hailes,' Matthew replied, keeping his eyes on her husband. 'Did you know that, Mr Hailes?'

Hailes had turned an ashen grey and was swallowing. 'Yes, I did, inspector. You see, Archie, Mr Ballantyne, tele-phoned earlier.'

'You knew?' Mrs Hailes demanded. 'Why didn't you tell me?'

'I didn't want to upset you, my dear,' Hailes said plain-tively, looking from her to Matthew.

Mrs Hailes rounded on Matthew. 'How was Kit killed?'

'He was stabbed in the heart.'

Her hand went to her mouth. 'Who would do such a thing?'

'That's what I'm trying to find out. We believe Mr Fair-bank was with a woman at the club after everyone else had left. Would you know who that woman was, Mr Hailes?'

'It would have been Daphne,' Mrs Hailes answered. 'Daphne's his wife, inspector.'

'Yes, I know,' Matthew said, 'but it wasn't Mrs Fairbank. Mr Hailes?'

Hailes shook his head. 'No, I don't know who it was.'

'What about this incident with the waiter? You were involved in that, weren't you?'

'Oh, that.' Mrs Hailes looked at her husband with contempt. 'I don't know what he was thinking getting involved in that, inspector.'

'You didn't approve, Mrs Hailes?'

'Well, Archie and Kit can be very amusing, inspector, but Eric has absolutely no sense of humour.'

'Oh, so it was a joke, was it, Mr Hailes?'

Hailes looked uncomfortable. 'It was Archie and Kit, inspector. They just pulled me into it.'

'Did you know the waiter?'

'No, he was just one of the staff.'

'Why are you asking about the waiter, inspector?' Mrs Hailes asked, then her eyes widened and her eyebrows rose. 'Did he do it? Did he kill Kit?' Before Matthew could reply, she went on. 'Can't say I'm surprised. Nasty looking chap, if you ask me. Surly. Always looking at you out of the corner of his eyes.'

Matthew ignored this. 'Did you know a Charles Calthrop, Mr Hailes?' he asked and saw a flicker of alarm cross the other man's face. 'That name appears to ring a bell?'

'No, no. It doesn't,' Hailes said, wiping his hands on his handkerchief. 'I've never heard of him.'

'It looked to me as if you recognised the name.'

'No, I didn't,' Hailes cried indignantly. 'I don't know the man and I don't know anything about Kit getting killed.'

'Eric, calm down,' Mrs Hailes said, embarrassed by her husband's behaviour.

'Don't tell me to calm down,' Hailes snapped. 'Police coming here, asking all these questions. Anyone would think I was a suspect.'

'He's not saying that. You're not saying that, are you, inspector?'

Matthew wasn't ready to say anything of the kind. 'There's no need to get worked up, Mr Hailes. These questions are just routine.'

'I'm glad to hear it,' Hailes said, taking a deep, steadying breath. 'Well, if that's all, inspector. I've got a lot to be getting on with.'

'He always says that and nothing ever gets done in that shed,' Mrs Hailes told Matthew, rolling her eyes.

But Hailes had already entered the shed, closing the door, and begun banging with a hammer.

'I will be leaving now, Mrs Hailes,' Matthew said, looking at Hailes through the shed window, 'but please tell your husband that I may be back to ask further questions. If and when that happens, I'd be grateful if he would be more obliging.'

Matthew walked away, hearing Mrs Hailes's indignant, 'Well, really!' as he went.

Matthew had barely got inside the door of the station when Sergeant Turkel called to him.

'Superintendent Mullinger wants to see you, sir. Said you're to go up as soon as you got in.'

Matthew nodded and climbed the stairs to the second floor. He nodded to Miss Halliwell, who glanced up from her typewriter and eyed Mullinger's door nervously. When Matthew knocked and entered, Mullinger was pacing.

'Where the devil have you been?' Mullinger demanded. 'I go into town for an important meeting and I come back to discover Christopher Fairbank has been murdered in his bed.'

Mullinger made it sound as if Matthew had deliberately arranged for a man to be killed just to spoil his day. 'Did you know Christopher Fairbank, sir?' Matthew asked.

'I met him once or twice. A fine man, Stannard, a fine man. That such a dreadful thing should happen to him. Who did it?'

'There are two potential suspects,' Matthew said. 'A waiter from the club and a woman Fairbanks was with. I've sent Sergeant Denham to talk with the waiter. I haven't been able to find out yet who the woman was.'

'A woman?' Mullinger said, his brow creasing.

'Mr Fairbank stayed at the club when the other members left and retired to an upstairs bedroom. He had a woman with him in the bedroom.'

'Well, couldn't this woman have been his wife?'

'Mrs Fairbank says she was at home. There's no one to corroborate her claim, but it seems more likely he was with another woman. Mr Fairbank was notorious for his womanising.'

Mullinger slumped down at his desk. 'Good God, Stannard, you don't want to listen to gossip.'

'It's more than gossip, sir. His wife confirms he was regularly unfaithful.'

Mullinger winced. 'Well, let's keep that sort of thing to ourselves. We don't want to tarnish a man's reputation with talk like that.'

'I am going to have to pursue it as a line of enquiry, sir,' Matthew said. 'If I'm going to find his killer.'

'You still haven't found the killer of that other man.'

Still? Matthew thought angrily. *And it's not for want of trying.* 'His body was only found a few days ago, sir.'

Mullinger glared up at Matthew. 'I would have thought that plenty of time for a man with your reputation, Stannard.'

'I am making progress, sir,' Matthew said, gritting his teeth. 'In fact, I've established there's a connection between the dead man and Fairbank.' That got Mullinger, Matthew saw with a swell of pleasure.

'What sort of connection?'

'Fairbank knew him. The dead man was Fairbank's guest at the charity auction held at the club.'

'So, whoever killed Fairbank killed this other man? The waiter fellow?'

'I'm not ready to say that. I need to make further enquiries. Unfortunately, the people who might be able to help most are reluctant to talk to me.'

'And who are they?'

'Fairbank's closest friends. I've already had a brief chat with them, but I shall have to talk to them again and—'

Mullinger jumped to his feet and waggled a finger at Matthew. 'Now, now, Stannard. I know who you're talking about and I don't like what you're suggesting.'

'Sir?'

'Ballantyne? Foucault?' Mullinger queried, his bushy eyebrows raising. 'That's who you mean, isn't it? Those men are two of our most distinguished residents, Stannard. I won't have you questioning them as if they're common criminals.'

'I'm not suggesting that, sir—'

'Good,' Mullinger cut him off. 'So, leave them alone. Explore your other avenues of enquiry.'

What other avenues? Matthew thought savagely. 'Sir, are you ordering me not to talk to the people who knew Mr Fairbank best?'

Mullinger resumed his seat. He put on his spectacles and looked up at Matthew over the rims. 'I trust I don't need to order you. Tread carefully, inspector. You're not in Hackney anymore.'

He flicked his hand at the door. Matthew was dismissed.

Chapter Twenty-Two

Dickie shook out a cigarette from the packet and offered it to the man sitting opposite.

'Thanks,' Harry Cole said, taking the cigarette and lighting it. 'I can't believe it. Him being murdered at the club. Do the police know who done it?'

'I couldn't say,' Dickie said. 'They've not released any information yet. But I expect they'll want to talk to you and to the other staff.'

'But why would they want to talk to me? I had nothing to do with it.'

Dickie patted the air to calm Cole. He hadn't meant to make the young man anxious. 'It'll just be trying to find out if you saw or overheard anything. Nothing to worry about.'

Cole relaxed. 'That's all right, then. What 'paper did you say you were from?'

'*The Chronicle.*' Dickie returned the cigarette packet to his coat pocket and took a puff of his pipe. 'Frank Greader said you could tell me stories about the Empire Club and its members.'

Cole twisted his pint glass on the cardboard coaster, his

brow creasing. 'I ain't sure I should. I mean, not if you're going to put it in the 'paper. I could lose me job.'

Dickie was ready for this reticence. 'I'm just collecting background information, Mr Cole. Nothing you tell me will have your name attached, I promise you.'

'Yeah?' Cole still looked doubtful. 'Well, if you promise. What do you want to know?'

'Just what you can tell me about the members. What goes on at the club that isn't public knowledge. That sort of thing.'

'I'm not sure I know all that much, other than the private parties that go on upstairs.'

Dickie leaned forward. 'But that's exactly the sort of thing I'm interested in. Who has these private parties? Which members?'

'The other members call them The Five. Bloody stupid name.'

'I've heard about The Five.' Dickie rattled off their surnames. 'That them?'

Cole nodded. 'Mr Yates, he's supposed to be in charge, but The Five practically rule the roost there. They do what they like and he's too much of a coward to stop them.'

'What do The Five get up to at these private parties?'

'Nasty stuff. I mean, they have lots of booze. All right, so what?' He shrugged. 'But they're taking drugs up there too. I know, because I've seen 'em snorting it up their noses. And then they turn really nasty, especially Spencer.'

'Violent?'

'That's right. I had a friend worked with me there. He was taking up some drinks, and one of 'em, I don't know which one, tripped him up, deliberate like. My pal falls flat on his face, spilling all the glasses and whatnot, and you know, he's not going to take that sort of thing from anyone, he don't care who they are. So, he jumps up, ready to punch someone's lights out, and that Spencer, he does the same. Only it ain't a fair fight because the big one, Ballantyne, he grabs hold of my pal, so he can't do anything. Spencer lands him a punch in the stomach and one on the nose. My pal's bleeding everywhere and can't do a thing to defend himself. And then they practically chucked him down the stairs. He complained to Yates about that, and you know what, that chump didn't do a thing. Didn't want to know.'

'Is your friend still working there?'

'No fear. He got out after that.'

'Would he talk to me?'

Cole made a face. 'I doubt it. He ain't proud of what happened, you see. But that's not the only story I could tell you.'

Dickie could see the young man was warming to his theme. He sipped at his pint, determined not to interrupt.

'There was a girl who used to work there,' Cole went on. 'Betty, her name was. Nice girl. Nothing like that between us,' he hastened to say as Dickie's eyebrows rose enquiringly. 'We were friends, that's all. Anyway, The Five, they wanted a couple of the girls to stay on after the club was shut for one of these private parties, you know, to serve them food and drinks.' Cole sighed and shook his head. 'Betty never told me what happened, but I heard The Five talking one night. They were laughing and joking about her and the other girl, saying things I'm not going to repeat, not even to you, and... well, Betty never came back. But I've seen her.' He met Dickie's eye. 'I've seen her in Stratford late at night, walking the streets.'

'You mean she's a prostitute?'

'She is now. She weren't before. Betty was a nice girl before she went to that private party and now she's a...a... what you called her. So, what does that tell you?'

'Betty... what?'

'Trantor. Betty Trantor.'

'You still in touch with her?'

Cole shook his head. 'But go down Stratford High Street late at night and I'll bet you'll find her.'

'Maybe I will,' Dickie said. 'Anything else?'

'And there was what they did last night,' Cole went on after another mouthful of his beer. 'I mean, I know Norman's a bit odd, but he didn't deserve what they did to him.'

Dickie was intrigued. 'What did they do?'

Cole told Dickie of Kelly's humiliation at the hands of The Five. 'I'm glad they didn't pick on me,' he said. 'Mind you, I'd have punched their faces in if they'd tried.'

'Any reason they picked on this Norman Kelly?'

'I don't think so. He was just close by.'

'Didn't anyone stop them?'

'The other members, they were all looking a bit uneasy. It was obvious they didn't like what was going on, but they didn't want to get involved. I tried to speak to Norman after it had happened, you know, see how he was. But he locked himself in the lavvie and refused to come out. He was still in there when we all left. Thinking about it, it wouldn't surprise me if Norman did that Fairbank in. And you know what? I wouldn't blame him.'

So, Norman Kelly might have still been in the club when everyone but Fairbank and whoever he was with in the bedroom had gone. That was interesting. An idea occurred to Dickie, and he reached inside his jacket pocket to take out a folded photograph he had been carrying around since learning of The Five. He had taken the snap at the charity auction. 'Kelly's not in this picture, is he?' he said, pushing their glasses aside and smoothing the photograph out on the table.

'This is taken at the club, ain't it? Am I in it?' Cole scanned the faces and stabbed a face in the crowd of revellers. 'That's me. Look.'

Dickie pretended an interest, then prompted, 'Norman Kelly. Is he there?'

Cole studied the photograph again. 'There he is,' he said, picking out a face in the top-right corner. 'That's Norman.'

Dickie twisted the photograph round to face him. Cole had pointed out a tall man with dark hair that hung in greasy strands around his ears and neck. His skin appeared dark, his countenance rather sullen.

'Does it help what I've told you?' Cole asked as Dickie put the photograph back in his pocket.

'It does,' Dickie nodded, wondering what else Harry Cole could tell him about The Five and the Empire Club. 'Let me get you another drink.'

Chapter Twenty-Three

Matthew had been working at his desk ever since his meeting with Mullinger. He'd avoided the other detectives, not trusting himself to utter a word, worried he might express to his colleagues exactly how he felt about their superintendent.

DC Pinder had knocked on his door an hour previously to tell him Sergeant Denham had called in to say he hadn't been able to talk with Norman Kelly, the waiter not being at home. Pinder added that a detective from the Yard had called to inform them that they had no record of a Charles Calthrop. With instructions from Mullinger not to pursue Fairbank's friends, Matthew was running out of options.

Denham returned about an hour later, entering Matthew's office gingerly. 'I'm back, sir,' he said.

Matthew nodded a greeting. 'Got the post-mortem report?'

Denham handed over the file he was carrying and stood by the desk while Matthew read Wallace's findings.

The cause of death had been the stab wound to the heart as suspected. The blade had penetrated to a depth of four inches and the wound matched one of the kitchen knives Barnes had sent over for examination. There were no fingerprints of any kind on the knife, suggesting the killer had wiped the handle clean before returning it to the drawer. Wallace had found traces of cocaine in Fairbank's nostrils and signs of the drug in his body. Semen was present on the body, as were vaginal secretions, showing Fairbank had engaged in sexual activity shortly before his death. Again, all as expected. Wallace's estimate of time of death hadn't changed, although he was prepared to say the killing had likely taken place in the early hours of the morning.

Matthew closed the file. Did the fact that the killer used a weapon that had been at hand rather than take his or her own imply the murder hadn't been premeditated? he wondered. Did it even matter?

'You can arrange for the return of the other knives to the club,' he told Denham as DC Barnes ducked in and handed him a large brown envelope containing the crime scene photographs. Matthew slid the black-and-white prints onto his desk. He examined them closely, but they didn't tell him anything he hadn't already noticed.

'So, you didn't find Norman Kelly?' he said as he put them back in the envelope.

Denham looked down at his feet sheepishly. 'No, sir. He wasn't at home and the fellow tenant I spoke with didn't know where he might be. I left my card for him to call. I did wonder if I should have taken a look in his room.'

'And did you?' Matthew asked, looking up at him.

'No, sir,' Denham said warily, and it was clear to Matthew he wasn't sure whether he had done right by not searching Kelly's room or not.

'Good,' Matthew said with a nod, and the sergeant relaxed. 'Because if you had searched his room, you would have committed an illegal act. Unless you have a warrant to search his room that I don't know about?'

'No, sir,' Denham assured Matthew.

'Well, that's something. Anything on the fingerprints on the champagne glasses other than Fairbank's?'

'Barnes was dealing with that, sir,' Denham reminded Matthew, and gestured for Barnes to come into the office again. 'Fingerprints,' he hissed at the detective constable.

'Oh, yes,' Barnes said and addressed himself to Matthew. 'There were fingerprints on the glass with the lipstick, but they don't match anything we have on file.'

'House to house enquiries?'

'Nothing so far, sir.'

It was frustrating, but Matthew had been here before and he reminded himself that leads could take time to materialise. 'We need to talk to this Norman Kelly. Contact local stations and ask them to put out an alert for him. Tell them that, if necessary, they can arrest him under suspicion of murder.'

Norman had only just stepped inside his front door when he was accosted by Mrs Coggs.

'You've been out a long while,' she said accusingly. 'In the cold and all.'

'Yes,' he sniffed, moving past her towards the stairs.

Norman had whiled away the hours walking the streets, sitting on benches in parks, trying to avoid the stares of other people. At least he'd had a coat to keep out much of the cold. He'd found it in the cloakroom at the club, one of the items he'd helped himself to before he left the previous night. It had been hanging, unwanted, on the hook for weeks. It was a decent overcoat, thick dark blue wool, real quality. But though the coat was warm and thick, he'd been in the cold too long for it to continue doing its job. He was hungry, too, and without any money in his pockets, the only food he had was in the old biscuit tin in his room. So, though he hated the four walls of his lodging house room

184

and the people in it, he had had no choice but to return home.

'You been up to no good?' she called after him.

He halted and turned to her in alarm. 'What do you mean?'

'This has always been a respectable house,' Mrs Coggs said. 'I don't know what the neighbours must think, me having the police at my door.'

'Police?' Norman scurried back down the stairs. 'The police have been here?'

'A detective. Nice young fella. Wanted to talk to you. Something about where you work. Said they're talking to all the staff.'

'What did you tell him?'

'What time you came in last night, and I told him what a racket you made. Waking me up.' She paused, expecting an apology. When she didn't get one, she went on savagely. 'He asked where you were, and of course, I said I didn't know, because I don't, do I? Couldn't tell him anything, I couldn't.' She took out the card Denham had given her and shoved it at Norman. 'He said you're to call him when you came in, and if you don't, he'll be back. Probably mob-handed, and I don't want that round here, so see you do.' She went back into her room, slamming the door behind her.

Norman's heart was pounding. He bolted up the stairs to his room and sank onto his bed. The police were looking for him and they would come back. They might knock on the door any minute. He couldn't just sit and wait for them to come for him.

Pulling his suitcase out from beneath the bed, Norman threw it open and tossed the few clothes he possessed into it, his comb and razor, and the packets of cigarettes he had taken from the club and the biscuit tin. He banged the suitcase shut, snapping the latches close.

Moving to the door, Norman opened it a fraction, listening for any sounds from below. He heard nothing. He tiptoed down the stairs, holding his breath as he passed Mrs Coggs's door and turned the latch. It clicked noisily. He pulled the door open, hoping it wouldn't squeal, and stepped outside, closing it softly behind him.

With a last look around, he hurried away into the night, not knowing where he was going, just knowing he had to go.

Chapter Twenty-Four

The church was freezing and Rosie Yates patted her gloved hands together to tempt some feeling back into her fingers. She wished she had pleaded a headache that morning; it wouldn't have been a complete lie. Ever since Friday she'd been fretting Tommy would find out that she'd done exactly what he told her not to do and spoken to the police. And what if she had been wrong about the dead man and he wasn't Charles Calthrop at all? What if that inspector had taken her words for truth and was chasing after the wrong man? What if she had made a hash of everything as her father always told her she did?

She should have told Tommy she didn't feel well enough to go to church. Tommy would have understood. He would have told her to stay in bed until her head was better, and she would have done, flicking through her magazines until he came home when she would declare her headache gone. Then she would bathe and dress and wander downstairs to check the cook was getting on with the Sunday lunch. Tommy would go to the sitting room, sink into his armchair, light his pipe and read *The Sunday Times*. She would join him, taking up the more sensationalist papers that made Tommy roll his eyes, curling up on the sofa as the fire crackled in the hearth. Rosie was enjoying this pleasant daydream when someone nudged her elbow.

'Oh, hello, Florrie,' she said without enthusiasm.

Florence Ballantyne grinned. 'What a to-do,' she declared gleefully.

'Do you mean Kit?'

'My dear, of course I mean Kit. What a thing to happen. When I heard, well, I burst into tears, Rosie, I did. Absolute floods of tears.'

'The shock, I expect.'

'Yes, I expect so. I simply had to come to church this morning and pray for Kit. And Daphne, of course,' Florence added with a careless shrug.

'Of course,' Rosie agreed loyally.

'I'll also pray for guidance.'

'Guidance?' Rosie asked, knowing her friend expected her to ask.

'Well, yes.' Florence sighed. 'The question is, do I tell the police about Sophie Sutton?'

'Sophie Sutton?' Rosie cried and heads turned towards her. She smiled at them, embarrassed by her outburst, and lowered her voice. 'What do you mean about Sophie Sutton?'

'Don't you remember what we were talking about in the hairdressers?' Florence said. 'I said then Sophie Sutton was planning something with Kit, didn't I? And that very night—'

'Yes, but you didn't mean,' Rosie cupped her hand around her mouth and whispered, 'killing him. You were talking about her and him doing… you know.'

'Yes, I meant that then, but now, I don't know. But I do know she was the reason Kit stayed behind at the club on Friday when everyone else left.' She looked around the church, seeking her husband and finding him deep in conversation with Adrian Foucault. Satisfied he wouldn't overhear her conversation, she continued. 'Archie doesn't know about Sophie Sutton, so he couldn't tell the detective anything. And to be honest, I don't think Archie would have told him even if he did know. Archie would never say anything that might harm a woman's reputation.'

Thinking of her own doubts about the rightness of her decision to talk to the police, Rosie said, 'Maybe you should keep this about Sophie to yourself, Florrie.' Florence made a noise of annoyance and Rosie guessed she'd said the wrong thing.

'If it were only her infidelity,' Florence said, a little shrilly, 'then I wouldn't think of breathing a word, Rosie, you know me. I don't take a moral stand on that kind of thing. Live and let live, I say. But Kit has been murdered, for heaven's sake.'

'Then I don't know why you're asking me,' Rosie snapped. 'It sounds like you've already made up your mind to tell the police.'

Florence gave Rosie a sharp glance. 'I suppose I have. I do think it's the right thing to do. So, I want to ask a favour. Rosie dear, can I come round to yours after church?'

'Come to ours? What for?'

'I can't talk to the police at our house. Archie wouldn't like it. And I can't go to the police station, can I? Someone might see me.'

Rosie reddened. She'd visited the police station, not worrying about being seen, only worrying that Tommy would find out.

'Tell me I can, Rosie dear. Be a good friend.'

Rosie cast a wary glance over her shoulder at Tommy. Tommy wouldn't like it – having Florence in their home, having the police come around. But Florence had grabbed both of her hands and was looking at her imploringly.

'Yes,' Rosie nodded reluctantly, 'of course you can.'

. . .

Dickie knocked out his pipe against the wall as the church doors opened and the congregation filed out. He stepped back as they walked past him, watching for one of the men he wanted to talk to. He saw him, talking to his wife just outside the church porch, and then them separating, the woman walking one way with another couple, Archibald Ballantyne heading straight for Dickie.

'Mr Ballantyne?' Dickie asked, putting his fingers to his hat.

Ballantyne halted and frowned at Dickie. 'Yes. Who are you?'

'Dickie Waite, *The Chronicle*. Can you give me a few words about the murder of Mr Christopher Fairbank? He was a friend of yours, wasn't he?'

'Yes, he was.' Ballantyne cleared his throat as he watched Dickie ready his notebook and pencil. 'Well, I'm very saddened by what happened to poor Kit Fairbank. He was the best of friends, an excellent companion and a great philanthropist. He will be sorely missed.'

'Any idea why he was killed?'

'I'm sure I don't know. I can't imagine why anyone would want to kill such a fine man as Kit.'

'Could it have been a jealous husband?' Dickie asked. 'Mr Fairbank was quite the ladies' man, I hear?'

Ballantyne had opened his mouth, ready to answer. He shut it again and glared at Dickie. 'Why, you—'

'Or maybe someone he cheated over an antique or painting?' Dickie went on, unabashed.

'You foul, little—' Ballantyne lunged for Dickie and grabbed his scarf. Dickie's amused expression, and the startled looks of people passing by, made Ballantyne rethink. He released Dickie, but stepped closer, so his face was inches

190

from Dickie's. 'You print a word of such allegations and I'll sue you and your damned newspaper for libel, you hear me?'

'It's only libellous if it's untrue, Mr Ballantyne, you know that,' Dickie said, knowing he sounded braver than he felt. The dark eyes bore into his, but Dickie saw hesitation in them, despite Ballantyne's bravado and threat.

'You'd have to prove it, chum, and you'll never be able to do that. Watch your back.' Ballantyne released him, shoving him away.

Dickie watched him go and straightened his scarf, tucking it back inside his coat. He saw his hands were shaking.

Ballantyne slammed his front door shut, startling Daisy who had been expecting her master and mistress back at this time and had come out of the kitchen to greet them with their coffee and cake.

'Is everything all right, Mr Ballantyne?' she asked warily.

'No, everything is not all right, Daisy,' Ballantyne said, throwing his hat and coat on the floor. He stared at them, his chest heaving.

She looked down at the tray. 'Do you want the coffee, sir?'

'Put it in there,' he replied, jerking his head at the sitting-room door. *That damned reporter!* he thought as he heard her set the tray down on the coffee table. *He'd found out some-thing, that much was obvious. But what exactly? Someone had talked. But who?*

There was a knock on the door. Certain it was the reporter following him for more information, Ballantyne yanked the door open, ready to give him another piece of his mind. He was taken by surprise for the second time that morning when he saw Howard Mullinger standing on his doorstep.

Mullinger appeared to be taken aback himself. 'I say, Archie. Are you all right?'

'What?' Ballantyne barked. 'Oh, yes, just a, er,... nothing. What do you want?'

'I just wanted to express my condolences,' Mullinger said, his neck turning purple with embarrassment. 'But if this is a bad time—'

'No, no,' Ballantyne said, halting Mullinger as he turned away. It might not be a good idea to upset a policeman who could prove useful. 'Come in.'

Mullinger stepped inside, glancing at the hat and coat lying on the floor. 'Terrible thing to have happened. You must be very upset.'

'That's a bloody understatement, Howard. Kit was my best friend. Hanging's too good for the bastard who killed him. Have you caught him yet?'

'The investigation is under way,' Mullinger said with an encouraging smile.

'What the hell does that mean?' Ballantyne snarled. 'Have you caught that bloody waiter or not?'

Mullinger swallowed. 'My men are having trouble locating him. But we'll get him, Archie. Don't you worry about that.'

'Well, don't take your time about it.' Ballantyne heaved a deep breath as Daisy, who had been lingering in the sitting room, came out and hurried to hang up her master's hat and coat. 'Get back to the kitchen,' he ordered, not wanting her fussing, and she scurried away.

'You don't seem quite yourself, Archie, if you don't mind me saying so,' Mullinger said, watching the kitchen door close. 'Has something happened?'

'You could say that,' Ballantyne said, running his hand through his hair. 'I had that bloody reporter from *The Chronicle* accost me outside the church.'

'What reporter?'

'That shabby fellow. Waite, I think his name is.'

'Oh, I know him. What did he want?'

'He was asking me about Kit. Wanted a comment for his rag. I thought I'd be obliging, give him what he wanted. You've got to do that with these fellows, otherwise they never leave you alone. Anyway, I told him I was upset and what a great loss Kit is and all that, and then he started asking impertinent questions. I fair lost my temper, I tell you, Howard.'

'I'm sorry you've been pestered, Archie. If there's anything I can do…'

Ballantyne stared at Mullinger, considering. 'As you've offered, there is, actually. You could have a word with the editor. Tell him to call his dog off. He'd listen to you, I'm sure.'

As he expected, Mullinger welcomed the flattery. 'You leave it to me, Archie. I'll give the editor a call and tell him what's what.'

'I'd appreciate it, Howard.' Ballantyne opened the door. 'Don't let me keep you.'

'Right, yes,' Mullinger said awkwardly, stepping down onto the front step, and Ballantyne knew he was hoping to be asked to stay. 'Give my regards to your wife.'

'I will,' Ballantyne nodded. 'And I'd appreciate it if you could keep me updated about the waiter. Let me know what's going on.'

'Of course,' Mullinger nodded. 'I'll let you know as soon as I have any news.'

'Thanks. And then we'll have to see if we can't get old Tommy Yates to sign off on your club membership, eh?' Ballantyne said with a wink.

Mullinger winked back.

Chapter Twenty-Five

Matthew rang the Yates's doorbell, hoping this visit wouldn't prove to be a waste of time like the other visits he had paid that morning, following up on the calls that had come in responding to the newspaper article. He was starting to regret having Dickie write the piece, not anticipating how many people would call in certain they knew the dead man, and they all had to be followed up. He'd already had to cancel leave for Denham, Pinder and Barnes. With two murders to solve, there was no possibility of taking time off.

Mr Yates opened the door. 'Good morning, inspector. Thank you for coming.'

Matthew wiped his shoes on the doormat and stepped in. 'You have something to tell me about Mr Fairbank, I understand?'

Yates shook his head. 'Not me. A friend of my wife's. She believes she has information that may be of some use. Mrs Archie Ballantyne. She's in the sitting room. If you'll follow me.'

Matthew followed, astonished to hear it was Florence Ballantyne who had wanted this meeting and wondering why he hadn't been called to her home.

Florence was sitting on the sofa, Rosie beside her. Matthew saw consternation on Rosie Yates's face and guessed she was worrying he'd say something that would alert her husband they had met before. She didn't need to worry. He wouldn't give her away if he could help it.

'Detective Inspector Stannard, Mrs Ballantyne,' Yates announced and gestured Matthew forward.

There was an air of barely suppressed excitement about Florence Ballantyne. Matthew had seen the look before and knew it was the look of a woman who found murder and the police wonderfully exciting and had no notion of the misery and pain the sudden, violent death of a loved one might cause. It was all a game to her, a bit of fun, something to pass the idle hours of her day.

'What do you have to tell me, Mrs Ballantyne?' Matthew asked, taking a seat on the sofa opposite.

Florence took a deep breath. 'I know why Kit Fairbank stayed at the club Friday night. He had a rendezvous with one of the women members.'

Yates gave an embarrassed cough and turned away to face the window.

Matthew noted the choice of word. A rendezvous. Florence Ballantyne made a sordid adulterous encounter sound romantic. 'Who was the woman, Mrs Ballantyne?' he asked as he took out his notebook.

'Mrs Sophie Sutton.' Florence enunciated the name carefully, watching Matthew as he wrote.

'And how do you know Mrs Sutton had a rendezvous with Mr Fairbank?'

'Because she said as much to me earlier in the evening. And she had been dropping hints all week that she and Kit had been...,' she shrugged and smiled, 'getting along well. And after what happened at the charity auction.'

'What happened at the charity auction?'

Florence glanced over at Rosie, whose cheeks reddened. 'They were selling kisses, inspector, for charity. And Kit bought a kiss from Sophie. He paid twenty pounds for it, and, well, let's just say he got his money's worth.'

'I see. And her husband? Was he aware of this relationship?'

'He was there for the kiss, of course, and they were quite blatant with their flirting. He didn't look at all pleased about it. But I have no idea if Andrew knew how far it had gone. I don't know, but maybe that's why he left the club early on Friday.'

'He left the club early?' Matthew asked. 'Alone?'

Florence nodded and Matthew felt a spark of optimism for the first time since arriving in Craynebrook. This wasn't a waste of time after all. He finally had something to go on. The woman's name, and not only that, another potential suspect in the form of her husband. But he had a question he needed an answer to.

'Why did you call me here, Mrs Ballantyne? Why not to your own home?'

Florence smoothed her skirt over her knees. 'I didn't want my husband to hear me talking to you, inspector, I confess. You see, he was very fond of Kit and to hear that he might have been up to something like…, well, I'll say it, adultery, would be very distressing.'

Matthew stared at her. Was she talking about the same Ballantyne he'd met yesterday morning? That Ballantyne wouldn't have turned a hair to hear of his friend's adultery, Matthew felt sure. 'You're saying your husband didn't know about this affair?'

'I doubt it very much.' Florence looked shocked at the idea. 'Men don't talk about things like that to each other, do they?'

She looked to Rosie for support. Rosie smiled weakly at Matthew and looked away.

The clock on the mantle chimed the half hour.

'Oh Lord,' Florence cried, 'is that the time? I must be going or I'll be late for lunch.' She rose and looked down at Matthew. 'Have I helped, inspector?'

'A great deal, Mrs Ballantyne,' Matthew assured her. 'Thank you.'

'I'm so glad. Well, goodbye.'

'I'll see you out,' Yates said and walked with Florence to the front door.

Matthew waited until the sitting-room door had closed. 'Did you know about Sophie Sutton's relationship with Mr Fairbank, Mrs Yates?'

Rosie shook her head. 'No, inspector. They only moved to Craynebrook in November and to be honest, I hardly know her. I saw the two of them flirting, but that was normal for Kit. Do you really think she killed him?'

'I will need to talk to her, Mrs Yates,' he said in answer.

'And what I told you about the other man,' Rosie whispered, casting a wary look at the sitting-room door. 'Have you found anything out?'

'Progress is being made,' he said.

'Oh, good. I've been worried I've set you off on the wrong path. And now you have Kit's murder to deal with. I'm sorry if I've been so much trouble to you.'

Stop apologising, Matthew wanted to say to her, but then her husband returned, shaking his head, and he decided it was time to pay a visit to Mr and Mrs Sutton.

The Suttons were at lunch when Matthew called and he was told by their maid that he would have to wait. Matthew didn't mind. It gave him the opportunity to look around their sitting room, to get a picture of the woman who was one of his two main suspects.

Rosie Yates said the Suttons had only recently moved to Craynebrook and it showed in the newness of the furniture and soft furnishings. Matthew didn't see any furniture that might have been a family heirloom, given to a bride or groom as a wedding present, only sofas and tables that had probably been ordered all at the same time from a department store's catalogue. It was tastefully done, Matthew conceded, but it lacked personality. The only item that seemed to have any personal significance was a wedding photograph perched on a small table in the corner of the room.

Matthew studied the bride and groom in the picture. Andrew Sutton, wearing his army uniform, was older than his wife, perhaps by as much as ten years, but handsome with his neat moustache and dark hair. Sophie Sutton had a striking face, not pretty exactly, but attractive in its way. Her wedding veil framed a face that expressed not happiness but satisfaction, as if marriage had been what she had set out to achieve and her choice of husband was irrelevant. Matthew looked into the eyes of Sophie Sutton and asked himself whether she was capable of sticking a knife in a man. He shifted his gaze to Andrew Sutton and asked the same question. The answer to both questions was the same: Yes.

Matthew straightened as he heard a man's voice in the hall. The sitting-room door opened and Andrew Sutton strode in. He went straight to the mantlepiece, opened a silver box and took out a cigarette. Matthew wondered if he realised he was there, getting his answer when Sutton lit his cigarette and turned to him.

'Is this about Christopher Fairbank?' Andrew Sutton said, and without waiting for an answer, 'I don't know what you think I can tell you.' He threw the spent match into the fire. 'I barely knew the man.'

'But you were acquainted. Your wife, particularly so.'

Sutton's eyes widened. 'What do you mean by that?'

Matthew ignored the question and glanced at the door. 'Will your wife be joining us?'

Sutton strode to the door and shouted into the hall. 'Sophie. Come in here.' He didn't speak again while they waited for her to appear.

'Yes?' Sophie Sutton put her head around the door, glanced at Matthew, then stared, wide-eyed, at her husband.

'He wants to talk to you too,' Sutton said.

Sophie looked terrified as she came into the room and sat down on the sofa. Matthew saw her hands were shaking as she fiddled with the pearls around her neck. He glanced back at the wedding photograph. The face was the same, but the expression was very different. There was no triumph in Sophie Sutton's eyes now. Now, she had the look of a cornered animal.

'Would you rather we speak alone, Mrs Sutton?' Matthew asked.

'No, she wouldn't,' Sutton answered for her. 'I'm not having you intimidate my wife.'

'That's not my intention, Mr Sutton,' Matthew said. 'Mrs Sutton?'

Sophie swallowed. 'You can ask whatever you want before my husband, inspector.'

He'd given her a chance. 'If that's what you want.' Matthew looked over at Sutton. 'I understand you left the club early, Mr Sutton?'

'Yes. I wasn't feeling well.'

'But you, Mrs Sutton, remained at the club?'

'That's right,' Sophie said.

'Why didn't you leave with your husband?'

'Because Andrew said I needn't.' She glanced up at her husband, as if for confirmation.

'I saw no reason why my wife shouldn't stay and enjoy her evening because of my indisposition, inspector,' Sutton said.

Matthew didn't believe that sentiment for a moment. He suspected Mr Sutton hadn't want his wife to create a scene. 'And what time did you leave, Mrs Sutton?'

'When everyone else did,' Sophie said. 'Around twelve-thirty.'

Matthew tapped his pencil against his notebook, keeping his eyes on her. 'Did you walk home from the club, Mrs Sutton, or did you drive?'

'I walked home,' she said, picking an imaginary speck of fluff from her skirt. 'Andrew had the car.'

'You walked home alone? At that late hour?'

'The moon was out. It was quite light, inspector.'

'Even so, surely you should have asked one of the other members for a lift? For your own safety.'

'Well,' she shrugged and gave a little laugh, 'I didn't. I walked. Is there a problem with my walking home, inspector?'

'There's a problem with the answers you're giving me, Mrs Sutton,' Matthew said. 'You see, a witness has come forward to say on Friday night you stayed behind at the Empire Club after all the other members left, saving Mr Fairbank.'

Sophie's eyelids flickered, and veins stood out on her neck as her jaw tightened. 'I can't think why anyone would say that. I left when everyone else did.'

'But no one offered to take you home. Are all the gentlemen members of the Empire Club so ungentlemanly?'

'I...no—' Sophie began and broke off. She sighed deeply. 'I wanted to walk.'

'How long did it take you to get home?'

'A half hour, perhaps. No longer. I'm sure I was back by one.'

Matthew turned to Sutton. 'Can you confirm the time your wife returned home, Mr Sutton?'

'If my wife says she was back by one o'clock, inspector, then she was back by one o'clock.'

'But did you hear her come in?'

Sutton's mouth twisted. 'Yes. I heard her come in at one o'clock.'

Matthew looked from one to the other, certain they were both lying. 'So, just to be clear, Mrs Sutton. You didn't stay behind at the club with Mr Fairbank on Friday night?'

Sophie looked Matthew straight in the eye. 'No, inspector, I did not. Whoever told you I did is lying.'

Chapter Twenty-Six

Bach was playing on the wireless, his *Church Cantata No.13,* according to the copy of the *Radio Times* lying open on Dickie's lap.

It had been a good lunch, roast pork with apple sauce, and the meal was sitting heavily on his stomach. That, and the rhythmic click-clack of Emma's knitting needles, was making him feel sleepy. Dickie shifted his backside forward in the chair, put his feet up on the footstool, laid his head against the antimacassar and closed his eyes. He had almost drifted off when someone knocked on the door.

'Who can that be?' Emma muttered, stuffing her knitting down the side of her armchair and going out to answer it.

Dickie cocked an ear to listen. He heard the door open, and a moment later, recognised the voice of Bill Edwards. He knew he could forget his afternoon nap as their voices and footsteps drew nearer.

'It's Bill for you,' Emma said, showing the editor in. 'I'll make some tea.'

Dickie sighed, lifting his feet off the footstool and sitting up. 'This can't be good,' he said, gesturing Edwards to the armchair. 'You coming round on a Sunday.'

Edwards stretched himself out in the chair, wiggling his toes before the coal fire. 'I don't enjoy doing this, Dickie, but needs must.'

'Tell me.'

'You've been bothering Archibald Ballantyne, haven't you?'

'I wouldn't say bothering. I tried to talk to him this morning.'

'And got right up his nose, to put it delicately. I had Superintendent Mullinger calling me up at home, telling me to tell you to leave him alone.'

'What's it got to do with Mullinger?' Dickie cried.

Edwards shrugged. 'You know what that lot are like. They all stick together.'

'And are you?'

'Am I what?'

'Telling me to leave Ballantyne alone?'

'I have to, Dickie,' Edwards said, spreading his hands. 'If I don't, we won't get anything from the police. Mullinger's already got his men's mouths shut up tight. If I go against him, he'll cut us off completely.'

'So what?' Dickie said sulkily. 'I can live with that.'

'Really? He'll complain to head office and that'll be you and me out of a job.'

'So, now we have the police and the privileged friends of the police dictating what we can write about?'

'It's how it works, Dickie. You know that.'

Dickie nodded and stared at the glowing coals in the fire.

'What was it all about with Ballantyne, anyway?' Edwards asked.

Dickie poked his tongue between two teeth, feeling a sliver of pork stuck there. He wasn't sure he wanted to tell Edwards what he'd found out. He didn't have proof, after all, just the testimony of a lifelong crook and a few rumours.

'Come on, Dickie,' Edwards said. 'Spit it out.'

Dickie decided he would. 'You wanted me writing profiles on Ballantyne and the people like him. Well, let's just say I've found out a few things that would make the profiles a lot more interesting.'

'Such as?'

'Corruption. Intimidation. Debauchery.'

Edwards frowned. 'You're joking?'

'No,' Dickie reached for the sherry bottle behind him on the sideboard and two glasses. 'I've spoken with a very respectable solicitor who's had personal experience of intimidation as well as a very disreputable villain who will tell many a lurid tale if the money's right.'

Edwards took the glass of sherry. 'Do you have any proof?'

'No,' Dickie admitted. 'Not yet.'

'Can you get any?' Edwards asked quietly.

Dickie gave him a sideways glance. 'I thought I had to leave Ballantyne alone?'

Edwards made a face and stared at the fire. Dickie knew the editor was weighing up the benefits of a juicy story with the loss of the superintendent's favour. Which side would he come down on?

'You're right,' Edwards said after a minute. 'Ballantyne's out of bounds.'

Emma came in with the tea and Dickie hid his sherry. She'd put Garibaldi biscuits on a plate and got their best china out for Edwards, not the chipped, mismatched crockery they normally used. She set it down on the table and poured. There was an unspoken rule between Edwards and Dickie not to talk about work in front of their wives, and so the conversation turned to other subjects while they drank. When tea was finished, Emma rose to pull the curtains and left them alone again, taking the teatray with her.

'It's a shame,' Edwards said when she had gone.

Dickie didn't know whether he was referring to his story or his wife, but he agreed all the same. 'Won't your wife be expecting you back?' he asked.

'Trying to get rid of me?'

Dickie shook his head. 'Just wondering why you're still here when you've done what you came to do and delivered your bad news.'

'It's warm in here,' Edwards grinned, nodding at the coal fire. He was about to take another sip of his sherry when a brick came crashing through the window.

Both men jumped out of the armchairs. Emma came rushing in from the kitchen.

'What was that?' she cried, and stared down at the brick that lay in the midst of shattered glass on her carpet.

Edwards hurried to the window and peered out through the jagged hole the brick had made in the glass. He saw a car speeding away.

'I saw them,' he said, turning back to Dickie. 'A black car with a beige roof driving off.'

Emma was crying as she bent to pick up the pieces of glass.

'Don't do that, Em.' Dickie pulled her to her feet. 'You'll cut yourself.'

'Why?' she said, staring at him in incomprehension. 'Why did they do this?'

Dickie glanced at Edwards. 'I don't know. But leave it. I'll clear it up.'

'Why would someone do this?' she asked again. 'My window.'

'I want you to go up to the bedroom, Em,' Dickie said sternly. 'Go upstairs and lie down.'

'Call the police, Dickie,' she said as she went.

'I'll call them,' Edwards said and went out into the hall.

Dickie heard him lift the receiver and ask for the police. He couldn't take his eyes off the brick. There was nothing wrapped around it, no note. Wasn't that what usually happened? A threatening note wrapped around a brick, so at least the recipient knew what he was being warned off of? Or maybe there was no need. Dickie knew exactly who had sent this brick, for he remembered the very same thing had happened to Joseph Palmer.

'They're sending someone now,' Edwards said, coming back into the room. 'Best not touch anything.'

'They can't get fingerprints off bricks, Bill,' Dickie said.

Edwards nodded resignedly. 'I'll wait down here if you want to see to Emma.'

'I better go up and see how she is,' Dickie agreed.

'Who?' Edwards muttered to himself as Dickie moved towards the door.

'Ballantyne,' Dickie said.

Their eyes met.

Edwards nodded, understanding. He gestured at the shards of glass on the red-patterned carpet. 'Do you still want to look into these rumours?'

Dickie didn't hesitate. 'Yes.'

'Then do it. Find the dirt. And Superintendent Mullinger can go boil his head.'

Chapter Twenty-Seven

Sophie listened for the banging of the front door, and only when she heard it, did she release the breath she had been holding.

He was gone. She was safe for now.

Sophie put her fingertips to her left cheek and winced, then rose to look in the mirror. Turning her head slightly to the right, she studied her reflection in the glass, her chin wobbling as she saw the black mark on her left cheek, exactly where Andrew had hit her.

She burst into tears, falling onto the sofa and burying her face in her hands. Her whole body shook with her sobs, and she stayed that way until her sobs became gasping breaths.

Sophie pulled a handkerchief from her sleeve and folded it to carefully wipe beneath her eyes, examining the cotton to see if her mascara had run. There were black smears on the cotton. She drew a deep shuddering breath that calmed her, made her think more clearly. She sat there for a few more minutes, working things out. Then she went upstairs to the bedroom, cleaned her face, remade it and patted her hair back into place. Downstairs, she put on her hat and coat, picked up her handbag and keys, and left the house, giving the door a tug to make sure it had shut.

She walked to the high street and through the park, making for the police station on the other side. She opened the door to the lobby and Sergeant Turkel, stationed behind the front desk, looked up, professional smile in place, and the question, 'Yes, madam?' already forming on his lips when his eyes fixed on the bruise on her cheek.

Sophie ignored his stare. 'I want to speak to Detective Inspector Stannard.'

'Of course, madam,' Turkel said, picking up the telephone. 'If I could take your name?'

'Mrs Sophie Sutton.'

'And what is it about?'

Sophie took a deep breath and raised her chin. 'I think my husband killed Christopher Fairbank.'

Matthew took Sophie into an interview room, telling DC Pinder to bring in tea as he closed the door.

When Turkel had called him with the news that Mrs Sutton wanted to see him because she believed her husband was a murderer, Matthew had almost choked on his biscuit. DC Barnes had just taken a report from one of the uniformed officers that a resident from St Jude's Avenue said they had seen a man sitting in a parked car around one o'clock on Friday night near the Empire Club. At one point, the man had got out of the car and walked towards the club to stare up at the windows. When he had turned back towards his car, the resident had got a good look at him. He was tall, broad-shouldered with dark hair and a moustache. Plenty of men could fit that description, Matthew knew, but it sounded a hell of a lot like Andrew Sutton to him.

'How did you get the bruise, Mrs Sutton?' Matthew asked, taking a seat opposite her.

'My husband, shortly after you left.'

'I'm sorry,' he said, feeling guilty. 'Because you were with Christopher Fairbank on Friday night?'

'Yes. We stayed at the club when everyone else had left and went up to the bedroom.'

'What time did you and Mr Fairbank go up to the bedroom?'

'About a quarter to one.'

'And you left when?'

'Just after two. And before you ask, Mr Fairbank was alive. I didn't kill him. Though, God knows, I had reason to.'

'What reason would that be, Mrs Sutton?'

'Remember what you said about the gentlemen of the Empire Club being ungentlemanly? Well, never a truer word spoken and all that. Kit got what he wanted and then there was no need to be charming anymore.'

'Which is why he left you to walk home alone?'

She nodded. 'But I didn't stab him, inspector.'

'You think your husband did?'

'Yes, I do.'

'And why do you think that?'

'Because when I turned the corner into my road, I saw him parking the car outside the house. I watched him as he hurried indoors. When I got in and went up to the bedroom, his clothes were thrown over the ottoman. Andrew always hangs up his clothes. And he was pretending to be asleep.'

'That's suspicious, I agree, but—'

'And after you'd gone, and after he did this,' she pointed at her cheek, 'he said Kit had been taught a lesson, that he couldn't make free with other men's wives and get away with it. That Kit got what he deserved.'

'That could be just talk—'

'And then he said he'd enjoyed the look on Kit's face when he stuck the knife in.' She raised her eyebrows at him. 'Does that answer your question, inspector?'

The door opened. DC Pinder deposited two cups of tea on the table and quickly departed.

'He actually said that?' Matthew said.

Sophie's lips twisted. She nodded. 'I'd say that was an admission of guilt, wouldn't you?'

Matthew considered a moment. He had to admit Andrew Sutton killing Fairbank made sense. But he studied Sophie's bruised cheek and reminded himself to be cautious.

'I will talk to your husband, Mrs Sutton,' he said.

'You mean you'll arrest him?'

'I'll have to see what he says first.'

'But I've told you what he said,' she cried. 'I've told you he was out when Kit was killed. What more do you need? Why can't you arrest him?'

'He may have an explanation for his movements, Mrs Sutton. An allegation of the kind you've made has to be investigated, not taken at face value.'

'You mean you don't believe me?'

'I didn't say that.'

'Of course you don't believe me. I'm only a woman, aren't I?' Sophie opened the clasp of her handbag and delved inside for her cigarette case. Shaking fingers extracted a cigarette and moved it to her lips. Her lighter wouldn't light. Matthew struck a match and held it to the tip of the cigarette.

'Mrs Sutton,' Matthew said, throwing the spent match in the ashtray, 'is there anywhere you could go? Relatives? Friends? I'm concerned for your safety if you return to the house.'

'So you should be if you're not going to arrest him.'

'You could lodge a complaint against your husband for assault.'

210

Wet blue eyes looked through the smoke at him. 'Can I do that?'

Matthew nodded.

'And he'd go to prison?'

'Probably not,' he sighed. 'He might be fined, or if it got to court, he would probably raise the matter of your infidelity and…'

'And he'd be the one to be pitied.' Sophie nodded knowingly. 'A poor man having to put up with an unfaithful and ungrateful wife. I see.' She stubbed her cigarette out in the metal ashtray. 'Thank you for being so direct, inspector. When will you question my husband?'

'I'll see him today.'

Sophie rose and grabbed the door handle.

'Just one question, Mrs Sutton,' Matthew halted her. 'When you were upstairs with Mr Fairbank, were you aware of anyone else in the club?'

She frowned. 'No. We were alone.'

'You're sure of that? There couldn't have been someone in one of the other rooms?'

'Are you saying there was?' Her cheeks coloured.

'Did you hear anyone?'

'No. But I suppose there might have been. It's a big house.'

Matthew nodded. 'Did Mr Fairbank say anything about the waiter he had embarrassed earlier in the evening?'

'He said he thought it had been a good joke.'

'And what did you say?'

'I don't think I said much, inspector. I had other things on my mind.'

'I'm sure you did,' he murmured as Sophie left the room. She hadn't touched her tea.

Chapter Twenty-Eight

Andrew Sutton was not pleased to see Matthew again.

'What is it this time?' he demanded, striding off into the sitting room, leaving Matthew and the police constable he'd brought with him to follow. 'I warn you, I'm not in the mood for this. My wife's decided to disappear and we're supposed to be having drinks with friends tonight. Whatever this is about, make it quick.'

'I need to ask you about Friday night,' Matthew said.

Sutton turned to Matthew. 'You've already done that. I've told you. I wasn't even at the club after ten o'clock.'

'Mrs Sutton has made a statement, contradicting what she told me earlier today, that she did in fact remain at the club alone with Mr Fairbank until two o'clock on Friday. She also claims you were parking your car and dashing into this house as she turned into the road after she'd left him. That would have been between two and two-thirty.'

'She's lying.' Sutton's face had turned stony. He leaned on the mantelpiece, one foot up on the fender. 'I was in bed.'

'I also have a witness who claims seeing a man sitting in a car near the Empire Club around 1 a.m. on Friday, and that this man got out of his car, looked up at the windows of the club, and returned to his car. The witness got a good look at the man and gave us a description.' Matthew paused for effect. 'The description matches you, Mr Sutton.'

Sutton stared at Matthew for a long moment. Then he said, 'This is ridiculous. I've told you where I was. That witness is obviously mistaken and my wife is an inveterate liar. She always has been. Ever since we married. You've no idea what I've had to put up with from her.'

'Did she deserve a blow to the face?' Matthew asked.

Sutton raised his chin a little higher, the thin lips tightening. 'I'd like you to leave, inspector.'

'I'm afraid I can't do that, Mr Sutton.'

'I insist you do.'

'If you refuse to answer my questions, then I'm going to have to arrest you.'

'Arrest me?' Sutton scoffed. 'For what?'

'On suspicion of murder.'

Sutton's mouth fell open. 'You're not serious?'

'I'm perfectly serious, sir. But I'd rather not arrest you at this stage.'

'Do you know who I am?' Sutton demanded.

Matthew sighed. How many times had he heard this question? 'The matter can be cleared up easily enough if you agree to take part in an identity parade.'

'I will certainly not agree. How dare you even suggest it? Get out of my house.'

'Then you leave me no choice. Mr Sutton, I'm arresting you on suspicion of murder. You do not have to say anything, but anything you do say may be taken down and used in evidence against you. Do you understand?'

Sutton blustered a response and Matthew ordered the constable to take him to the station. Sophie Sutton had got what she wanted after all.

. . .

'Inspector? Could I have a word?'

Matthew had been heading towards the stairs up to CID, his mind busy on the questions he would ask Andrew Sutton and the arrangements that needed to be made for the identity parade. He didn't have time to answer questions from the Press.

'I'm sorry, Mr Waite,' he said, waving Dickie away. 'I can't stop to talk.'

'It's not for the 'paper, inspector,' Dickie called. 'It's about Fairbank.'

Matthew turned back. 'What about him?'

'I have information for you. I think it might be helpful.'

'Might, Mr Waite?'

Dickie shrugged. 'Let me tell you what I've got and you can decide.'

Matthew checked his watch. 'Ten minutes. Come up.' He jerked his head for Dickie to follow him up the stairs.

'It's busy,' Dickie observed as they passed through CID into Matthew's office. All the telephones were ringing.

'Your article caused quite a response,' Matthew said, throwing himself into his chair and offering Dickie the other on the opposite side of the desk. 'A lot of it will be rubbish, but it all has to be checked. So, what do you have for me?' He frowned as Dickie sighed and stared down at his hands in his lap. 'Are you all right, Mr Waite?'

'No, not really,' Dickie confessed. 'I had a brick come through my window this afternoon, inspector. It's rather shaken me up.'

'A brick? Did you report it?'

'Yes. My editor was with me at the time and he telephoned the police. They sent a young constable out. He's taken it all down in his notebook.'

Matthew frowned. 'I'm sorry that's happened to you, Mr Waite, but what has it to do with the Fairbank murder?'

'I'm not entirely sure it has,' Dickie admitted, 'but I've been making enquiries for the profiles I'm writing. I've heard rumours about a group of men nicknamed The Five. According to the gossip, these men are very different to what most people think they are. So, I started to dig a little deeper.'

'Who are The Five?'

'Ballantyne, Fairbank, Foucault, Spencer and Hailes. Do you know them?'

'I've met them,' Matthew nodded.

'And what did you think?'

Matthew gave him a smile.

'Well,' Dickie said, nodding understanding, 'they have a reputation at the Empire Club and the other Craynebrook clubs for being the life and soul of the party, especially Ballantyne and Fairbank. But I've discovered they also have a reputation amongst the criminal classes. Ballantyne and Foucault for taking money from the people they defend. Fairbank for cheating people on art and antique deals. Spencer takes backhanders for council building works. I'm not sure what Hailes gets up to, but he's one of them, so the talk is that he's dodgy too.'

'Do you have evidence for any of this?'

'Nothing in black and white. Just the statements of people I've talked to. But I think evidence could be found if you knew where to look.'

Matthew drummed his fingers on the edge of his desk. 'What's this got to do with a brick through your window?'

'I tried to interview Ballantyne this morning and I got a flea in my ear for my trouble. And this afternoon, I get the brick through the window. The same thing happened to one of the people I spoke to. He's a solicitor, an old school friend of mine. He overheard a conversation between Ballantyne and a client he'd got acquitted where the client was talking about giving him the money for getting him off. My friend reported this conversation to the judge and he got a brick through the window. Nothing ever came of his statement to the judge. Hushed up, you see.'

'You told the police this?'

Dickie nodded. 'But I'm telling you because you might have to cast your net further afield for Fairbank's killer. The kind of people they were mixed up with probably wouldn't hesitate to kill.'

'I already have two suspects for Fairbank's murder, Mr Waite.'

Dickie leant forward on the desk. 'Two? I know there's this waiter chap—'

'How do you know about the waiter?' Matthew cut in.

'I've spoken with a member of the Empire Club staff. He told me what Ballantyne and Fairbank did to Norman Kelly.'

'What's his name?'

'I'm not telling you his name, inspector. You have your confidential sources, I have mine. Who's the other suspect?'

'You really expect me to tell you?' Matthew asked, raising an eyebrow.

'No,' Dickie sighed. 'So, if you have two suspects in your sight, then what I've told you is of no use?'

'It's of interest,' Matthew said. 'But with two murders on my hands, it's not the right time for me to be looking into rumours of corruption.'

'Even if they might be connected?'

'You don't have any proof, Mr Waite,' Matthew reminded him. 'I realise that as a reporter you're keen to have a scoop, but I can't give it to you.'

Dickie drew a deep breath. 'I understand. But at least tell me you'll bear what I've said in mind.'

'I will,' Matthew promised, 'and I'm grateful for the

information. But I do have a lot to get through and it's already been a very long day. So, if you don't mind, DC Barnes will show you out.'

It was a subdued Andrew Sutton that Denham escorted from the police cell at eight o'clock the next morning. His clothing was rumpled, his hair uncombed, his face unshaven, and as he entered the interview room, Matthew could tell he'd decided to cooperate. Perhaps his solicitor, who pulled out a chair for his client before taking his own, had advised him it would be wise. Whatever the reason, Matthew was glad.

'Now, Mr Sutton—' Matthew began.

'I want to make a statement,' Sutton cut him off. He took a deep breath. 'I was outside the Empire Club in my car on Friday night. I had left the club around 10 p.m. because I was feeling unwell, but I returned later because I suspected my wife was staying at the club to engage in carnal relations with Christopher Fairbank.'

'What time did you return to the club?' Matthew asked, surprised by this admission.

'I think it was about a quarter past one. I knew the club would be closed by half-past twelve. When Sophie hadn't come home by one, I guessed what she was doing, and I got in the car and drove to the club.'

'Why did you sit outside in your car? Why not go in?'

'I didn't know what to do. I had the idea of walking in on them, but when it came to it, I baulked, I suppose. The idea of the scene it would create was repugnant to me.'

'How long did you sit in your car?'

'Until Sophie came out at about two. I was surprised she was alone and realised Fairbank must still be in the club.'

'Did you then confront Mr Fairbank?'

'No. I didn't go into the club.' Sutton held up his hands as

Matthew opened his mouth to ask why. 'I had no idea what I would say to him or what I would do. I thought I would look ridiculous. He was so arrogant, so confident, that I had the idea he wouldn't be at all ashamed or apologetic. So, I drove home.' He put a hand over his eyes. 'I know how I must sound. A coward who won't fight for his wife. I'm not proud of myself.'

A man who takes his anger out on his wife rather than the man who cuckolded him, Matthew thought as the solicitor murmured something in Sutton's ear.

'I did not kill Christopher Fairbank,' Sutton said, stabbing the tabletop with his finger with each word. 'I've never even been upstairs at the club.'

'Your wife said you made certain statements about the death of Mr Fairbank,' Matthew said, pulling out the typed copy of his notes made during his interview with Sophie. 'She said, and I quote, "he said Kit had been taught a lesson, that he couldn't make free with other men's wives and get away with it. That he got what he deserved". And lastly, that you "enjoyed the look on his face when he stuck the knife in".' Matthew looked up at Sutton's horrified face. 'Did you say those words, Mr Sutton?'

The solicitor touched Sutton's arm and whispered in his ear again. Sutton nodded and looked at Matthew. 'I did say Fairbank had been taught a lesson, that he got what he deserved. But I did not say I stuck the knife in. That is a lie.'

Matthew studied Sutton's face. He'd looked into the eyes of many liars over the years and he didn't think Sutton was one of them. But still…

'You'll remain in detention, Mr Sutton, while we continue with our enquires.' He told the police constable on the door to take Sutton back to his cell.

'What do you think, sir?' Denham asked when they were alone.

'I think he's telling the truth,' Matthew said. 'I think most men, when they've found out that their wives have been unfaithful and the man has been killed, would say something similar.'

'But the plunging the knife in?' Denham queried. 'That's pretty damning, isn't it?'

'Oh, I wouldn't be surprised if that was a little embellishment on Mrs Sutton's part.'

'Really? What a cow,' Denham shook his head. 'That's the kind of statement that could get a man hung.'

'Maybe that's what she's hoping for,' Matthew shrugged. 'I want Sutton's fingerprints checked against all the prints lifted from the first floor of the club. If Sutton never went upstairs as he claims, then we shouldn't find his fingerprints there and it might help to corroborate his story. And you can tell Sergeant Turkel we won't be needing the identity parade after all.'

Chapter Twenty-Nine

Denham yawned as the silence at the end of the line went on. This was the fifth call he'd made to police stations in East London to check the alerts were still out for Norman Kelly. He flipped through his notebook as he waited, rereading the notes he had written following his interview with Mrs Coggs. If only he'd found Norman Kelly then. The murder enquiry would be over. Mullinger would be happy. Stannard would forget his slip of the tongue in front of Mr Yates, and he wouldn't have had to endure the cold shoulder of his wife in bed the previous night. And all because Norman Kelly was on the run and he'd had to work. It wasn't his fault Sunday leave had been cancelled and he couldn't go with her to her parents in Enfield for the day as planned. Not that he'd wanted to go. An entire day with his in-laws was not his idea of fun. Not that he'd ever say so to his wife, of course.

'Yes, I'm still here,' he said, jerking awake as someone spoke at the other end of the line. 'Still nothing? All right. Thanks.'

He hung up just as DC Pinder, sitting across from him, did the same. Pinder made a face.

'Who'd you have?' Denham asked, nodding at his colleague's telephone.

'A man who claimed the prime minister killed our dead man because he found out he was a spy. These people. They're off their heads.'

Both men's telephones began ringing.

'Here we go again,' Pinder grimaced and picked up the receiver.

Denham answered his telephone, scraping his chair back to spring to his feet as Mullinger walked into CID. 'Mr Yates?' he said, greeting the superintendent with raised eyebrows as the voice at the other end of the line spoke. 'Yes, hello. This is Sergeant Denham... No, Inspector Stannard isn't here at the moment. Can I help?.... The club?... Clear up? No, I'm sorry, Mr Yates. The inspector wants the club to remain closed for the time being... No, I'm sorry... It's not possible, I'm afraid—'

'Give me that.' Mullinger snatched the telephone from Denham's hand. 'Mr Yates?... Yes, good morning. Superintendent Mullinger here. What seems to be the problem?... I see... Well, I don't see why you can't reopen.'

'Sir,' Denham whispered. 'Inspector Stannard ordered for the club to remain closed—'

Mullinger waved at Denham to be quiet. 'Yes, I understand there is some confusion... But by all means, open the club, Mr Yates... Not at all, you're very welcome... Yes, yes, I'll look forward to that... Goodbye, Mr Yates.' The superintendent hung up. 'Where is Inspector Stannard?'

'He's downstairs, sir, releasing Andrew Sutton.'

'Releasing him?'

'Yes, sir. Lack of evidence.'

'I see. Well, carry on.'

Mullinger strode out of the office. Denham sank into his chair and met Pinder's eye.

'The inspector's going to hit the bloody roof,' Pinder said, shaking his head.

Denham nodded. He had a feeling it was going to be another of those days.

Matthew watched Andrew Sutton and his solicitor shaking hands outside on the pavement through the glass of the station's front doors. Not a single fingerprint of Sutton's had been found anywhere on the club's first floor, and without evidence to prove he was there, Matthew had nothing to justify holding him. He'd had to let him go, and his optimism of the previous day, when he had been hoping he had his murderer, had left him.

'You've released Andrew Sutton,' a voice behind him said.

Matthew groaned inwardly as he turned to face the superintendent. 'Yes, sir. I had nothing to hold him on.'

'Pity,' Mullinger said. 'And the wife? Is she a suspect?'

'I don't think so. I believe she left when she said she did and that Fairbank was still alive. I've told Mr Sutton that they must stay in Craynebrook for the time being.'

Mullinger nodded. 'I was just up in CID. It's very busy. The telephones are ringing non-stop.'

'Yes, there's been quite a response to the article calling for information.'

'An article I did not authorise, Stannard,' Mullinger reminded him. 'Any new leads?'

'Nothing plausible as yet, sir.'

Mullinger grunted, and Matthew could have sworn there was pleasure in it that the article had caused nothing but extra work. 'So, this waiter fellow is still your main suspect?'

'Yes, sir. He's absconded from his lodging and we've

alerted all neighbouring stations to be on the lookout for him.'

'It's taking too blasted long, Stannard. People are expecting an arrest to be made and a man charged.'

'What people, sir?' Matthew wondered.

'The public, Stannard,' Mullinger said, but Matthew suspected that wasn't who he had meant. 'That waiter left at liberty presents a danger to the public.'

'If he's guilty.'

'Good God, Stannard, what more proof do you need? Fairbank and his friends handled him a little roughly in some jape and he took his revenge. He had the motive, he had the means, and he had the opportunity. And he's disappeared. Of course he did it. So, just pull your finger out and find him.'

Mullinger grabbed the door handle to leave, then paused and turned back. 'When I was in CID, Mr Yates telephoned to find out if he could reopen the club. I've told him he could.'

'What?' Matthew cried. 'Sir, the club has to remain closed until our enquiry's over. There could be evidence—'

'Nonsense. The place has been searched. Any evidence has been dealt with. You can't expect it to remain closed indefinitely.'

'But we've no way of knowing what's relevant at the club yet,' Matthew protested, his voice rising. 'A lead may turn up that points to something we've overlooked there. The club has to stay closed.'

'It does not.' Mullinger's voice rose even louder than Matthew's. 'That's my order, Stannard. I won't have it contradicted by you. Is that understood?'

Matthew looked away and saw Sergeant Turkel at his desk, pretending he wasn't there but looking at the two of them out of the corner of his eyes. 'Sir, this is my investigation. I must be allowed to conduct it as I see fit.'

223

'You'll conduct it as I see fit,' Mullinger growled. 'And if you don't, if you prove unable to find this killer, then know this, Stannard, I'll have you out of here faster than you can blink.'

Chapter Thirty

Thomas Yates unlocked the gates of the Empire Club and pushed them open with a feeling sigh. He hadn't wanted to call the police to ask if the club could be reopened but he'd had so many members asking if it would be that he'd had no choice. When Sergeant Denham had told him no, he'd been relieved. He could say to the members, *I'm sorry, but the police say the club must stay closed. It's out of my hands.* But then the superintendent had interfered and said it could be opened, so now he didn't have an excuse. So, here he was, opening the club. Rosie had wanted to come with him. He'd put his foot down and said no to that. He didn't want her here, seeing what he would see.

'Afternoon, Mr Yates.'

He jumped at the voice. 'Oh, Miss Cooke,' he said, almost laughing with relief. 'You quite startled me. What are you doing here?'

'It's my shift,' Sally Cooke said.

'Is it?' He tried to remember. 'Well, it's very good of you to turn up. No one else has.'

She nodded at the house. 'You are going in?'

'Yes. The police say we can reopen so I need to…' he

looked up at the first-floor windows and grimaced, 'tidy things up. I asked Mrs Briggs if she would do it, but she refused. I don't blame her, of course, but it is what we pay her for.'

'I can tidy the room, Mr Yates,' Sally said. 'I don't mind.'

'Oh, no, I couldn't ask—'

'I don't mind, Mr Yates,' she repeated, smiling at him.

'Well, if you're sure? It's very decent of you, Miss Cooke. Very decent indeed.'

They walked up the path together and Yates unlocked the front doors. Sally headed for the cloakroom and hung up her hat, coat and handbag. Yates followed and hung up his hat and coat, then watched as Sally mounted the stairs, impressed by her readiness to get on with the job. He followed her lead and started up the stairs.

Sally had already thrown the dirty pillowcases on the floor by the time he reached the bedroom doorway. He watched as she pulled the bottom sheet from the mattress, crumpling it up in her arms.

'I thought it might be stained,' she said, seeing him standing there. 'But there's not a drop of blood on it.'

'The wound was to the heart,' Yates said, trying not to look at the bed, 'and apparently he was on his back.'

'It means you don't have to change the mattress, anyway,' she said brightly and threw the dirty sheet onto the landing.

Yates turned to the wall, studying the floral patterned wallpaper.

'What are you looking for?' Sally asked.

'The police said there was a hole in the wall.' Yates put the flat of his hand on the wall and swept it over the surface. A fingertip dipped. 'Yes, here it is.'

Sally peered over his shoulder. 'Why is there a hole?'

'It's a peephole, the inspector said. It goes all the way

through to the room next door. Someone has been spying on the people in this room.'

'Who?'

Yates shrugged. 'I've no idea. I didn't know there was a peephole.'

Sally rushed out of the room. He hurried after her as she ducked into the junk-room and saw her find the peephole and put her eye to it.

'You can see right in,' she said breathlessly.

'The police think a camera might have been set up there.' Yates pointed at the three indentations in the carpet. 'Those marks might have been made by a tripod.'

'Someone was taking photographs?'

'It's disgraceful,' Yates shuddered. 'That one of the members should be so depraved.' He looked up. Sally was staring at him. 'Miss Cooke?'

'You didn't know about this?' she asked, pointing to the hole.

'I most certainly did not!' he cried indignantly. 'If I had, I would never have allowed it to remain. As it is, I'm going to put something in it so it can't be used in that way again.' And to prove it, he strode over to his office and came back screwing up a few sheets of paper. 'Let me get there,' he said, and Sally moved aside. He pushed the paper into the hole, only stopping once he was satisfied it was completely plugged up. Then he put the painting of *The Hay Wain* back on its hook. 'I shall keep this door locked.' He shooed Sally out of the room. 'No one will have access to it again.' Yates took out a bunch of keys from his trouser pocket, selected one and locked the door. He straightened and looked at Sally. She was watching him with interest. 'I'm not sure I should reopen the club,' he said, putting the keys back in his pocket.

'You said the police gave you permission.'

'Oh, yes, I'm allowed to. I just don't know if it's a good

idea. I'm learning things about this place and the people in it that I never imagined.'

'You must reopen, Mr Yates,' Sally said, putting a hand on his arm.

'Must I? I'm not just thinking of myself. I'm thinking of the staff as well. You won't feel unsafe working here?'

'Don't worry about me. I'm learning to look after myself. You have to be strong, Mr Yates. If you act weak, you'll be treated as weak, and people will take advantage. Don't give them the chance.'

He patted her arm. 'What a very remarkable young lady you are, Miss Cooke. I shall endeavour to follow your advice.'

The Empire Club, normally almost empty on a Monday evening, was heaving.

The members had turned out in their droves, all eager to be where a murder had taken place and all pretending that wasn't the reason they had come. Some had even wandered up to the first floor and gone into the bedroom where Fairbank had been killed and come back down expressing their disappointment that there was nothing to see.

Yates loathed them. Suddenly and emphatically loathed them. How had he ever thought they were worth his efforts? These people, who had thought Fairbank so witty, so charming, so worth knowing, had come to gossip and giggle about his death over cocktails and canapés.

The treasurer sat in the lounge in an armchair by the bay window, a table separating him from Rosie in the other chair. He looked across at his wife and felt a sharp pang of love for her. She wasn't like the other women here. She wasn't gossiping about Fairbank. Rosie hadn't been up to the bedroom to see the scene of the crime. She hadn't even wanted to come tonight and had only decided to do so when she realised her husband would be comforted by her presence.

Rosie reached across the table and plucked at his sleeve. 'Are you all right, darling?'

'Look at them,' he said in a low voice, nodding at the others in the room. 'Vultures. That's what they are.'

'Oh, Tommy,' she said, putting her pretty head to one side, 'it won't be for much longer. As soon as you can find someone to take over, we'll leave. That's what we discussed, remember?'

'I remember,' he said gratefully, 'and it won't be a moment too soon.' He frowned. A hush had come over the room, and then people began whispering to each other. 'What is it?' he asked.

'It's Daphne,' someone answered him. 'She's here.'

'Here?' Yates cried, getting to his feet.

'She's gone upstairs,' a woman by the door exclaimed excitedly.

This was all he needed. The dead man's widow turning up to do or say God knew what. What if she became hysterical and started screaming or tearing her hair out? Grief-stricken women did things like that, didn't they? And then he'd prob-ably have to call the police and have them crawling all over the club again. Oh no, he couldn't bear it.

'Rosie,' Yates said, pulling his wife out of her chair. 'Go after her. See what she's up to.'

'Oh, Tommy, I can't,' Rosie said, trying to pull away.

He didn't let her go. 'Please, Rosie.'

'But what do I say?' she said, allowing him to propel her towards the door.

'You'll know what to say,' Yates said as he gently pushed

her in the direction of the stairs. 'You're good at that sort of thing.'

'You did what?' Eric Hailes hissed as Donald Spencer stepped away from the billiard table and picked up his whisky.

'A brick, Eric,' Spencer said, watching Ballantyne line up his cue with the white ball. 'Just so he got the message.'

'You bloody idiot.'

'Calm down, Eric,' Ballantyne said as the white ball clicked against the red. 'It was just a little warning to keep his nose out of our business.'

'But a reporter, Archie!' Hailes said despairingly. 'He can write about us in his newspaper. We could be all over the front page.'

'If he prints a single word, we'll sue. And besides, I got Mullinger to have a word with the editor. You know Mullinger will do anything if he thinks he can get in with us. He'll silence the little bastard, don't you worry.'

'I do worry, that's the problem.'

'Then don't. Have a drink,' Spencer said, refilling Hailes's glass, 'and calm down.'

Hailes downed the whisky. 'Have they caught anyone yet?'

'Not yet,' Ballantyne said. 'Mullinger telephoned me today and said they'd questioned Andrew Sutton but had to let him go. Lack of evidence. And Sophie's in the clear, too, apparently. So, it's looking like it was that waiter after all.'

'Couldn't take a joke,' Spencer muttered, chalking his cue and leaning over the table to take a shot. His eyes moved to the doorway as Sally Cooke entered with a tray of canapés and offered them to Ballantyne.

Hailes rubbed his sweating forehead. 'Are we safe, Archie? I mean, we both joined in with Kit, didn't we? Is he going to come after us?'

Ballantyne sighed. 'Even if he does have some idea of coming for us, Eric, we're on to him, aren't we? We'll see him coming.'

'You think so?' Hailes shook his head at Sally's canapés.

'I do think so, and so does Adrian.'

'And where the hell is Adrian?' Hailes demanded, watching as Sally offered the tray to Spencer.

Spencer took three of the canapés, looking Sally up and down with a shameless interest.

'Adrian's at home this evening,' Ballantyne said as Sally left the room. 'Said he had a lot of paperwork to get through.'

'You'd think he'd make an effort to be here tonight,' Hailes muttered.

'Why?' Spencer said. 'What difference does it make whether he's here or not?'

'Well, I mean…' Hailes shrugged.

'What the bloody hell does "well, I mean" mean?'

'To pay his respects, Donald,' Hailes said angrily. 'Not that you'd know what those are.'

'Kit wouldn't expect it,' Spencer said, sending one of the white balls shooting across the green baize. He cursed as it bounced off the side cushion. 'And you think everyone downstairs is here tonight to pay their respects? They've just come to satisfy their curiosity. They're loving having a juicy murder to talk about.'

'Oh Lord,' Ballantyne murmured, gesturing with his eyes towards the hall.

Spencer and Hailes followed his gaze and saw Daphne Fairbank pass by the doorway.

'What's she doing here?' Hailes hissed.

'Probably come to gloat,' Spencer said with a grin.

Rosie crept up the stairs, wishing someone else would tell her they'd see to Daphne so she could go back to Tommy with a clear conscience. But no one came to her rescue, and she turned into the narrow corridor to see Daphne standing in the doorway of the room where her husband had been murdered.

'Daphne?' she called softly so as not to startle her. 'Are you all right?'

'Yes, I'm fine,' Daphne said, moving further into the room.

Rosie went after her, knowing that the room had been tidied and there would be no trace of the terrible thing that had happened there. 'You really shouldn't be here, you know.'

'Kit was here,' Daphne explained.

A lump rose in Rosie's throat. 'I understand you wanting to be near where he was…'

Daphne slowly turned her head towards Rosie, her dark eyes drilling into hers. 'Don't be ridiculous, Rosie. You know what my marriage was.'

'Then… why?'

'I just wanted to see for myself where he brought his women.'

'Which women?'

The corner of Daphne's mouth curled. 'Many of the women downstairs, I imagine. I wonder how long it took for them to discover what Kit was really like.'

Rosie shifted her feet, feeling distinctly uncomfortable. She hoped Daphne wasn't going to ask her any questions about Kit's affairs. And what, Rosie wondered, did she mean by what Kit was really like?

'Was it Sophie Sutton?' Daphne said, breaking into her thoughts.

'Sophie Sutton?'

'Was she with Kit Friday night? I know you know. I can see it in your face.'

'Yes, I believe so.'

'Is she here tonight?'

Rosie shook her head.

'Is she keeping away because everyone knows?'

'I don't know what everyone knows. But Florence knew it was her, and you know what Florence is like.'

Daphne smiled coldly. 'Yes, I know what Florence is like. I'll bet she's having a whale of a time downstairs, gossiping about my dead husband and his whores. She never slept with Kit, you know, even though she pretends he had a fancy for her. Kit would never touch anything that belonged to Archie. Any other woman, though, was fair game. He had the sense not to try for you.'

Rosie coloured. 'Let's go back downstairs, Daphne. Tommy and I will take you home.'

'That won't be necessary, thank you. But I do have a favour to ask of you.' She opened her handbag and took out a brown envelope. 'Would you ask your husband to give this to the police? I really don't want to talk to them again.'

Rosie took the envelope. 'What is it?'

'Something that may be of use to them. I found it hidden in my husband's bedroom. The police didn't find it when they searched but they didn't know where to look. I advise you not to look at what's inside.'

'I wouldn't dream of looking inside,' Rosie said, horrified by the insinuation she pried into private papers.

Daphne smiled. 'Thank you. Well, I shall stop being a nuisance to you and go home. You can tell your husband I won't be back, and that I won't be renewing my membership.'

Rosie watched Daphne go down the stairs and sighed with relief. Looking down at the envelope she held, her fingers feeling the hard edges of whatever was inside, she wondered what Tommy would say when she told him he must have yet another encounter with Inspector Stannard.

Chapter Thirty-One

Miss Harriet Bird rose from her bed at a quarter past seven and washed briskly in the tiny functional bathroom. Mr Foucault had had the bathroom installed a few years earlier for her sole use and Miss Bird had been grateful for the consideration he had shown in making this arrangement. It would have been most unsuitable for her, an unmarried woman, to share a bathroom with an unmarried gentleman of Mr Foucault's station.

She brushed, plaited and pinned her long, dark hair around her skull in a style that had remained unchanged since entering her thirties, and climbed into her ankle-length black dress with its white lace collar, smoothing out any wrinkles in the fabric. She checked her appearance in the mirror, nodded satisfaction with it, and stepped out into the narrow hall, emerging from behind the green baize door that separated her employer's house from her quarters. She padded softly down the carpeted staircase to the kitchen. Mr Foucault liked his breakfast, always taken in bed, by 8 a.m. and it would never do to be late.

While she waited for the kettle to boil, Miss Bird set about gathering the breakfast things – the tea tray, the toast rack, the eggcup and spoon – and considered what she would give Mr Foucault for his dinner. Veal perhaps or pork chops with a mustard sauce.

Fifteen minutes later and Miss Bird had her employer's breakfast ready. Carrying the breakfast tray out into the hall, she mounted the stairs, noting with some little annoyance that the study door was open and a light had been left on. She would see to them when she came back downstairs.

She reached Mr Foucault's bedroom door and rapped lightly on the wood. There was no answer, but that wasn't unusual. Mr Foucault didn't always respond and Miss Bird knew she wouldn't see anything she shouldn't when she entered and wished him a good morning. Bachelor though he was, Mr Foucault had never disgraced himself by bringing women back to his house.

Miss Bird set the tray down on the table at the end of the bed, moving to the window and pulling back the curtains to let the daylight in. She turned to the bed, ready to make her morning greeting, and blinked in surprise.

Mr Foucault was not in bed. The blankets and sheets were undisturbed; there was no indentation in the pillow to suggest Mr Foucault had laid his head there. Miss Bird racked her brains. Had she forgotten an instruction? Had Mr Foucault told her he was spending the night elsewhere and so wouldn't need breakfast this morning? She shook her head as if that might dislodge a memory, but no. She couldn't remember anything of the kind. How very odd!

Miss Bird went out into the hall and frowned at the bath-room door. Could he perhaps be in there, having risen earlier than usual? She put her ear to the door and listened. Nothing. Gingerly, she tried the knob. It turned, and the door opened. The bathroom was empty. How very peculiar this was, Miss Bird thought as she returned to the bedroom and picked up the breakfast tray, annoyed all her work was now wasted. No, not wasted, she told herself as she went back down the stairs. She would eat the boiled egg and toast and drink the tea. No sense throwing it away and doing another breakfast for herself.

Miss Bird reached the bottom of the stairs for the second time that morning and remembered the light still on in her master's study. She set the tray down on the hall table and headed for the study door. Pushing it open wider, she entered, making a noise of surprise as she saw Mr Foucault sitting at the bureau on the other side of the room, his back towards her.

'I'm sorry, Mr Foucault,' she said. 'I didn't realise you had already risen.'

Mr Foucault didn't answer. In fact, he didn't move. Miss Bird edged closer.

'Mr Foucault?' she asked, her heart starting to flutter. Something, she didn't know what or why, was telling her something was wrong. She reached his chair and her breath caught in her throat. There was a long gash in her employer's throat and blood had soaked into his smoking jacket. Miss Bird rocked backwards at the sight, her sharp ears picking up a strange squelching noise. Her gaze travelled downwards to her feet, and it was only then she saw a bright shade of red against the blue carpeted floor. Miss Bird's hand went to her mouth as she felt a scream rising up her throat. She didn't want to scream, didn't want to do anything as undignified as screeching. So instead, she ran out of the room and snatched up the telephone from the hall table.

'Number, please,' the operator's tinny voice said.

'Please put me through to the police,' Miss Bird replied.

What in God's name is happening? Matthew wondered as he stepped inside Adrian Foucault's house for the second time in four days. His bewilderment must have showed on his face because Denham raised his eyebrows understandingly as he emerged from a doorway on Matthew's left.

'Morning, sir,' he said. 'In here.'

Matthew followed his sergeant into the study.

'Mr Adrian Foucault,' Denham said, gesturing at the body slumped in the captain's chair. 'Found by his housekeeper at five to eight this morning. I've put her in the kitchen. Watch where you put your feet, sir. There's blood around him on the carpet.'

'How is the housekeeper?' Matthew asked, stepping carefully up to Foucault.

'Quite calm, I'd say. Doesn't seem the hysterical type. Very prim and proper.'

'Thank God for that,' Matthew said under his breath. He winced as he saw the wound in Foucault's neck. 'A knife again,' he said, straightening.

'Or a razor?' Denham suggested.

Matthew shook his head. 'The cut's not sharp enough. The edges are a little ragged.'

'Very well observed, inspector,' a voice behind Matthew said.

'Morning, Mr Wallace,' Matthew said, turning.

'Well, you are keeping me busy, aren't you?' Wallace said with a wry smile, setting his medical bag down on the Chesterfield.

'It's not through choice,' Matthew assured him.

'No, indeed. May I?' Wallace pointed at the body.

Matthew stepped to the side. 'Just mind the blood on the carpet.'

Wallace peered at the neck wound as Matthew had done. 'Exsanguination,' he declared.

'You what?' Denham asked.

'He was bled out, sergeant,' Wallace explained. 'One cut

clean across the throat. No arterial spray. You see his hands are covered in blood. His instinctive reaction once the cut was made would be to put his hands to his throat. It wouldn't have taken long for him to die.'

'Time of death?' Matthew asked.

Wallace felt Foucault's limbs. 'Rigor is still present and well set in, so I would say death occurred between ten last night and seven this morning, with it being more likely last night.'

'I see,' Matthew said. 'Thank you, Mr Wallace. I'll let you carry on. If you want me, I'll be in the kitchen.'

'Very well, inspector.' Wallace waved a hand as Matthew and Denham left the room.

Prim and proper seemed to Matthew a very apt description of Miss Bird. She sat bolt upright at the kitchen table, the ubiquitous cup of tea before her, and her dark eyes fixed upon Matthew as he entered. She said nothing but watched his every movement as he pulled out a chair and sat down opposite.

'Good morning, Miss Bird,' he said, thinking how inaccurate that greeting was. 'I'm Inspector Stannard. How are you feeling?'

'I'm perfectly well,' Miss Bird said, adding, 'thank you.'

'I'm going to have to ask you some questions.'

'Of course you must, inspector, and I will answer you as best I can.'

'Thank you. You discovered Mr Foucault's body at five to eight, I understand?'

'Yes. I had prepared his breakfast.' Her gaze shifted to the tray at the end of the table with its untouched breakfast. 'I took it up to his bedroom as usual. He wasn't there, which I thought was very odd indeed. He wasn't in the bathroom either. So I brought the tray back downstairs and remembered I'd seen the light on in his study. I thought he'd gone to bed having forgotten to switch it off, so I went in to do so, and saw—' She paused and took a deep breath.

'You're doing extremely well, Miss Bird,' Matthew said encouragingly.

She ran a finger over a severely plucked eyebrow. 'I saw Mr Foucault at his bureau. I thought he was working, and I went over and saw that he was, in fact, dead.'

'When did you see him last?'

'At nine last night when I went upstairs to my room.'

'Is nine your normal hour for retiring?'

'Around nine, yes. I tidy the kitchen after dinner and then go up, usually no later than nine-thirty. I don't like to intrude upon Mr Foucault's leisure hours.'

'Where is your room?'

'At the top of the house.'

'Far enough away not to hear anything that might happen on the ground floor?'

'Mr Foucault was never one for making a noise, inspector. But no. I would never be able to hear him when he was playing music on the gramophone, for instance.'

'Was he playing music last night?'

'He was. Mozart's *The Magic Flute*.'

'And what was he doing when you retired?'

'He was working at his bureau.'

'Was he expecting any visitors?'

'I don't believe so. He never said he was.'

'And he would have said so?'

'He would usually have me open a bottle of wine or provide food if he was expecting guests. And I think it unlikely he would have been working if he was expecting company. He always made a point of closing the bureau if he had guests.'

240

'Had Mr Foucault been to bed last night?'

'No. The bed was as I had left it. I turned it down before retiring.'

'Do you know if Mr Foucault had had an argument with anyone?'

'You're asking if Mr Foucault had any enemies who might wish to kill him?' Miss Bird's tone was almost incredulous.

'I am,' Matthew admitted.

'I knew very little about Mr Foucault's private life and nothing about his professional, inspector, but I cannot believe that anyone would wish him harm. He was a very decent man.'

Matthew nodded, wondering how Miss Bird's opinion of Adrian Foucault could be so different from what Dickie Waite had told him.

'I'd like you to take a look at the kitchen knives, Miss Bird,' he said. 'Can you tell me if any are missing or out of place?'

Miss Bird rose and pulled out a drawer from one of the kitchen cupboards. 'No, all the knives are here, as I left them.' She closed the drawer and turned to Matthew. Her face changed. She looked back at the drawer, realised why Matthew had asked about the knives, and shivered.

Matthew got to his feet. 'Thank you, Miss Bird. You've been extremely helpful. We'll be in the house for quite some time, but I'd like you to remain in case I need to talk to you again.'

Miss Bird gave a brisk nod. 'I'll be here should you need me, inspector.'

Matthew sent Denham out to question the neighbours while he returned to the study. Wallace had gone and the photographer was packing his equipment away. He assured Matthew he would have the prints developed straight away. The mortuary van turned up a few minutes later and Matthew watched as two men placed Foucault on a stretcher and carried him out of the house.

Matthew had Foucault's study all to himself. He sat down in the chair Foucault had been sitting in, checking there wasn't any blood on the green leather or polished wood, and looked down at the papers the dead man had been working on. It was a trial brief and Foucault had been making notes, underlining words in a witness statement, writing down questions to raise. Matthew set these papers aside and opened the bureau's cubby holes.

He found money, notes rolled up with a rubber band, and a lot of papers. Many were bills and receipts for household and personal items, but there were also a lot to do with the barrister's work. Matthew found a large red account ledger and his eyes widened in disbelief at the fees Foucault had charged for his services. He set this to one side and continued his examination.

His interest deepened when he came upon a smaller account ledger, tucked away at the back of the top drawer as if it had been hidden there. What piqued Matthew's interest more than the figures written in the right-hand column was the fact that the entries describing the payments appeared to have been written in some kind of shorthand. To his eyes, it looked a lot like code. He searched for Foucault's bank statements, found them neatly filed in a large folder, and drew them out to cross-reference against the sums in the large red ledger. The figures didn't quite match. The amounts were all there, but there were additional sums on the statement, all round figures – fifty pounds, eighty pounds, and on one occasion, one hundred and twenty pounds. The reference showed the amounts had been paid into the account in person and in cash.

Matthew searched the desk for invoices, found them filed neatly in a folder in the bottom drawer. He found the ones for the current year and checked them against the incoming amounts on the statement. They were all accounted for.

'So, what were these other payments for?' Matthew murmured, thinking of what Dickie had told him about The Five.

He rifled through a pile of papers he found pushed to the back of the bureau. More bills, some letters. Matthew was about to put them back when his finger brushed over the metal of a paperclip and he drew out the sheet of paper it was attached to. Beneath the paperclip was a midnight blue matchbook with 'The Twilight Club' printed on the front, and beneath that a letterhead bearing the same name but with the addition of a Soho address and telephone number. The letterhead was blank save for a handwritten inscription that took up half the page. It read: *Adrian, old chap. What do you think of this? Charles.*

Matthew frowned. There was something about the handwriting that was familiar, but he couldn't immediately place it. He scanned down to the bottom to a series of typewritten names: 'Owners: Charles Calthrop, Adrian Foucault, Archibald Ballantyne, Christopher Fairbank. Donald Spencer, Eric Hailes'.

His breath caught in his throat. Calthrop, Fairbank, Foucault, in partnership together and all dead!

'Sir?'

Matthew jumped. He hadn't heard Denham come into the room.

'Yes, Denham, what is it?'

'Nothing from the neighbours. No one saw or heard anything last night.' He glanced at the bureau. 'Anything interesting in the desk, sir?'

'Yes. Very.' Matthew gathered up the ledgers and the other papers of interest. 'I'm taking these back to the station.'

Thomas Yates was waiting for Matthew in the station's entrance lobby. 'I need a word in private, inspector,' he said miserably.

Matthew could have done without Yates just then, but he nodded and took the elderly treasurer into the private room. He set Foucault's paperwork on the table. 'What's this about, Mr Yates?'

Yates passed him a brown envelope. 'Daphne Fairbank gave this to my wife last night at the club. She asked if I would give it to you.'

Matthew took the envelope and peered inside. 'Photographs?' he said to Yates, tipping the envelope up so the prints dropped into his hand.

'I'm afraid so.'

Matthew's eyebrow rose as he took in the topmost photograph. It showed a naked Christopher Fairbank in sexual congress with a woman. Matthew recognised the room. It was the same bedroom he'd been killed in. He shuffled through the other pictures. They were all of Fairbank in similar situations.

'My wife, fortunately, didn't look inside the envelope,' Yates said. 'I looked because I wanted to know what Daphne Fairbank was involving me in.'

'Mr Fairbank is in all of these,' Matthew said, shuffling through them again. 'But there's a different woman in each. Do you know any of these women?'

Yates nodded. 'I'm afraid I know all of them, inspector. They are all members of the Empire Club.'

Chapter Thirty-Two

It had taken Dickie all day to regain his composure. He'd always known he wasn't a particularly brave man, but he hadn't realised just how much of a coward he was until the brick had come through his window. He'd heard stories from other reporters over the years of how they'd been threatened when they'd been chasing a story and they'd boasted of how they just got on with the job. Had that been hollow boasting? Dickie wondered as he walked down the high street.

But now Dickie's fear had passed, mutated into a kind of defiance, an anger that Ballantyne thought he could get away with scaring him and his wife. If Ballantyne had thought such a threat would frighten him off, he was in for a rude surprise. With Edwards backing him up, Dickie was ready to do all he could to expose Ballantyne and his friends.

Dickie caught the eye of a woman leaning against a shop doorway. She looked frozen half to death, not surprising considering what she was wearing – a thin print dress, more suited to spring than winter, and a shabby coat – and there was no meat on her bones to insulate her.

'Hello, duckie,' she said, the smile she gave him getting

nowhere near her sunken eyes. 'Looking for company, are you?'

'Looking for a lady,' he said, realising lady was not the right word for the kind of woman he was hoping to find. 'Betty Trantor?'

Her eyes narrowed. 'You police?'

Dickie shook his head. 'No, nothing like that. I'd just like to talk to her about something. Do you know where I can find her?'

'Well, I shouldn't,' the woman said, looking him up and down, then raising an eyebrow suggestively.

It took Dickie a moment to work out what she wanted. He dug into his coat pocket and pulled out a handful of coins. He showed them to her. 'It's all I've got, love,' he lied.

She scooped the coins out of his hand. 'She'll be down there in the bank doorway. That's her spot. Don't you tell her I told you where to find her, though.'

Dickie promised he wouldn't and set off towards the bank. As he drew near, he saw a woman standing just outside. She smiled at him as she approached. 'Hello, darling. You—'

'You don't have to do that,' Dickie said, holding up his hand. 'I'm not a punter. Are you Betty Trantor?'

The woman straightened. 'Who wants to know?'

'I'm not the police. My name's Dickie Waite and I'm a reporter.' He reached out to her as Betty turned away. 'Please. I've come here specifically to meet you.'

She turned back to him. 'Why?'

'I met an old friend of yours. Harry Cole. You used to work with him at the Empire Club.'

Betty shook her head. 'I don't want to talk about that place. Harry shouldn't have told you about me. Bugger off, will you? Leave me alone.'

'I'm trying to expose them. The Five. Please talk to me, Miss Trantor. There are things I think only you can tell me.'

246

She bit her lip, still undecided but at least willing to listen.

'Let me buy you a drink,' he pleaded. 'You must be freezing. Let's go in the pub over there and have a chat. Yes?'

Betty looked towards the pub. It was an inviting prospect, Dickie hoped, with its sound of cheerful voices and the yellow glow of its lights. Better than standing out in the cold.

'All right, then,' Betty said.

'Thank you,' Dickie said, and gestured her towards the pub.

Dickie got a gin and orange for Betty, a whisky for himself. Betty cupped the glass with hands white with cold, and closed her eyes in pleasure as she took a mouthful and the alcohol warmed her throat.

'Better?' Dickie asked.

'A bit,' she acknowledged, and took another mouthful. 'So, what do you want to ask me?'

'What happened to you at the Empire Club,' Dickie said. 'How it made you end up like this.'

'What did Harry tell you?'

'Just that you were one kind of girl when he knew you at the Empire Club and now you're this.' He gestured at her. 'He doesn't know what happened exactly. Just that you were at one of The Five's private parties.'

Betty twisted the glass on the coaster. 'It's not easy for me to talk about. I mean, I ain't never told anyone, not what really happened. I'm not sure I can.'

'I'd appreciate it if you'd try.' Dickie reached into his pocket and took out his wallet. 'I can give you something for your time.'

He waited for her to say no, not really expecting a refusal, and she didn't make one. Hiding the ten-shilling note beneath his fingers, he slid it across the table to her. There was no mistaking what Betty Trantor was, and he didn't want people thinking he was paying for more than her time.

Betty put the note in her handbag. 'Are you really going to write about them?'

Dickie nodded. 'But I don't need to mention your name in the newspaper, if that's what's worrying you. You'll just be a source, that's all.' He didn't add that if anything came of his article, if the police decided to get involved, that he would probably have to give her name to them. 'Wouldn't it feel good to tell what happened to you? To get back at them?'

'Easy for you to say,' Betty laughed hollowly. 'All right. I'll tell you. You can't think any worse of me than you do already, I suppose.' She took another mouthful of her gin and orange. 'I was asked by Mr Yates – he's the treasurer of the club – if I wanted to wait at table for some of the members in the private room upstairs after hours. These members had given me decent tips, so I jumped at the chance to earn some extra money. I said yes, me and this other girl.' She took a deep breath. 'The private dinner was late, around ten o'clock. The kitchen staff prepared all the food. Me and the other girl just had to serve it. Which we did and everything was all right. We cleared the table and took all the crockery and cutlery downstairs to wash up. One of them, the big one, Mr Ballantyne, said to come back up when we'd done. He didn't say what for, and to be honest, we didn't give it a second thought, just said we would.

'Everyone else had gone by the time we went up. We went into the dining room, and they were all drinking. Two of them were taking drugs. I don't know what kind, but they had lines of white powder on the dining table and they were sniffing it up their noses. Mr Ballantyne told us we'd been so good, we deserved a drink. He gave us champagne and it was nice. I hadn't had champagne before and I liked it. We had another and another, and... well, I suppose we got a little tipsy. The girl I was with had gone over to the two taking the drugs, and they got her to take some. She got really silly, I mean, falling about all over the place and talking like there was no tomorrow. I started to feel sick and said I'd had enough and that I was going to go home. That was when Mr Ballantyne grabbed me and said I wasn't going anywhere.

'I tried to get away, but his friend, Mr Fairbank, took hold of my ankles, and then I was practically turned upside down. My head was spinning. I remember him throwing me down on the dining table and someone grabbing hold of my wrists. My knickers were pulled off and...' she looked up at Dickie defiantly, 'he did it to me. I remember screaming and him putting a hand over my mouth to shut me up. When he'd finished, they swapped places, and Mr Ballantyne did it to me too. I was hurting so much, all I could do was cry. I remember looking over to my friend, wondering why she wasn't helping me, and she was on the other end of the table, with that Spencer on top of her. I don't think she was awake, though. She didn't know what was being done to her.' Betty sniffed and tilted her head back. Dickie had seen his wife do the same thing when she was trying not to cry. 'We were there all night. They all took their turn with us. Then they left, laughing. I couldn't stay at the club, not after that, but I had trouble getting another job. When I did, I usually messed it up until no one would give me a character reference. So, all I could do to earn a living was to go on the streets. Charge for what they took from me.'

'I'm so sorry,' Dickie said, his stomach turning at the story she'd told. He'd suspected it would be something of this sort. Sex and booze. The men doing what they wanted. 'Did you never think of going to the police? Reporting them for rape?'

She smiled ruefully. 'Do you honestly think I would have

been believed? They would have denied it ever happened or said I was drunk and wanted it.'

Dickie nodded. Betty was right. The Five would be believed before her. 'What happened to your friend?'

'She died, I heard, after she tried to get rid of the baby one of them gave her.' Betty finished her drink. 'So, are you going to write about me and what they did?'

'I am,' Dickie said.

'Much good it'll do. It won't make any difference, Mr Waite. They're untouchable.'

'I'm going to try and change that,' he said. He glanced up and saw a man at the bar watching them. 'Someone you know?' he asked.

Betty turned in the direction he nodded. 'Yeah,' she said, her unease returning. 'That's Jack. He takes care of me. He'll be wondering what I'm doing here, talking to you, instead of working.'

Dickie understood. Jack was her pimp. 'I don't want to get you into trouble, so I'll be off now. Thanks for talking to me. I know it can't have been easy.'

'Nothing's easy for me, Mr Waite,' Betty said. 'Not since that night.'

It was cold in the Gents and not even the overcoat Norman wore was keeping him warm any longer. He'd lost his suitcase, stolen from him while he slept on a park bench, and so he had nothing left. He needed to eat, and to eat, he needed money. And to get money, he had to do what he had hoped he would never have to do again.

Norman had been waiting in the public lavatory for twenty minutes, waiting for someone who wanted what he was offering and was willing to pay. There had been an uncomfortable moment, when he'd thought he'd correctly read a signal and moved into the cubicle to wait. But the man hadn't followed him in. He'd poked his head back out to discover why not, and the man was still standing where he'd left him, frowning at Norman. Had he changed his mind or was he not the kind of man Norman had thought he was? Norman's heart had banged painfully in his chest. This was a danger moment, he knew. If he'd got it wrong, he could end up black and blue. He didn't want to go through that again. But he was lucky. The man turned on his heel and hurried out of the public convenience, and Norman breathed again.

There had been two other men, men who had come in to urinate and had watched Norman with suspicion as they washed their hands before leaving. He was thinking of giving up when his luck turned. A man came in, glanced at Norman in the mirror, and Norman knew this time he'd read the signal right. He went into the cubicle and the man's footsteps slapped on the wet tiled floor, coming closer until he was inside with Norman. Norman asked what he wanted and the man told him. Norman named a price – not too much nor, he hoped, too little – and the man agreed.

Halfway through the deed, black booted feet appeared in the gap at the bottom of the cubicle door. Norman's companion pushed him away, cursing and desperately rear-ranging his clothing.

'They're in here,' a voice said.

'All right. Get 'em out,' said another.

A fist pounded on the door. 'Come on, you two. Out you come.'

Norman put his hands flat against the door. He shook his head at his companion, feeling tears pricking at his eyes. He didn't want to go out there.

'Out!' the voice bellowed. 'Police!'

Norman whimpered as his companion pulled him out of the way and unlocked the door. 'Constable,' he heard him say. 'Thank goodness you're here. This man,' he pointed at Norman, 'followed me into the cubicle—'

'Yeah, yeah. Tell it to the judge,' the constable said, turning the man around and clapping the irons on him.

A sergeant came up to the cubicle where Norman was cowering. 'Time to face the music, chum. Come on.' He reached in and grabbed hold of Norman's sleeve, pulling him out.

'Let me go. Please,' Norman begged, the tears flowing freely.

'Enough of that,' the sergeant snapped. 'Don't make it difficult for yourself.'

But Norman kept his hands behind his back, jerking them away when the sergeant reached for them to put on the hand-cuffs. The sergeant, patience spent, shoved Norman against the wall. 'Behave yourself,' he shouted, the words bouncing off the tiled walls. Norman winced and surrendered. The cuffs were put on. 'What's your name?' the sergeant demanded as he searched Norman.

'Luke Williams,' Norman said.

The sergeant pulled out a crumpled, dirty handkerchief from Norman's trouser pocket, made a sound of disgust and stuffed it back. He found Norman's wallet and opened it. 'Broke, are you?' he said, as he opened the notes section and found it empty save for a wrinkled photograph of a man and a woman posing against a front door in old-fashioned clothing, a little boy standing between them. He found a library card and studied it. 'Luke Williams, eh?' he said, raising an eyebrow at Norman. 'So, what you doing with a library card for Norman Kelly?'

Norman didn't answer. The sergeant frowned. 'Are you

Norman Kelly?' He gave Norman a shove to encourage him to answer.

Norman nodded.

'Well, well. Half the police in East London are looking for you, chum,' he said, grabbing Norman's arm and pushing him towards the exit. 'There's an inspector who's going to be very pleased to see you.'

Chapter Thirty-Three

Matthew hurried down the stairs to reach the telephone before Mr Levitt was roused. 'Hello?' he panted as he checked his wristwatch. It was twenty to two. He'd only been asleep for an hour and a half.

'Inspector Stannard? Sergeant Richards here. Sorry to disturb you so late, but I thought you'd want to know. We just had a call in from Leytonstone nick. They've picked up Norman Kelly.'

Thank God, Matthew mouthed, closing his eyes in silent prayer. Now, Mullinger might get off his back. He'd given Matthew a mouthful when he'd found out about Foucault's murder, accusing him of being lax in finding the killer and how Matthew was in danger of undermining the public's faith in the police. Matthew had endured it all without saying a word, not that the superintendent had given him any opportunity to speak.

'They found him in a Gents lavvie,' Sergeant Richards went on, 'doing you know what. So, they're charging him with that and then they say you can have him. Do you want me to make the arrangements to bring him here in the morning?'

'Yes, I do,' Matthew said, wide awake now. 'And let the other stations know he's been found so they don't waste any time looking for him.'

'Will do,' Richards said.

'Middle of the bleeding night again,' Mr Levitt said as Matthew hung up the telephone. 'What d'ya have to say about that?'

'Nothing, Mr Levitt.'

'Nothing?' Mr Levitt cried as Matthew climbed the stairs. 'Not even a bleeding apology for getting me out of bed? You listening to me, Stannard?'

Matthew closed his front door and sank back against the wood, listening as Levitt muttered and shuffled back into his flat. He didn't care what the grumpy old sod said. Kelly had been caught and Matthew had found his killer. Mullinger would be satisfied and everyone at the station would stop wondering whether he was up to being an inspector.

He climbed back into bed, not noticing the chill of the sheets as he pulled them up to his armpits. Closing his eyes, he tried to get back to sleep, but it was no use. His brain was too busy trying to put all the pieces of his investigation together.

At 5 a.m., Matthew gave up. He rose, washed and dressed and made breakfast. While he ate his porridge, he worked out all the questions he would need to ask Norman Kelly later that morning.

Mullinger held the receiver to his ear, a smile playing upon his lips.

'Archie?' he cried when the connection was made. 'Howard Mullinger here… Yes… Sorry to call you so early, but I wanted to pass on the good news. The waiter has been caught… That's right…. Yes, he'll be questioned this

morning and I'll get my man to charge him by this afternoon…. So, you can rest easy now, old chap… Not at all. The
least I can do…Yes. That would be lovely. Goodbye.'

He set the receiver in the cradle and smiled to himself.
He'd be a member of the Empire Club before the week
was out.

Chapter Thirty-Four

Matthew's first impression of Norman Kelly was that he didn't look like a killer.

Kelly sat huddled in his chair, his overcoat collar pulled up, his chin sunken into it. He looked up at Matthew and Denham furtively as they entered the interview room as if he was expecting to be hit.

'Mr Kelly,' Matthew began, taking a seat at the table opposite, 'I'm Detective Inspector Matthew Stannard and this is Detective Sergeant Justin Denham. Do you understand why you're here?'

'I didn't do anything.' The words came out cracked and quiet.

'Well, that's not true, is it, Mr Kelly? You were arrested by the other officers because you were caught performing an illegal act on another man in a public place.'

'No, that wasn't… it was a mistake.'

Matthew heard Denham snort.

'The man you were with has admitted the offence,' Matthew said, reading from the notes the arresting officers had given Denham. 'He has subsequently been charged and released.'

Norman looked up, his eyes widening. 'So, if I admit what we were doing, I'll be released too?'

Matthew shook his head. 'You'll be charged for that offence. However, I need to ask you questions about other matters, Mr Kelly.'

'What other matters?'

'Relating to the Empire Club and some of its members.'

Norman sighed. 'All right. I admit I took the cigarettes and this.' He tore the overcoat off and threw it on the table. 'So, just charge me for theft or whatever it is and let me go. Please.'

'What are you talking about?' Denham said. 'Stealing cigarettes and a coat?'

Norman looked from Matthew to Denham and back again. 'I took them from the club. I wasn't going to go back there, not after what they did to me, and I took some packets of cigarettes from the stores and that coat. It had been hanging up in the cloakroom for weeks. No one wanted it, so I took it. I didn't see anything wrong with that.'

Denham removed the overcoat from the table, folding it up and laying it over his knees.

'You're not here because of theft, Mr Kelly,' Matthew said. 'You're here to answer questions about the murders of Christopher Fairbank and Adrian Foucault.'

Norman's eyes grew wide. 'They're dead?' he gasped.

'Oh, Jesus,' Denham said impatiently. 'You know they are. You killed them.'

Matthew nudged Denham beneath the table with his foot to keep his mouth shut. Denham was there to take notes, not to talk to Kelly, certainly not to make bold statements and provoke their main suspect. Denham got the hint. He cleared his throat and began scribbling in his notebook.

Matthew reread Denham's report of his conversation with

Mrs Coggs. 'Where were you between 12.30 a.m. and 7 a.m. Saturday morning, Mr Kelly?'

Norman still looked stunned by Denham's words and it took him a moment to answer. 'I was at home,' he said.

'We've spoken to your neighbour, Mrs Coggs. She says you didn't come in until half-past three in the morning. You woke her up.'

'No, she's wrong,' Norman said, looking away. 'I was in bed.'

'She also said you came in crying at half-past three. Why were you crying, Mr Kelly?'

'I was upset.'

'What about?'

'I don't want to talk about it.'

'Was it because you'd been humiliated at the Empire Club?'

Norman looked up at Matthew. 'You know what happened?'

Matthew nodded. 'That must have been a horrible experience. What did you do after they let you go?'

'I hid in the lavatory. I couldn't face anyone. I wanted to be left alone.'

'How long did you stay in the lavatory?'

'I don't know. Until it went quiet.'

'An hour? Two?'

'I don't know. I just waited until everyone had gone.'

Matthew flipped through the pages in his file to the section on Foucault. 'Where were you on Monday night, Mr Kelly?'

'Just around.'

'Around in Craynebrook?'

Norman shook his head.

'You weren't at home,' Matthew pointed out. 'And you

were picked up by the police in Leytonstone, which isn't that far away.'

'I wasn't here,' Norman said. 'I wouldn't come back here.'

'Were you with anyone who could confirm your whereabouts on Monday night?'

'No. I wasn't with anyone. I stayed away from people until last night when I went into the Gents.'

Matthew sighed silently. Norman Kelly might not have anyone to corroborate his whereabouts for both murders, but neither did Matthew have any evidence that put him at the scene of either crime. He had a feeling he would have to keep on at Norman Kelly with his questions until he gave in and confessed to killing Fairbank and Foucault.

If he killed them, Matthew reminded himself. He was experiencing feelings of doubt. Kelly had every reason and opportunity to kill those men, and yet he'd seemed genuinely surprised to hear they were dead. But maybe he was just a good actor. After all, Matthew had no other likely suspects, not since he'd let Andrew Sutton go, and Sophie Sutton had never really been in his sights. Kelly had to be the killer. Matthew just needed to find the evidence to prove it.

'All right, Mr Kelly,' he said, closing his file. 'I'm going to put you back in the cell while we carry out further enquiries. We'll talk again later.'

Chapter Thirty-Five

Lund was in the office when Matthew and Denham returned to CID.

'Kelly coughed yet?' he asked as Matthew threw his file on his desk and lit a cigarette.

'No,' Matthew said. 'He's denying everything. I've put him back in a cell for the time being.'

Lund made a disapproving face, then took a bite out of his slice of toast and wiped away the blackcurrant jam that dribbled down his chin. 'That's just giving him time to pull himself together again. You've got to keep at 'em when they refuse to talk. Just hammer away. They always break in the end.'

'I know,' Matthew nodded, knowing Lund was right. 'But I prefer to have evidence that they can't argue with.'

'And you haven't got it against Kelly?'

'There's no fingerprint evidence. Nothing to prove he was in the bedroom at the club or at Foucault's house. He wasn't carrying a knife when he was picked up and he had no money on him.'

'So what?' Lund shrugged. 'He wore gloves and got rid of the knife.'

'Maybe,' Matthew conceded, 'but then, if he was broke, surely he would have taken something from Foucault's house to sell? Or taken the money from his desk? There was plenty in there.'

'Maybe he's an idiot,' Lund muttered.

'Or maybe he didn't do it.' As soon as Matthew spoke his thought aloud, he wished he hadn't.

Lund stared at him, toast halted on its way to his mouth. 'You're not actually thinking that, are you? What other suspects you got? I heard you let that Sutton bloke go because you had nothing on him. You let the wife off without even blinking. If you don't pin the murders on this Kelly, you'll be back to square one.'

'I know,' Matthew muttered unhappily as his telephone rang. He snatched up the receiver. 'Stannard…' He sighed. 'All right, Miss Halliwell. I'll come right up.'

'The Super wants you?' Lund asked.

Matthew nodded and stubbed out his cigarette.

Matthew knocked on the door and poked his head inside. 'You wanted to see me, sir?'

'Yes, Stannard,' Mullinger said, setting down his fountain pen and leaning back in his chair. 'You have this Norman Kelly in custody. Why haven't you interviewed him yet?'

'I have interviewed him, sir,' Matthew frowned.

'No, you haven't,' Mullinger retorted. 'He's downstairs in a cell.'

'That's right, sir. He's there while I make further enquiries.'

'Do you mean to say you've interviewed him and not charged him? What the devil are you playing at, Stannard?'

'Mr Kelly is denying the murders, sir,' Matthew said.

'And I don't have the evidence at present to prove he is guilty.'

'Don't talk nonsense. He absconded from his lodgings as soon as he knew we were after him. Of course he's guilty.' Mullinger flicked his hand at the door. 'Charge him.'

'I can't do that, sir,' Matthew said. 'Not yet.'

Mullinger glared at him. 'Stannard,' he said after a tense moment, 'I've told Archie Ballantyne we will have charged Kelly by no later than this afternoon. I trust you're not going to make a liar of me?'

'You told Mr Ballantyne…?' Matthew stared at the superintendent. 'I don't understand. Why would you do that?'

'He asked to be kept informed,' Mullinger said indignantly.

'Sir,' Matthew cried, 'Mr Ballantyne shouldn't have been told anything at all. And as for charging Kelly, I can only do that after I've questioned him and I have the evidence to prove he's guilty.'

Mullinger banged his hand down on the desk. 'He is guilty. Kelly had the motive, he had the opportunities, and he had the means for both murders. He is a criminal and a degenerate. What more do you need?'

'Evidence,' Matthew shot back. 'Proof he committed the murders.'

Mullinger rose from behind his desk. His body blocked out the light coming in from the window. 'You are treading on very thin ice with me, inspector,' he snarled. 'Now, I am telling you to charge Norman Kelly with both murders and you will do it or I will have you thrown out of this force before you can blink. Is that understood?'

Blood was rushing in Matthew's ears. His hands were curling into fists at his side. 'Understood,' he said.

. . .

'Well, what did the Super say?' Lund asked as Matthew stormed back into the office.

'Mind your own business,' Matthew snapped, dragging out his chair and dropping into it.

'Oh dear,' Lund said with a chuckle. 'Didn't go well, did it? What did he do? Read you the Riot Act?'

'He told me to charge Kelly,' Matthew said. 'It doesn't matter, apparently, whether I can prove he's guilty. He's decided Kelly is guilty and that's enough.'

'He's the boss, Stannard,' Lund said, picking up the telephone. 'End of the day, that's all it comes down to.'

'You mean you'd charge Kelly? Without any evidence?'

'Bloody right I would,' Lund said with a shrug. 'He probably is guilty. And I'd rather do what the Super says than refuse and have him against me.'

'And what if Kelly's innocent?' Matthew asked.

'Then he'll be acquitted at trial, won't he? It won't be your problem. You'll have done your job. Do what the Super wants. Charge the bastard and move on. After all, you've still got that other killing to clear up, haven't you?' Lund rubbed his stomach. 'Think I'll pop out and get myself a bun. Do you want anything?'

Matthew shook his head. As Lund left, Denham entered. 'Should I give Kelly back his overcoat, sir? It's cold in the cells.'

Matthew shook his head. 'He said it wasn't his. We should have it returned to its rightful owner. Have a look inside. See if there's a name in it.'

Denham held the overcoat up to look. 'No name. Just the tailor's label. Rose & Harper. Maybe I should—'

'What did you say?' Matthew sat up and held out his hand for the overcoat. Denham gave it to him and Matthew stared at the label.

'What is it, sir?' Denham asked.

Matthew searched his In tray for the file on his conman. Finding it, he rifled through the pages until he came to the report he'd filed of his conversation with Adam Gibson.

'What is it?' Denham asked again.

'This is our conman's overcoat,' Matthew cried. 'Mr Gibson said Rupert Caine bought an overcoat as well as the tails. And—' He jumped up from his chair, pushed Denham aside and hurried over to the evidence box that held the personal belongings of the conman. He found the wristwatch with the engraving. 'Signed by N,' Matthew said, showing it to Denham.

'You think Kelly gave him that watch?' Denham asked.

Matthew read and reread the engraving. 'Get Kelly back in the interview room, Denham. I've got more questions to ask him.'

Chapter Thirty-Six

Matthew lit a cigarette and patted the overcoat folded on the table. 'You claim you stole this overcoat from the cloakroom at the Empire Club? Do you know who it belonged to?'

Norman shook his head.

'Do you know a man called Charles Calthrop?'

'No.'

'Rupert Caine? Stephen Carter? Cyril Pargeter?'

'I don't know any of those names.'

'What about this?' Matthew put the wristwatch in front of Norman. 'Do you recognise this watch?'

Norman shook his head.

Matthew turned the watch over. 'There's an engraving. You see it's signed 'N'. Is that you, Mr Kelly?'

'No. I don't know anything about a watch.'

'Did you argue with the man you gave this watch to?'

'I didn't. Why would I give a man a watch?'

'Because you were friends,' Matthew said. 'Or more than friends?'

Norman put his hands to his face. 'Stop. Please.'

'What was his real name?'

'Who?'

'The man whose body you dumped on the common.'

'What? I didn't—'

'Why did you kill him?'

'I don't know what you're talking about. Stop asking me all these questions. I haven't done anything.'

'Did he humiliate you like the others? Like Fairbank and Foucault? Is that why you killed him?'

Norman banged both his fists down on the table. 'STOP IT!' he screamed. 'I didn't kill anyone. Go away. Leave me alone. I'm not talking to you anymore. '

He twisted around on his chair, turning his back to Matthew and Denham, and his body began to shudder with his sobs.

Matthew slammed the file shut and scraped back his chair. He yanked the door open and strode out, biting the inside of his cheek to stop himself from shouting in frustration.

'I reckon he did it,' Denham said as he handed Matthew a cup of tea. He'd put Norman back in the cell, still crying, and put the overcoat in the evidence box.

Matthew knocked his cigarette against the ashtray. 'Why?'

'Why do I think he did it?'

'Why would he kill them?' Matthew pointed Denham to the chair.

'The first one, the conman.' Denham shrugged. 'Lovers' tiff? The other two because of what they did to him.'

'Why so different? They were killed in different ways,' Matthew explained when Denham frowned. 'The conman was bashed on the head. Fairbank and Foucault with a knife.'

'He used whatever came to hand.'

Matthew shook his head. 'He doesn't have a car. Never

even had a licence. How did he get the body to the common? Who was the other person who helped him dump the body? How did he know Foucault was at home on Monday? And why Foucault? Foucault was a bystander when the others pulled his trousers down. Why not kill Ballantyne next? There's too many things that don't add up.'

'You are going to charge him, though, aren't you, sir?'

Matthew took a long drag on his cigarette. 'Not yet.'

Denham opened his mouth to speak, then muttered, 'Christ,' and got to his feet. Matthew turned his head to see what had alarmed the sergeant, and quickly stubbed out his cigarette and got to his feet too.

'Well?' Mullinger demanded before he'd even got through the door.

Matthew jerked his head at Denham to get out, grateful he closed the door after him. 'I'm not convinced of Kelly's guilt, sir.'

'You mean you haven't charged him,' Mullinger nodded. His neck had turned purple. 'Despite everything I said.'

'I'm sorry, sir, but I can't charge a man for three murders unless I'm certain he's guilty.'

'Three murders?'

Matthew cursed himself for letting that slip. 'There appears to be a connection between Norman Kelly and the man found on the common. I don't know the nature of that connection yet, but…'

'Are you telling me you can clear up all three murders with one charge? And you haven't charged him?'

'Sir, I can't—'

Mullinger cut him off. 'I'm going to show you something.' He held up the *Evening Standard* he had been clutching and showed the front page to Matthew. 'Read it,' he barked. '"Three murders. Police baffled." Craynebrook is in the national newspapers, Stannard. This article claims

Craynebrook residents are living in fear. We are being ridiculed.' He threw the newspaper on Matthew's desk. 'I won't have my station dragged through the dirt because of you. I am giving you one last chance. Charge him.'

Matthew's heart was banging in his chest. He took a deep breath. 'No, sir.'

The purple hue of his neck rose to flood Mullinger's face. He looked as if he was about to burst. He turned and yanked the door open. 'LUND!' he yelled, and the portly detective came running in from the corridor.

'Yes, sir?'

'I want you to interview Norman Kelly. Don't let him out of that interview room until you have his confession.'

Lund shot a look at Matthew. 'I thought Norman Kelly was DI Stannard's case.'

'Not any more,' Mullinger said. 'It's yours. When it's done, Lund, come and tell me.'

'Yes, sir,' Lund said as Mullinger strode out.

Chapter Thirty-Seven

Donald Spencer closed his office door, telling his secretary, who was hovering with her notepad, that he wasn't taking calls. He picked up his telephone and gave a number to the operator. He drummed his fingers impatiently on the blotter as he waited to be connected.

'Don?' Ballantyne answered. 'Why are you calling me at work?'

'I've just heard that bloody reporter is still sniffing around.'

'But I thought you dealt with him. Didn't you say—'

'I put a brick through his window, Archie, but he's still working on a story about us.'

'How do you know?'

'Someone I know told me one of his tarts was in The Dog and Duck in Stratford having a drink with the reporter. He thought he was a punter at first, but it became obvious he wasn't interested in a bit of How's-Your-Father. He was getting her to talk.'

'And did she?'

'Oh, yes. My friend said she was jabbering away.'

'How does your friend know it was the reporter?'

'Because he asked the tart who he was and she told him. Said the reporter was writing a piece on prostitutes and wanted to talk to some of the girls.'

'Who was the tart?'

'That one we had at the club a year or so ago. One of the waitresses.'

'I don't remember.'

'I know who she is. I've used her a few times.'

'Well, shut her mouth, for Christ's sake,' Ballantyne said, his voice rising with alarm. When he spoke again, it was lower, as if he'd realised he could be overhead. 'But be discreet, Don. Don't do anything that will draw attention to us.'

'I can do that, Archie, don't panic. But shutting one tart's mouth might not be enough. If this reporter is determined to find out about us, there's any number of people he can talk to. I can't silence them all.'

'For Christ's sake,' Ballantyne said again, and Spencer could picture his friend wiping a face wet with sweat. 'What do we do?'

'I'll deal with the tart,' Spencer said. 'But maybe I should put it around that we're not happy people are blabbing? What do you think?'

'Will it do any good?'

'It can't hurt.'

'I suppose so,' Ballantyne reluctantly agreed. 'I heard from Mullinger this morning that they've got the waiter and they're going to charge him today. We're going to be in the public eye over the next few weeks, so we—'

'Need to behave ourselves,' Spencer chuckled.

'Don,' Ballantyne growled. 'I'm serious. We can't afford to slip up.'

'All right, all right. Keep your hair on. I'll deal with the tart after work.'

'Good. Florence is going out with the girls tonight, so I'll be at the club this evening. Meet me there and tell me what happened.'

'What about Eric?'

There was silence for a few moments as Ballantyne considered. 'Let's leave him out of it. His agitation gets on my nerves and he's no bloody help anyway.'

'Fine. I'll see you tonight,' Spencer said and hung up.

He unlocked his desk drawer and took out an envelope. A prime plot of council land was being sold and at least three property developers wanted to buy it. Inside the envelope was another envelope marked Private and Confidential and addressed 'For the eyes of Donald Spencer only', and inside that was a wad of notes amounting to one hundred pounds. Spencer knew that if he was to do as Ballantyne told him and not make any slip-ups, then he should return the money. But one hundred pounds in his hand was too tempting. He put the money into his briefcase and stamped the property developer's tender with Approved.

Spencer smiled to himself. Ballantyne need never know.

Chapter Thirty-Eight

Matthew had to get out of the station. He couldn't stay in CID, where the other detectives were trying not to look at him, and Lund would come back gloating he'd got Norman Kelly to confess. So, he pocketed the Fairbank photographs Thomas Yates had given him, grabbed his hat and coat, and set off for Soho to explore the only lead he had left – the photographer's stamp.

Matthew discovered Leslie Heller's photographic studio was a dingy, dark room he rented at the back of a bookshop. The books on the shelves at the front of the shop were of the usual kind, the type of material that would appeal to the majority of the reading public. But Matthew knew there would be a section of the bookshop that would have books of interest only to a very specific clientele, the type of reader who preferred illustrations with their stories and would take their purchases out of the shop wrapped in brown paper so the titles couldn't be seen. The bookshop owner didn't quail at the presentation of Matthew's warrant card. Matthew guessed he'd been raided so often, the police held no fear for him anymore. Matthew asked for Leslie Heller and the bookshop owner directed him to the room in the back.

Matthew didn't bother to knock. He opened the door and walked into a room where strips of negatives hung from string tacked from one side to the other, where chemical smells mingled with stale smoke and body odour. Matthew could feel his eyes watering.

'Who are you?' a scrawny, pigeon-chested, lanky haired man of around fifty demanded.

'Police,' Matthew said, looking around. As well as the negatives, there were also photographs hanging from the strings and dripping into trays on a workbench. His lips curled in disgust at the images they depicted.

'Oh, for Christ's sake,' Heller said. 'Can't you lot leave me alone? This is harassment.'

'Calm down, Mr Heller,' Matthew said. 'I'm not here to arrest you. I just want some information.'

'Yeah?' Heller frowned as he wiped his hands on a dirty tea towel. 'What kind of information?'

Matthew passed him the photographs. 'Did you take these?'

Heller shuffled through the prints. 'These were a while ago. I didn't take them. I just developed them for a customer.'

'Who was the customer?'

Heller took a bent cigarette from his top pocket and lit it. 'Can't tell you that,' he said as he blew smoke into the air. 'Client confidentiality, ain't it?'

'Don't give me that,' Matthew said. 'I want the name. If you don't tell me, I will arrest you and you can spend the next twenty-four hours in a cell. And while you're in there, I'll have this room cleared out, your equipment and materials will be put into police storage, and you won't have a business to slither back to.'

Heller snorted. 'You can't do that.'

'I can do that. I'm on a murder enquiry and your name is on important evidence.' Matthew pointed at the photographs.

The photographer stared down at the prints. 'Murder?'

'The man in the photograph has been murdered.'

'Bloody hell,' Heller breathed. 'All right. This fella,' he pointed at Fairbank, 'bought the prints. He gave me the negatives to develop.'

'So, they were his photographs? He took them?'

'I don't know if he took them. I think it was probably his friend who took them. He's the one with the interest.'

'Who was his friend?'

Heller took a deep breath, considering. 'Fella called Adrian Foucault.'

Matthew's breath caught in his throat. 'Adrian Foucault came here with Christopher Fairbank?'

'If Fairbank's the bloke in these prints, yeah. I never knew his name. But Foucault's been coming to me for years.'

'For what, exactly?'

Heller shrugged. 'These sort of pictures. He likes to look. He also helps himself to my equipment when he's taken some snaps he don't want me to see.'

'And you let him?'

'He pays me for it, and I ain't going to say no to the likes of him.'

It all became clear. Foucault had made the peephole at the club. He'd set up a camera in the junk-room. And it was he who had taken the photographs of Fairbank in action, presumably with Fairbank's permission. Had Foucault been there the night Fairbank was killed? Had he taken pictures of Fairbank and Sophie Sutton? And if he had, where were they now?

Matthew took another look around the room, then looked Heller up and down. 'How did Mr Foucault come to be acquainted with someone like you, Mr Heller?'

Heller's lip curled. 'You really don't like me, do you, copper?'

275

'Give me a reason to.'

Heller laughed, not at all offended. 'Everyone around here knows Foucault and his friends. They've got a taste for what Soho offers.'

'The prostitutes?'

'Them,' Heller nodded, 'and more. Foucault and his chums were thinking of setting up in business here.'

Matthew raised an eyebrow in surprise. 'What kind of business?'

'The nightclub kind of business. There was a place just around the corner they was thinking of taking to open up a club. Foucault and the others looked around it and everything. But it must have fallen through because nothing came of it. There's an Itie cafe in there now.'

'Did this nightclub have a name?' Matthew asked, thinking of the letterhead he'd found in Foucault's desk.

'I don't think it got that far.'

'Have you heard of a man called Charles Calthrop?'

Heller's mouth twisted into a pucker. 'Might have done.'

'Have you or not?'

'I've heard of him, yeah.'

'And?'

Heller sighed. 'He's a conman. Goes by a lot of names. Calthrop ain't his real one.'

'I'm aware he had aliases.' Matthew rattled the names off.

'I've heard a couple of those,' Heller nodded. 'Haven't seen him for a long time, though. He ain't been around here.'

'That's because he's dead,' Matthew said. 'He was murdered, his body dumped. So, I need to know what you know about him.'

'Poor sod,' Heller said. 'All right, I'll tell you the one thing I do know and then you can bugger off. Agreed?'

Matthew nodded. 'Agreed.'

'Right then.' Heller threw his spent cigarette away and lit another. 'His real name was Kenneth Croft.'

Chapter Thirty-Nine

Denham picked at his nails as he waited in the corridor outside the interview room.

Blimey, but it had been awkward in CID after the superintendent had left. Denham and the others all looked at each other, eyes wide, waiting for an almighty row to blow up between Lund and Stannard. But there was no row. Lund had gone into the inspectors' office and closed the door. There had been no raised voices, just the murmur of Lund's voice as he spoke to Stannard. Denham had seen Stannard hand over his files, then put on his hat and coat and open the door.

Denham, like Pinder and Barnes, had put his head down and not looked up as Stannard had left the office. They didn't even speak once they were alone. It was all too shocking. None of them quite knew what to say. A few minutes later, Lund had come out of his office and told Denham to put Kelly in the interview room.

So, here Denham was, waiting for Lund to arrive. He straightened as he heard the inspector's heavy footsteps on the stairs.

'He in there, Denham?' Lund asked as he turned into the corridor.

Denham nodded. 'He's still upset, sir.'

Lund made a face like he didn't care. 'He's going to get a lot more upset once I've started on him. Got everything? Good. And if he asks for a cup of tea or a fag, you don't give him one. Right?'

'Right, sir.'

Lund threw the door open. 'Right, Norman. Are you going to save us some time and confess or you going to string this out?' He banged his file down on the table, making Norman jump.

'I didn't do anything,' Norman said, watching Lund warily as he took a seat opposite.

'Well, that's not true, is it? You were picked up for performing an obscene act, which I'm not even going to put into words, it's so disgusting, and you admitted to DI Stannard that you stole cigarettes and an overcoat from the club you worked at.'

'Where is DI Stannard?' Norman asked.

'Not here. I am. So, come on. Tell me why you killed them.'

'I didn't, you bloody bastard—'

Lund slapped Norman hard across the side of his head. 'Talk to me like that again, son, and you'll get worse.' He flipped through the file Matthew had given him. 'So, what we have is you having your revenge on Fairbank and Foucault for pulling your trousers down and showing your knickers, or whatever men like you wear. So, what was the reason for killing the other bloke? The one you left on Craynebrook common?'

'I told Inspector Stannard,' Norman said, holding a hand up to his cheek. 'I had nothing to do with those men. I haven't killed anyone.'

Lund slapped him on the other cheek. 'Wrong answer, Norman. Try again.'

. . .

Donald Spencer turned into the street, his Alvis hugging the kerb. He drove slowly, glancing every now and then at the road ahead, but keeping his gaze on the people walking along the street, and mainly on the women who lingered. He had passed three such women when he saw the one he was searching for. He pulled up and leant over to wind the passenger window down.

Taking her cue, the woman came up to the door and ducked her head inside the open window. 'Want business, luv?' came her automatic question. She broke off, her eyes widening as she realised who sat in the driver's seat.

'Hello, Betty,' Spencer said, giving her a wolfish smile. 'How's tricks?'

'I didn't know it was you, Mr Spencer,' Betty said, and began pulling her head out of the window.

He halted her with a 'Get in.'

'No—,' she began before she could stop herself. 'I mean, I ain't free.'

'Get in,' he said again, the smile gone.

Betty hesitated for a second or two before she opened the passenger door and climbed in.

'Wind the window up,' he said, releasing the handbrake and pulling out into the road. 'Don't want you getting a chill, do we?'

'Where are we going?' Betty asked, clutching her handbag tightly on her lap.

'For a drive,' Spencer answered. He could feel her nervousness and it made him smile. 'So, here's the thing. A little bird has told me you've been blabbing your mouth off, Betty. To a reporter, of all people.'

'I 'aven't been talking, Mr Spencer. I wouldn't.'

'Don't lie to me. You were seen. An old buffer, name of Dickie Waite. He works for *The Chronicle*.'

Betty swallowed. 'Oh, him.' She tried to laugh but it came out false and tremulous. 'He just wanted to find out about the girls, you know. What it's like working on the streets. He's writing something in his 'paper, he said.'

Spencer turned the car into a side street and parked, switching the engine off. He twisted in his seat to face her.

'I thought we was going for a drive,' she said, swallowing.

He took hold of her chin and twisted her head to face him. 'Tell me what he really wanted, Betty. And don't lie this time.'

Betty gave the gentlest of tugs to see if he would release her, then gave up when his fingers gripped tighter. 'He was asking about Mr Ballantyne and Mr Fairbank mostly.'

'What about them?'

'About the parties you have at the club.'

'And what did you tell him?'

'Nothing, really. Just that I'd waitressed at one. I didn't tell him nothing about you, Mr Spencer, I swear.'

'I really hope you're telling me the truth, Betty.'

'I am, Mr Spencer.'

Spencer put his hand inside his overcoat pocket and withdrew a gun. He put the tip of it to Betty's temple. 'Because if I find out you've told him anything you shouldn't, I'm going to put a hole through your pretty head. You understand?'

Tears burst from Betty's eyes. They fell down her cheeks as she nodded.

'Good girl,' Spencer smiled, keeping the gun at her temple for a few seconds longer before putting it back inside his pocket. 'Now, get out.'

Betty fumbled for the door handle and all but fell out of

the car in her hurry. Spencer watched her in the rear-view mirror as she ran down the street and turned out of sight. He'd frightened her enough, he reckoned, to keep her mouth shut from now on.

Chapter Forty

Matthew was feeling dog-tired by the time he put his key in the lock and opened his front door. He was holding his breath, hoping Mr Levitt wouldn't appear and give him an earful. He wasn't sure he would take it with his usual equanimity, and he really didn't want to get into an argument with his cantankerous neighbour. He tiptoed up the stairs to his flat's front door. As he opened it, he heard humming.

'Hello?' he called warily.

'Mattie? That you?'

Matthew relaxed as he recognised his sister's voice. 'Yeah, it's me. What are you doing here?'

Pat poked her head out of a doorway. 'Georgie brought home a load of sausages. There were too many for us to eat before they'd go off, so I thought I'd bring you some.' She frowned. 'You look knackered, Mattie. Are you all right?'

Matthew hung up his hat and coat. 'I'm all right.' *Ask,* he mentally begged. *Please ask me what's wrong.*

'What's happened?' Pat asked. 'No, wait. I've got the kettle on. Go and sit down and you can tell me over a cuppa.'

Matthew obeyed, falling into his armchair and resting his head against the back until Pat bustled in with the tea tray.

His sister had put Garibaldi biscuits on a plate, biscuits he hadn't bought, and knew Pat had done her usual and restocked his frequently bare cupboards.

'Come on, then,' she said, pouring the tea. 'Tell me what's wrong.'

He took the cup and saucer she held out, grateful for her no-nonsense instruction. 'My superintendent took the murder case away from me today. Gave it to the other inspector in front of everyone.'

Pat's face fell. 'Why did he do that?'

'There have been two murders over the last four days, both connected. Two men, members of the same club, close friends. There was an incident at the club where they humiliated a waiter. I sent my sergeant to talk to this waiter, but he did a runner, so it seemed obvious he had something to hide and that he was the killer. There were other possible suspects, but they didn't seem as likely. Anyway, we finally got hold of this waiter and I questioned him.' Matthew sighed as he rubbed his forehead, trying to rub away the ache that had been pounding for hours. 'I have to admit, he still seemed a likely suspect, but I don't know. He just didn't seem a killer.' He shrugged at Pat, unable to explain why. 'I wanted to check up on some of the things he'd told us, but my superintendent told me to charge him. He said he was the killer and everyone wanted to see him charged, so I had to charge him.'

'You refused, didn't you?' Pat nodded knowingly.

'Yeah,' Matthew sighed. 'I wasn't ready to charge him, Pat. And it wouldn't have been fair.'

'Fair?' Pat cried. 'If he was a killer—'

'*If* he was the killer,' Matthew burst out. 'I wasn't convinced. And I can't charge a man when I have doubts about his guilt. After all, he could hang for these killings if I get it wrong.'

'So, are you going to get fired?'

'You don't get fired in this job, not unless you've done something really bad. You get transferred or demoted. I could be knocked back down to Uniform if Mullinger has a mind to.'

'Oh, Mattie.' Pat looked as if she was about to cry.

Matthew mustered a smile. 'Don't worry about me, Pat. I'll be all right.'

'Oh,' she slapped at his hand, 'you always say don't worry, knowing full well I never stop.'

He grinned and reached behind to a cupboard, drawing out a half-empty bottle of whisky.

'What you doing, Mattie?' Pat asked wearily.

'Making the tea a little more interesting,' he said as he poured a drop of the whisky into his cup. 'Want some?'

Pat shook her head. 'Don't get drunk,' she pleaded. 'Especially not alone. It's not the answer.'

'Just something to help me sleep.'

'I'm doing you something to eat,' his sister declared, getting up and heading to the kitchen. He heard her banging a frying pan on the gas ring, and soon, the smell of sizzling sausages filled his nostrils. Within fifteen minutes, Pat presented Matthew with a sausage sandwich dripping with brown sauce.

'Eat that up,' she said, stuffing the cork into the whisky bottle and putting it away. 'I'm not going until it's all gone.'

Matthew ate while Pat went around his small flat tidying, plumping up cushions, stuffing his dirty laundry in the washbag she'd bought with her and washing up the dirty dishes. She came back into the sitting room as he finished the last crust of his sandwich.

She took the empty plate from him. 'I'll 'phone you tomorrow.'

'You don't have to—'

'I will 'phone you tomorrow.'

Matthew nodded, smiling at her insistence. 'Thanks.'

Pat leant over and ruffled his hair, an impulsive, distraction gesture he knew she always did when she was in danger of becoming over-emotional. 'What am I going to do with you?'

It was a question that didn't need an answer. Pat said goodbye and Matthew heard his front door close. He reached back into the cupboard and took out the whisky bottle.

Ballantyne downed the brandy, looked mournfully at the empty glass, and set it down on the table. He raised his arm, clicked his fingers, and Sally Cooke hurried over to the armchair.

'Yes, sir?'

'Another brandy, here, and bring me a cigar.'

'Right away, sir.' Sally left, stepping aside in the doorway to allow Donald Spencer to enter the smoking room.

'Archie?' he called.

Ballantyne peered around the side of his armchair whose high back had been hiding him from view. 'Over here.'

Spencer strode over and sat down on the arm of the chair opposite. 'I've seen the tart. Frightened her enough to keep her mouth shut. She won't be talking to anyone else.'

'Good.'

Spencer wondered at Ballantyne's downcast expression. 'What's the matter?'

Ballantyne turned incredulous eyes upon him. 'What's the matter? Are you serious? Or just simple?'

'It's too bad about Kit and Adrian,' Spencer nodded.

'They were my friends, Don,' Ballantyne said. 'Things aren't going to be the same without them.' He looked around the smoking room. 'This place, for example. I've been sitting here, thinking.'

'About what?'

Ballantyne sighed. 'That it might be time to move on.'

'Where to?'

'The country, maybe. Florrie has always talked about living in a cottage.'

Spencer snorted. 'You're not the country squire sort, Archie. Village fetes and agricultural shows? You'll be bored within a week, deflowering all the village virgins within two. And you couldn't keep all your antics quiet in a village like you can here in town.'

Ballantyne shook his head, wanting to contradict Spencer but knowing he was probably right. Florence might yearn for a cottage with roses growing around the front door but what would he do with himself in such a place? Even so, it would be good to get away for a while. The last few months had been nothing but stress. He needed to unwind. Speaking of which…

'Where's that damn brandy?' he shouted.

Spencer followed Ballantyne's gaze towards the smoking-room door as Sally Cooke entered with a silver tray bearing a glass of brandy and a cigar. She offered them to Ballantyne.

'Took your time,' he muttered, snatching the cigar from the tray and pointing for her to put the glass on the table. 'You'd best keep your hands off,' Ballantyne said as he saw Spencer watching Sally as she left the room. 'There's too many eyeballs on us.'

'Not what I'm thinking, old boy,' Spencer said, his eyes narrowing.

'And you'd best keep off the powder, too.'

'Why? You said they'd caught that waiter and they'd be charging him. We don't have to worry about the police sniffing round anymore.'

'There'll be a trial, won't there?' Ballantyne asked, exasperation creeping into his voice. 'We're going to be right in the public eye then and—'

Spencer waved him quiet. 'All right. You've made your point.' He studied Ballantyne whose eyes were closing. 'You look done in, Archie. You ought to call it a night.'

Ballantyne nodded. 'I'll toddle off home once I've had my cigar.'

'Think I'll pop down The King George. Bit livelier in there. This place is like the grave tonight.'

'A rather unfortunate choice of words, Don,' Ballantyne said, his voice a little slurred.

Spencer grinned and rose. 'See you, Archie.'

Ballantyne waved his cigar at him as Spencer left and picked up his glass. He really did miss his friends. Don was all right in his way, but he didn't share the same tastes as Kit and Adrian, and as for Eric… that little weasel was becoming more of an old woman every day. No, despite what Don had said, it might be time for a change of scene. But not the countryside. Upon reflection, that really did sound too dull. Maybe another part of town, or even abroad. Paris or Monte Carlo. Yes, that would be fun. To enjoy a bit of glamour for a change. He'd talk about it with Florrie when he got home if she wasn't too tired.

If I'm not too tired, more like, he mused, smiling to himself. *I must have been overdoing it lately. I can hardly keep my eyes open.*

Chapter Forty-One

The ringing of his alarm clock woke Matthew at 5 a.m. He clambered out of bed, putting the kettle on the gas to make a cup of coffee, hoping the caffeine would clear his head. At 6 a.m., he telephoned the station and told the desk sergeant he wouldn't be in until much later as he would be following up a lead in Essex. Matthew didn't elaborate, didn't tell the sergeant what he'd gone on to find out about Kenneth Croft at Scotland Yard after leaving Soho. He didn't want Mullinger telling him to forget about Croft, that there wasn't any need for him to follow up on leads on his murder now they had their killer. But if he also admitted the truth to himself, he couldn't face being in the station today.

'Morning, Justin,' Sergeant Copley said as Denham clattered down the stairs to the custody area. 'You're in early.'

'Got a busy day. Inspector Lund passed me all the paper-work to do on our chap here,' he jerked his head at the cells. 'You know what he's like. Never does anything he can get someone else to do.'

Copley grinned, understanding. 'How's Stannard doing?'

Denham made a face. 'I don't know. He's called in this morning that he's going to be out all day following up a lead in Essex.'

'A likely story. Bet he just couldn't face the music here. Is it true what everyone's saying? Stannard going to get the boot?'

'Where did you hear that?'

'Mavis,' Copley said. It was common knowledge that if there wasn't exactly a passionate romance between the custody sergeant and Miss Halliwell, there was, at the very least, an understanding. 'She said Old Mouldy had had her put through a call to the Chief Commissioner and that he was talking about the inspector in less than rosy terms. She reckons he's after getting rid of him.'

'Oh.'

'You sound disappointed.'

'Well,' Denham shrugged, 'I quite like him. I mean, yeah, he's a bit of a tartar, but he knows what he's doing. And at least he doesn't palm all his work off on others.'

'I wouldn't mind seeing him gone,' Copley said, dropping two cubes of sugar into his mug, 'the way Mavis keeps going on about him. "Isn't Inspector Stannard handsome? Isn't he smart? Why don't you dress like him, Tommy?" As if I can go about like him when I'm in Uniform and he's in CID and he probably earns twice as much as me.'

Denham grinned. 'You looked in on Kelly yet?'

'I was about to when you came down. You want him for another interview?'

'No. I just wanted to see how he is. Lund was pretty hard on him yesterday and you know what his sort are like.'

Copley nodded. 'Cry babies. Come on then,' he said, grabbing the metal ring with the keys to the cells. 'Let's go and see him.'

Denham followed Copley down the narrow corridor to the

cells, watching as the sergeant fitted one of the keys into the lock and turned it. 'What's up?' he asked as Copley grunted.

'I can't open the blooming door. It's stuck.' Copley slid back the wicket and peered inside. 'Christ Almighty. Give me a hand here.'

'What is it?' Denham asked, lending his shoulder to the door. He had his answer when the door shifted and he stumbled into the cell.

Norman Kelly had fashioned a rope from the torn strips of his shirt and tied one end to the frame of the wicket. The other he had looped around his neck. His eyes were starting from their sockets and his tongue had swollen so that it bulged from his mouth.

'Jesus,' Copley said, his hand over his mouth.

'Call the doctor,' Denham said, untying the knot.

'He's dead, Justin. Look at him.'

Denham had freed Kelly from the noose and was lowering his body to the floor. He felt for a pulse. The skin was cold. Copley was right. Kelly was very dead. Scrambling to his feet, Denham forced himself to take several deep breaths. 'We're still going to need the doctor,' he said. 'And you better tell the Super what's happened.'

Copley hurried away and Denham heard him on the telephone, calling desperately for a doctor. Denham looked back down at Kelly and shook his head. 'You silly sod,' he whispered, leaning over to close the staring eyes.

Chapter Forty-Two

Matthew had spent the train journey going through the copy of the file Scotland Yard had given him on Kenneth Croft. Even without comparing the fingerprints, there was no doubt in Matthew's mind that the dead man from Craynebrook common and Kenneth Croft were one and the same. The mugshots paper-clipped to the file showed a good-looking man of around twenty years, his face bearing the plumpness of youth, and Matthew could easily see how people would find that boyish face appealing, and once it had matured, charming. He'd flicked through the arrest reports, discovering Croft's criminal past. He had begun his criminal career as a thief, stealing from shops and lifting goods from lorries, and had progressed to confidence tricks. Croft hadn't been very successful at either, for he had invariably been caught, and sentenced to serve time in prison — twenty-eight days in 1924, two months in 1926, and six months in 1927. Then nothing. No arrests, no prison sentences. It was as if Kenneth Croft had disappeared off the face of the planet. Either that, or he'd given up defrauding people.

But Matthew knew that wasn't true. Kenneth Croft had been actively engaged in confidence tricks the previous year, all of which appeared to have been highly successful. So what had changed in Kenneth Croft's life to make him a better conman?

An idea came to Matthew as the train pulled into Colchester station. Was it because he had acquired a partner, someone who was clever and skilled at deception and who made Croft more careful? He knew Croft had been working with someone. The driver he'd shown off outside Rose & Harper proved that. Had that driver been Norman Kelly?

Matthew took a cab to the address given in Croft's file as his next of kin. It was the address for a Mr and Mrs Croft, and Matthew approached the front door with trepidation; it was never easy telling people their loved one was dead.

His knock was answered by a man in his early sixties. The resemblance to Kenneth's mugshot was striking.

'Mr Croft?' Matthew asked, showing his warrant card.

The man had spectacles hanging from a chain around his neck and he put them on his nose to read it. He sighed. 'Is it about Ken?'

'It is,' Matthew said, his gaze shifting to the woman who had come to stand by Mr Croft's side. She looked older than her husband and there was a yellow tinge to her skin.

'This is my wife. It's about Ken,' he told her.

'Is he all right?' she asked. 'We haven't heard from him for weeks.'

'Could I come in, Mrs Croft?' Matthew asked and caught Mr Croft's eye. He saw the look of understanding pass across the older man's face and knew he had already guessed the reason for Matthew's visit.

Mrs Croft gestured him inside and directed him to a small sitting room that reminded him of his childhood. Battered armchairs with stained antimacassars were sited around a coal fire, a rickety oak table was shoved against the wall with woven placemats and salt and pepper pots its permanent ornamentation. On the mantelpiece were framed photographs of Kenneth – him as a young boy wearing shorts and too-big boots, him wearing an apron standing by his father in what looked like a hardware shop, and him wearing an army uniform from the Great War.

'Please sit down, inspector,' Mr Croft said, pointing Matthew to one of the armchairs and gently pushing his wife into the other. He pulled over a dining chair from the table, set it next to his wife and took hold of her hand. Mrs Croft looked up at her husband in surprise and Matthew knew that, unlike him, she hadn't guessed the news was bad.

'When did you last hear from your son, Mr Croft?' Matthew asked.

'The end of November,' Mr Croft said. 'He telephoned to wish my wife a happy birthday.'

'And nothing from him since?'

They both shook their heads.

Matthew took a deep breath. 'I'm afraid I have some bad news for you. A body I believe to be your son was found on Craynebrook common last week.'

Mrs Croft gave a cry and covered her mouth with her left hand. The right gripped her husband's. Mr Croft's mouth tightened and he turned his head away.

'I'm very sorry,' Matthew said.

'Last week?' Mr Croft asked.

'The body had no identification on him. It's taken this long to find out who he was.'

'Nobody recognised him?'

Matthew hesitated. 'I'm afraid the face was unrecognisable. Your son had been badly beaten shortly before his death.' He winced as Mrs Croft's whimpers became sobs. 'And he had been where he was found for a few weeks, so animals had....' He didn't need to go on.

'I see,' Mr Croft nodded.

Mrs Croft looked across at Matthew with red, wet eyes. 'Who killed him?'

'We're still investigating, but we have a suspect in custody. Does the name Norman Kelly mean anything to you? Christopher Fairbank? Adrian Foucault?'

Mrs Croft looked up at her husband. 'We don't know them, do we, Dennis?'

Mr Croft shook his head. 'Never heard of any of them, inspector.'

'I'm sorry to have to ask these questions, Mr Croft,' Matthew went on, 'but are you aware of what your son did for a living?'

'We know it wasn't decent,' Mr Croft said archly. 'He'd been in trouble with the police before, but I suppose you know that.'

'He'd gone into confidence tricks, Mr Croft,' Matthew said. 'I've spoken with men he defrauded out of many hundreds of pounds.'

'He always said he only took money from people who could afford to lose it and who ought to know better. It doesn't make it right, I know, but…' Mr Croft trailed off with a shrug.

Mrs Croft suddenly let out a cry and turned to Matthew. 'What about Nancy? Is she all right?'

'Who's Nancy, Mrs Croft?' Matthew asked.

'She's his girl,' Mr Croft answered. 'Well, Ken said they were married, but I don't think they were.'

'I'm not aware of any Nancy, Mr Croft,' Matthew said, his mind turning to Croft's wristwatch and the inscription from 'N'. Could it have been from Nancy, not Norman? 'What can you tell me about her?'

'We only met her the once,' Mr Croft said. 'Ken brought her to see us last year. Pretty girl, tall, a bit on the skinny side, but nice enough.'

'I didn't like her,' Mrs Croft cut in, wiping her nose with her handkerchief. 'I could see straightaway the kind of girl she was.'

'And what was that, Mrs Croft?'

'Like she was too good for everyone. I saw her looking round here turning her nose up. She made Kenny worse, I could see it. She kept telling him she had to have this and that, things he couldn't afford. If it wasn't for her, he might have given up all his bad ways for good.'

'You don't know that, Ethel,' Mr Croft shook his head. 'They were made for each other, even you have to admit that. Nancy made him happy.'

Mrs Croft gave a disapproving 'Huh' and wiped her nose again. 'If you don't know about her, inspector, where is she?'

'I don't know, Mrs Croft,' Matthew said. 'I will try to find out.'

'She left him, I suppose. Found someone richer who can give her what she wants. Oh, Kenny!' Mrs Croft started crying again.

'Do you know her surname, Mr Croft?' Matthew asked.

'Ken did tell us…' He looked towards the ceiling as he tried to recall the name.

'Price,' Mrs Croft said without hesitation. 'Nancy Price.'

'And do you know where she came from?'

'She came from round here. He met her when he came home to see us. At the fun fair in the park.'

'Does she have family locally?'

Mrs Croft shook her head. 'I don't know. We never met her family.'

Matthew asked a few more questions, but it became clear the Crofts knew nothing about Nancy that would help him find her. 'Well,' he said, getting to his feet. 'Thank you for your time. You've been very helpful and I'm very sorry about your son.'

He said goodbye to Mrs Croft, who seemed to barely notice his going. Mr Croft saw him out.

'I want to see my boy, inspector,' he said as Matthew stepped out onto the front step.

'The body will need to be formally identified,' Matthew nodded. 'I'll make the arrangements for you to come to Craynebrook and do that.'

'Thank you, inspector. You know, Ken wasn't perfect, but he didn't deserve to end up thrown away like rubbish. I hope you catch the bastard who killed him.'

'I'm going to do my best,' Matthew assured him.

Chapter Forty-Three

Florence Ballantyne winced as Daisy wrenched back the bedroom curtains and let the harsh sunlight in.

'Good morning, madam,' Daisy said brightly, coming to stand beside the bed. Her figure blocked out the sun and Florence managed to open one eye.

'It's too early to be so cheery, Daisy,' she said, pushing herself up and sinking against the cushioned satin headboard with a sigh. She put her fingers to her head to check her hairnet was still in place. 'I didn't get in until gone two.'

'It's gone ten, madam. Nice night, was it? Did you enjoy the show?'

Florence moaned a response, leaning forward as Daisy put her bed jacket around her shoulders. She slid her arms into the sleeves and tied its straps in a bow beneath her chin. Daisy placed a breakfast tray on her lap, and the aroma of kippers filled Florence's nostrils.

'I said I would have porridge this morning, Daisy. You know I don't like kippers when I breakfast in bed. They make the room smell.'

'Sorry, madam,' Daisy said unapologetically. 'I'll open

the window, shall I?' She didn't wait for an answer and unhooked the latch to open the top window.

'Have you taken Mr Ballantyne's breakfast in to him yet?'

'He's not in his room, madam,' Daisy said. 'I took his tray in but he weren't there.'

'Not there?' Florence frowned. 'Did he say he was going out early?'

'Not to me, madam. Last I saw the master was last night when he said he was going to the club. Will that be all, madam?'

'Yes. Thank you, Daisy.'

Florence picked at her kippers, taking small mouthfuls. After about five minutes, she picked up the telephone receiver from her bedside – installed at great expense the previous year, a present from Archie so she could call her friends from the comfort of bed – and gave the operator a number. The line connected and she said, 'Rosie?... Hello, dear... Yes, it's me. Could you ask your husband if he saw Archie at the club last night?... What's that?... Oh, Tommy wasn't there?... No, no, nothing wrong. It's just that Archie didn't come home last night and I'm wondering where he is, that's all. I thought he may have stayed at the club... Oh, would you? Yes, if you could ask Tommy to find out, I'd be so very grateful.... Call me back?... You're a darling.'

Florence hung up the telephone. She'd lost her appetite for the kippers and moved the breakfast tray to the side. She rose, slipping her feet into her feathered mules and left her bedroom, crossing the hall to her husband's room and looking at the bed that hadn't been slept in.

Oh, stop panicking, she told herself going back to her room. After all, this wasn't the first time Archie had stayed out all night. It was just what had happened to Kit and Adrian that was making her worry. But then, she didn't need to worry, did she? Archie had told her the police had caught the man who killed them, so he was perfectly safe.

Yes, Archie was perfectly safe, but oh, she did wish Tommy Yates would hurry up and call and tell her Archie was snoring peacefully in one of the club bedrooms.

Chapter Forty-Four

Matthew left the Crofts and found a telephone box. Closing the door, he opened the directory hanging from a chain beneath the telephone and flipped through to the Ps. Running his fingers down the columns, he stopped when he came to the Prices. There were three and he found himself wishing Nancy had a more unusual name. He picked up the receiver and dialled the first number. He asked for Nancy and was told there was no one called Nancy there. He dialled the second number and did the same, only to receive the same answer. Praying the third would be the right one, Matthew dialled the number.

'Can I speak with Nancy please?' he asked.

'Nancy don't live here anymore,' the voice said. 'Who are you?'

Matthew introduced himself. 'Are you Mrs Price?'

'That's right. I'm Nancy's mother. What's she done?'

'I need to talk to you, Mrs Price,' Matthew said. 'May I come round?'

There was loud sigh and then Mrs Price said, 'Suppose so.'

Before Matthew could doublecheck the address listed in the telephone directory, Mrs Price had hung up.

Matthew's knock was answered by a rather plain young woman about twenty years old. He showed her his warrant card and she called over her shoulder, 'Mum! It's that policeman who 'phoned!'

An older woman came out of the kitchen at the end of the passage, wiping her hands on her apron. 'Tell him to come in, Ruby.'

Matthew thanked Ruby as she opened the door wider and he stepped in. 'Go in,' she said, pointing him towards a door to the right.

The sitting room was smaller than the Crofts and smelt of overboiled cabbage. 'Well, sit down,' Mrs Price said, taking a seat on a threadbare settee, pulling her hem over her fat, vein-streaked knees as Matthew sat down on a dining chair. Ruby came in and sat down beside her mother.

'Well, come on, then,' Mrs Price said. 'Tell us what's she done.'

'I'm not sure she's done anything, Mrs Price,' Matthew said. 'I'd just like to find out a little about her. When did you last see Nancy?'

'Eighteen months or more, ain't it, Ruby?' Mrs Price said, nudging her daughter's elbow.

'About that, yeah,' Ruby nodded.

'We had a row,' Mrs Price explained, 'about that fella she met. A wrong 'un, if ever I saw one. Oily, he was. Had the gift of the gab, but I saw right through him.' She looked pleased with herself. 'Told Nance to give him the elbow, didn't I? But she wouldn't 'ave it. "You don't know him", she said. "He ain't what you think". I told her he was exactly like I thought, and she'd be sorry when she found out what he was

302

really like.' Mrs Price sniffed. 'Haven't heard a peep from her since.'

'Nancy never liked being told what she could and couldn't do,' Ruby said.

'Right little madam,' Mrs Price said. 'We weren't good enough for her. Told us so to my face, she did. "I want more than this, Mum", she said. And she thought she was going to get it with him. I told her, all she'd get from him was a baby with no ring on her finger and no money to look after it.'

Matthew, sensing Mrs Price would carry on in this vein all day if he let her, cut in. 'Does the name Norman Kelly mean anything to either of you?'

'Who is he?' Mrs Price asked. 'Another bloke she's hitched up with?'

'Do you recognise the name?' he persisted.

Mrs Price pursed her lips and shook her head.

'Miss Price?'

'No, I've never heard of him,' Ruby said.

'I see,' Matthew said, disappointed. He glanced up at the mantelpiece. 'Is that Nancy?' he asked, pointing to a picture of a young woman with her arm around Ruby that had been partially covered by other framed photographs.

'Yes, that's her,' Mrs Price said as Ruby fetched it down from the mantelpiece and handed it to Matthew. 'Taken three years ago on your birthday, weren't it, Ruby?'

'Pretty, ain't she?' Ruby asked Matthew.

He nodded. 'Would it be possible to borrow this photograph for a little while, Mrs Price?'

'Take it,' she said with a shrug, and Matthew eased the photograph out of the frame and put the picture at the back of his notebook. He handed the empty frame back to Ruby.

'Can you tell me what kind of person your daughter is, Mrs Price?'

'A show off, inspector, that's what she is. Always wanting

to be looked at. Never happier than when she's the centre of attention. Remember when she joined the amateur dramatics society, Ruby? All those plays she was in? Up there on the stage at the town hall, showing off what she'd got, sometimes barely a stitch on.'

'She loved to dress up,' Ruby smiled, 'and putting on make-up. I remember one time there was a knock at the door, and I opened it, and an old woman was standing on the doorstep. I asked her what she wanted, and she told me she was my long-lost aunt and all this and that, and I believed her. I asked her in and then she took off her wig and it was Nancy all the time.'

'See what I mean?' Mrs Price said to Matthew. 'Showing off.'

'No, Mum, it weren't that,' Ruby protested. 'She was just having a bit of fun.'

'What? Pretending to be what she wasn't? Nancy did too much of that if you ask me.'

'She liked to dress up?' Matthew asked, a thought wriggling its way into his mind.

Ruby nodded enthusiastically. 'She dressed up as a soldier in a red coat and hat one time when one of the boys was ill and couldn't be in the play. She played his part and she was wonderful.'

'Ain't right,' Mrs Price said, shaking her head. 'Girls dressing up as boys. God knows what the neighbours thought when they saw her like that.'

The chauffeur, Matthew thought. Nancy Price had been Croft's bloody driver. It hadn't been Norman Kelly, after all. 'Do you have any idea where Nancy is now?'

'No, we ain't,' Mrs Price said, 'and I don't want to know. She's turned her back on us, inspector, and we don't want to have any more to do with her. If you find her, you tell her to keep away.'

Chapter Forty-Five

Thomas Yates was feeling guilty. He'd rowed with Rosie, complaining at her volunteering him to go to the club to find Florence Ballantyne's errant husband, and he'd walked out, slamming the front door. What was Rosie doing now? he wondered. Had he made her cry? What a brute he was. He would buy her some flowers after he'd been to the club to make it up to her.

Yates opened up the club's front doors and stepped inside. It was colder inside than out and he shivered, tugging the opening of his overcoat tighter and sinking his chin into his muffler. 'Ballantyne?' he called, and waited for an answer. None came, and he tutted, letting the doors close behind him.

He mounted the stairs and reached the landing. 'Ballantyne?' he called again. He walked towards the bedrooms and opened the first door. The room was empty, the bed still made. Taking a deep breath, he opened the door of the bedroom where Fairbank had been killed. He let the breath out when he saw the bare mattress and nothing else. Ballantyne wasn't there.

Yates went back downstairs. He searched the kitchen and saw nothing out of the ordinary. The function room was empty, so was the lounge. He returned to the hall and saw a light shining in the smoking room. So that's where Ballantyne was. He went in.

'Ballantyne,' he said, seeing a foot sticking out at the base of the armchair on the far side of the room with its back towards him. 'We've had your wife on the telephone, worried about you. You might have called her and set her mind at rest. Ballantyne?'

Yates moved to the side of the chair and looked down. His breath caught in his throat. Ballantyne's eyes were closed. He looked for all the world as if he were asleep. Yates might have thought so too were it not for the knife sticking out of his chest.

Chapter Forty-Six

It was the afternoon before Matthew got back to the station. There was no one on the front desk and the telephone was ringing. He reached over the counter and answered it, taking down a message before hanging up. 'Sergeant Turkel,' he called, but received no answer.

Matthew went up to CID. The office was empty and telephones were ringing here too. He hurried around the desks, answering one after another, taking messages, and promising the callers they would be called back as soon as an officer became available. He heard heels clacking in the corridor outside, and a moment later, a flustered Miss Halliwell entered, her arms full of files. He called her name, making her jump.

'Oh, inspector,' she said breathlessly. 'I didn't see you there.'

'Where is everyone?' he asked, gesturing at the empty office.

Miss Halliwell dropped the files on DC Pinder's desk and pinned a stray strand of hair back into place. 'Most of the men are at the Empire Club. The others are downstairs in the cells.'

'Why are they at the Empire Club?'

She frowned at him. 'Don't you know?'

'I've been out all day,' he explained impatiently.

'Archibald Ballantyne was found dead there this morning. And the others are down in the cells because one of the prisoners killed himself.' Miss Halliwell sighed. 'It's all happening today.'

'Which one?' Matthew asked.

'What?'

'Which prisoner?' he cried.

She put her hand on her hip and glared at him. 'Norman Kelly, of course.'

Matthew ran to the Empire Club. A large crowd had gathered around the gates and one of the uniformed constables was doing his best to hold them back. He saw Matthew and let him through to the house.

'Stannard!' Lund shouted from the end of the hall when he saw Matthew. 'What the bloody hell are you doing here?'

'I just heard what happened,' Matthew panted, peering into the smoking room where he saw Dr Wallace bending over an armchair. 'Was Ballantyne found in there? When was he killed?'

'This isn't your case anymore,' Lund said, grabbing hold of Matthew's arm and pulling him away from the door.

Matthew jerked his arm away. 'When?'

Lund huffed. 'Last night, the doc said.'

'When Kelly was in custody?'

Lund bristled. 'Don't you bloody start—' He broke off as Matthew pushed past him into the smoking room. 'This is my case, Stannard.'

Wallace looked up as the two men entered. 'Afternoon, Inspector Stannard,' he said. 'We meet again.'

308

'Was it a knife?' Matthew asked.

'Stannard!' Lund snarled.

'Yes, inspector,' Wallace replied, ignoring Lund. 'Stabbed in the heart again.' He followed Matthew's gaze which had moved from the dead Archibald Ballantyne to the empty brandy glass on the table beside him. 'Ah, yes. Well spotted.'

Matthew peered inside the glass. There was a white powdery residue at the bottom. 'He was drugged?'

'I'd say so,' Wallace nodded. 'Can't tell you with what until I do the post-mortem and run the tests.'

'You didn't tell me about that.' Lund glared at Wallace.

'You should have seen it for yourself, Inspector Lund,' Wallace shot back.

Lund's mouth tightened as he looked from the pathologist to Matthew. 'What is it?' he shouted as Denham came into the room.

Denham hesitated, seeing Matthew. 'Sorry to interrupt, sir, but Mr Yates is asking if he can go.'

'Was it Mr Yates who found the body?' Matthew asked Denham.

'Yes, sir.'

'I need to speak to him.'

'On yer bike, Stannard.' Lund said, turning to Matthew and putting a hand on his chest. 'You're not talking to anyone. This is my bloody case. You've got no business being here.'

Matthew pushed the hand away. 'I am going to talk to Mr Yates, Lund, whether you like it or not.'

The two men kept their eyes on each other, neither willing to back down. But there was something in Matthew's eyes that persuaded Lund not to argue further.

'All right,' he said. 'Talk to him if you want. See if I care.'

'Thank you,' Matthew said, then turned to the staring sergeant. 'Take me to Mr Yates, Denham.'

Chapter Forty-Seven

Thomas Yates was sitting in one of the lounge's armchairs, a hand rubbing his chin as he stared into the cold fireplace. He didn't get up as Matthew approached.

'Mr Yates?'

Yates sighed. 'I don't know what the world's coming to, inspector. Why is this happening?'

'Get him a drink,' Matthew murmured to Denham. 'Not tea. Something stronger.' Denham hurried off and Matthew took a seat opposite Yates. 'I'm afraid I need to ask you some questions.'

'I can't tell you anything. I wasn't here last night.'

'Not about last night. About the night of the charity auction.'

Yates turned a frowning face on Matthew. 'The charity auction?'

'TOMMY!' a woman screeched and both men turned towards the door as Rosie Yates rushed in.

'What are you doing here?' Yates cried, half-rising as Rosie grabbed his hand. She pushed him back into the chair and knelt beside him. 'I told you to stay at home.'

'I couldn't. I knew you'd need me. Are you all right?'

'Inspector,' Yates appealed, 'please take my wife away.'

Matthew stretched out an arm towards her but she slapped his hand away.

'Don't you dare try to get rid of me,' Rosie said, all timidity gone. 'I'm staying.'

Denham came in with a glass of brandy. He hesitated as he saw Rosie, but Matthew jerked his head to give the drink to Yates. Denham passed it to the treasurer.

'Drink that, Mr Yates,' Matthew ordered.

Yates didn't protest. He took a mouthful of the brandy, and colour came into his cheeks.

'Better, darling?' Rosie asked, moving to a footstool Denham brought over for her.

Yates nodded. 'The inspector needs to ask me some questions, my dear.'

'Actually, Mrs Yates,' Matthew said, 'you might be able to help too. On the night of the charity auction, do you remember seeing this woman?' He passed her the photograph of Nancy Price.

'She does look familiar,' Rosie said, her brow creasing. 'Oh yes, I remember her now. How silly of me. Her hair was different, shorter, and she was wearing a lovely green dress. I remember thinking how pretty she looked.'

'Did you talk to her? Was she with Mr Calthrop?'

'I don't know who she was with. I think there were a lot of new people there that night.'

'The members had been allowed to invite who they wanted,' Yates explained. 'We wanted a good turnout for the auction, you see.'

'Millicent,' Rosie said. 'That was her name.'

'Not Nancy?' Matthew asked.

'No,' she looked up at him with her clear blue eyes. 'Definitely Millicent. We were in the Ladies at the same time and, well, you know how it is, you start talking.'

Matthew had no idea how ladies behaved in the lavatory, but he nodded to encourage her to continue.

'I remember she was looking a little worried,' Rosie went on, 'and I asked her if she was quite well. She smiled and said she was, but I could tell something was wrong. So I said she could tell me what was bothering her and she just shrugged and said she didn't really want to go to a private party her husband had agreed to. How she wished they could just leave then.'

'What private party was she referring to?' Matthew asked.

'I didn't ask, but...' Rosie looked sideways at her husband, 'I supposed she meant one of their parties.'

Yates's face registered his understanding.

Matthew turned to Yates. 'Whose parties, Mr Yates?' he asked, believing he already knew the answer.

'The Five, inspector.'

Matthew nodded. 'The Five being Fairbank, Foucault, Ballantyne, Spencer and Hailes?'

Yates nodded.

'Do you know where these parties took place?'

'Upstairs in the private dining room.'

'And The Five had a party there on the night of the charity auction?'

'Yes. Just before midnight, Ballantyne told me he and the others would be staying on.'

'And a terrible state they left the dining room in, inspector,' Rosie said. 'Tommy had the cleaning woman complaining to him about all the mess she had to clear up.'

Matthew remembered the knickers he'd found at the back of the fireplace, part of the mess The Five caused that Mrs Briggs must have missed. What else had she missed?

He got to his feet. 'I need to take another look upstairs.'

. . .

Matthew had asked Yates to accompany him. Yates had agreed but told Rosie she was to remain downstairs. She didn't argue this time.

'Has this room been used since the night of the charity auction, Mr Yates?' Matthew asked as he opened the dining-room door.

'I don't believe so,' Yates said, standing just outside. 'What are you looking for, inspector?'

'I don't know until I find it,' Matthew said, moving around the dining table. 'If I find it.'

'You think something happened in here that night?'

'I think it's possible. Millicent was with Charles Calthrop and he wasn't seen alive after that night. From what your wife has just said, they were coming up here with The Five, three of whom are now dead.'

'But why?' Yates threw up his hands. 'Why all this killing?'

Matthew worked his way around the table, this time paying greater attention to the furniture in the room. The knickers had gone unnoticed by Mrs Briggs behind the fire grate; perhaps something else had gone unnoticed behind the sideboard or under the chair legs. He was almost back at the door when his eyes caught sight of dark specks against the white woodwork of the doorframe. They were down low, almost at floor level. He wouldn't have noticed them if he hadn't been standing anywhere other than where he was. He bent down.

'Found something, inspector?' Yates asked, peering around the door.

'Can you turn the lights on, please, Mr Yates?' Matthew asked as he peered closer.

The lights came on and Matthew leant back so he wasn't casting a shadow on the frame.

'What is it?' Yates said, staring too.

'I think that's blood,' Matthew murmured. He put his fingers to the burgundy-coloured carpet beneath the red specks. They came away with a red stain upon the tips.

Matthew rose, taking out his handkerchief and wiping his fingers. 'No one's to come into this room, Mr Yates,' he said, gently pushing the treasurer aside and closing the door.

'Did you say blood, inspector?'

'I did,' Matthew nodded, moving to the stairs and shouting for Denham.

'Yes, sir?' Denham called up from the bottom step.

'If Dr Wallace is still here,' Matthew said, 'tell him I need him to take samples of a section of carpet up here.'

'Yes, sir.' Denham hurried away, almost knocking Lund over as he came up the stairs.

'What are you up to, Stannard?' Lund demanded.

'I'm up to solving a murder,' Matthew said.

'You're not solving anything. This is my case. If you're holding anything back from me—'

'We got the wrong man,' Matthew interrupted. 'Kelly couldn't have killed Ballantyne.'

'Maybe not, but there's nothing to say he didn't kill the others.'

'All the killings are linked. Whoever did the other two, it stands to reason killed Ballantyne. Unless you're saying there's two knife-wielding maniacs going around Crayne-brook killing men from this club?'

'I'm saying, smart arse, that Kelly must have had an accomplice. If he wasn't guilty, why did he kill himself?'

'You tell me.'

'What are you getting at?' Lund growled. 'He was guilty. Don't try to twist it into something it ain't.'

'I'm not trying to twist anything, Lund,' Matthew said. 'I'm just trying to catch a killer, same as you.'

Chapter Forty-Eight

Superintendent Mullinger hung up the telephone and buried his face in his hands. What a mess! What a bloody awful mess! And now he had to clear it up. The Assistant Commissioner's words kept going around in his head – *death in custody, neglectful officers, duty of care, public enquiry, station practices will be looked into, statement to the Press*, and most worrying of all, *heads will roll*. Whose head? Mullinger wondered despairingly.

And it was so unfair. It wasn't his fault Kelly had killed himself. If only Kelly had confessed to killing Fairbank and Foucault, there might have been a way out of the mess. But he hadn't confessed, and now Ballantyne had been murdered, and it looked like a killer was still on the loose.

Mullinger hadn't dared go to the Empire Club. He couldn't face the gaggle of reporters he suspected would be outside, demanding comments, questioning him on how he could let three eminent men be killed and still be no closer to catching their killer. Lund was there, of course, and he had to hope he would find a clue to lead him to the killer. But there was a nagging doubt at the back of Mullinger's mind. Lund was a good man, always doing what Mullinger expected of him, but he wasn't assiduous and he wasn't clever, and Mullinger suspected cleverness would be key in catching this particular killer.

Clever, like that bastard Stannard was clever. Where had he been all day? In Essex, following up on a lead on that conman, as if a nobody like him mattered after the deaths of these three men. Mullinger wished Stannard had never come to his station. He hadn't wanted him, hadn't wanted a detective with a taste for publicity in his station. But had he been consulted? Like hell he had. Just a letter in the post telling him to expect Stannard, as if he was the luckiest superintendent in the world.

It was Stannard who had brought Kelly to the station. If he hadn't, and if Stannard had charged Kelly when he'd been told to, the suicide would never have happened, at least not under Mullinger's roof. Kelly would have been gone; he would have been someone else's problem. Instead, Mullinger now had to make a statement to the Press, expressing regret, sympathy, and assurances that enquiries would be made to find out how such a terrible thing could happen. The Press would ignore all that, of course, and print that it was all his fault, that Superintendent Mullinger had allowed a man to kill himself and ask what sort of a station he was running where things like a death in custody could happen.

Well, at least he wouldn't have to put up with Stannard for much longer. The transfer he'd submitted should be processed soon and Stannard would be at another station, some other superintendent's problem. With any luck, the top brass would listen to his suggestion that Stannard be demoted. He'd been promoted too soon, that was the problem. Got ideas above his station. Far better for him, for everyone, if he had stayed a sergeant. And after this fiasco, he might even be put back in Uniform. That would teach the insubordinate bastard a lesson. And he'd be sure to say Stannard was leaving when he spoke to the Press. Let them make a story out of that.

The telephone on Mullinger's desk rang. He answered it. It was Miss Halliwell, telling him she had a reporter from *The Chronicle* on the line wanting to speak with him.

Superintendent Mullinger sighed and fished in his drawer for his bottle of aspirin. 'Put him through.'

Matthew walked into the council building and asked to see Donald Spencer. Spencer was in a meeting, he was informed by the secretary, and would Matthew care to wait. Matthew didn't have the time nor the patience to wait, and he threw open the door to Spencer's office.

'What the hell—?' Spencer cried, jumping up from behind his desk. The bespectacled man sitting on the other side turned and stared at Matthew with interest.

'I need to speak to you, Mr Spencer.'

'Can't you see I'm in a meeting?'

'This can't wait.'

Spencer sighed and nodded at his companion. 'Geoffrey, get out for a minute. This better be important,' he said after Geoffrey had obliged. He put his feet up on the desk and leaned back in his chair. He didn't invite Matthew to take a seat.

'Are you aware Archibald Ballantyne is dead, Mr Spencer?' Matthew asked.

Spencer whipped his feet off the desk and sat up. 'Archie's dead?'

'He was killed last night at the Empire Club, presumably by the same person who murdered your friends, Fairbank and Foucault.'

'But you had the man who killed them. Archie said you'd arrested him.'

'A man was helping us with our enquiries, but it was never confirmed he was the killer. And as he was in custody at the time of Mr Ballantyne's murder, he couldn't have been responsible.'

'Then who the devil is?' Spencer demanded.

'I thought perhaps you might know.'

Spencer looked taken aback. 'Why would I know?'

'Charles and Millicent Calthrop. Remember them?'

There was a flicker of surprise in Spencer's eyes. Matthew knew he was lying when he said, 'No.'

'They were at the charity auction at the Empire Club, brought there as guests of Christopher Fairbank. They attended a private party with you and your friends in the dining room upstairs. In the private dining room in which blood has been found.'

Spencer met Matthew's eye and held it for a long moment. 'You're going to have to explain why you're telling me this, inspector. I don't quite know what you're getting at.'

'I'm hoping you can tell me something about that party, Mr Spencer.'

'I didn't know there was a private party that night,' Spencer said, a smile playing upon his lips as he regained his composure. He shrugged and shook his head. 'I should be annoyed, them having a shindig without me. Still, you can't be angry with the dead, can you?

'I shall have to speak to Mr Hailes about it, then.'

The smile faltered just a little. 'I don't think Eric knew about it either.' Spencer tapped his finger on the desk. 'In fact, now I remember. Eric left with me that night. I drove him home.'

'What about The Twilight Club?' Matthew asked. 'Ever heard of that?'

Spencer shook his head. 'No.'

'And yet your name is on a Twilight Club letterhead which I found in Mr Foucault's desk.'

There was surprise in Spencer's eyes but no alarm. 'Was it really? How very odd.'

Matthew's fist clenched in his pocket. 'I think I should warn you, Mr Spencer, that it's possible you may be a target for the killer.'

'Me? Surely not?'

'Your friends have been killed, for reasons as yet unknown. It would be wise to be vigilant.'

'Oh, I will be, inspector,' Spencer said. 'Thank you for the warning. Now, if you don't mind, I think I've kept Geoffrey waiting long enough.'

Spencer waited a whole minute after Matthew had left before picking up the telephone.

'Eric? That you?' he asked when the line connected.

'Yes, it's me.' Hailes replied in surprise. 'What's the matter?'

'I've just had that copper here,' Spencer said. 'Did you know Archie's been killed?'

'WHAT?' Hailes yelled down the line.

Spencer winced. 'Keep your voice down, you bloody fool. I take it that means you didn't?'

'When? How?'

'Last night at the club. I don't know how. The copper didn't say. But it wasn't that waiter. He was in a police cell when it happened.'

'But if not him, who?'

Spencer chewed on his bottom lip. 'I have an idea.'

'Tell me.'

'Not until I'm sure. But the copper said I might be a target, which means you might be too. So, keep a look out.'

'I knew it,' Hailes whimpered. 'I knew we were in danger.'

'Stop your snivelling. The copper thinks he's on to something about Calthrop. He's found blood in the dining room at the club. You'll get a visit and he'll try and trip you up. Don't let him. I told him we left the club together and didn't go to any private party that night, only the others did. You must say the same, you hear me?... Eric, answer me.'

'Yes, yes, I heard.'

'Don't do anything stupid.'

'I won't. But…'

'But what?'

'Well, don't you know people who can find this maniac and get rid of him?'

'I'm not trusting this to anyone else, Eric. I'll deal with it,' Spencer promised and hung up.

He took out a key and unlocked the top drawer of his desk. Smiling, he took out the pistol he had used to frighten Betty Trantor and held it in his hands. It was a Luger he'd picked up off a dead Hun in the Great War; the poor bastard hadn't even fired it before he died, so it had a full magazine. Spencer gripped the handle and felt the weight of it. It felt good, natural.

It was, he thought, as he shut one eye and lined up the muzzle with the picture of the king hanging on the opposite wall, a pity he hadn't yet had reason to use it.

Chapter Forty-Nine

Matthew telephoned the stockbroking house where Eric Hailes worked, asking to speak with him. The broker's secretary apologised but informed Matthew that Mr Hailes had left for the day. Matthew thanked her and hung up, certain Spencer had warned his friend to make himself scarce. He made his way back to the station.

Denham was standing in his office doorway talking to Lund when Matthew entered. He stepped aside with a 'Sorry, sir,' and looked from Matthew to Lund with unease. Out of the corner of his eye, Matthew saw Lund jerk his head at Denham, and Denham departed, closing the door behind him.

'So, where you been?' Lund asked sourly.

'I paid Donald Spencer a visit,' Matthew said.

'What for?'

'To find out what he knew about the private party upstairs at the club. And to warn him.'

'Warn him about what?'

'That he might be the killer's next target. If he was involved.'

'Involved in what?' Lund made a noise of impatience.

'For Christ's sake, talk to me, Stannard. Tell me what you're thinking.'

Matthew had been about to light a cigarette. Instead, he threw his box of matches aside and sank back in his chair. 'I think the three men who have been killed, and possibly Spencer and Hailes, were involved in the murder of the man they knew as Charles Calthrop.'

'You're joking?' Lund said.

'Why?' Matthew wanted to know. 'Because of their social standing, they can't possibly have been involved in murder? I wouldn't have taken you for a snob, Lund.'

'All right, all right,' Lund said, patting the air. 'Why'd they kill him?'

Matthew shrugged. 'It's only a guess, but I think they worked out he was a conman. I think he may have been trying to get them to invest in a nightclub that didn't exist. Somehow, they found out it was a fake and they decided to get their own back.'

Lund considered this. 'So, who killed Ballantyne? And the others, if you're right about Kelly?'

'Calthrop's real name was Kenneth Croft. He had taken up with a young woman called Nancy Price about eighteen months ago. If I'm right, she's the killer, murdering them in revenge for Croft.'

'A woman?' Lund shook his head in disbelief. 'So, where does Kelly come in?'

'I don't know,' Matthew admitted. 'But I don't think he killed anyone.'

Lund cursed and threw his half-eaten roll at the wall. Cheddar cheese spilled all over the floor. 'How long have you had a name for the dead man?'

'Since late yesterday afternoon,' Matthew said. 'But I only learned about Nancy Price this morning.'

'And where is she?'

'I'm guessing she's somewhere local,' Matthew said, snatching up his matches and lighting his cigarette. 'So, it's a case of telephoning around the local hotels, boarding houses and letting agents to see if her name appears anywhere.'

Lund sighed. 'That's a lot of calling around. How are we going to manage that when everybody's tied up with Ballantyne and Kelly?'

'We'll have to do it,' Matthew said. He went out into the main office and picked up the stack of telephone directories. He came back to his desk and held one out to Lund. 'You going to give me a hand?'

The police closed the club as soon as the mortuary van drove Ballantyne's body away. A constable was posted on the gates to ensure no one got in and the crowd of onlookers thinned and eventually drifted away.

Sally Cooke had been one of the onlookers, waiting to see if the club would reopen and she would be able to work, but she supposed that no one would want to be in the club, not now two of its members had been killed there.

She turned away from the club gates and headed for the high street, burying her chin in the folds of her woollen scarf, keeping her hands stuffed deep in her pockets. Remembering she had nothing to eat at home, Sally decided to stop and buy something for her tea. Not that she had much of an appetite these days, but she had to keep herself healthy, at least for a little while longer.

Sally called in at the grocers and bought a small loaf of bread, six eggs and a pound of tea. Then she made for home, one small room at the back of a large house which she had to access via a side alley. It was a far cry from what she had been used to, when she had a flat in Mayfair or Chelsea or Knightsbridge, and when she had slept between Egyptian cotton sheets and drank champagne out of crystal glasses. Those days were gone. They would never come again. But then, she didn't want them to.

As Sally heaved her shopping beneath her arm and fit her key into the lock, she heard footsteps behind her. She turned, and her breath caught in her throat.

The man walking down the alley towards her lit a match and put it to the end of his cigarette. The flame danced in his eyes and she saw his teeth as his lips widened into a wolfish grin.

Donald Spencer threw the spent match away. 'Hello, Nancy.'

Chapter Fifty

'Or is it Sally? Or Millicent? You're going to have to tell me what to call you.' Spencer leaned in closer. 'What's the matter? Cat got your tongue?'

Nancy Price backed away. 'What are you doing here?'

'Bit of luck really. I was driving home past the club and saw you standing outside. I'd been wondering how to find you and there you were.' He looked at the door behind her. 'Aren't you going to ask me in?'

Nancy shook her head.

Spencer slipped his hand inside his coat pocket and drew out the Luger. He pointed it at her forehead. 'Ask me in, Nancy.'

The telephone calls, which had so far yielded no information on Nancy Price, had been delegated to the junior detectives as soon as they became free. Matthew and Lund had turned to rereading the witness statements taken after the Fairbank and Foucault murders, searching for clues.

'It has to be an inside job, doesn't it?' Lund asked as he flipped another page. 'Otherwise, how would this Nancy

Price know where to find the men to kill them? She has to know someone at the Empire Club who told her that Fairbank was staying behind at the club on Friday, that Ballantyne was there last night. But then,' he groaned, 'how would she know that Foucault wasn't there on Monday?' He looked up at Matthew. 'What is it?'

'Oh, Christ, I've been so stupid!' Matthew cried, drawing the surprised gazes of the men in the outer office. 'She's one of the staff.' He took out one of the statements. 'You interviewed Yates this morning after he found Ballantyne and he said he wasn't at the club last night, but that he thought it would be fine because he didn't expect many members to turn up and Sally Cooke was very able and reliable to manage on her own. And here.' He grabbed another of Yates's statements. 'The club was busy on Monday night and he was grateful Sally Cooke had turned up because she did such a splendid job. And Yates was interviewing for new staff on the Friday before Fairbank's murder. Sally Cooke is Nancy Price.'

'You sure about this, Stannard?' Lund asked doubtfully as Matthew grabbed another file and began riffling through the pages. 'I mean, if she was this Nancy, wouldn't The Five have recognised her?'

Matthew shook his head. 'She used to be in her local amateur dramatics' society. Her sister told me how she loved to dress up and disguise herself. That's what she's done. Ah, got it.' He ran his fingers down a list of names.

Lund moved to look over his shoulder. 'What have you got there?'

'The names and addresses of all the members and staff Mr Yates gave me after Fairbank's murder. And there she is. Sally Cooke. And we've got an address.' Matthew shouted for Denham.

Denham's chair scraped noisily as he jumped up from his desk and poked his head around the doorframe. 'Yes, sir?'

'I need cars and Uniform straightaway.'

Nancy backed up against the small sink. She gripped the cold ceramic edge to steady herself.

Spencer put his hand up to her face and removed the spectacles she wore as part of her disguise. He tossed them onto the draining board. Then he tugged the wig from her head to reveal Nancy's blond hair. He chuckled to himself. 'Clever. Very clever. I didn't recognise you at first. But there was something about you that seemed familiar. It just took me a while to work out who you were.

'What are you going to do?' Nancy asked. 'Are you going to shoot me?'

'Only if you insist on making a fuss. If you be a good girl and behave yourself, I'll hand you over to the police.'

'I'll tell them what you did,' she said. 'They'll arrest you too.'

Spencer shook his head. 'I don't think so. I'll deny everything you say and who do you think they'll believe? A man like me or a whore like you?'

'I'm not a whore.'

'If you say so. My question still stands. Who will they believe?'

'So, you're not going to shoot me?' Nancy nodded at the pistol.

'No,' Spencer said regretfully. 'Truth is, I'd like to, but the police need to hang someone for the murders. Best their case is closed.'

'I haven't finished yet.'

Spencer threw back his head and laughed. It was so loud in the small room. Nancy reached down into the sink and

328

curled her fingers around the knife she had left there that morning.

'Yes, you did very well to get three of us,' Spencer said, smiling. 'If I have one criticism, it's that you didn't kill Eric first. He's such a whiny little sod.' He looked around the small room. 'Don't you even have a telephone here? Bugger, it looks like I'm going to have to take you to the police myself. What a bore.' He waved the pistol towards the door. 'Go on. Move.'

Nancy stayed where she was.

'Move,' Spencer said in a voice that was growing annoyed. 'I'll drag you there if I have to.'

Nancy lifted the knife out of the sink, keeping it hidden behind her back. 'I'm not going anywhere with you.'

Spencer swore and lunged at Nancy. He grabbed her arm and dragged her towards him. Nancy cried out and brought up the knife, ready to plunge it into his neck. But Spencer saw the knife and he twisted away. The blade caught him on the arm, piercing the sleeve of his coat and penetrating the flesh beneath. He hissed in pain.

'You bitch,' he snarled, and made a grab for her arm.

Nancy bent backwards, overbalancing and falling to the ground with a thud, but she still had the knife. Spencer loomed over her, and she thrust the knife upwards, sinking it into him.

Spencer didn't make a sound, but his eyes widened in surprise. He staggered backwards, his hands pressed to his stomach. Blood oozed between his fingers. Anger filled his face, and he raised his right arm and pointed the pistol at her. But Nancy kicked at his hand and the pistol fell from his fingers. She snatched it up. Spencer was on his knees. She pointed the gun at him.

And then she heard the siren.

Nancy yanked open the door and ran out into the night.

Chapter Fifty-One

The police car screeched to a stop. Matthew threw open the door and jumped out. Lund clambered out after him. Three uniformed officers were already charging down the side alley towards Sally Cooke's room and Matthew quickened his pace. As he drew near the door, one of the constables called out, 'We've got a wounded man here.'

'Who is it?' Lund shouted as he came up behind Matthew and followed him into the room.

'It's Donald Spencer,' Matthew answered in surprise.

He stared down at the man lying on the floor. A constable was holding a tea towel, snatched from the draining board, to Spencer's stomach. It was soaked in blood. Spencer's face was grey. His eyes were closed.

'We'd better get him seen to before he croaks it,' Lund said, and gave orders to the constables to get Spencer into the police car and drive him to the hospital.

The uniforms carried Spencer out, two constables holding an ankle each, one holding him beneath the armpits. Denham, who had been travelling in a second car and had only just arrived, stood back to let them pass.

'So, where's this Nancy Price?' Lund asked. 'And what was Spencer doing here?'

'God knows,' Matthew said, staring around the room. 'We need to put out an alert for Nancy. Her handbag's here,' he said, pointing at the floor where Nancy's bag had fallen during her struggle with Spencer, 'so she may not have any money on her to hole up in a hotel or similar. She'll probably be on foot trying to get out of the area.'

'We should catch up with her before too long, then,' Lund said.

Matthew sighed in frustration. They'd been so close to catching Nancy and she'd got away. And now Spencer was wounded, perhaps even dead already, and Nancy Price was free to finish her mission and kill Hailes.

Hailes!

'I know where she's going,' Matthew cried.

'Where?' Lund asked.

'To kill Eric Hailes. Stay here, just in case she comes back.' Matthew rushed out of the door, Denham quickly getting out of his way.

'Stannard!' Lund called after him.

Matthew skidded to a halt halfway up the alley. 'What?'

'Don't go on your own, you bloody fool. She's already killed three men, maybe four.' Lund nodded at Denham. 'Go with him. And don't let him treat her like a lady.'

Eric Hailes flushed the toilet and moved to the basin to wash his hands. Over and over went the bar of soap in his hands as the water flowed, and his mind went back to his last conversation with Spencer. It was all right for Don to say he would deal with the killer, but when? How long would it be before Don got rid of whoever it was? And in the meantime, he was fair game.

Hailes dried his hands on the towel and wished it was safe to go out of the house. He would have loved to nip down to the pub and drink himself silly without Doris moaning in his ear. He'd tried to explain to his wife why it was necessary to lock all the windows and doors without telling her exactly why he was a target, but she'd looked at him like he was an idiot.

'Why would anyone want to kill you?' she sneered.

He'd almost blurted out what he'd done, just to prove he wasn't as worthless as she thought him, but he'd held his tongue. He laughed as an idea came to him. What if the killer got Doris and he wasn't touched? Oh, wouldn't that be wonderful! To be free of her nagging and her constant put-downs.

Hailes jumped as the front door knocker was banged three times. Yanking open the bathroom door, he hurried down the hall. He reached the landing and saw with horror that Doris was at the front door, drawing back the bolt.

'NO!' he yelled, running down the stairs as Doris turned the latch.

He was too late. The door was thrown open, sending Doris stumbling backwards to fall on her backside. Hailes, frozen on the bottom step of the stairs, watched in horror as Nancy entered and pointed a pistol at him.

'It's you? No, please,' he begged, holding out his hands. Distantly, he heard Doris whimpering. He wanted to run, to flee back up the stairs, but his legs wouldn't work.

'Shut up!' Nancy screamed at Doris, and Doris clamped her hands over her mouth, muffling her sobs.

'I'm sorry,' Hailes said. 'I'm sorry for what happened. But you don't have to do this.'

'I do,' Nancy panted, tears running down her face. 'I've killed all the others. You're the last.'

'They made me do it,' Hailes screamed. 'I didn't want to.'

'I don't want to hear your excuses.' Nancy raised the pistol and grasped it with both hands. 'I just want to make you pay.'

Hailes could see her finger tightening around the trigger. Then out of the corner of his eye, he saw Doris clamber to her feet. She hurled herself at Nancy, pushing her over onto the floor, and for a split second, he thought Doris was trying to protect him. But then his wife ran out of the house screaming, and Hailes looked after her in horror, astonished by her betrayal.

Hailes willed himself to move and his legs finally obeyed. He hurtled around the bottom of the staircase, heading for the kitchen door. He heard footsteps and knew Nancy was chasing him. He grabbed the handle of the kitchen door and yanked it downwards, but the door, always prone to sticking, refused to open. *This is it*, he thought. *I'm going to die.* He slumped against the door and closed his eyes.

And then there were shouts and other footsteps, and he dared to open them. A man had thrown his arms around Nancy, pinning her arms to her side, and was pulling her backwards down the hall. Another man wrenched the pistol from Nancy's hand.

Nancy was screaming, whether in pain or frustration, Hailes didn't know, and he didn't care. He was alive and that was all that mattered.

Chapter Fifty-Two

Matthew poured brandy into a glass and passed it to Eric Hailes. Hailes gulped it down, coughing as the spirit burned his throat. He held the glass out to Matthew, wanting another.

'I think you should stick at one,' Matthew said, taking a seat on the sofa.

Hailes cradled the empty glass. 'Has she gone?'

Matthew nodded. 'Miss Price has been taken to the station.'

'You should take her to a nuthouse. She was going to kill me!'

'I know. Why?'

Hailes shrugged. 'I don't know. The woman's mad. She must be.' He looked down at his empty glass mournfully. 'Can't I have another?'

'I need you sober, Mr Hailes,' Matthew said. 'When you're calmer, we'll go to the station and you can make a statement.'

'Do I have to? You've got the bitch. Isn't that enough?'

'There are questions I need answers to.'

'But I don't know anything,' Hailes protested.

Matthew lit a cigarette. 'Miss Price attacked Donald Spencer earlier this evening. He's in hospital as we speak.'

Hailes's eyes widened. 'He's not dead?'

'No, but he's in a serious state. Miss Price killed your other three friends, attacked Mr Spencer and came after you. Do you really expect me to believe you don't know why?'

Hailes looked towards the closed sitting-room door. 'Where's my wife?'

'She's with one of my men in your dining room. Mrs Hailes is very upset, but maybe she will tell me what this is all about.'

'Doris doesn't know anything about it,' Hailes burst out with a scornful laugh.

'Anything about what, Mr Hailes?' Matthew asked quietly.

'About—' Hailes broke off and shook his head. 'I don't know.'

The door opened and Denham put his head in. 'The car's back, sir.'

'Good.' Matthew stubbed out his cigarette and rose, straightening his jacket. 'Mr Hailes? If you could come along with me, please.'

Nancy Price looked a mess. Her hair was unbrushed and her face was still covered in the make-up she had used to disguise herself as Sally Cooke. She was barely recognisable as the girl in the photograph her family had given Matthew.

She hadn't said a word since Matthew had wrestled her to the ground at Hailes's house. Hadn't given her name to the custody sergeant when he booked her in, hadn't responded to the offer of tea, hadn't spoken when asked if she wanted a solicitor. Matthew had the unhappy feeling she wasn't going to talk to him at all.

'How are you feeling, Miss Price?' he asked, offering her a cigarette.

Nancy turned her face to the wall.

Matthew took out a cigarette for himself and lit it, leaving the packet in front of Nancy. 'Mr Spencer is in a critical condition in hospital. I expect that disappoints you. You wanted him dead, didn't you?'

Nancy said nothing.

'Mr Hailes on the other hand is very much alive and in this station making a statement. He claims to have no idea why you would want to kill him or his friends.'

Nancy's eyes flicked at Matthew, and for the briefest of moments, he thought she was going to talk. But she looked away again, folding her arms even tighter across her chest.

'I'd like to know why you killed those three men,' Matthew said. 'Why you attacked Mr Spencer and Mr Hailes. I'm not good at one-sided conversations, Miss Price,' he said, growing irritated by her continued silence. 'If you're not going to talk to me, I'm going to tell you why I think you've done this.'

Was that a shrug he saw?

'All right, then,' Matthew said. 'This is what I think. You and Kenneth Croft were planning to con these men out of some money. Quite a lot of money by having them invest in a non-existent nightclub in Soho. Somehow, they found out it was a con, but instead of reporting you to the police, they decided to deal with you themselves. Fairbank invited you and Mr Croft to the charity auction at the Empire Club, keeping up the pretence that you were all still friends. You were then invited to a private party when everyone else left the club. You didn't want to go to that party. You told Mrs Yates so in the Ladies lavatory, but you went all the same. At that party, Mr Croft was killed, by one or other of the men or by all of them. His body was dumped on Craynebrook common. I don't know what they did with you or why they let you go, but when Mr Croft's body was found, you decided to take your revenge. You got a job at the club posing as a waitress. You stayed behind to kill Fairbank that same night. You found out that Foucault was at home on Monday and you went to his house and killed him. You killed Ballantyne by drugging him first, perhaps because he recognised you and you didn't want to have a struggle. How am I doing so far?'

Nancy was listening. He could see her looking at him out of the tail of her eye.

'Did you invite Spencer to your room or did he come unannounced? I don't think you're stupid. I don't think you would have invited him there, so I'm going to work along the lines that he realised who you were and followed you. Was the pistol his? Perhaps he was going to shoot you, then claim it was done in self-defence. But you fought back and you stabbed him. You took his pistol and made your way to Eric Hailes to finish what you'd started.' Matthew took a long drag on his cigarette and blew the smoke out. 'How much have I got right?'

He waited. The silence lengthened, but he continued to wait. He was going to get her to talk if it killed him.

'He wasn't going to shoot me,' she said at last. Her voice was cracked and croaky. 'Spencer was going to bring me to you.'

'Anything else?'

'Ballantyne didn't recognise me. I just thought it would be easier to kill him if he was drugged. It was easier, but far less satisfying.'

'But everything else?'

'True.'

Matthew glanced down at Denham's notepad, making sure he had taken this last down. 'I'm going to need a statement from you, Miss Price, confessing to the murders and the attacks.'

Nancy nodded. 'Are you going to charge the other two with murder? They killed Ken.'

'You saw them?'

'They did it right in front of me. Hit him over the head with a cricket bat as soon as we got in the dining room upstairs.' Nancy squeezed her eyes shut. 'I wish I could get that image out of my mind, but I see it all the time. That's why I did it, inspector. And I'd do it again.' She took up the packet of cigarettes and slid one out. Matthew lit it for her.

'Why kill the other three?' he asked.

Nancy took a deep drag of the cigarette. 'Because.'

'Because what?'

She glared at him. 'Just because.'

Matthew thought of the knickers he had found and reasoned he knew why. He wouldn't press her to tell him. 'Sergeant Denham will take down your statement and get you to sign it,' he said. 'Just one thing. Did you know Norman Kelly?'

Nancy shook her head. 'No. Who is he?'

'He was a waiter at the club. You never met him?'

She sighed. 'I don't think so.' Nancy's face suddenly screwed up and tears fell down her cheeks.

Matthew gave her his handkerchief, one of the ones Georgie had given him with his initials embroidered in the corner. Nodding at Denham, he left the interview room.

'Well?' Lund asked as Matthew walked into their office in CID.

'Miss Price has admitted the killings and the attacks. Denham's taking her statement now.'

Lund blew out a puff of air. 'Thank God for that. Why did she do it?'

'She claims Spencer and Hailes killed Kenneth Croft. Hit him over the head with a cricket bat. But she didn't say why she killed the other three. Maybe it was just because they were there.'

'I suppose it doesn't really matter why. You interviewed Hailes yet?'

Matthew shook his head. 'Not yet. We're waiting on his solicitor to arrive and I suspect it's going to be a waste of time. His solicitor will advise him not to say a word, and to be honest, we don't have anything on him other than Miss Price's say-so. How's Spencer?'

'Still out of it. The doc said we can't see him for a day or two. He lost a lot of blood.'

'But he's going to live?'

Lund nodded. 'So the doc says. When he wakes up, you can charge him with murder. Quite a haul for you, isn't it?'

It wasn't said with jealousy. In fact, Matthew could have sworn he detected a note of apology in Lund's words.

'I'm just glad it's over,' Matthew said with feeling.

Chapter Fifty-Three

Matthew was being made to stand while Mullinger read Nancy Price's confession.

'Three murders and two attacks.' Mullinger shook his head. 'It's hard to believe a woman capable of such things.' He closed the file and looked up at Matthew. 'These accusations she makes against Hailes and Spencer. Any truth in them?'

'I think so, although we can't question Spencer yet and Hailes is making no comment, as advised by his solicitor. I've got officers searching both their houses, but as yet nothing. Although, there is Spencer's car. It was parked outside Miss Price's room. It's a two-tone Alvis, beige and black, the same colouring as the car seen driving across the common when we think the body was dumped. I've asked Dr Wallace to have a look in it to see if there's any traces of a dead body being in there.'

'No sign of this cricket bat Miss Price says they killed Croft with?'

Matthew shook his head. 'But Dr Wallace confirms a cricket bat fits the description of the murder weapon. Her story rings true.'

'Incredible,' Mullinger murmured. 'Men like that.' He cleared his throat and handed the file back to Matthew. 'Very good. Keep on at Hailes for the time being.'

'You read that Miss Price didn't know Norman Kelly, sir,' Matthew said.

Mullinger cleared his throat. 'Yes, I saw that. It seems you were wrong about his involvement, Stannard.'

'*I* was wrong?'

'Kelly was guilty of nothing more than committing obscene acts and petty thefts. Still, this is not the time to go into all that. Let's concentrate on getting evidence against Hailes and Spencer. You may go.'

Matthew left Mullinger's office, tempted to slam the door behind him. What a bastard Mullinger was! Pretending it was his idea to pin the murders on Kelly. Why, he had a good mind to—

'Inspector?' Miss Halliwell broke into his thoughts.

'Yes?' he snapped.

'The front desk called while you were in with Mr Mullinger. There's a Miss Bird waiting to see you. Sergeant Turkel has put her in the front interview room.'

'I'm sorry for disturbing you, inspector,' Miss Bird said as Matthew entered the front interview room, 'but I have found something I think should be in your hands.'

Matthew forced a smile onto his face, not finding it easy because Mullinger's accusative words were still going round in his head. He watched as Miss Bird opened the shopping bag she carried and drew out a large, leather-bound book. She pushed it across the table to him.

'I've been packing away Mr Foucault's belongings at the house as per his solicitor's instructions. There is a cousin who inherits, and he means to sell the house, you see, otherwise I wouldn't have presumed to concern myself with such matters. I was packing his books away, opening each to ensure there weren't any bookmarks between the pages. When I opened that book there... well, you'll see what I found. No,' she said sharply as Matthew made to open the front cover, putting a gloved hand over his. 'I'd prefer you to wait, inspector. I have no desire to see them again and it would be rather embarrassing for me. You will see that Mr Foucault cut a recess into the pages and used it as a hiding space for those items he wanted to keep secret. I daresay you'll understand why he felt the need to do this when you see what he put in there. Suffice to say, Mr Foucault was not the man I believed him to be and I refuse to have anything more to do with him. So, if you'll excuse me, inspector, that's all I came to do and now I'll be on my way.'

Matthew stepped aside and Miss Bird hurried from the room without even giving him a chance to thank her. He sat down at the table and opened the book. His eyes widened in surprise. Inside the book, in a recess cut out as Miss Bird had described, were photographs, not of Fairbank in bed this time, but of the private dining room at the Empire Club.

He flipped through the prints. The photographs were a series of pictures taken in quick succession. The first photograph showed Foucault's face close to the lens, seemingly checking something on the camera. The second and third showed Fairbank and Ballantyne alternately holding Nancy Price down on the dining table. In one photograph, Ballantyne was taking his pleasure; in another, Fairbank. In the fourth, behind them, by the door, near where Matthew had found the blood, stood Spencer and Hailes. Both men were in their shirtsleeves, their bowties untied, their winged collars askew. Their faces seemed darker in hue, suggesting they'd been exerting themselves, and Matthew saw why. At their feet, lay the battered body of Kenneth Croft. In Spencer's hand was a cricket bat.

Matthew burst into the interview room where Eric Hailes was sitting with his solicitor. Denham was on the other side of the table, looking fed up. From the emptiness of his notepad, it seemed Hailes was sticking to his No Comment policy. Matthew sat down next to Denham and glared at Hailes.

'Mr Hailes, do you still deny knowing why Miss Price murdered your friends and tried to kill you and Mr Spencer?'

'Inspector,' the solicitor cut in with a delicate cough, 'my client hasn't denied anything. My client is exercising his right not to say a word. Silence is not proof of guilt.'

Matthew took a deep breath, then put the photographs in front of Hailes. Hailes looked down at them, and his face paled.

'Do you want to explain these, Mr Hailes?' Matthew asked. 'You see here,' he pointed at the photograph that showed Foucault. 'This shows Mr Foucault setting up the camera and making sure it works. We've checked. Mr Foucault is the only one of your friends to own a camera. This second photograph shows Miss Nancy Price being held by the wrists on the dining table while Mr Ballantyne rapes her. The third shows Ballantyne holding Miss Price down while Mr Fairbank rapes her. This fourth picture shows you and Mr Spencer standing over the bloody and battered body of Mr Kenneth Croft, and in Mr Spencer's hand is the cricket bat that killed him. I'd say this bears out Miss Price's story very well. Do you still have nothing to say?'

The solicitor, who had looked on in horror as Matthew went through the photographs, swallowed and whispered something in Hailes's ear. Hailes looked up at Matthew, his light brown eyes fixed and staring. He opened his mouth and whispered, 'No comment.'

Matthew's jaw tightened. He rose. 'Stand up,' he said to Hailes. Hailes looked to his solicitor for instruction, and his solicitor nodded. Hailes got shakily to his feet.

Matthew stared him straight in the eye. 'Eric Hailes, I'm arresting you for the murder of Mr Kenneth Croft.'

Chapter Fifty-Four

Deputy Assistant Commissioner Eliot Campbell sipped at his tea as he waited in the office of Superintendent Howard Mullinger. He took a look at his wristwatch, watched the minute hand moving around the watch face, and sighed with impatience. If he had to wait much longer, he would be late home and his wife would have to entertain their dinner guests alone. He took another sip of tea, and his ears caught the sound of voices in the outer office. That was Miss Halliwell, he reasoned, telling her boss he had a visitor. A moment later, the door opened.

'I'm so sorry, Deputy Assistant Commissioner,' Mullinger blustered as he entered, hand already outstretched. 'My meeting rather overran and I had no idea you were coming. I hope you haven't been waiting long?'

'Well, some little time,' Campbell said, shaking the hand. 'But your secretary,' he smiled at Miss Halliwell hovering in the doorway, 'made me quite comfortable.'

'Good,' Mullinger said, and nodded at Miss Halliwell to close the door. He sat down at his desk. 'So, to what do I owe the pleasure?'

'The Commissioner wanted me to pop in,' Campbell

began, 'to see how matters stood following the regrettable death of Mr Kelly in custody.'

Mullinger swallowed nervously. 'The inquest established that Kelly's death was a suicide, which there was, of course, no doubt it was, and has exonerated us, that is, the police, of any neglect of duty.'

Campbell grunted. 'That was good of the coroner, if not entirely accurate. I've read the custody logs, Superintendent. The officer on duty did not carry out every cell check he was supposed to.'

'That officer will be disciplined,' Mullinger assured him quickly.

'Of course he will. I know you'll see to that. But what troubles the Commissioner and myself is why Kelly was in such a state that he felt compelled to take his own life.' Campbell looked meaningfully at Mullinger.

'I really couldn't say,' Mullinger began carefully. 'Kelly was extremely uncooperative and not at all forthcoming during interviews. He worked himself up into quite a state, I understand, when Detective Inspector Stannard was questioning him.'

'Yes, I've read the reports made of the interviews with both Stannard and Lund. It's evident that, as you say, Kelly was in something of a state during questioning, but it's clear that DI Stannard had doubts over his guilt and ceased his questioning to investigate further. At that point, DI Lund takes over the questioning. Why was that?'

Mullinger began fiddling with items on his desk. 'I felt DI Stannard wasn't making any progress with Kelly. He was allowing Kelly to lead him down garden paths, to drag the matter out. I thought DI Lund might have more success.' He swallowed uneasily as Campbell studied him.

'He didn't, though, did he? Kelly never swayed from his

original denial. DI Lund was forced to put him back in the cell without getting a confession.'

'That is true, as I understand it,' Mullinger nodded. 'Of course, the questioning was entirely in the inspectors' hands.'

'But you're ultimately responsible for what happens in your station, Superintendent,' Campbell pointed out. He took another sip of his tea. 'Did DI Lund get rough with Kelly?'

Mullinger's mouth fell open. 'I'm sure he did not, sir.'

'But you were keen to get a confession from Kelly? Even though, as it turns out, he was perfectly innocent.'

'That was not apparent at the time, sir. In fact, it was DI Stannard who first identified him as a main suspect—'

'Yes, DI Stannard. From all I've read in the reports, Stannard was doing his job, identifying and questioning a suspect. And, of course, he has now made three arrests, clearing up all four murders.'

'That is true, but—'

'Which makes me wonder why on earth you want him transferred, Superintendent. And not only transferred. You've recommended a demotion. Promoted before he was ready, you stated in your letter. Care to explain how you reached such a conclusion?'

'I...er... I...'

'Perhaps you'd now like to rescind that transfer request,' Campbell suggested, 'in view of the very excellent job Inspector Stannard has done since he's been here?'

'Yes,' Mullinger said, staring down at his blotter. 'I think, upon reflection, I would like to rescind that request. An excellent officer, as you say.'

'Then we need say no more about the matter. It's regrettable that we will never understand why Mr Kelly felt it necessary to kill himself. But the least said, soonest mended, on that matter, wouldn't you say, Superintendent?'

Mullinger nodded.

Campbell smiled. 'I'm glad we understand one another.'

Chapter Fifty-Five

'This is a nice place,' Dickie said as he and Matthew took their drinks over to a vacant table. 'Your sister's, you say?'

Matthew nodded. 'And her husband's. They took it over about two years ago now. You should have seen it before they came here. To call it a dump would be generous.'

Dickie smiled, then his face grew serious. 'Why did you ask me to meet you for a drink, inspector?'

Matthew stared into his beer. 'I wanted to find out if you were going ahead with the story about The Five. It's just that I haven't seen anything in *The Chronicle* about them. I know the brick through the window was frightening, but there's no reason now why you shouldn't pursue the story. Three of The Five are dead, the other two are awaiting trial for murder. They're not going to get off, not with the evidence we managed to gather. You're safe from them.'

Dickie nodded. 'I hear what you're saying and I agree. But my editor thinks there's no point in drawing attention to rotten apples in our midst. The Empire Club has closed, never to reopen as a social club. All the members are pretending they never knew The Five. Some are even moving away. The

Suttons have put their house up for sale. No one's interested, apparently.'

'You mean your editor's been got at.'

Dickie met Matthew's eye. 'I expect so.'

'Who wouldn't want the story to be known?' Matthew wondered.

'Oh, there's plenty of people who had dealings with The Five. Most of them legit, I expect, but there's always one or two matters that are best kept out of sight.' Dickie shrugged. 'I've got the trials to cover in a few months' time. I'll get a story then. Not the happiest of stories, admittedly.'

'Nancy Price might hang,' Matthew said miserably.

'She is guilty of murder, inspector,' Dickie said. 'Three times over. I don't expect many people are mourning the loss of those three men, but still.'

'You don't know what they did to her,' Matthew said, shaking his head. 'To say she was provoked into killing them is an understatement.'

Dickie wiped his mouth with the back of his hand. 'What did they do to her?'

'They raped her, at least two of them, Ballantyne and Fairbank. Maybe the others did as well, I don't know, and Miss Price won't say.'

'They've done that before,' Dickie said quietly. 'One of the people I spoke with had been a waitress at the club. She was asked to work at one of their private parties, her and another of the girls, and they were both raped. But she went on the street, inspector. She didn't kill anyone in revenge.'

'People react differently, Mr Waite,' Matthew said. He thought for a moment. 'Would she testify at Miss Price's trial if you asked her? Speak on Miss Price's behalf? It could help, show that rape was a pattern of behaviour for The Five, that they regularly abused women and anyone else they felt like, certain they could get away with it.'

'You want me to ask the people I spoke with if they'd be prepared to stand up in a witness box and tell their deepest, darkest secrets? You do realise one of them's a prostitute, the other a lifelong crook? They're not exactly the best of witnesses.'

'Would you at least talk to them? Ask them?'

'All right, leave it with me.' Dickie nodded and took a mouthful of beer. 'And what about you? Rumour has it Mouldy Mullinger wanted you out of his station.'

'Where did you hear that?'

'I have my sources,' Dickie grinned. 'Is it true? Are you leaving?'

'It's probably true he'd like to get rid of me,' Matthew said. 'But I haven't heard anything, so as far as I know, I'm staying.'

'And you want to stay?' Dickie asked doubtfully. 'Knowing that?'

Matthew shrugged. 'I've got to work somewhere. Better the devil you know.'

Dickie nodded, then smiled over Matthew's shoulder as Pat came up to the table.

'You going to be sitting here all night or you coming up to see Mum?' she demanded of Matthew. 'She'll moan if she finds out you've been here and not gone up.'

'Mr Waite, this is my sister, Pat,' Matthew said, his cheeks reddening.

'Pleased to meet you, Mr Waite,' Pat nodded at Dickie. 'Well, Mattie?'

'I'm coming,' Matthew said, finishing his pint.

'Are you staying to tea, Mr Waite?' Pat asked.

Dickie glanced at Matthew, who avoided his eyes. 'Well, I don't want to intrude, Mrs...'

'Harris,' Pat said. 'And don't give me any of that fancy how-you-do. We don't stand on ceremony here. Any friend of

Mattie's is always welcome. Now, come on, if you're coming.' She waved at them to follow.

'Sorry, inspector,' Dickie said, as they made their way towards the bar. 'I didn't mean to let your sister think we were friends.'

'It's fine. Really,' Matthew said. 'And you can stop calling me inspector. My name's Matthew.'

'Well, then, you better call me Dickie now we're friends. You know,' he added as they passed through to the hall behind the bar, 'you're a very unusual policeman.'

Matthew looked back at Dickie and grinned. 'It's been said before.'

Also by C. K. Harewood

Under Cover of Darkness (exclusive to subscribers)

Echoes of a Murder

Death of a Blackbird

Scan the QR code to visit www.ckharewood.com

Printed in Great Britain
by Amazon

47370302R00202